Sacrifice
FLY

Sacrifice
FLY

TIM O'MARA

Minotaur Books ♨ New York

SACRIFICE FLY. Copyright © 2012 by Tim O'Mara. All rights reserved. Printed in the United States of America. For information address St. Martin's Press, 175 Fifth Avenue, New York, N.Y. 10010.

www.minotaurbooks.com

Design by Omar Chapa

ISBN 978-1-250-00898-5 (hardcover)
ISBN 978-1-250-00899-2 (e-book)

First Edition: October 2012

10 9 8 7 6 5 4 3 2 1

In memory of my father, Thomas O'Mara,
who always had books around the house, and
in honor of my mother, Patricia O'Mara,
who always threatened to write one

Acknowledgments

ALTHOUGH I DID ALL THE TYPING, the writing was helped along by many people.

Thanks to all the kids, parents, and dedicated educators I've worked with at IS 71, JHS 126, IS 49, and, of course, The Computer School.

Words beyond thank you to the special folks at Camp Ramapo/Anchorage who put me on the right trail, especially the Stempels, the Kosbergs, John Kernochan, and Mike Kunin.

I owe the Joes Stark and Capobianco, for advice fiscal and physical, respectively.

The Kerwins and the Carrolls loaned me their living rooms in times of need.

Dallas Murphy's Writing Group helped beyond measure, especially Matt Fenton, Allison Field, Brad Carroll, Mark Miano, Liz Maguire, and, of course, Dallas.

My wonderful agents, Maura Teitelbaum and Erin Niumata, wooed me when I needed wooing and led me to my terrific editor at Minotaur Books, Matt Martz. You all made my book better. Thank you.

Love and thanks go out to my Missouri in-laws—Les and Cynthia Bushmann, and Maggie and Elise Williams—for putting up with the kid from New York.

I'd be neglectful if I did not thank the following: Tony and Diane Ianuzzi, Jim and Josephine Levine, Greg Boyer, Drew Orangeo, Teddy's, The Center for Fiction, Wayne Kral, Harold James, Sharon Bowers, Jonathan

Rabb, Rob Roznowski, Lisa Herbold, Matt Bennett, and Gene and Janice Bushmann. You all played your parts well.

A great, big tip of the hat to Mike Herron: a good reader, terrific writer, and above all, a great friend.

Thanks to my siblings—Jack, Ann, and Erin—and their families. Not to play favorites, but an extra-big shout-out to my brother, Sgt. Mike O'Mara, of the Nassau County Police Department. Your respect and reverence for the job rubbed off on both Raymond and me. We both owe you much.

Finally, this process was made all the more meaningful because of my amazing wife, Kate Bushmann, and our talented daughter, Eloise. Thanks for getting me home safely.

Sacrifice
FLY

Chapter 1

I WAS ABOUT TO GET RUN OVER.

I thought about moving left, maybe right, but my knees were having no part of it. So I tightened the grip on my umbrella, braced myself, and waited for the impact.

When he was less than ten feet away, he slammed on his brakes and skidded to a stop. With his back to me, he moved his head up and down, admiring the four-foot-long black comma left on the pavement. I took off my sunglasses as he spun his bike around and checked me out.

"Hey," he said, leaning over the handlebars. "Ain't you that teacher from school?"

"Yep," I said, slipping my sunglasses into my front shirt pocket. I rubbed my lower lip and flipped through my mental yearbook. It took about ten seconds. "Ain't you that kid from Miss Levine's class?"

He didn't answer, choosing instead to look over his shoulder at his friends, who were too busy putting the piece of plywood back on top of the cinder blocks to notice him shooting the shit with *that* teacher from school. He turned back to me, wiped his hand across his forehead, and blew the sweat off his brown fingertips. Four o'clock on the second-to-last Tuesday in May, and the temperature was over ninety.

"Whachoo doin' here?" he finally said. "Afta school and all?"

"Homework patrol," I said. "You do yours yet?"

"Ahh, that's wack." His grin faded. "Ain't no homework patrol. Is there?"

"Not yet," I said and shifted my umbrella to my left hand. "I'm here to see someone."

"He in trouble?"

"I hope not," I said.

I wasn't sure the little daredevil heard me as he raced back to his buddies singing out, "Somebody's in trouble," happy in the knowledge it wasn't him. This time.

I looked up at the towering building in front of me. Twenty-plus stories of aging air conditioners, Dominican and Puerto Rican flags hanging from balconies that were used to store old furniture, to park bikes, and to hang wet clothes out to dry. Frankie Rivas lived up there with his grandmother. Frankie was one of my eighth graders, and I was doing a home visit on this tropical Tuesday in Williamsburg, Brooklyn, because I hadn't seen the kid in almost two weeks and I got tired of listening to a busy signal every time I called.

The two glass doors that made up the front entrance to the building were propped open, allowing the outside air—and anyone who wanted—to come in. Above me, in faded gold script, was a sign informing me that this was, indeed, Building One of Roberto Clemente Plaza. "Plaza" sounded far better than "the projects," which always made me think the people living here were part of an experiment. Or "housing complex," something someone did not live in so much as suffer from. No, "plaza" would do just fine; this one was named after the late, great Pittsburgh Pirate who died a few months after getting his three thousandth hit.

I stepped into what passed for a lobby and went over to the intercom to the left of the bulletin board. I punched in Frankie's apartment number and waited for a response. After thirty seconds, I tried again. Nothing. The elevator dinged, and as I turned, the door opened and a Hassidic family stepped out. The father was dressed in black from hat to shoes, and was followed by his wife and six kids: four girls in matching plaid skirts and two boys dressed like their father. You've got to have some kind of faith to dress in black in this kind of heat.

The door to the elevator stayed open, and I moved toward it. I stopped when a voice behind me said, "Somebody in trouble?" An older black man in a maintenance uniform and pushing a mop bucket was coming through the front door.

"I'm here to see Frankie Rivas," I said. "Or Matilda Santos? They're in 1705."

He motioned with his head and said, "You buzz up?"

"I tried. No answer."

He went over to the buttons and pressed the apartment number as the elevator door shut. "She expecting ya?"

"No. I tried calling but the phone's been busy. For two days."

He gave me a look, not unlike the one I got from the kid on the bike outside, readjusted his belt, and said, "You a cop?"

"I'm Frankie's teacher."

He took a moment to get a better look at me. "You look familiar."

"I work over at the middle school."

"Which one?"

I told him.

"All my kids're grown and gone," he said. He walked over to the desk on the other side of the elevator, reached over the top, and pulled out a clipboard. "Don't know no one over at the school no more." He handed me the clipboard. "Go ahead and sign in. Make it official."

I took the pen that was hanging by a string from the clipboard and noticed as I put down the date of my visit that no one had signed in for two days. Official. I handed the clipboard back. He checked out my name and whispered it out loud.

"Raymond Dawn," he said, mispronouncing my last name. "Raymond Dawn."

"Donne," I said. "Like finished."

He said it a third time, this time correctly, checking out my face. I looked over his shoulder at the yellow-and-brown tiled mosaic of Roberto Clemente embedded into the wall. The legendary ballplayer's flawless swing, frozen in tile forever.

"You know Frankie?" I asked.

"Oh, yeah," he said. "Everybody knows Lefty. Don't know why the grandmother ain't picking up. Saw her go on up with Elsa and some bags of groceries not more than an hour ago."

"Seen him lately?"

He thought about that. "Not in over a week, I guess. Maybe more'n that." He looked back at the clipboard and mouthed my name one more time. "Whyn't you go on up, Mr. Donne. I'll try her again. Maybe by the time you get up to the seventeenth, she'll be answering."

"Thanks."

I turned and pushed the Up button to the elevator when I heard his fingers snap behind me. "I remember you now," he said.

I took a deep breath and wished for a cold bottle of water.

"You used to work around here." He touched his finger to the clipboard, tapped it a few times until it came to him. "You *was* a cop, right?"

"A long time ago. Yeah."

"And now you a teacher?"

"Yes."

"What'sa matter, mister? You don't wanna be popular?"

I shrugged and gave him a polite smile. How slow was this damn elevator? As if on cue, it appeared and I walked in.

"I'll see ya on the way out, Mr. Donne," he said, as if I'd be interested in carrying on the conversation. I raised my umbrella to him as the doors closed.

The elevator smelled of ammonia and artificial lemon. In less than a minute, the doors opened up onto the seventeenth floor, and I followed the arrows to number 1705. Two dark-skinned girls in shorts and T-shirts but no shoes were blocking the hallway, lying on their stomachs, moving crayons across a large sheet of poster paper. I cleared my throat. They stopped and looked up at me. The one to my right slid over a centimeter, and I took the opportunity to squeeze by. I got to 1705 and pushed the black rectangle just below the peephole. It made a hollow thud, and I waited a full thirty seconds before trying again. The girls looked over at me. I gave them my best teacher smile. They went back to their artwork.

"*¿Quien es?*" a voice from the other side of the door asked.

I leaned in, my ear about an inch from the peephole, and said, "Mrs. Santos?"

"*Sí. ¿Quien es?*"

"It's Mr. Donne, ma'am. Frankie's teacher?"

A few seconds later, she said, "Frankie no here."

I raised my voice a notch. "Mrs. Santos, this is Raymond Donne. Frankie's teacher. I need to speak with you or your grandson." One of the girls gave me a mean look as the other placed a finger to her lips, shushing me.

"*Ay Dios.*" The sound of a lock turning was followed closely by the door being opened just enough for me to see the chain on the other side. A pair of bright blue eyes appeared, just over the chain. "Frankie's teacher?" she said. "Senor Donne?"

"Yes." My voice was lower now. "I need to speak with you. Would you mind if I—"

"Frankie," she said. "He is in trouble?"

"You can say that, yeah." The hint of cooler air and the smell of meat cooking wafted into the hallway. I remembered how thirsty I was. "He hasn't been coming to school."

"Frankie no here," she repeated. "He stay at his father's."

"Mrs. Santos, it's been seven days, and if he—"

"*¿Siete días?*"

"Yes, ma'am. Seven school days." I unfolded the printout of Frankie's attendance and held it up for her to see. "Since Friday of last week." She didn't quite get that, and I wasn't sure how to say it in Spanish. I tried anyway. "*¿El Viernes de . . . semana pasado?*"

Part of it got through because she said, *"Ay Dios,"* again and then, "That is when he start to stay with the father."

"*¿Donde . . . ?* Where does the father live?"

"*El Sud,*" she answered. The Southside.

"Do you have a phone number for him?"

"No. No have a phone. He have the, *¿cómo se dice?* the cell."

"Okay. Do you have his cell phone number?" I asked, remembering my own cell phone, which was sitting in a drawer back at my apartment, unused and uncharged for over a year now.

"No. He no give."

This was becoming a big waste of time. "Mrs. Santos, I need to speak to someone about Frankie's attendance. He's in danger of not graduating if he misses much more school."

"No graduate?"

"Yes. No graduate. And as his legal guardian, you are—"

"No," she said. "I am not the . . . I no have the, *¿como se dice?* . . . "

"Custody?"

"*Sí. La custodia.* The father," she said with obvious disgust. "He have the custody."

"Mrs. Santos, this is the only address the school has for Frankie. You are the emergency contact. According to all my records, he lives here with you."

"*Sí,*" she said. "Most of the time . . . *Pero Francisco,* the father, he takes Frankie, and I no can do nothing. *El Derecho,*" she added. The Law. "Is best for Frankie to be here, I know."

The blue eyes stared back at me over the chain, filling up with tears. They're being wasted on me, I thought.

"And you have no way to reach the father?"

"I have his . . . his address."

"Can you give it to me, please?"

"*Sí,*" she said. "*Espera.*"

Yeah, I thought as she shut the door on me, I'll wait. Not so long ago, I'd be waiting on the other side of the door breathing cooler air. Maybe get a glass of water. When I knocked on someone's door with my nightstick— always with the nightstick—it would be my decision whether or not I waited in the hall or entered the residence. A tip of the hat, a certain tone of voice, and a little "Mind if I come in?" and I would be on the other side.

I heard a door open down the hall. A woman's voice yelled out, "Maria!" The two girls got to their knees, shoved all the crayons into their pockets, and ran down the hall. A few seconds later, Mrs. Santos's door reopened. Her small hand eased through the opening, thin gray fingers clasping a piece of paper.

"*Aquí,*" she said. "Is where the father lives."

I looked at the address. It was on my way home if I walked from here.

"You tell the father," Mrs. Santos continued, "*es necesario que* Frankie be in school. You tell him he will be in trouble Frankie no go to school."

"I'm not trying to get anyone in trouble, Mrs. Santos. But if Frankie does not graduate, he won't be going to high school next year."

She thought about that and then gave me a long look.

"You," she said, "you are the one who got Frankie—the *scolar* . . . "

"Scholarship," I finished for her. "I got him the tryout for Coach Keenan, yes."

"You watch Frankie play? He pitch real good."

Didn't matter how good he pitched. He flunks eighth grade, and he can kiss the free ride to Catholic school good-bye. And it'll be at least five years before Eddie Keenan even looks at another kid of mine.

"Yeah," I said. "He's very good."

"You tell the father. No school? Trouble."

Before I could answer, the door shut and the locks slid back into place. My conversation with Frankie Rivas's grandmother was over.

Chapter 2

THE ELEVATOR DOORS OPENED onto the sixteenth floor and were about to shut again when a voice called out, "Hold that, please!" I stopped the door from closing. A Hispanic woman in her mid-twenties slid in between the doors. She was wearing black pants and a black, short-sleeved shirt with the logo of a margarita glass over the left pocket along with *"El Azteca"* written in script.

"Who is in trouble now?" she asked me.

"Why does everyone ask me that?"

"No offense," she said, "but a white guy riding the elevator at Clemente? Somebody is either in trouble, or you took a wrong turn off the bridge."

"Raymond Donne," I said. "Frankie Rivas's teacher."

Her face softened. I got a smile and an offer of her hand. I took it. "Elsa," she said.

"How was your shopping trip with Mrs. Santos?" I asked.

"How did you . . . ?"

"Maintenance guy downstairs."

"Maintenance?" She laughed. "Harold pushes a wet mop around and takes a break to smoke every ten minutes. Has plenty of time to talk, though." She took a few seconds before adding, "*Is* Frankie in trouble?"

"I hope not," I said. "I'm heading over to see him at his father's now."

She let out a disgusted sigh.

"Your opinion of the father?" I asked.

"That man is a father when he's in the mood. Or when he needs something."

"Grandmother says Frankie's been with him for a week and a half now."

"That's longer than usual. I guess he needed something bad."

The doors opened, and Elsa and I stepped out into the lobby. We both spotted Harold on the other side of the glass door, outside finishing up a cigarette. We exited the building, and the heat slapped me in the face.

"Elsa," Harold said. "You know Mr. Donne here?"

"We just met."

"You be careful what you say 'round him, girl." He lowered his voice to a conspiratorial whisper. "Used to be a policeman."

Elsa gave me a long look and said, "Really?"

Harold said, "Yup. Take care now."

Elsa and I walked to the street. I turned to the left. She was going the other way, toward the J and M subway trains.

"It was nice meeting you, Mr. Donne."

"Same here."

"Are you going to bring Frankie home?"

"I'll see what I can do," I said, because it sounded better than "I don't know."

"Then maybe we will see each other again."

"Maybe," I said, pointing at the logo on her shirt. "Say hi to Maria for me."

"You know Maria?"

"My first assignment was Midtown North. She took good care of us."

Elsa smiled and said, "I'll tell her."

I got about a block before getting light-headed. I needed water an hour ago. The air-conditioning in the corner bodega felt so good I wanted to stay for a couple of hours. I bought a large bottled water and stepped back outside before I changed my mind.

By the time I got to the next corner, my water was gone. I tossed the bottle into an overflowing trash basket and waited for the light to turn. A couple of guys were sitting on milk crates in front of the laundromat, their boom box blaring what passed for hip hop these days, and drinking out of brown paper bags. First day the temperature hits ninety, it's summertime in the 'Burg. Don't make no difference what the calendar says. Time to kick it. Worry about the rules come winter. Bad time to be a cop. Or a school-teacher. The two caught me looking at them; the one on the left reached down and lowered the volume on the radio.

"You see something you like?" he asked.

I shook my head. "You looked familiar," I said. "Sorry."

The other guy said, "Maybe you the one look familiar. Cop."

I shook my head as the light went green. "Have a nice day," I said.

"Fuck you, five-oh." They both laughed and bumped fists. I crossed the street, not missing my old job one bit.

The Williamsburg Bridge was in full rush-hour mode as I walked under it. Cars and trucks crawling in the direction of Manhattan, the traffic coming into Brooklyn not much better. The subway just ambled along. Back in the days when my knees worked the way they were supposed to, one of my favorite things to do was to take my bike over the bridge into Manhattan and ride along the other side of the East River. On the way back, I'd stop in the middle and watch as the river traffic flowed by and listen as the cars and trucks hummed along.

I got to the fenced-in parking lot on the corner of Rivas's block. It wasn't too long ago that the blocks around here would be filled day and night with the smell of sugar from the Domino factory by the river. For over a hundred years it stood there, the largest sugar factory on the planet. It was bought a couple years ago by some brothers from the Dominican Republic, two of the richest landowners down there and heroes to the people in this neighborhood. The kind of guys who wielded enough power in this country that they could get the president on the phone and talk about sugar tariffs and federal tax breaks and political contributions. The same guys who sold the place off to real estate developers a while back, leaving a few hundred neighborhood folks out of work.

Man, this block used to smell sweet.

Frankie's dad lived in one of an identical pair of adjacent buildings across the street from where I stood. At least they used to be identical. The one on the left sported new windows, flower boxes, and a recent paint job. The one on the right had what must have been the original windows—even from across the street, I could see they didn't sit right anymore—and a paint job at least a decade old. I found myself wondering how much

more in rent the tenants in the one on the left paid. Frankie's dad lived in
the one on the right.

I crossed over, stepped up to the buttons, and buzzed. No answer. I
tried again. No answer. I reached over and tried the front door. Unlocked.
I climbed the three flights up to Rivas's apartment. My knees were throbbing and ready to call it a day. I knocked on the apartment door, waited half
a minute, and knocked again with my umbrella. The sound reminded me of
my nightstick. I did it again. In the middle of my third attempt, a door behind
me opened.

"Jesus," a man's voice said. I turned, and for the second time that day,
a pair of eyes looked at me from over a chain lock. "Ya gonna wake the dead
with that knocking."

"I'm looking for Francisco Rivas," I said. "Senior."

"He buzz you in?"

"Front door's unlocked. I think it's busted."

"Shit. Again?" The eyes watched me a little longer, and the voice said,
"You a cop?"

I caught the aroma of marijuana coming into the hallway and said,
"No."

"He owe you money?"

"I'm from his kid's school."

"Milagros?"

Frankie's sister. I'd forgotten she lived with the father.

"Frankie's."

"Christ," he said. "About time."

I took a step closer. "What's that mean?"

"Been hanging around here all week. During school hours. Almost
took my head off throwing that damn ball against the front of the building. You the truant officer?"

"I'm from the school. You know if he's home?"

"The kid or the father?"

"Either one."

"Not answering, huh?" I didn't justify that with an answer, and it took
a few seconds for him to say, "Oh, yeah. Why else would you be—"

"Have you seen Mr. Rivas around lately?"

"Two, three days ago maybe. Maybe longer. You sure you ain't a cop?"

I took another step toward his door. "If I were," I said, "what would stop me from entering your apartment and locating the source of that smell?"

"Ever hear of a warrant?"

"Sure, I think it was right after the lecture on reasonable cause."

"Shit," he said. "Hold on a second." He shut the door, and when he opened it again he handed me a key. "Here. Rivas had a habit of forgettin' his."

I took the key. "Just like that?"

"Hey. You either a cop, one of his lowlife friends, or from the school, like you said. Any way I play it, ain't no positive for me carrying on this conversation. Rivas gives ya shit about that key, tell him you told me you was a cop, and reasonable cause and shit. You can also tell him to keep the damn thing."

Without waiting for a response, he shut the door. I knocked on Rivas's door one more time, and when I again got no answer, looked at the key in my hand. Technically, what I was about to do was breaking the law. However, I didn't see myself getting into any real trouble, as all I wanted to do was verify that no one was at home. Then at school the next day, I could call the attendance guy and report Frankie's absences. If Rivas was home, I'd talk my way around why I had his key and opened his door. After all, he was the one keeping his kid out of school. If he were angry enough to call the cops on me, he would be opening himself up to some unwanted scrutiny.

I stuck the key in the lock and turned. I eased the door open, let go, and waited for it to swing fully open.

"Mr. Rivas?" I called. "Frankie?"

Silence. Still in the doorway, I looked at the room in front of me. To my left, there was a couch with a crumpled sheet and blanket tucked behind the cushions and hanging over the front. A sleeping bag with a pillow was on the floor, halfway under the coffee table, which was covered with fast-food wrappers and half-empty soda bottles. The smell of stale smoke and a cheap air freshener hung in the air. The windows were closed, the air conditioner silent.

No one had been here for days.

I took my umbrella and hooked it around the leg of the coffee table. I pulled it toward me and used it to make sure the door didn't swing back and close on me. A cop I used to work with got stuck in an apartment with a pit bull once. Swore the place was empty. It took him thirty seconds and four bullets to get the dog off his leg. Last I heard, he was spending his early retirement in a reclining chair, a remote control in one hand and a can of beer in the other.

I waited and listened for a few seconds—a small hallway off to the right, a dining table to my left—before I stepped into the living room. Against the far wall, directly under the painting of a smiling Jesus touching two children on their heads, was an entertainment center with a flat-screen TV, VCR, DVD, and CD players and enough movies to start a rental service.

I walked into the kitchen. All the drawers and cabinets were open. The floor was a mess of silverware, broken plates and cups, a blender, and a toaster oven. The refrigerator door was covered with schoolwork, a post-card from some place that had palm trees, and a child's drawing of a white house with a red barn along its side. I opened the fridge: half a loaf of bread, a jar of jelly, and a container of milk, which I opened. It was beginning to turn.

I went back into the living room and crossed over to the other side of the apartment. There were two doors to choose from. I tried the one on my left. It was the bathroom, and it was in the same shape as the kitchen. The medicine chest had been tossed, towels were on the floor, and the shower curtain ripped from its rod. A litter box was on the side of the toilet, untouched and clean. I backed out and shut the door.

The door to my right was shut. I knocked, maybe because it had to be the bedroom and a certain amount of privacy was expected. I turned the knob and slowly pushed. An orange cat sprinted out between my legs followed by the smells of shit and piss. Beneath those odors was another smell, and I knew what I'd find when I fully opened the door to Rivas's bedroom.

It took my eyes a few seconds to adjust to the darkness of the bedroom. I let the bedroom door swing all the way open, allowing a little more light into the room. I could make out a lump on the bed, almost like someone had dumped a pile of dirty clothes. Almost.

I moved toward the bed, reached out with my umbrella, and poked the lump on the bed. It didn't give. Another step—my eyes able to make out more than just shapes now—and I could tell that the lump of clothes on the bed had a person inside.

I stumbled back a few feet and hit the wall. Instinctively, I reached over, found the light switch, and flicked it on.

The dead guy looked as if he'd been sitting on the edge of the bed and just fell back, his legs dangling over the side. And there I was—like a fucking rookie—standing stupid in the middle of a crime scene. The last two things I noticed before stumbling out of the room were a dark stain on the floor below the dead guy's feet and that he was clutching a child's book bag with a bright yellow flower painted on its back pocket.

The next thing I know, I'm knocking on the neighbor's door with my umbrella.

Loud enough to wake the dead.

Chapter 3

"MR. DONNE?"

I turned and looked up into the face of the patrolman who earlier had instructed me to wait outside. He was standing on the step above the one I was sitting on. The shine on his belt and holster told me he'd been on the streets for maybe three months. A bright red zit was forming above his lip among the facial hairs he hoped would one day grow into a mustache.

"Detective Royce wants me to tell you that he appreciates your patience," he said.

"Big black guy in the suit?" I asked.

"That would be him," the cop said. He raised his hand to show me a five-dollar bill. "He wants to know if you'd like a water or something from the corner."

"How much longer before I can go?" I asked.

He shrugged. "Crime Scene guys are almost done."

"They notice the flower?"

He looked at me like I was starting to lose it in the heat.

"Sir?"

"The flower," I repeated. "On the book bag. There was no blood on it."

"I'm sure they did." He took the steps down to the sidewalk. "Something to drink, sir?"

"Yeah. Water would be good. How much more time did you say?"

"They gotta finish up in the apartment, and the detective needs you to talk to the youth officers." Youth officers, when they were available, dealt with crimes committed by—or against—juveniles. "They should be here in a few minutes."

"A few minutes real time?" I asked. "Or a few minutes police time?"

He smiled. "A few minutes, sir."

About an hour later—after finishing my water, watching the Crime Scene people leave, and telling the youth officers everything I could about Frankie—I was leaning against the railing on the steps outside Rivas's apartment when Detective Royce came out of the building. He walked right past me, over to a car that was parked across the street. He took off his jacket and, before tossing it through the open passenger's window, removed something from one of the pockets. As he crossed back over, he was slapping a pack of cigarettes against his palm. When he got to the steps, he looked up at me and said, "D.O.N.N.E.?"

"That's how it's spelled," I said.

"First name . . . Raymond?"

"Yes."

"Hmmm." He opened the pack of smokes and stuck one in his mouth. "We got a chief by that name over at One Police Plaza."

"Yeah. I've got an uncle by that name who's a chief over at One P.P."

"Shit." He thought about that for a moment, took the unlit cigarette from his mouth, and let out an imaginary plume of smoke. After putting it back between his lips, he sat down, reached inside his jacket, and pulled out a small notepad and a pen. "You're Chief Donne's nephew?"

"Sorry."

He looked at my umbrella and said, "You used to work out of the Nine-Oh, right?"

I nodded. If he knew my story, he knew enough not to mention it.

"Wanna tell me what you were doing here?"

"Like I told the officer upstairs," I said. "Looking for Frankie Rivas."

"I heard that. But why you? Don't they have folks for that?"

"Attendance teachers, yeah. And after the kid's out for two weeks, they put him on their list of homes to visit." I told him about Frankie's scholarship to Our Lady, how it was contingent upon his grades and attendance, and how waiting two weeks wouldn't work.

"That the only reason?"

"Yes, Detective," I said. "That's the only reason."

"Grandma hasn't seen the boy in ten days, huh?" he asked.

"That's what she told me."

Royce wrote that down. "Guy across the way says that he hasn't seen anybody around for the past coupla days."

"He didn't strike me as the type who gets out a lot."

"Picked up on that, huh?" The detective grinned. "Guy had all his windows open and the AC going full blast. Think he mighta been hiding something?"

"Crossed my mind," I said. "How fast before you start the mobilization?"

"It's started. Officers should be over at the grandmother's, and they'll canvas the neighborhood—both neighborhoods—and work their way out from there."

"Right," I said, knowing the mobilization would have to include the East River. *The news will be all over this,* I thought.

"Any idea where they might have gone?" Royce asked.

"Assuming they're not with whoever killed the father?"

"Assuming that, yes."

"No. I don't. Any idea exactly what happened up there, Detective?"

"Exactly? No. Crime Scene seems to think it's a combination of a blunt instrument to the head and some sort of blow to the face. Nose is where all the blood came from. There's also a decent-size dent just above the left ear." He paused. "You say the kid was a baseball player?"

"Yeah."

"There's no bats in the apartment."

"He probably keeps them at his grandmother's."

"Yeah," Royce said. "I guess we'll find out."

"Detective," I said. "Frankie did not kill his father."

"Gotta check out all possibilities, Mr. Donne." He was studying my reaction. I tried not to give him one. "You know that. Neighbor said the kid's in special education."

"Yes, Detective. Frankie's a grade or two behind in reading and math. I teach a small group of kids. Right now I have eleven. None of them is violent."

Royce took the still-unlit cigarette from his mouth and rolled it between his thumb and forefinger. It was a full thirty seconds before he spoke again.

"You noticed the book bag the victim was holding?"

"I did."

"And the lack of blood on the flower?"

"Yes."

"Means two things," he said. "One: you were a bit too involved in my crime scene. I'll let that go, considering you discovered the DB and got a bit edgy."

"Thanks."

"Two: the bag found its way into his arms after the bleeding was done. Bag was empty, by the way. There's a lot of blood at the feet of the vic, who we are presently identifying as Francisco Rivas, Senior. You ever meet the man?"

"No. I only dealt with the grandmother."

"Looks like the book bag belongs to the sister." He looked at his notebook. "Milagros. You wouldn't have a contact on her, would ya?"

"No," I said. "Her school should."

"Have to wait until morning then." He stood up and flicked the cigarette into the street. Then he pulled a card out of his shirt pocket. "You think of anything useful, give me a call."

"That's it?" I took the card. "I can go?"

"Unless there's something you left out of your statement. You came. You saw. You called it in. And you don't strike me as the type who would enjoy waiting around for the newspapers to show up. I can have Officer Sikes take you home if you want."

I thought about the cop with the zit. "He's got a driver's license?"

Royce laughed. "Pre-req for the job."

"Thanks, but I could use the walk."

"You sure? You don't look too good."

"My first dead body in a while," I said, easing myself up. "Another water, I'll be fine."

"Whatever you say, Mr. Donne."

With that, Detective Royce went back to his crime scene, and I made my way home.

Halfway home, my knees had just about given up, so I took a seat on a bench just inside McCarren Park, more than a little angry with myself. I knew before I pushed the bedroom door all the way open what I'd find on the other side. I knew it would take me somewhere I'd been before and hoped to never go again. I should have turned around and gone home. I opened the door anyway.

The door to my father's study is open. Just a couple of inches, but this door is never open. If it were up to him, my dad would put a lock on it. The Door is to be kept closed.

I put my bag down and approach. I stop about a foot or two away.

"Dad?" I say into the dark space between the door and the molding. "We're home."

I hear my mother's voice behind me talking to my sister, Rachel, but I'm too focused on the open door to pay attention to what she is saying.

I curl up my right index finger and tap my knuckle against The Door *three times.*

"Dad?" I try again. "We're back."

At first I think the smell is some sort of cleanser. It has a bite to it that reminds me of the stuff my mom uses on the tub. The smell gets stronger when I push the door open a bit more, and now I'm reminded of the taste you get when you put a penny in your mouth.

I think about reaching in, switching on the light, but if my dad is in there and napping, he's not going to be happy if I wake him. Mom, Rachel, and I have been out in Montauk all weekend. Dad stayed home to get some work done, but he didn't really want to come anyway. He rarely does.

Maybe he brought in some food a couple of days ago and forgot about it. Maybe that's what I smell.

My dad is lying facedown on the floor. I turn to call for my mom, but she's already behind me. She pushes me aside and rushes to my father's body. I watch as she kneels down next to him, like she's about to pray.

"Goddamn," she whispers. Then she looks up at me. "Raymond," she screams as if I've interrupted a private conversation. "Take Rachel and go upstairs! Now!"

Before I can protest, she gets to her feet and pushes me out of the room. The door slams in my face and I go to find my sister.

•   •   •

The smell of death stays with you. It doesn't just get into your nose and lungs, it gets deep inside you: into your blood and your gut and your dreams. If I believed in a soul, it'd probably get into that, too. Now, under the trees of the park, the smell of Frankie's father's death was mixing with the smell of my father's.

Some doors should stay shut.

I looked out at the park and took a deep breath. No one has ever quite explained to me exactly where Williamsburg ends and Greenpoint begins. Longtime residents of the area still argue over which streets belong to which neighborhood. The cops, they just cared whether it was the Nine-O or the Nine-Four. It didn't really matter all that much, unless you were trying to sell your house, then Greenpoint sounded a hell of a lot better than Williamsburg. But one thing was agreed upon: right smack in the middle was McCarren Park.

The bench I was on faced the soccer fields where a Polish team was getting ready to play an Hispanic team, the sidelines filling with supporters talking loudly in both languages. Behind me were the Little League fields—where Frankie would sometimes play—so small that, with the two games going on at the same time, the outfielders from each game had to stand side by side. Add to those the bikers, joggers, skateboarders, rollerbladers, handball players, and families looking to grab any piece of green they could find, you had yourself a microcosm of Brooklyn.

Sitting all by itself across the street, like a neglected step-kid, was McCarren Pool, the largest public pool in the city system. It had been decades since it last opened its gates to swimmers. Every three or four years the local politicians would stand up and announce their plans to reopen and "revitalize" the pool. And after all the votes were counted, you wouldn't hear another word until the next election. No one was quite willing to say out loud that the reason the pool had closed, and would more than likely stay closed, was because it was just about impossible to secure a pool that size that was visited by the Polish, Italians, Blacks, and the Hispanics—and where were the Hasidim going to swim? So the pool just sits there, its walls crumbling a bit more each year, weeds and trees growing from its floors. A reminder of a kinder, gentler time that maybe never really was, when swimming in a public pool meant just that.

I got up and walked over to the Avenue to grab a hero at the pizza place. By the time I got home, the Yankee game would be on and, with any luck, I'd be asleep by the fifth inning. As I waited by the window for my food, the old Polish man walked by. Dressed in his usual green plaid jacket and black pants—no matter the season—he was yelling out his usual crazy Polish rant. I used to get a smile out of his act until the guy I bought kielbasa from told me that his loud rants were usually about the family he'd lost to the Germans in the concentration camps. I wondered what he smelled when he went to bed.

I took my hero and began the five-minute walk down to my apartment. The Avenue was packed: people shopping for dinner, some for clothes, and others running into the local hangouts for a quick drink before going home.

Shit. It was Tuesday. I'd promised Mikey I'd take his shift tonight. I looked at my watch. Seven thirty. I went over to the car service around the block and lucked into a driver just getting on duty. Two minutes and five dollars later, he dropped me off at The LineUp.

Chapter 4

EMO THE MOLE'S REAL NAME was Edgar Martinez O'Brien, and Edgar was as proud of his Puerto Rican–Irish heritage as he was of the job that had earned him his nickname. I poured him a pint of Bass and placed it next to his can of tomato juice as he fiddled with his cell phone.

"Thank you, sir," he said and raised his glass to toast. "Five, seven, four." Which, to those of us in the know, meant that Edgar had five years, seven months, and four days until he could collect his pension from the New York City Transit Authority. Edgar did communications work for the subway system. "Nice surprise seeing you here on a Tuesday, Raymond."

"Helping out Mikey," I said. "He's got a big date."

"Oh, yeah?" Edgar said. "With which hand?"

He looked around to see who was laughing. No one. Kevin and Petey—two ex-cops who'd put their papers in on the exact same day over four years ago—just gave him blank stares and went back to watching the weather on the silent TV above the bar.

Edgar cleared his throat and lifted his cell phone. "Wanna see something cool?"

"Not in the mood right now, Edgar."

"Watch." He ignored my response. "I mean, listen."

He motioned with his head to where Nicky G was on the pay phone, leaning against the wall, the phone cradled between his shoulder and ear, and the racing form folded under his arm. Edgar pressed a few buttons on his cell and then held it out to me.

"Get a load of this."

"Edgar, I'm busy. Just—"

He pushed the phone at me. "Just listen. Geez."

I took the phone to shut him up and put it to my ear.

"Honey," a raspy voice said. "I sweartagod, I just got here. I'm gonna grab a quick burger with the boys—maybe watch a few innings—and come right on home."

Nicky G lying to his wife. And I was listening to it on Edgar's cell phone.

I handed the phone back to Edgar. "Nice trick," I said.

"Trick?" He grabbed the phone. "Took me half an hour to set that up. Had to get special wiring, a miniature—"

"It's also illegal, Edgar."

"Illegal, shmillegal. I'm just having some fun."

"Don't let any of the guys around here in on your fun. Or Mrs. Mac. They might take your fun away from you."

Edgar folded up his cell phone and stuck it in his pocket. He took a sip of Bass and replaced it with a little tomato juice.

"Whatsa matter, Ray?" he asked. "Bad day with the kiddies?"

"School was fine. Leave it alone, Edgar."

I reached under the bar, pulled out the *Daily News* and handed it to Edgar, knowing the sports section had a better chance of shutting him up than I did. As he flipped to the back pages, I went down to the other end of the bar to tend to the two twenty-something ladies who were finishing up their light beers.

"Two more?"

"Please," said the one on the right. "Do you know if those two officers from last Tuesday night will be coming in tonight, Ray?"

Last Tuesday? It took me the same amount of time to get their beers as it did for me to remember last Tuesday night.

"Mullins and Glass?" I said. "I don't know. They may be with their girlfriends."

"They got girlfriends?" the one on the left said.

"That didn't come up in conversation?"

"No," the one on the right said. "It did not."

"Must have slipped their minds." I looked over my shoulder. "You want me to see if Edgar's available?"

"Emo?" they both whispered. "When we want a date with a cop wannabe, we'll let you know," the one on the left said and then slammed the bills in front of her. "Could you give us some quarters for the pool table, Ray? I feel like slapping some balls around."

I did as they asked and got a couple more for Petey and Kevin. Nicky G—now finished lying to his wife—was also finished with his burger. I put another vodka tonic in front of him. Back at the other end, Edgar was tapping the newspaper.

"You see the San Diego game last night?" he asked.

"I don't have satellite."

"Gotta get that package, Ray. Great investment. You should talk to Mrs. McVernon about putting one in here. I could even install it if she wants. Be great for business." He tapped the page again. "Guy pitched a complete game shutout. Eighty-four pitches."

"Eighty-four pitches?" I said.

"Yep. Bee-you-tee-full." He closed his eyes. "That's . . . nine point three pitches per inning. Talk about getting the job done."

"How'd the other guy do?" I asked.

"Huh?"

"The other pitcher. How'd he do?"

Edgar moved his finger along the bottom of the box score and said, "Heh. Pitched a three hitter, struck out six. Walked none. Tough loss."

I nodded. A good pitcher will do that. Your opposite number's up there on the mound throwing bullets, you'd better come out with your A game.

"Hey, that reminds me," Edgar said. "Mets're on. You mind?"

I grabbed the remote from under the bar and switched the TV to the Mets game.

"I'm keeping the sound off, though."

"No problem, Ray," Edgar said. "It's only the Mets. Geez, what is the matter with you tonight? You sure you didn't have a bad day at work?"

"My day was fine, Edgar."

"Bull dinkey. C'mon. You can tell me." He leaned forward and lowered his voice. "You're the only one around here tells me anything."

I looked into Edgar's desperate eyes and felt like going back to the other end of the bar. Instead, I took a deep breath and said, "I was over on South Third and Driggs today, looking for one of my students."

"Isn't that the block where the cops found a DB this afternoon?"

"How did you . . . ?" Edgar had a police scanner. Also illegal. "I called it in."

"You? Called in a DB?"

"The DB . . ." I said, ". . . the dead body was my kid's father."

"Shit," he said. "They know who did it?"

"Not unless I missed something in the last couple of hours."

"You find the kid?"

"No."

"Think he did it?"

"See, Edgar," I took the remote and put it back under the bar, "that's why no one around here tells you shit. You run your mouth too goddamned much."

He raised his hands, put a sad look on his face, and said, "Sorry."

The sound of beer bottles hitting the bar came from behind me. One of the ball-slapping ladies was holding up two fingers. When I walked the two beers over to her, she said, "And two shots of Jack."

I poured them and told her the round was on me.

"Why's that?" she asked.

"To apologize for men everywhere."

She looked at the two shot glasses and smiled. "It's a start."

I went back to work. Busy work: moving the bar rag around, washing out pint glasses, and cutting up lemons and limes. All the while, keeping one eye on the floor behind the bar. One overlooked spill or piece of ice and I could find myself on my knees and calling it an early night. I looked over at the ball game and then at Edgar, who was giving me the wounded-puppy look.

"I'm sorry, Ray," he said. "You know I get excited about this stuff. I don't know the kid, I just—"

"Okay, Edgar. Relax. I didn't mean to jump down your throat. It's been a long day."

"No, no. I should be apologizing to you. I mean, it's your student out there, missing." He looked up at the game, and with his eyes still on the TV, he said, "What're you gonna do now?"

"About what?"

"About the missing kid. His old man getting killed."

"Edgar, you miss out on the last five years of my life? I'm not a cop anymore."

"Yeah, but . . ."

"But what? You think this is—" Just over Edgar's shoulder, the front door opened and Mrs. McVernon walked in. What was she doing back here?

I came in over an hour ago and she went home. She gave me a small smile and gestured with her finger for me to join her at the other end of the bar. Maybe she came in to save me from Edgar.

"Is everything okay?" I asked.

"I need a favor," she said, fingering the small gold replica of her dead husband's badge that hung from a chain around her neck. She did that whenever she wanted to remind her audience of her husband. "It's a big one, I'm afraid. So you feel free to just say no."

"Okay."

"I just got a phone call from Billy," she said.

It took me a second. "Morris?"

"Yes."

"And . . . ?"

"You know he has his yearly barbecue with the boys?"

My old partner's "Q" was the social event of the spring for about fifty or sixty cops each year. I'd missed the last couple.

"Yeah," I said, not wanting to talk about it. "What about it?"

"Well . . . it's this Saturday . . . and he's having work done on his house that's lasting longer than the contractors said."

I nodded. I looked down the other end of the bar, hoping a thirsty customer would give me a way out of this conversation. No luck.

"So," Mrs. Mac continued, "he wants to have the Q here."

"Here?" Christ. "What'd you tell him?"

"That I would get back to him after I worked out the details."

"I don't know, Mrs. Mac. You'd need to clear out the outside area for the grills," I said.

"The Freddies will do that," she said, referring to the twin Dominican brothers who worked the kitchen for her and whose parents showed little imagination when it came to naming their baby boys. "Billy said he'd have all the food delivered here and I can order enough beer to handle the extra business."

"Sounds like a good deal, Mrs. Mac."

"Yes," she said, again playing with the miniature badge.

"But . . . ?"

"I want . . . I need . . . you to work it for me."

"I don't work on Saturday," I said, a bit too harsh.

"That's why I'm asking for a favor, Raymond."

"Mikey'll be here. You won't need me." And I don't need this.

"That's not true, Raymond," she said. "You know those boys. You can handle them. Make sure things don't get too . . . rowdy."

Right.

"Mrs. Mac," I said. "I haven't seen Billy—or 'the boys'—in a long time."

"He said five years."

"You had a long talk with Billy, Mrs. Mac."

"I'm sorry to ask, Raymond, but it would mean a lot of money for the bar, and I love those boys dearly, and my Henry would roll over in his grave if he knew I missed an opportunity to help Billy out."

This woman could give lessons in guilt. Her Henry graduated from the police academy with my uncle about a hundred years ago. As Uncle Ray worked his way up the ladder, Henry McVernon stayed on the streets, eventually making detective. A couple of years back—not long after he'd bought The LineUp—it caught up with him in the form of a massive heart attack. Just like my father. I wasn't the only ex-cop who picked up a weekly shift at the place to help his widow keep it going. No wages, just tips. And now a favor. A big one.

"You don't think Mikey can handle it?" Why should she? I didn't.

"He's coming in early, but no, not by himself. I need you."

"I appreciate your confidence, Mrs. Mac, but I don't think I'd be too comfortable around all those guys."

"Like I said, Raymond. Feel free to say no."

I thought I just did.

"Mikey'll work the bar?"

"With a little help from you. I hope."

"And Gloria's going to be here?"

"She's bringing her sister. The Freddies will do the cooking."

It sounded to me as if Mrs. Mac had already said yes to Billy.

"You told Billy that you'd be asking me to work it?"

"He couldn't have been happier," she said. "In fact, he says it will help 'dispel the idea' he's had that you've been avoiding him."

"I haven't been avoiding anybody, Mrs. Mac."

"You have nothing to explain to me, Raymond. I'm just passing on what Billy said."

After a few seconds, and against my better judgment, I heard myself say, "Then how could I possibly say no?"

"You'll do it?"

"I'll work the first couple of hours."

"And we'll see what happens."

"Yeah."

She came around the side of the bar and kissed me on the cheek. "Thank you, Raymond. And if my Henry were still alive, he'd thank you, too." She took me by the hands and stepped back. "What's that smile for?"

"Your Henry should have taken you into the interrogation room with him. Suspects wouldn't have stood a chance."

"Don't think the idea didn't cross his mind, young man." She squeezed my hands. "Thank you, Raymond. And remember, it's a school night. Last call is at eleven thirty."

"Go home, Mrs. Mac."

"Yes," she said. "This time to stay."

As she passed behind Edgar, he put his hand in the air. Mrs. Mac grabbed it, gave it a kiss, and said, "Good night, Emo."

"What was that about?" Edgar asked as the door shut behind Mrs. Mac.

"Billy Morris is having a party here this weekend."

"The Q?"

"Yeah," I said. "The Q. And don't get any—"

"Oh, come on, Raymond," he pleaded. "I will sit here at my end of the bar and keep my mouth shut. I promise."

"Edgar . . ." Asking Edgar to keep his mouth shut in a room full of cops was like asking a cat to pay no attention to the canaries at the window. "You ask one unsolicited question or bother anyone with one of your *tricks,* I'll throw you out myself. You understand?"

"Jeez, Raymond. I'm not a kid, you know."

"Tell me you understand, Edgar."

"I understand, Raymond."

"Good." I ignored the wounded-puppy look. "You ready for another TJ and Bass?"

"Yeah."

"It's on me."

"Thank you."

"Don't mention it."

Chapter 5

WEDNESDAY MORNING, JUST after eight, and the main office was already buzzing. Two unhappy kids sat on the big wooden bench with their two even-unhappier parents. Mary and Edna were working the phones. Mary was saying, "Yes, I have told them many times that you've been waiting for their papers. I can't go home and do it for them." Edna was explaining, "That's why Mr. Thomas sent a memo home asking parents—*sí, entiendo*—to schedule doctor's appointments after three o'clock. The teachers can't teach the kids—I said that I understand, *entiendo*—*si los niños no estan en la escuela, los maestros no pueden enseñarlos.* Yes, ma'am. You have a nice day, too."

I grabbed the papers out of my mailbox and turned to leave, looking forward to getting to my classroom and throwing myself into the day. I had forced myself out of bed. Staying home would have just given me more time to think about Frankie and his sister. I needed controlled chaos.

"Mr. Donne."

"Mary," I said, stopping at the door.

"The district office called for you this morning."

"How're they doing over there?"

"They still have not received your end-of-the-year paperwork."

"That's because I haven't done it yet."

"I told them you'd fax it over by Friday, the latest."

"That's very optimistic of you."

"Raymond, you know how they are. What would you like me to tell them when they call back?"

"Tell them I'm busy teaching my kids and haven't had the time yet. But if any of them wants to come over and watch my class for half a day, I'd be more than happy to get the paperwork done."

"Also," she picked up a slip of paper, "Mrs. Simpkins called wanting to know why Eric was not getting any homework."

"What did you tell her?"

"That Mr. Donne—with rare exception—gives homework every day Monday through Thursday until the end of June."

"Thank you, Mary," I said.

"Get those forms done, Raymond."

I was two steps out of the office when my name was called again. Ron Thomas, the principal. He was wearing a white dress shirt with the sleeves rolled up, blue tie, and gray pants. One of the many former athletes turned gym teachers turned administrators in the system. This morning, he did not look happy with his career choice.

"Mr. Donne," he said, "I've gotten phone calls this morning from the *News*, the *Post*, and Channels 2 and 7." He pulled me aside and lowered his voice. "Asking about Francisco Rivas and his father's murder yesterday."

"They think it was over the weekend."

"What?"

"The cops. They think Frankie's dad was killed over the weekend."

"Whatever. They're looking for information on the boy."

"Did you give them any?"

"Just that he was—is—a student here in good academic standing and expected to graduate and attend high school in the fall. That is correct, right?"

"Yes."

"And they asked for you."

"For me?"

He shook his head. "Not by name, but they wanted to speak to his teacher. Seems one of the radio stations reported that the body was discovered by a schoolteacher. Was that you?"

Some reporter got to the young cop. "Yeah."

"Jesus, Ray. Why the hell would you—"

"I was looking for Frankie," I said.

"Great. Now the papers'll be all over us."

"Don't let them in and don't take their calls."

"Right." He rubbed his eyes. "The ELA scores are due in this week, and I don't expect good news. It's all I need to have the reading and writing scores of my eighth grade posted all over the papers along with the story of one of our students missing and his father murdered."

This must be real tough for you, I thought.

Ron calmed down and said, "You used to be a cop, Ray. Are they going to be here?"

"They'll want to see his records, talk to his friends."

"We have to allow that?"

"They're not the papers, Ron. Yes, you have to allow that."

"Shit."

"I need to grab some coffee before the kids show up, Ron."

Before I could do that, my boss grabbed my shoulder. "When they get here, could you sit in? You know how these guys think. You could answer their questions . . . better than I could."

"If you think it'll help, Ron, sure."

"Thanks, Ray."

On my way downstairs, I was almost run over by Elaine Stiles, the school counselor. She was carrying a box filled with manila folders.

"Raymond," she said, brushing her hair out of her face while balancing the box on her hip. "Hi. Sorry. I've got to run these records over to the high school. Then back here for the special ed rec . . . Oh my god, did you hear about Frankie's father?"

"Yeah."

"Jesus, huh? Did they find Frankie yet?"

"Not that I know of."

"Do they think he's—?"

"He's officially reported as missing. Along with his sister."

"Right. His sister." She looked at me and then at the box she was carrying. "I got to go. But, hey, when I get back I need five minutes to talk about Lisa King."

"Only five?"

"Something's up. I'm trying to get her into a high school other than . . . you know where . . . but I'm getting no help from her, and less from her parents."

"What can I do?"

"That's what the five minutes are for. 'Bye."

A minute later, I opened my classroom door. Almost eighty degrees outside and they still had the heat on in the building. Something about having to use up the school's oil allotment for this year or we wouldn't get the same for the next. I opened the windows, got the fan going, started a pot of coffee, and went over to my desk to finish grading the previous day's math quizzes. So far, only two of my kids had passed. Eric Simpkins was not one of them. Must have been all the homework I wasn't giving.

I finished the papers, poured myself a cup of coffee, and went back to my desk to wait for the students. Ten minutes later, nine of my eleven kids had shown up. No Lisa King. Again. And, of course, no Frankie.

After Eric put his things away in the back closet, I called him up to my desk.

"What's up, Mr. D?" he asked.

"Got a call from your mom this morning, E."

"Yeah? What she want?"

"She wanted to know why I stopped giving homework."

He pursed his lips, thought about it, and said, "Where she get that idea?"

I pulled out some work he had handed in the day before and held it out to him. "Your work's been getting sloppier lately, E. Doing it on the playground or the lunchroom?"

He shrugged. "Both, I guess."

"You can't do that and expect to get it done well. The lunchroom's too loud and the playground . . . You need to do it at home, where it's quiet."

"No offense, Mr. D, but you ain't never been to my house."

"For the rest of the year, Eric, you do your homework at home. And your mom signs it."

"Ahhh, Mr. D. I ain't no second grader."

"So don't whine like one. You broke one of my big rules, E. You used me in a lie. Now you pay the price."

"Damn. That ain't—"

"Isn't," I corrected him. "It *isn't* fair, and I don't care. Take it like a man. In six weeks—less—you'll be out of here for good."

That brought a smile to his face. "Ah ight," he said. Then he added, "Damn, kids in the yard were saying something about Frankie's pops."

"Sit down," I said. "I was just about to talk to you guys about it."

* * *

"Divide both sides by three."

Dougie raised his hand. "Why divide? Can't we just subtract?"

"If the unknown—the variable, N—is being multiplied by three, then you have to do the opposite to get it by itself."

Dougie looked around at the other kids. None of them looked back.

"I don't get it," he said.

"What's two times three, Dougie?" I asked.

"Six."

"Six divided by three?"

"Two."

"So, we're back to two."

"Yeah," he said, "but . . ."

"Whatever N is, if it's being multiplied by three, I can get it by itself by dividing by three." I gave the class a hopeful look. "We call that . . ."

"Isolating the variable," a small voice from the back said.

"Thank you, Annie. Isolating the variable. And whatever I do to the left of the equal sign, I'd better do to the right." I put my arms out and turned my hands palms up. "Balance."

The bell rang, end of the period. The boys jumped up. They had gym next.

"Whoa!" I said. "Me. Not the bell. You'll finish the problems on page two forty-eight. At home," I added, my eyes on Eric. I looked at my watch, then at the class.

"You may go."

The kids had been gone for about ten minutes and I was on my third cup of coffee, when Elaine Stiles walked into my room.

"Got any more of that?" she asked.

I pointed to the machine in the back. As she went over to it, I allowed myself to admire the way her skirt fit, and how it exposed just enough of her tanned legs from above her knees down to the low-cut leather boots she wore. Hard to believe this woman is fifteen years older than I am and has a daughter who'll be in college next year. She returned with her coffee, smoothed out her skirt, and sat in the chair next to my desk.

"I need to talk to you about Lisa, but this thing with Frankie has got me . . ."

"Yeah," I said. "Me, too."

I told her about my day yesterday. When I had finished, she said, "Oh my god, Raymond. That must have been horrible."

More than you know. "It was."

"What are the police doing about Frankie and his sister?"

"Treating them as missing children. They do what's called a mobilization, a search from the last known location and work out from there. They'll check the parks, vacant buildings."

I left out the part about the river, but Elaine's face filled with concern as she considered the possibilities.

"They don't think they're . . ."

"They're considering all possibilities, Elaine. That's all I can tell you." I took a final sip of coffee and tossed the cup into the wastebasket. "Lisa King?"

"Lisa King," she began, "has not been accepted to any of the high schools to which she applied." I knew that. "She's been wait-listed for a couple, but I'm not getting my hopes up. I can try and maybe get her into one of the alternative sites, but I need more from her and her family. If something doesn't happen soon, she's going around the block."

"Around the block" was the euphemism for the high school that the local kids went to when they were not accepted to the ones they applied to. Its claim to fame was that it was one of the first city schools to have permanent metal detectors installed at the entrances.

"Why no help from home?" I asked.

"I don't know. That's why I need your help."

"Me?"

"I've called the father and asked him to come in."

"Is he back with the family?"

"It seems like it."

Lisa King's mother had kicked the father out last year and filed a restraining order against him. Seems that Mr. King had a taste for alcohol and believed that more was better than less. When he tied one on—every two weeks or whenever payday was—he'd get angry and take it out on his wife. Mom finally had enough after Lisa stepped between the two of them one time and ended up missing a week of school. That's what it takes some-times. Now he was back home.

"He said he'd be in tomorrow," Elaine said. "Around ten. I checked your schedule. You're free that period."

"Is his wife going to be with him?"

"I don't know. She's working now. Does it matter?"

"Probably not. I'd just like to see the two of them together. Get a feel for the dynamic." Elaine smiled. "What?" I asked.

"You," she said. "'Dynamic.' You sound like a counselor."

"Right." I paused for a few seconds. "Okay. I'll see what I can do."

"Thanks, Raymond." She stood up, looked over at my blackboard, and said, "Algebra this late in the year?"

"They have to at least see it before they go to high school."

She turned to leave and stopped when she got to the door.

"He's going to be fine, right?" she asked. "Frankie?"

"Absolutely," I said. "He'll be back before you know it."

"Promise?"

"I'll see you later, Elaine."

After she left, I went to the board. All those equations. Variables. Unknowns.

I picked up the eraser and wiped them away.

My class was on the ground floor, and with the windows open I was con-stantly wiping dust and soot from every flat surface in the room. I'd start in the back by the sink and work my way forward. There wasn't much of a graffiti problem. My kids had me for five subjects, five days a week, and each one had his or her own desk. It's not like they could write stuff and get away with it. The worst I had to deal with was numbers from math problems, checking the spelling of words, and the random doodles of the eighth-grade mind. Until I got to Frankie's desk.

The upper-left section of Frankie's desk was covered with his auto-graph, one right on top of the other: FRANCISCO RIVAS, JR.

I'd told him that, as much as I appreciated and encouraged his self-confidence, I'd appreciate it more if he'd practice in his notebook.

"Ahh, Mr. D," he said last time we had this talk, "you should be thank-ing me."

"How do you figure that?" I asked.

"When I'm pitching for the Yanks and you're still teaching here, this desk'll be worth some serious green. You can sell it, make enough to get some good tickets to watch me play."

"You're going to make me pay to watch you pitch?"

"I can't be asking the boss for tickets all the time. Got a family to think about."

"Until that day comes, try to keep my desks a little cleaner. You make the Yankees—hell, you even make the Mets—you can come back here and write on every single desk I've got."

"I'm gonna do that, Mr. D," he said. *"You watch."*

I left Frankie's autographs alone and sat down at his desk. I'd do that from time to time, get a feel for what my students were seeing. I reached inside and pulled out his spiral notebook. I began flipping through the pages and saw more autographs, pictures of baseballs, the *N* and *Y* interlocking to form the Yankees insignia. On the inside of the back cover was a photo of a large, white house with a smaller structure—a garage, maybe a barn—off to the side. Underneath the photo were listings from a real estate section for houses up in Ulster County in the half-million-dollar range. Frankie had written SIGNING BONUS on the bottom of the page.

I placed my palms down on his desk and shut my eyes. I could see his father's body, the yellow flower on his sister's bloodless book bag, the near-empty refrigerator. I picked my hands up and slammed them down on the desk.

"Goddamn it!"

I don't know how long I sat there with my eyes closed, but when I opened them again, Lisa King was standing just inside the doorway, her book bag hanging over her shoulder.

"You okay?" she asked.

"Yeah." I looked at my watch. "Nice of you to join us."

She shrugged. "Slept late."

"Did you sleep through the last two days?"

She shrugged again, went over to her desk, and placed her bag on the seat.

"What we got now?"

"Five more minutes of gym. Then lunch and back here for one period. Good timing."

"Shoulda just stayed home."

"That's a choice," I answered. "I spoke to Ms. Stiles this morning."

"So?"

"So, if you had your hopes on a certain high school . . ."

"I'm just gonna go around the block."

"'Around the block,'" I repeated. "That's assuming you get out of the eighth grade."

Another shrug, like she didn't have a care in the world.

"Second, a kid like you'd get lost in that place."

"I'll be fine."

"No, Lisa." I stood. "You will not be fine. You have any idea what the dropout rate at that place is?"

"You saying I'm dumb?"

Jesus. "I'm not saying you're dumb." I took a moment to check myself. "Your dad's coming up tomorrow."

Now she cared. "You called my dad?"

"Ms. Stiles did. Yes."

"Ahhhhh!" She looked at me and waved her hand as if slapping away a fly. "All y'all need to mind your own business."

"You *are* our business, Lisa," I said. "Whether you like it or not."

"Nah, nah," she said and ran her hand from her forehead to the back of her neck. I noticed a slight discoloration two inches above her left eye.

"What's that mark on your face?" I asked.

She turned away and headed toward the door. "Nothing, okay?"

I followed her. "No, it's not okay." I grabbed her elbow to stop her from leaving the room and got a close-up look at the mark above her eye. "Where'd you get that bruise?"

"Nowhere." She shook my hand off her arm. "I'm going to gym."

"Lisa," I tried, "I can't help you unless you talk to me."

She raised her eyebrows. "I guess you can't help me then."

She walked out into the hallway. Again, I followed and called her name.

"Go help the other kids, Mr. D," she said, not bothering to turn around. "They need it more than I do."

I couldn't think of a response to that, so I just watched as the kid who didn't need my help made a right turn into the staircase. The gym was the other way.

•   •   •

A few hours later, the kids were gone, the windows were shut, and I went up to the main office to check my mailbox before going home. Mary was slipping her pocketbook over her shoulder when she spotted me.

"Oh, Ray," she said. "Mr. Thomas said not to worry about the meeting with the police. He took care of it over the phone."

"Really?" I said, surprised by the disappointed tone in my voice.

"That's what he told—" The phone rang, stopping her in mid-sentence. She picked up and mumbled her standard greeting. She pressed a button and held it out to me.

"Tell them they'll have it tomorrow," I said. "Whatever it is."

"It's a female," Mary whispered. "Sounds cute."

And you sound like my mother, I thought. I walked through the swinging gate and took the phone.

"This is Raymond Donne."

"Mr. Donne, this is Elsa. Mrs. Santos's neighbor. From yesterday?"

"Yes," I said.

"It's Mrs. Santos. Her apartment was broken into."

Shit. "Did the cops get there yet?"

A pause and then, "She did not call the police."

"Elsa," I said, "she has to call the police. Where is she now?"

"My mother and I are with her here. In her apartment."

"In her— Elsa, you have to call the police. Now."

"She called the church."

"Excuse me?"

"You said yesterday that you were a policeman."

"Five years ago. Why are you calling me?"

"What is the church going to do, Mr. Donne? Please come over."

"If she doesn't want to call the police, what makes you think she'll want to see me?"

"It would make me feel better, Mr. Donne. She is very stubborn and will not listen to me or my mother."

I took a moment to look at the clock. I wanted to go home. I said, "I'd like to, Elsa, but . . ."

"Thank you, Mr. Donne. Thank you."

"Call the police," I said, but she'd already hung up.

Chapter 6

WITH HAROLD NOWHERE TO BE found, I took the elevator straight up to the seventeenth floor. Elsa was standing outside Mrs. Santos's apartment when I turned the corner.

"Mr. Donne," Elsa said as she stepped toward me. "Thank you for coming."

"Did you get her to call the police?"

"She is inside," she said. "With my mother and Mr. Cruz."

"Another neighbor?"

"He's from the church."

"Did he convince her to call the cops?"

"Come inside," Elsa said. "Have something to drink. Some water, iced tea." She lowered her voice. "If Mrs. Santos asks, you came by to check on Frankie."

"You didn't tell her you called me?"

"Come," she said, pulling on my elbow.

I pulled back while we were still in the doorway. "Are you going to answer any of my questions?"

"No," she said. "I did not tell her I called you. No, Mr. Cruz has not convinced her to call the police. Now can we go inside?"

Good-looking women can get away with talking like that sometimes. Use their tone of voice to imply a sense of superiority and vulnerability at the same time. I put my hand on the doorknob and turned it a few times.

"What are you doing?" Elsa asked.

"The lock doesn't seem to have been forced," I said. I ran my hand over the wood and brass plating. "No scratches on the door."

"Come inside," she said, pulling me again. This time I went without a fight.

We walked through a narrow hallway, past a dozen or so pictures on the wall, some black-and-white, some in color. Elsa led me into the main room, where an elderly woman in a wheelchair held hands with another woman of about the same age, who sat in a metal folding chair. They looked over at Elsa and me as we entered. I could tell from the blue eyes that the woman in the wheelchair was Frankie's grandmother. The wheelchair had a decal on the side: a blue snake wrapped around a white cross. The words EC MEDICAL were written under the logo.

"Mommy," Elsa said. "Senora Santos. This is Mr. Donne. Frankie's teacher. *El maestro de la escuela.*"

I stepped forward and offered my hand to Mrs. Santos.

"*¿Qué tu quiere?*" she asked, looking at my hand.

"I came by to see if there's any news about Frankie." I withdrew my hand. "If you've heard from the police."

She let out a hiss and said, "*La policía.*" She looked at the other woman and they commiserated by shaking their heads.

I turned to Elsa. "Maybe I should go."

Before she could answer, a man's voice came from another room.

"*Si, immediatemente,*" he was saying. "'As soon as possible' would mean immediately, would it not?" A pause. "Thank you, Johnny."

I heard the refrigerator door close. A man came out of the kitchen, holding a glass of water in each hand. He acknowledged my presence with a slight nod of his head and handed the glasses to the two older women. He whispered something in Spanish and they both smiled. He turned his attention to me.

"Elijah Cruz," he said with just a hint of a Spanish accent. We shook hands and he held mine in a tight grip until I said, "Raymond Donne."

Elijah Cruz appeared to be a few years older than I. His dark hair was cut short, and his goatee had a few flecks of gray in it. He was wearing a white shirt with the sleeves rolled up, a black tie, and black pants. A cell phone was clipped to his belt.

"You are from Francisco's school," he said.

"I'm his teacher."

He nodded. "Senora Santos told me you were here yesterday looking for Francisco. It was you who found Mr. Rivas?"

"How did you know that?"

"The detective who came by last evening—Detective Royce—mentioned it. That must have been quite a shock for you."

"You could say that."

He gave me a sympathetic smile. "Unfortunately, there is no new information regarding Francisco or his sister. And now"—he placed his hand on Mrs. Santos's shoulder—"to add to her miseries, her apartment has been violated."

Elsa's mother whispered something to Frankie's grandmother, and again the two women shook their heads. I took a quick look around the room. I'd never been inside the apartment, but everything looked pretty much the way I guessed it should. There was an oxygen tank in the corner of the living room, the same snake and white cross on its side.

"Was anything taken?" I asked Mrs. Santos, but she was not looking at me, so Elijah Cruz answered.

"She does not believe so."

"I didn't notice any damage to the front door. Who else has a key to the apartment?"

Cruz translated my question for Mrs. Santos.

"Solamente Francisco . . . y Johnny," she said to Cruz just above a whisper.

"Her grandson and the super," Cruz told me.

Mrs. Santos looked at me and for the first time since I'd entered her home, addressed me directly.

"You no think Frankie came home and not tell me?" she asked.

"No," I said, noticing all the eyes in the room on me now. "I don't think anything. It's just a routine question." *Shit, Ray. Could you sound more like a cop?*

"He no come home without telling me," Mrs. Santos said to Elsa's mother. *"Imposible."*

She started to breathe a bit heavier, and Elsa's mother went to the corner of the living room and wheeled over the oxygen tank. She took the opportunity to throw a distrustful look my way before she handed the blue mask to Mrs. Santos, who took it and placed it over her nose and mouth. As I watched her breathing, Elijah Cruz took me by the arm.

"Perhaps we should talk outside, Mr. Donne."

"Yeah," I said. "Maybe we should." I gave Elsa a look and motioned with my head toward the front door. She nodded and mouthed, "Thank you."

When we got to the hallway, we were met by a gray-haired man in a blue denim shirt with the name JOHNNY written on it in gold script. He placed his toolbox on the floor, took Cruz by the hands, and held them.

"Johnny," Cruz said. "Thank you for coming so quickly. I am very grateful. As is Senora Santos. This is Mr. Donne."

"Mucho gusto," Johnny said, shaking my hand.

"I'm impressed," I said. "It takes me a week to get my super to return my phone calls."

Johnny smiled. "Senor Cruz, he call. I am not too busy. I come."

Elijah Cruz put his hand on Johnny's shoulder.

"Johnny is a member of the church, Mr. Donne. We look out for each other."

"Si," Johnny said.

"Let us leave you to your work, Johnny," Cruz said.

"Mucho gusto, Senor Donne." Johnny picked up his toolbox, gave us a smile, and stepped over to the door to get to his work.

"I apologize for Senora Santos, Mr. Donne," Cruz said. "She is very tired and very upset. The police, the newspapers. And now"—he pointed to where Johnny was crouched down removing the old lock—"this."

"Where was she when the break-in occurred?" I asked.

Cruz smiled and said, "Detective Royce said you were a police officer once." He paused. "The church. *Las Mujeres*—our women's group— meets Wednesday afternoons. It is as much a prayer group as it is an opportunity for the women to share time and food with each other."

"I'm confused," I said. "You work at the church, Mr. Cruz?"

"No, I would not say that. I am a parishioner, like Johnny and Senora Santos."

"Who makes a phone call and gets the super here in world-record time."

"I am not without a certain amount of influence, Mr. Donne. I am in the fortunate position to help the church financially. The members appreciate and respect that." He reached into his shirt pocket and handed me a business card.

"EC Medical Supplies," I said, recognizing the snake and the cross. "The wheelchair and oxygen tank?"

"That is my company, yes."

"I didn't know that Mrs. Santos was ill."

"Chronic bronchitis," he said. "She will be with us for a long time, but she does need assistance. Especially in a time like this."

"I've got to be honest with you, Mr. Cruz," I said, slipping the card into my back pocket. "I'm concerned that she called you and not the police."

"But not surprised."

"Excuse me?"

"Senora Santos trusts me, Mr. Donne. She does not trust the police. You were a policeman for how long?"

"Long enough," I said. "Why?"

"Would it offend you if I suggested that this is the first time you were ever in a Puerto Rican woman's apartment without the authority that comes with the uniform?"

"I'm not easily offended, Mr. Cruz."

"Good." He smiled. "If you give *la abuela* the choice between calling the police or her church, she will choose the church every time, Mr. Donne."

"I understand that, but—"

"If I felt that Senora Santos was in real danger, I would call the police myself."

"You don't think her apartment being broken into puts her in real danger?"

"I am considering the very real possibility," he said, lowering his voice, "that her apartment was not broken into."

"Excuse me?"

"You looked around," he said. "Did anything seem out of the ordinary?"

"No."

"And the front door?"

"Seemed fine," I said. "But then why are you so quick to replace the lock?"

"Because it will make her feel safer, Mr. Donne. Do you want to be the one to tell her that her imagination and stress of the past few days has gotten the better of her?"

"No."

"Then we have the lock changed, and she feels a bit more secure. She told me when she returned home, her front door was open. I believe that in her hurry to get to *Las Mujeres,* she may have neglected to close her door. She has had a lot on her mind the past few days, yes?"

"This women's group," I said. "*Las Mujeres.* They meet every Wednesday?"

"Yes."

"Then it is also a very real possibility that if someone did break into her apartment, they knew she'd be at the church for a few hours."

He nodded. "That is true."

"It's also true her former son-in-law was murdered and her grandchildren are missing. Whoever is responsible may be behind her apartment being broken into."

"That is possible."

"But you won't offer that possibility to Mrs. Santos?"

"No," he said. "I will not."

"Then I think I should."

"She will not accept it coming from—"

"A white guy?" I said.

"An outsider," Cruz said. "During your years as a policeman, how many times were you welcomed into the home of a Puerto Rican?"

"I wouldn't say I was ever *welcomed.* I went where I was needed."

"Our people do not look at it like that."

"Then why do they call the police?"

"Most have no one else to call," he said. "Senora Santos does. You have to understand, Mr. Donne, the Puerto Rican is not comfortable asking for help from outsiders. It is our experience that no one knocks at our door without wanting something. It is part of our history. Part of who we are and where we come from. You have to knock many times before you are invited inside."

"I've just been inside."

"You were not invited by Mrs. Santos. Nor welcomed, I'm afraid. I will handle this."

"You can ensure her safety?"

Before he could answer, his cell phone rang. He took it from his belt, flipped it open, and said, "I have to take this. Excuse me." He walked a few steps away and lowered his voice. "Yes. I have told them that many times. They are to go ahead with the procedure and they will be reimbursed. Yes. Call me when it is done." He closed the phone.

"So," I said, "I pretty much wasted my time coming over here?"

Cruz stepped back over and touched me on the elbow, a little gesture reminding me who was in charge here. He was good.

"Your willingness to help has not gone unnoticed. I am sure that Elsa appreciates your coming over."

"You know that she called me?"

"I suspected as much. She looks out for Senora Santos."

"And so do you," I said.

"Yes. And this time will be no exception. Senora Santos will stay downstairs tonight. Now, this may be a good time for you to say good-bye to her."

"Why don't you do that for me, Mr. Cruz? I'm not sure she wants to see me again."

"Even though she did not invite you, Mr. Donne, I believe she would appreciate the respect of your saying good-bye."

We stepped back into the apartment, and this time, when I got to the pictures on the wall, I stopped to look at them. There were some old photos, black-and-whites of palm trees and beaches. Puerto Rico. Most of the newer ones, the ones in color, were of Frankie: in his baseball uniform, graduating from elementary school, with someone I guessed was his sister, Milagros. They were standing in front of the big, white house I recognized from the picture in Frankie's notebook. Next to that one was a picture of a pregnant woman standing next to a young Frankie. The woman had the same dark eyes, the same hopeful smile.

"Is this Frankie's mother?" I asked Cruz.

"Yes," he said.

"How did she die?"

"Non-Hodgkins lymphoma," he said.

"Cancer?"

"Cancer of the blood, yes. The lymphocytes turn malignant and start to crowd out the healthy white blood cells."

"You a doctor, too?"

"I spent two years in medical school before I chose another path. It helps to understand what afflicts the people I help." He touched the photo. "Christina was diagnosed just before she became pregnant with Milagros. She could not undergo treatment while pregnant, and by the time Milagros was born the disease had spread too far."

"How long did she live?"

"Another three years. A credit to her strength."

I looked again at the photo, this time focusing on the smile that would be gone too soon. She was putting forth one hell of a front for her son.

"When you grow up in the projects," Cruz said, "and experience the hardships that Christina faced, you don't consider that it will be your own body that betrays you."

We stood there for another moment before he said, "Come. Say good-bye."

Mrs. Santos and Elsa's mother were at the table, drinking their waters. Elsa stepped out of the kitchen, drying her hands with a towel.

"Mr. Donne," she said, so the ladies would realize I was back. "Thank you for coming."

"I wanted to say good-bye." I looked at the two women. They didn't look back. I nodded and said, "Good-bye."

Elijah Cruz took my hand again. "Thank you, Mr. Donne. Perhaps you will knock on Mrs. Santos's door again someday."

I gave him a small smile. "Perhaps."

"I will walk you out, Mr. Donne," Elsa said.

"Elsa!" her mother hissed.

"Mommy, shhh!" She waved her hand at her mother. "I'll be right back." She led me out into the hallway. "I am sorry about that, Mr. Donne. They don't mean to be rude."

"It's okay, Elsa. And please, call me Raymond." She nodded. "That photo on the wall," I said. "The large, white house?"

"The 'mansion'? It's Anita's. She lives upstate."

"Ulster County?" I asked, remembering the real estate ads from Frankie's book.

"Highland, yes. Why?"

"Just wondering."

She pressed the Down button for the elevator. As we waited, she said, "Anita is Frankie's mother's cousin. The house was a wedding gift from her husband."

"She married well."

"She married rich. She wanted that life. I guess we all did. Anita, Christina, and I would talk for hours as kids about the life we would have after getting out of here. Anita's dreams came true." She drifted off for a few seconds. "Anita's husband, John, owns the travel agency where Frankie's father works—worked."

"That's a long commute from Highland."

"They have an apartment here in Williamsburg. John owns some buildings in the neighborhood."

"You see her much?"

Elsa snorted. "Only during the holidays. If her husband allows her to visit the projects. 'Slumming,' they call it and expect me to laugh along with them."

"Is that what Anita calls it?"

"She pretends to mimic him, but I can tell it makes her a little uncomfortable. I think she is beginning to feel the same way he does."

"Some people have a problem with where they came from."

"Some people," Elsa said, "have a problem with where they end up."

The elevator arrived. I reached over and held the door before it could close.

"Thank you, Mr.—Raymond."

"For what?" I asked. "I didn't do anything."

"You came because I asked you to. Even though Mrs. Santos does not appreciate it, I do. I feel better knowing that someone besides her church was here."

"It's not your church?"

"No. My mother and I are Catholics. And you?"

"Raised Catholic," I said. "But I got over it."

She smiled. "Thank you."

I stepped inside the elevator, pressed the button for the lobby, and tipped an imaginary cap. "Ma'am."

As the door closed, Elsa's smile got a little bigger. Maybe this wasn't a complete waste after all.

Down in the lobby, Harold was pushing a wet mop across the floor. When he spotted me coming out of the elevator, he took the opportunity to stop his work and meet me at the exit.

"Still no sign of Lefty, huh?" he asked.

"No," I said. "You see any strangers around here today, Harold?"

"Strangers? Nope. Why you ask?"

"No reason."

"Then why you ask?"

"See ya around, Harold."

He looked at my umbrella. "How's the leg, Mr. Donne?"

I ignored the question and left the building. I wanted to call the cops, let them know what might have happened up in Mrs. Santos's apartment. I decided it wouldn't do any good. She wouldn't tell them anything. When I got to the street, I went over to the pay phone and dialed nine-one-one. When the operator asked me the nature of my emergency, I said a crazy man was outside the Clemente Houses threatening people with a broken bottle.

If someone were watching Mrs. Santos's apartment, I wanted them to see some police.

I wasn't ready to go home yet. Since it was pushing six, I figured I'd head over to The LineUp, grab some dinner, and check in with Mrs. Mac about Saturday's party. The place was filling up with the after-work crowd—I waved to a few cops I recognized—but I managed to get the last stool at the bar. Right next to Edgar. Lucky me.

"They get the kid yet?"

"Hello, Edgar," I said. "I'm fine, thanks. You?"

"Good, man. How's the case going?"

Mikey came over, placed a bottle of Bud in front of me, and said, "Thanks again for last night, Ray. I owe ya."

"How'd it go?"

"Let's just say I owe ya big," he said. "You eating?"

"Yeah. BLT with turkey."

"Extra B?"

"Absolutely."

"Chips?"

I nodded.

"Glad you're still on that health kick. Be back in a sec."

"Anyway," Edgar said, as if Mikey had interrupted an actual conversation, "how's the case going? Papers said the kid might be a suspect."

"Edgar," I said, "I'm not involved in any case."

"The cops didn't call you about the missing kids?"

"His name's Frankie," I said. "The sister's Milagros. And I don't give a shit what the papers said. He didn't kill his dad. The cops called the school and got some background on Frankie, that's all."

Edgar leaned over. "They asking you for help?"

"No. They're not."

"Why not, man? You found the body. You used to be a cop."

"Used to be, Edgar." I tapped the side of my head with my forefinger. "Think."

"Come on, Raymond. One call to your uncle, and you—"

"The cops are not going to let me nose around because of who my uncle is. You want to know how the case is progressing, keep reading the papers. Maybe they'll actually print a few facts. Or stay at home and listen to your illegal scanner."

Edgar gave me a look, took a sip from his pint, and said, "I like you better when you're on the other side of the bar." He slid off his stool and headed toward the men's room.

"Me, too," I said.

"You're too young to be talking to yourself, Raymond."

I spun around. "And they said your husband was good at surveillance," I said, accepting a kiss on the cheek from Mrs. McVernon.

"Taught him everything he knew," she said. "How are you?"

"I'm fine." I could tell she wasn't buying that, so I added, "I was hoping that Frankie and his sister would show up today. The longer they're out there, the . . ."

"Greater the chance something bad happened to them?"

"Yeah." Spoken like a cop's wife.

"I'm sure they'll be fine, Raymond. Probably be home for dinner tomorrow."

"That'd be nice," I said.

"I just got off the phone with Billy. We're all set for Saturday. He's tickled pink that you'll be here."

Nice redirection. "Billy Morris does not get 'tickled pink,' Mrs. Mac."

"Anyways, we're all staffed, the distributor's going to make an extra delivery tomorrow so we'll be stocked for the Q, and Billy's taking care of the food."

"Then you don't really need me," I said.

"Don't even think of it, Ray," Mikey said as he put my dinner in front of me. "You are here Saturday."

"What happened to owing me one?"

"I'll owe ya two, after the Q." He laughed. "Hey, that rhymes." He turned away and headed to the other end of the bar singing, "Owe ya two, after the Q."

Edgar returned. "Easy, Mrs. Mac. Raymond's not in a very good mood this evening."

"He's just fine, Emo." Mrs. Mac patted me on the shoulder. "He's just got a lot on his mind these days. You boys enjoy the night. I'm going home to call my grandson."

"I'll see you Saturday," I said.

"Is noon too early?"

"It's fine, but as soon as the Q gets rolling, so do I."

"Thank you, Raymond. Good night, Emo."

Edgar bowed his head. "Ma'am." When Mrs. Mac had gone, Edgar turned back to me. "Why can't you be that nice to me?"

"Mrs. Mac doesn't ask a lot of stupid questions."

"I thought teachers didn't believe in stupid questions."

"Yeah, a lot of people think that." I took a bite of my sandwich, a sip of beer, and pointed at the newspaper in front of Edgar. "Let me see the sports pages."

Edgar knew this was my way of ending any further conversation. He sighed and slid the paper to me. I turned right to the box scores: the only part of the paper I could trust. Box scores don't lie or imply, they just are, and if you know how to read them—I mean really read them—you can get the whole story of a game you didn't see a single pitch of. Life would be a lot less confusing if people could just sum up their days in little one-by-three-inch boxes.

I checked out a half dozen games before I finished my dinner. I pushed the paper away, and signaled to Mikey for another beer. I also pointed at Edgar's. The least I could do was buy him a round after making him pout. He gave me a smile, and we clinked glasses. All made up.

"So," he said. "Whatta you do next?"

"About what?"

"The missing kids." He lowered his voice. "And the dead guy. What's your next move?"

"Edgar, you are this close"—I held my forefinger an inch away from my thumb—"to getting knocked off your stool."

I didn't think he heard me. "You're just going to let the cops handle it?"

"That's what they get paid to do, Edgar. Some of them are pretty good at it."

"Yeah, but if they don't get anywhere by the weekend, it's old news. Even I know that."

He had a point there, but I'd be damned if I admitted it. Anyway, what the hell was I going to do?

"Edgar," I said, "I gave up my dreams of being Jim Rockford a while ago. Pretty much after I figured out he got his ass kicked every time I watched a rerun."

"I always wanted to be Barney," Edgar said. "From *Mission: Impossible*."

"Good luck with that," I said. "Grow the fuck up."

"Here's what I think we should do," he went on. "First—"

"Edgar, I swear to god, if you don't drop this, I'll not only knock you on your ass, I'll ban you from the Q."

He studied my face for a few seconds, looking for signs that I was bluffing. When he finally summoned the courage to speak again, he said, "You wouldn't do that. You promised."

"Watch me," I said. "Leave it alone. I'm serious about this."

We locked eyes for a bit, and then he said, "Fine." He got off his barstool, took back his paper, and folded it under his arm. He reached into his pocket and pulled out a twenty-dollar bill. "I'll pay for my own drinks, thank you very much." And with those final words, Edgar Martinez O'Brien spun around and exited The LineUp.

Mikey came over and said, "Damn, Ray. What'd ya say to get him to storm out like that?"

"Could have been a couple of things, I guess."

"Well," Mikey said as he cleared away Edgar's unfinished beer, "if you remember any of them, tell me so I can try them sometime."

I managed a small grin as he placed another Bud in front of me. I felt a small sense of regret for the way I'd spoken to Edgar, but it passed.

Can't stand the heat? Stay the hell out of cop bars.

Chapter 7

"YOU SURE YOU DON'T WANT a cup?" I placed my coffee mug down by my grade book. "I've got plenty."

"I'm fine," Lisa King's father said, making sure I knew he was the kind of guy who took nothing from nobody.

He was sitting in the biggest chair I had, which was too small for him. He kept his hands on the table, and I could see the grease under his fingernails. He wore a blue denim shirt, "East River Boat" stitched above the left breast pocket. On the other side was his name, "William K," written in red script. Judging from the flecks of gray in his short Afro, I figured he had about eight years on me. He smelled of smoke, like someone who smokes in their car with the windows shut. I opened up the nearest window as far as it would go and then sat down across from Lisa's father.

"I'm not sure why Ms. Stiles called me out of work, Mr. Donne," he said, as he looked at his watch. "Lisa's mom usually handles all the school stuff. Said you didn't even call her."

"Right," I said, ignoring his point. "And I am sorry to cut into your day like this, but we have some concerns about Lisa that we felt might be better addressed with you."

He considered that with a nod and a grimace. "She step into it again?"

"Not exactly."

"Then what?" he asked, folding his hands in front of him. "Exactly."

I had decided earlier to start off with the academics, then work up to the big stuff.

"Well," I began, "it's not one particular incident, it's more of a series of . . ." This is why I don't dance. I'm not good at it. "We're afraid that Lisa might have to repeat the eighth grade, Mr. King. Or at the very least, attend summer school."

His eyebrows pushed upward and then came back down into a tight squeeze, which caused his whole face to wrinkle.

"I don't . . . her mother told me she was doing good."

"She was," I said. "Well enough to pass, anyway. But the last five or six weeks"—I turned my grade book around so he could read it as my finger ran across a series of x's and zeros—"she hasn't been handing in any homework, she's been late or absent nearly every day, and she's going to have trouble meeting the state standards on the tests."

Mr. King blinked a few times before saying, "I heard something about that on the news. What's that mean? 'Failure to meet state standards?'"

"Every eighth grader is required to demonstrate a certain level of proficiency on the . . ."

I could practically smell the bullshit coming out of my mouth. "The city is no longer promoting eighth graders if they don't meet the levels set by the state on the reading and math tests."

"But I saw her report card," he said. "She passed everything, right?"

"Those are the grades I give, Mr. King. And she barely passed. She keeps up the way she's going, she will fail the fourth marking period and end up back here again next year."

We sat in silence as he thought about that, the look on his face telling me that I was just one more person in his life telling him shit he didn't want to hear.

"She here today?" he asked.

"She showed up at nine thirty."

"Nine thirty." He bit his lower lip. "She left the house before I did, and I leave at eight. Don't take no hour and a half to get to school." He closed his eyes and made a visible effort to control his anger. "Lemme get this straight, now. You're telling me that if she starts passing and getting her ass to school on time, she'll move on to high school?"

"That's what I'm telling you," I said. "Yes."

"Then that's what she's gonna do. I'll see to that."

He started to get up, but I wasn't done. "That's not all, Mr. King."

"Jesus," he said as he sat back down. "Something else?"

"Lisa came in yesterday with a bruise above her left eye."

"Told me she got that in gym. Volleyball hit her."

"Lisa doesn't participate in gym, Mr. King. She never comes prepared and has to sit in the bleachers with her homework."

He shook his head. "So she fails gym. That gonna leave her behind?"

"That's not the point," I said and waited, like I used to do behind the two-way mirror, watching the detectives go after a guy. It wouldn't take long, I thought.

"Then what is the . . ." Here it comes. "Ah, no. You didn't call me in here to talk about Lisa's grades." As he stood up he pushed the table hard enough to make a little coffee splash over the side of my cup. I stayed seated as he leaned over and placed his hands back on the table. "You think I hit my little girl?"

I thought about getting up, but wasn't sure if he'd take that as a challenge. So I sat there and spoke in an even tone designed to remind him whose meeting this was. "She got that bruise from somewhere, Mr. King."

"Not from me." My first thought was that he wanted to come at me over the table. Or at least flip the damn thing. "I know you all think you know what happened at the house last year, and maybe you do. Some of it, anyways. But you don't know everything. I never . . ." He slapped his hands down on the table, making me jump back a bit. A small stream of coffee made its way to the edge of the table. Mr. King took half a minute before he continued, calmer now. "I made a lot of mistakes last year," he said. "But I ain't never hit my little girl."

"No," I said. "Just your wife."

"Yeah," he said, pointing his finger at me. "Lisa told me you used to be a cop."

"What's that got to do with anything?"

"I know how you all think. Think just because my lips're moving, I'm lying."

"You have a lot of experience with cops, Mr. King?"

"Give me that bullshit. I grew up in this neighborhood. I was getting rousted by the cops when you was still playing Little League with all your little friends out in the 'burbs. Yeah, Mr. Donne, I got plenty experience being looked at like I'm lying. But you ain't no cop anymore." He slid his chair gently under the table. "So I guess I'll be going now."

"Lisa got that bruise from somewhere, Mr. King," I said again.

He stopped and then turned back.

"I know what you people say," he said. "Folks don't change. Some asshole hits his wife once, well, he's just gonna keep on hitting her." He took a breath. "I did hit my wife. Once." A small smile crept onto his face. "You don't do nothing hurtful to that woman twice. She threw my ass out and told me not come back. Ever. And she meant it."

I stood, the safety of ten feet and the table between us, my heart still beating a bit too fast.

"What's your point, Mr. King?"

"You know why people don't change?"

"Tell me."

" 'Cause they ain't got no reason to. Plain and simple. They ain't got no reason." He slapped his hand against his chest. "That's what makes me different. I got a reason. And I'm changing." He stopped for a few seconds, deciding whether to keep the conversation going. "After a few months outta the house, I called my wife. Said, 'What's it gonna take? You let me back home?' And she told me." He held out his thumb. " 'Stop drinking.' I said I could do that." He extended his forefinger. " 'Get some counseling.' I'm doing that." The middle finger. " 'You don't never raise a hand to me again.' I said I could do that, and I'm keeping that promise. I am keeping that promise." He turned the fingers into a fist and placed it over his heart. "That woman and those girls? That's my reason to change. I almost lost them once, and that's not gonna happen again." He filled his chest up with air and let it out slowly. "You can either believe that or not. That's up to you all."

We stood there, looking at each other. I was waiting to see if he'd leave, now that he'd had his say. He was waiting for me to challenge what he said.

"I didn't call you in here to cause you grief or bring any more trouble into your house, Mr. King. But my first responsibility here is to Lisa."

He nodded. "Mine, too. I'll find out where she got that bruise and . . ."

"And what?"

He shook his head. "I don't know. Yet. But I will protect me and mine."

"You understand we're required by law to call in any suspicion of abuse."

"Figured you'da done that by now."

"I wanted to talk to you first."

That seemed to surprise him. "And what'd you decide?"

Good question. You gave a good speech, I thought. But, like you said, I'm used to people lying to me.

"We'll let you know," I said.

"You do that," he said and headed toward the door just as Elaine Stiles was coming in. It took her a moment to realize who he was.

"Oh, Mr. King," she said. "I thought I had missed you."

"You did," he said as he slipped past her and out of my room.

From the doorway, Elaine gave me a questioning look.

"That went well," I said.

She stepped over to the table. "What happened?"

I went over the conversation with her. How I started with Lisa's grades and ended with asking about the bruise above her eye.

"Ray," she said when I was done, "did you talk to him as a teacher?"

"As opposed to what?"

"The cop thing you do."

"What cop thing?"

She shook her head. "You squint your eyes just a touch and lean forward. Then you lower your voice and talk. Real. Slow."

"You've seen me do this?"

"Whenever you feel the control is slipping away and you have to take it back."

"Elaine," I said, "with all due respect, don't talk to me like I'm one of the kids."

"I'm not," she said. "I'm just asking how you spoke to him."

"I told him about our concerns and our responsibility to call in any suspected abuse."

Elaine waited before going on. I grabbed a couple of paper towels and wiped up the coffee from the table and the floor.

"Do you think he hit Lisa?" she asked.

"Are you asking me as a teacher? Or as someone who does that 'cop thing'?"

"Come on, Ray. I didn't mean any—"

"He said Lisa told him she got that bruise from a volleyball in gym."

She smirked. "Lisa's biggest risk in gym is getting a paper cut."

"I told him that. That's when he got defensive on me. I don't know, Elaine. There's a part of me that thinks he's being straight. My gut says no, he didn't hit Lisa."

"Is she in today?" I nodded. "I'll talk to her. See what she has to say now that we've met with her dad." The bell rang. "I'd hate to make that phone call and we're wrong."

"Or," I pointed out, "we don't make that phone call and we're wrong."

"Yeah," Elaine said. "There's that, too."

The sound of kids filled the hallway. I walked her back to the door.

"It's been a long year, Mr. Donne," she said.

I thought about Frankie. "It's been a long two days, Ms. Stiles."

"Yeah. Let's talk before you leave?"

"Absolutely."

She turned and headed down the hallway as my students started to gather outside my door. Elaine took Lisa by the elbow and led her away. Eric Simpkins had a big grin on his face as he stopped in my doorway. He held out his hand to bump my fist.

I ignored the gesture.

"Take out your Lit books," I said, ushering the kids into my room. "I want to see the Whitman homework out on your desks. Now."

The final bell of the day had rung, the kids were gone, and I was standing at my desk going through Frankie's notebook, page by page, when Elaine walked in.

"Lisa told me that she got the bruise when she was hanging around with a group of neighborhood kids. They're older, her parents don't want her hanging around with them, so she made up the volleyball story."

"You believe her?"

"No," she said. "I called her mom, you know, a kind of end-of-the-year, let's-all-get-through-this-together conversation. I mentioned the latenesses and the absences, asked how things were at home, and she said fine."

"So . . ."

"So if she's right and things are fine, a phone call to Children's Services will screw with these people's lives. The girls will be removed. You want to talk about gut feelings?"

"Go ahead."

"It's not perfect at the King house, but the family's working. I don't want to ruin any progress they've made if we both have doubts that her father hit her."

I sat down at my desk and turned a few more pages in Frankie's note-book. "What if we're wrong?"

"I don't think we are. We're both kind of good at this sort of thing."

"Yeah."

I turned to the back of the notebook and looked at the picture of the house and the real estate ads.

"Anita's house," Elaine said.

"You know it?"

"Frankie talks about it in our sessions. He loves that place."

"So does his sister," I said. "There was a drawing of it on the fridge at her dad's place. Looked just like the photo."

"You know," Elaine said after a few seconds of silence, "that's come up in our talks. Frankie said that house was the place he felt the safest."

I pointed to the cut-outs from the newspaper. "He's already planning to buy a house."

Elaine smiled. Maybe for the first time that day.

"Hey," she said, "the police would know about Anita, right? About the house? From talking to his grandmother."

"I don't know."

"We know about it."

"We know Frankie better than the cops," I reminded her.

She thought about that for a few seconds. "Shouldn't we . . . bring it to their attention?"

"*We?*"

She smiled again. "You."

"Detective Royce—the guy assigned to the case—said if I thought of anything that might be of use, I should call him." I reached into the back pocket of my bag and pulled out his card. There were two numbers listed. One was the precinct, the other a cell phone.

"You'll call him?" Elaine asked.

"This is something."

"It is."

"The precinct's kind of on my way home." If I walked five blocks out of my way.

"You want a ride?"

"No. I'll be fine."

"Call me," she said, "and let me know what happens."

"Nothing's going to happen, Elaine. I probably won't even get to talk to him."

"Call me anyway. Or we'll talk tomorrow."

"Okay," I said as I stood up. "Let's talk tomorrow."

After she left, I carefully removed the tape from around the picture of Anita's house and put it in my book bag. It probably would be a wasted trip, I told myself. Royce may not even be there, and what would I do then? "Hey, I'm Ray Donne? Used to work here. Now I'm a schoolteacher, and I was wondering . . ."

Before I could talk myself out of going, I went to the back closet to get my jacket and umbrella. I was glad to have the umbrella. No way I wanted to walk back into my old house looking like a cripple.

And who knew? Maybe it would finally rain.

Chapter 8

I WAS STANDING ON THE OTHER side of the avenue, outside the Korean deli across from the precinct, finishing up a pint of water, wondering how you could possibly make a profit selling a dozen roses for eight bucks. I made little circles with the bottle and watched as my last sip went around and around. When that last sip was gone, I stood there, figuring out to the nearest tenths place how much one orange would cost if five went for a buck nineteen.

"You want nickel back for that?" I turned to see the owner of the place. Back when I used to come here five days a week, he'd be behind the cash register at seven when I got my morning coffee and then again at six when I'd grab a paper to take home. If he recognized me now, five years later, he didn't let on. Funny how that is in this city. You see people every day, on the street, at the deli, and never know their names. Then you fall thirty feet, and your whole life changes.

"Excuse me?"

"You redeem." He pointed to the empty bottle. "Five cents."

"No," I said. "Here."

I handed it to him. As he took it, he kept his eyes on mine.

"How come," he finally said, "you not work here no more?"

"You remember me?"

"Oh, sure." Big smile now. "Large coffee, three sugars, very little half-and-half."

"Wow," I said. "I'm a teacher now."

"Ah," he answered, as if that explained it all. "Good job."

"Yeah."

We looked at each other for a few seconds, and when neither one of us could think of anything else, he said, "You take care."

"Yeah," I said. "You, too."

After he went back inside, I faced the building I was afraid to enter. Still the same dull, grayish green bricks, the same smog-frosted windows on the second floor. I remember being able to see out but never being able to see in.

The front door opened and shut every thirty seconds or so. Strangers in uniform going in; strangers in civilian clothes coming out. I wondered what my chances were of Royce coming out, saving me from going in. Having already waited for twenty minutes, I knew the answer. I crossed the avenue.

The closer I got to the front door, the more I began to question the visit. What did I have? A photo of a house a hundred miles north of here. That should be enough to keep a dialogue going for a whole five seconds. Then what? Cops are territorial by nature, and that's with their own kind. I was a schoolteacher now. Royce was not going to discuss the case with me because he liked me. Shit. Maybe he didn't even like me.

"Hey," someone said from behind me. "You going in or what?"

Before I could turn, a guy in jeans and a T-shirt and with a bag slung over his shoulder reached around me and opened the door. As it was closing, I stepped forward and held it so it wouldn't shut. I took a deep breath and walked through.

Everything seemed smaller, like the first—and only—time I returned to my old high school. I moved aside as two young Hispanic officers breezed past me, two kids who couldn't wait to hit the streets. A familiar smell hung in the air as the door shut behind them. I took a few more steps in to get away from the activity of the front door area. The uniformed officer working the front desk was so engrossed in his paperwork that I could have just walked past unquestioned: left to the lockers, right to the administrative offices, or a buttonhook upstairs to the detective squad. I chose to check in.

The cop at the desk was busy, but not with official business. He was tapping a pen against his folded copy of the *Times,* opened to the crossword. He had a phone cradled between his neck and shoulder. I had the feeling he might have forgotten it was there. After a half minute of me standing there holding my umbrella in front of me, he acknowledged my presence.

"Help ya?" he asked without looking up.

"I'm here to see one of your detectives," I said.

"Nature of complaint?"

I went for humorous. "It's too damned hot."

Now he looked up. "Nature of complaint."

"I don't have one. I'm here to speak with Detective Royce about a case we . . . regarding a case he's working on."

"You working?"

"Not as a cop," I said. "No."

"Okay. Didn't mean to offend you. Sir." He slid a clipboard in front of me and spun it around. "Sign in."

I took the pen that was attached to the clipboard by a string and put down my name, time, and destination. When I finished, I turned it around.

"Okay if I go on up?"

"I have to let the detective know you're here." He punched a button on the phone in front of him. "Might take a few." He looked back down at his puzzle. I did the same. Reading upside down was just one of the skills I had picked up in the classroom.

"Ten across," I said.

"What about it?" His eyes were still on the puzzle.

"You've written 'aviary.'"

"Yeah?"

"Should be apiary," I said.

"The difference being . . ."

"Birds are kept in aviaries. Bees are housed in apiaries."

He considered that for a while and said, "Guess that works." With the phone still between his ear and shoulder, he changed the *v* to a *p*. "That'd make eleven down pine and not vine." He decided to look up at me again. "Whatta you? One of them upside-down-reading nature lovers?"

"No," I said. "Just know the difference between the birds and the bees."

He pressed another button, or the same one, and, getting no response, he took the phone and hung it up. His head was still cocked to the side. Maybe that's why he was at a desk and had to live that way for the rest of his life.

"You know where ya going?" he asked.

"I've been here before," I said. "A long time ago."

"Then by all means." He gestured toward the stairs like a bored game-show host. "Go right on up."

"Thanks."

"Thank you," he said, and went back to his puzzle.

I turned to go upstairs and watched as two uniforms escorted a very unhappy man with his hands cuffed behind him down the stairs. Besides the cuffs, what caught my attention—and the other reason the man may have been unhappy—was the recent black eye he was sporting. He mumbled something about "fucking cops" and "my fucking eye." The officer on his right jerked the man's arm.

"Keep fucking yapping, Julio," the officer said. "Could be a rough ride to the courthouse."

Shit. I turned back to the desk to avoid eye contact.

"Holy fucking shit," Jack Knight said. "Raymond Fucking Donne."

"Jack," I said calmly, turning to face the voice from the past.

Jack looked me up and down and smirked, like I'd failed inspection. He let go of Julio's arm and took a step toward me.

"What the fuck brings you down to the old house? Registering a citizen's complaint?" He turned to his partner. "This here's Raymond Donne, Hector. We used to work the same streets. Back when we all spoke English."

I looked at Hector and gave him a sympathetic nod.

"I speak English, Jack," he said, as if this weren't the first time.

"Yeah," Jack said. "But not as a first language. Whyn't you take Julio out to the car, Hector. I'm gonna catch up with my old bud here for a few minutes."

Hector led Julio out the main door, and Jack turned back to me. "Tell me your uncle didn't pull some strings and you're not fucking coming back to the job, Ray. Please."

"No, Jack. I just swung by to see if *fucking* was still your favorite adjective."

Jack shook his head. "Still the fuck—still the wise guy. Heard you was teaching now."

"You heard right," I said.

"That figures. Always trying to help people. Never did quite have the fucking balls for this job, did ya, Raymond?"

"Whatever," I said. For Jack, helping people and being a cop were mutually exclusive. I motioned with my head at the door Hector and Julio had just gone through. "I see you've still got that gentle touch with suspects, huh?"

Again, Jack smiled. "Julio's not exactly the most coordinated of civilians. He banged his head while being escorted back to the precinct."

"Good to see you, Jack," I lied. "Try to stay out of trouble." I got a few steps toward the stairs before Jack grabbed my arm.

"You still got that judging look on your face, Ray. You got no fucking idea what it's like these days on the streets. I don't think you ever did."

I looked Jack in the eyes and then down at where he was squeezing my arm. "You might want to let go of me now, Jack. Unlike Julio, I will make a complaint."

"Fucking pussy." He threw my arm back at me. "I'm this close to getting my shield, Ray. Bet you never thought you'd see that happen. And I'm getting it on my own, not because of who my uncle is." He made a point of looking all around the room we were in. "I'm one of the few white guys left around this house, and I'll be damned if I let them take it all."

It was always "us" and "them" with Jack. I almost felt sorry for him. Almost.

"See ya, Jack." I made my way up the stairs without looking back. If Jack had anything else to say, I didn't hear it.

The walk up left me winded, and I had to lean against the wooden railing at the top of the steps to catch my breath. Everywhere I went these days, I was reminded of how out of shape I was. It cut deep to have it happen here, too. I swung open the gate and stepped into the detective squad. I saw Royce right away, sitting behind his desk, sipping from a huge water bottle while talking on the phone.

"Can I help you, sir?"

The question came from my left, from the police adminstrative assistant who sat behind a desk. PAAs are basically the doormen to the squad room, inquiring as to the reason for your visit, making sure the person you're hoping to see wants to see you, answering phones, and doing other civilian stuff.

"I'm here to see Detective Royce."

"Is he expecting you, Mister . . ."

"Donne." I spelled it for him. "Not really. I have an open invite."

"Sir?"

I gestured toward Royce, still on the phone. "Could you just tell him that Raymond Donne is here to see him?"

"Certainly." He pressed a button on his phone, and I heard a buzz from inside the squad room. Royce looked over and squinted. It took him a few seconds, but he eventually waved me in.

"Thanks," I said to the PAA, but he was already on the phone.

Royce's desk was identical to the half dozen others spread out around the large room: gray and cluttered. File cabinets were lined up against the back wall, flanked by a copy machine and a large coffeemaker. The air up here was different from the air downstairs. It had a hazy quality to it, like the fog was rolling in. Most of the light came from the overhead fluorescents, but some found its way in through the almost opaque windows. When I got to his desk, Royce was still talking on the phone. He gestured for me to sit.

"Seven o'clock," he said. "I know, but I'll be there for the second half. She won't even look for me until the end of the game. I do understand. That's why I'm on my way out." That last part was as much for me as for the person on the other end. "I love you, too. Bye." He hung up and shook my hand. "You got kids?"

"No."

"Married?"

"Nope."

"Good for you, Mr. Donne." He leaned back and picked up a carton of Chinese takeout. "I take that back. Get married. Have kids. Best two things I ever did." He noticed my umbrella. "Change in the forecast?"

I shrugged. "Just wishing for some rain."

Royce picked up a plastic fork and began stabbing at the remains of the carton.

"I thought detectives were required to eat Chinese food with chopsticks," I said.

"Oh, yeah. But only when we're having late-night meetings with beautiful assistant district attorneys who come by to show off their legs and discuss particularly tough cases they take personally." He pulled out his fork, which had found a shrimp, and put it in his mouth. "You ever see an assistant district attorney for Kings County?"

"Not for a while now."

"You're not missing anything. Fucking cop shows." He moved the noodles around a little more, didn't see anything he liked, and dumped the rest of the carton into his wastebasket. "What can I do for you, Mr. Donne?"

I cleared my throat. "I had to drop some papers off at the district office and figured I'd swing by here and see what the latest on the Rivas case was."

He nodded. "Just in the neighborhood, huh?"

"At the D.O. Yeah."

"Right." He took a sip of water. "Well, the *latest* on the Rivas case is that there is no *latest* on the Rivas case. The kids're still missing, the father's still lying in the morgue, and we don't know who did it. Thanks for coming by."

"You interviewed the family?" I asked.

"Yeah. We started doing that in murder cases about a year ago. I spent an hour with the grandmother."

"Any other family members?"

"Junior lives most of the time with his *abuela*. Milagros stayed with the dad. Closer to her school. Spoke to all the cousins in the area. Nothing."

He was talking tough to shut me up and get me to leave.

"What about his aunt upstate?" I was thinking about the photo in my pocket.

Royce gave me a confused look and then picked up a notebook from his desk. After flipping through the pages for a bit, he said, "Cousin. Anita Roberts. Wife of Rivas's employer, John Roberts. Telephone interview on Wednesday, 1430. Hadn't seen the vic for over a week." He flipped the notebook shut. "Have a nice night, Mr. Donne."

"Phone interview? You didn't go over and see him?"

"Oh," he said, leaning back in his chair and clasping his hands behind his head. "Go over and see him? I didn't think of that. Maybe I need to take your uncle's course in interrogation techniques again."

I wanted to come back with a smart retort of my own, but thought better of it.

"Of course I went over to see him. Twice. He wasn't there. Had a couple of nice chats with his assistant. Nice-looking woman, so it wasn't a complete waste of my time. Didn't care much for our dead guy. Not that anyone I've spoken with did. Eight interviews: family, neighbors, coworkers. Not one nice word about Mr. Rivas."

"So you settled for a phone interview with his boss?"

"Settled?" Royce leaned forward. I could smell the spicy shrimp on his breath. "I didn't settle for shit. I got what I could and moved on. You might think about doing the same."

Back inside for ten minutes and I got the guy annoyed with me.

"I'm sorry, Detective," I said. "I just thought—"

"Don't," he said. "Don't just think. You come into my place of business and tell me how I should conduct my investigation?" He put his hand on top of a pile of files that was almost twelve inches high. "One of many investigations I am currently involved in."

"That's not why I came here, Detective."

Royce picked up a framed photo from his desk and handed it to me. His daughter, I figured. About nine years old and the owner of a smile that could sell toothpaste.

"See that beautiful little girl?" he asked.

"Yeah."

"She's got a soccer game tonight." He looked at his watch. "Starts in a half hour out on Long Island. I missed the last two soccer games running around for this job. I am not going to miss tonight's." He moved the wastebasket with his foot. "So I shove shrimp lo mein down my throat, make a few more phone calls, and drop something off for my boss downtown. And if I don't hit too much traffic on the Belt Parkway, I just might make it to Baldwin in time for the second half and see my little girl play soccer."

I sat there quietly as Royce took another sip of water. When he was finished, he looked at me with a forced smile.

"You have any idea what it's like being a black soccer dad in the middle of Nassau County?"

"No."

"It ain't easy," was the answer. "I want those folks seeing that Quinn's got two parents that care about her. It's important to put that out there." He gave me a long look before asking, "You from the Island or Jersey?"

I smiled. A white ex-cop and now schoolteacher? Had to be Long Island or New Jersey. I didn't have that Westchester County look.

"I grew up not far from Baldwin."

"Any black friends growing up?"

"No, but there was one kid in my high school. Parents lived over in the military houses. Marines. Named him James. James *Brown*."

Royce laughed. "Why do parents do that shit to their kids?"

"Got me."

He grabbed a folder from the top of the pile and slid it into his bag.

"All right," he said. "Sorry if I came on a little rude. It's been a long one."

"Forget it," I said. "I should have called first."

"Yeah," he said, "you should have. But then I would have told you not to bother coming by and you would have had to come up with something better than 'I was dropping something off at the D.O.,' and where would we be then?"

I smiled, and pushed a little more. "You done with Roberts?"

"He's working from home this week. He's having some work done on it, and his wife's pregnant with their second kid, so he's staying up there. And no, as much as I'd love a ride up to the country, I am not planning on driving an hour and a half both ways just to see him say what I've heard him say over the phone. I got enough. He owns the travel agency, and Rivas was a kind of glorified gofer. Messenger, handyman around the apartments that Roberts owned, shit like that. I'll talk more with him when he gets back to Brooklyn."

"He say anything about Frankie and Milagros?" I touched my pocket where the photo of Roberts's house still was. "Where they might be or might've gone?"

"He didn't say." Royce stood and picked up his bag. "You make it sound like Junior and his sis left on their own. You got something to share with me, Mr. Donne?"

"I'm just putting the possibility out there, Detective."

"And if they did—get out of there before their dad got whacked—why haven't they contacted anyone? Grandma, the neighbors, Roberts?"

"That's a good question."

"Believe me, Mr. Donne. Everything that can be done is being done. All things are being considered, and all questions are being asked. I'm good at this."

"I wasn't trying to imply anything to the contrary." I stood, and with nothing much left to say, I said, "Thanks for your time."

"Appreciate you coming by." We shook hands. "Call next time you're gonna be in the neighborhood. Give me a chance to get my notes in order."

"I'll do that," I said and turned to leave.

"This the first time it's getting to you, Mr. Donne?"

"Getting to me?"

"That achy feeling in your gut. That you're not a part of this"—he made a sweeping gesture that took in the entire squad room—"anymore. Out of the loop."

"Detective," I said, "I just stopped by to see—"

"I'm sure I'll be dropping by in about five years myself, Mr. Donne. Just wanting to say hi, make a little small talk. My wife's already preparing for it."

"Good-bye, Detective Royce."

"We both got our jobs to do, Mr. Donne," he said as I started to walk away. "Just remember, this here . . . this here is my classroom."

"Absolutely." When I got to the PAA's desk, I turned back. "Good luck with your daughter's game tonight."

"Thanks."

A minute later I was standing across the street, looking up at the gray, hazy sky, the picture of Cousin Anita's house still in my pocket. Despite Royce's assurances, I couldn't shake the feeling that he was not doing all that could be done to find Frankie and Milagros. The mountain of files on his desk proved that. I knew how things worked, how the shit just kept coming. There was a time when I lived off the juice that came from that shit piling up. The nonstop flow of other people's problems. I'd walk into the house in my civilian clothes and come back out in blue, ready to take on whatever came my way. My gun, my shield, my radio—all just shovels to clean up other people's shit.

I gave the precinct one last look and headed off to the subway.

Chapter 9

FOR THE PAST TWO YEARS, SINCE my sister bought a condo in Rego Park, Queens, we've been having dinner together on the third Thursday of each month. I'm not sure how it started, but it's the closest thing we have to a family tradition, and we do our best to keep it going. Whatever is going on in our lives—bad breakups, job changes, missing kids—we get together. This was her month to pick up the check, so I was in her neighborhood. I found her standing in front of the restaurant, her cell phone up to her ear.

"Hey," I said.

Rachel flipped the phone shut. "You're late," she said. "You're never late."

"Subway." I gave her a hug. "Sorry."

"Are you okay?" she asked, taking a step back and giving me a long look.

"Yeah. Why?"

"For starters? You look like shit."

"It's this lighting." I looked up at the restaurant's neon sign. "Fuji-yama. Japanese, huh?"

"It's a shame you left the police force, Ray. Your deductive skills . . ." —she snapped her fingers—"sharp as ever. But, seriously. You do look like shit."

"It's been a long week. I haven't been sleeping too well."

"You can tell me all about it over drinks and dinner."

The way the host greeted my sister, you'd have thought she owned the place. We were escorted to a center table, and the guy pulled out Rachel's chair and said, "Two sakes?"

"Yes, Jimmy, please. My brother needs one."

"Brother?" Jimmy said. "Ahh. I thought maybe . . ." He shook his head and walked away to get our drinks.

"Have you two been close long?" I asked.

"I designed his menu and Web page," Rachel explained. "And he's crazy about me. So, why do you look like death?"

"It's a shame you left the greeting-card business, Rachel."

"I didn't leave. I'm management now."

"How's that going?"

"About what I expected. More money, more headaches. Kenny was too cheap to fill my old position, so I'm doing my new job and training a series of bimbos to do research." She raised her hand to cut me off. "Yes, big brother, greeting-card companies do research. It's not all 'Sorry your dog died. Here's a card.'"

"Did you write that one?"

"Now," she said, ignoring me, "he wants me to go to L.A. this week with one of his floozies for the annual trade show. Easier if I just killed the chick. And you?"

"Teaching's teaching," I said. "The year's almost over, so it's a lot of keeping the kids focused until graduation and getting the end-of-the-year bullshit done."

"That's not all, though."

"What do you mean?"

Before she could answer, Jimmy came over with a tray that held two small, porcelain cups that looked like they came out of a five-year-old's tea set. He placed the cups in front of us and poured sake into both. "You ready to order now?" he asked.

I reached for the menu. Rachel put her hand on mine and turned to Jimmy. "Two combination platters. Sushi and sashimi." To me, she added, "I'll explain the difference."

"Very good, Miss Rachel," Jimmy said.

"I know you, Ray," Rachel said after Jimmy left. "You'll look at the menu for ten minutes, get pissed off, and then ask for my opinion. I just wanted to save us some time." She raised her glass. We clinked and drank. "Okay?"

"Yeah," I said. "I'd rather have a beer, though."

"That's what makes these nights so special. I take you to new and exciting places, where you get to experience new and exciting tastes. You take me to get a hamburger."

"I took you to the Polish place on Bedford Avenue last month."

"Where I had the fabulous roast pork and pickled beets and you had a burger."

"They make a good burger."

"You're getting predictable in your old age, Ray. Life is more than just Budweiser and Yankee games." She took another sip. "You call Mom back?"

"Not yet, but that didn't stop her from leaving a five-minute message on my machine last night. Good news about Cousin Patty."

"Aunt Evelyn six, Mom zero. You know she's waiting to hear from you about the memorial service, right?"

"Speaking of future grandchildren," I said, changing the subject, "you still seeing that guy? Alan?"

"Alex," she corrected me. "No."

"What happened? I thought things were going well."

"For six weeks. We're going out less than two months, and he brings up the 'M' word."

"Marriage?"

"Money. As in, 'Can I borrow some?' "

I almost spit out my sake. "You're kidding me."

"I wish. Seems he and some college buddies have this great idea for a new business, and all he needs is five thousand dollars to get in. What are you smiling about?"

"You're getting better," I said.

"At what?"

"Two years ago you'd have been out five thousand dollars."

"I wasn't that bad," she said.

"You were close. Now you just need to take a little more time before bringing them home to meet Mom."

"Maybe if you brought someone home once in a while . . ."

"I'm enjoying this time of celibacy."

"Celibacy indicates a conscious choice, Ray. You . . . are not getting laid."

"Let's not argue semantics, Rache."

"Because you'd lose?"

"Because I'd like to have a nice dinner. Even if it is raw fish and warm rice wine."

Of which I took another sip as Jimmy came back to our table with two oversize plates of food and another vase of sake.

"Enjoy," he said, and he gave my little sister a smile before leaving again.

I watched as Rachel poured soy sauce into a small dish and added some wasabi.

"What are you waiting for, Ray?" she asked.

"A fork."

She raised her chopsticks, showed them to me, and, as if she'd been doing it her whole life, picked up a piece of fish, dipped it in the soy-wasabi, and placed it in her mouth. "Use your fingers if you want," she said. "It's okay, but be careful of the wasabi. It'll clear your nasal passages down to your intestines."

"I know what wasabi is."

I picked up a piece of something red wrapped in rice and smelled it. Not bad. I dunked it in some of Rachel's soy sauce mixture. She was right about its decongestive qualities, and I caught her smiling as she sipped her wine. We ate in silence until half my plate was finished.

"What else?" Rachel said.

"What else what?"

"What else is going on? School and what else?"

"How much time you got?" I asked.

She raised two more fingers to Jimmy and pointed at the sake. "At least that much."

I told her about Frankie and his father and Milagros. She let me talk for about five minutes without interrupting. Rachel was always good that way.

"Jesus, Ray," she said when I was finished. "No wonder you look like you do."

"I'm fine. Just need to get more sleep."

"You found a dead body. One of your students is missing. How can you say you're fine?"

"I don't know, Rache. I just am. Why are you looking at me like that?"

"You know who you sound like?"

"Oh, please," I said. "Not tonight."

"Because you know I'm right."

"Because you were ten when he died. You don't know what he sounded like."

"Oh, right. I forgot. Only you know what Dad was like." She wiped her mouth. "Maybe one of these days you'll enlighten me. Tell me all the things I don't know."

"Let's change the subject, huh?" I said.

"See?" Rachel pointed at me, pushing it. The wine was taking effect. "That's just what he would have done. Change the subject when things got hot."

"No," I said. "He would've reached across the table and smacked me upside the head. Then he would have changed the subject."

She shook her head. "It's been a long time, Ray. It's time to move on."

"Your shrink tell you that?"

"Don't," she said. "Don't you dare make light of my therapy. If you had—"

"Then don't you make light of my experience. You weren't the one who got hit, Rachel. You weren't the one whose stomach dropped when his car pulled into the driveway, wondering what he was going to find wrong this time."

You weren't the one to find him dead in his study.

My little sister paused, and gave me a look that bordered on pity.

"A lot of years, Ray," she repeated. "How long are you going to let him do this to you?"

"I don't know, Rachel." I stood up. "Maybe when the dreams stop." I turned and walked in the direction of the men's room. When I got there, I ran the water until it got real cold and splashed my face. As I was drying off, I checked out my face in the mirror. Rachel was right about one thing: I did look like shit.

When I got back to the table, Jimmy was taking the plates away and a younger man was putting two dishes of green ice cream on the table. After they left, Rachel said, "Ice cream makes everything better." I sat down. "I didn't know you were still having the dreams, Ray."

"Forget it. They're not as bad," I said, "and they're not as often."

"You going to call Mom?"

"Eventually."

"The memorial service is a week and a half away, Ray. If you don't go, she's going to have a lot of explaining to do."

"Tell people I'm out of town. Couldn't be avoided."

"The church has been planning this for months," she reminded me.

"Why does the church suddenly want to build a garden in his honor?" I asked.

"Mom wanted to do something for the church and the church wanted to do something for Mom. Why is that so hard to understand?"

"A lot of time has passed, that's all," I said.

"That's exactly my point." She put her hand on mine. "Let it go. For Mom." When I didn't respond, she said, "You're picking your thumbs again."

"What?" I asked.

"Your thumbs." She turned my hand over. "You used to do that when we were kids. Before a game or a big test. When'd you pick up that nasty habit again?"

"I don't know," I said, taking my hand back and looking at the thumb. The skin on the inside part was red and flaky.

"It's your student, isn't it? Frankie."

"What?"

"You're blowing it off like it'll take care of itself. Like you're gonna be at school tomorrow and he's just going to show up like nothing happened."

"You don't know what you're talking about, Rachel."

"What's so special about this kid?"

"Beside the fact that his dad was murdered and he and his sister are missing?"

"That's not what I mean," she said. "You got this kid a scholarship for high school. You called in a favor from Eddie Keenan. Shit, Ray. You went to his house. You don't do stuff like that. At least you haven't for a while. Why now? Why this kid?"

"Because this kid can throw a baseball eighty miles an hour."

"No," Rachel said. "There's more. What was his dad like?"

"How the hell am I supposed to know?"

"You talked to him every day. You're going to tell me you never talked about his dad?"

"Once in a while," I admitted.

"And?"

"And the guy was an asshole, okay?"

"Frankie told you that?"

"He didn't have to," I said. "No home phone, no work phone, just a cell phone number he wouldn't let his son give out. Frankie lived with his grandmother, five minutes from his dad. What kind of father does that? Frankie'd show up every once in a while with a new pair of hundred-dollar sneakers and say his dad told him he 'got paid.' Give me a break."

"Where'd he get the money?"

"Frankie wouldn't say, and I didn't ask. I think we can assume he wasn't driving around behind the sneaker truck waiting for a pair in his son's size to fall off." I took a sip of sake. "Took him a week to sign the acceptance letter for Our Lady. Woulda been just as happy if Frankie ended up in some dumping ground with a thousand other nine-digit numbers."

Rachel smiled. "So you took care of him?"

"I took care of getting him a shot at a decent high school."

"Our Lady is a little more than decent, Ray."

"And Eddie Keenan did me a solid."

"Sounds like he's getting something in return."

"Damn straight he is." I scooped up a little of the ice cream. It mixed nicely with the taste of the wine. "I stopped by the precinct today."

"What made you— You're kidding me?"

"I had some information I wanted to share with the detective on the case, and he pretty much told me to bug off."

"What'd you expect? A Junior Detective badge and a 'Go get him, Ray'?"

"I don't know what I expected," I said. "No, that's not true. I got pretty much what I expected. Fifteen minutes of his time, a little respect for the walking wounded, and 'Don't let the door hit you in the ass on the way out, Mr. Donne.'"

Rachel smiled. "Fifteen minutes, huh?"

"Thirteen of them were for Uncle Ray. I wanted to see how they're progressing. I got the feeling if nothing happens by the weekend, this guy's moving on. He has to."

"At least you tried."

"It didn't get me anywhere. I might as well have gone home and taken a nap."

"But you didn't," Rachel said as she stood up. She came around the table and kissed me on the cheek. "You did something. Who knows? Maybe the detective'll think about what you said and act on it."

"Maybe Frankie'll just waltz into my classroom tomorrow."

"I'm going to the ladies' room," she said and pulled two bills out of her pocket. "If Jimmy comes back before I do, give him this."

I looked at the bills: both twenties. "We drank more than this," I said.

"Jimmy tries not to charge me," Rachel explained. "It's a compromise."

A few minutes later, we walked outside and Rachel found the rare, unoccupied Queens cab. She gave me a long hug.

"Call Mom," she said.

"I will."

"And stop being so hard on yourself. And your thumbs."

"Go home, Rachel."

"I love you, Raymond."

"Me, too."

I watched as the cab took my little sister home.

Chapter 10

I AM UP ON THE FIRE ESCAPE AGAIN. The metal creaking. Fog rolling in.

"You planning on staying up there forever?"

I'm trying to hold on to the metal railing, but it's slippery, and my hands keep coming off. It's hard to breathe.

"I am not getting you out of this one. You are on your own."

Two lights are blinking, a red one on my left, green on the right. There's a slight buzz as each light comes on and then fades out.

"You hear me?"

I hear you, Dad. I always hear you. And I don't want your help. How about that?

"You really think you know what you're doing, don't you?"

Leave me alone, and I'll figure it out. You're good at that, right? Leaving me alone. Isn't that what you—the sound of the fire escape pulling away from the wall. I grab onto the railing and close my eyes to concentrate, but it doesn't help.

Fucker.

Another voice now. A kid's voice.

Shut up.

White mother FUCKER.

I said, Shut the fuck up.

Whatchoo gonna do, Casper? Can't do shit.

The fire escape starts to move back and forth, like a rowboat caught in a storm.

"All right." My father's voice again. "Give me your hand."

I said I don't want your help.

"You don't know what you want. Give me your—"

I do not want—

"THEN STOP ACTING LIKE A GODDAMNED CHILD, GET DOWN FROM THERE AND DO SOMETHING!"

I start to cough and wipe my hand across my wet face. Maybe it's the fog. Maybe I'm crying. I don't know what to do.

"Then you're going to be up there for quite some time, aren't you?"

It's not as easy as you think.

"It's not as hard as you make it. Do something."

Do what?

Except for the buzzing of the lights and the creaking of the metal as it continues to move away from its support, there is silence.

Do what?

The fire escape jerks to the left, sending me to my knees. I grab the railing, but my feet fall through the slats.

Do what? I say again.

The fire escape breaks free from the building and I am falling.

Before I hit the ground, I sit up in my bed, breathing heavy and drenched in sweat. My dream father's voice echoes in my head.

Do something.

Do something.

Once you've driven through the Bronx, you're officially out of New York City. It's not for another half hour, though—where the Tappan Zee Bridge crosses the Hudson River—that the departure is truly experienced. About halfway across, just before you enter Rockland County, if the air is clear enough, you can look south and see the Manhattan skyline in the distance, promising you that it'll be there if you decide to come home again.

Royce had told me he'd spoken twice on the phone to John Roberts—Rivas's boss and the husband of Frankie's cousin Anita—and saw no reason to rush a third conversation. What exactly was I expecting to achieve by borrowing my sister's car and taking a day off from school for a ninety-minute car ride north that Royce wasn't willing to take?

The radio was a mix of Springsteen and static when I took the exit ramp off the thruway. I made the right onto Highland and spotted a diner. A cheeseburger with fries and two iced teas later, I was fully fed, caffein-ated, and had directions to the Roberts house.

There were only eight houses on Bevier Court, and even if I hadn't known the address, there'd be no mistaking the huge white house I parked in front of. It looked just like the photo I was holding. From what I could tell, it was the last original house on the block, but there was enough scaf-folding along the side to launch a space shuttle.

I tossed my umbrella into the backseat, grabbed my suit jacket, and stepped out of the car. The suit—last worn at a wake or a wedding or a court date—was too tight in the waist, but it was the only one I owned.

As I adjusted my tie and stepped onto the driveway, I could see that the scaffolding went around to the back of the house. Roberts was expanding the top floor. Royce had told me Roberts was expecting another child. At the end of the driveway was the small barnlike structure I had seen in the crayon drawing of the house. It looked as if it served as a garage.

The sound of laughter came from somewhere inside the house, fol-lowed by the side door crashing open. A young girl—long blond hair, maybe three years old—in a flowery sundress came screaming down the steps, fol-lowed by a very pregnant dark-haired woman wearing an identical dress. The girl let the woman catch her, and she received a bunch of tickles in return. The girl's skin was a shade lighter than her mother's. They both stopped laughing when they noticed me. The daughter looked at me curi-ously, the mother with annoyance.

"I told you people," she said, "my husband is handling everything with the loan, and he is not going to be home until this evening."

Here I was trying for cop, and I got banker.

"Mrs. Roberts?" I asked.

"Yes," she said, still annoyed.

"My name is Donne, and I'd like to talk to you about—"

"I told you," she said. "John will not be home—"

"—your cousin Frankie."

She gave me a worried look and put her hand on her daughter's head. "Frankie?" she said, her tone a mix of excitement and concern. "Have you found them?"

"No," I said. "We have . . . they have not been found. That's why I'm here."

"My husband told you people . . . Detective Ross, I think . . . we don't know anything about where they are." Back to annoyed. "Don't you people talk to each other?"

"Detective Royce," I corrected. "Of course we do, it's just that—"

"As a matter of fact, my husband is down in the city today and planning on talking personally to Detective . . . Royce. So I'm afraid you have wasted a trip, Detective . . ."

"My name's Raymond Donne, Mrs. Roberts."

"Well, Detective Donne, you'll just have to drive back down and talk to my husband there. I'm sorry."

Anita Roberts took her daughter by the hand and started walking to the back of the house. The little girl gave me a smile as she looked at me over her shoulder.

"Elsa told me to say hello," I lied.

Anita stopped and turned back to me.

"You spoke to Elsa?"

"Absolutely. She's been quite cooperative." I took a few steps forward. "She gave me the impression that you'd do the same."

I listened to the wind blowing through the trees and the siren calls of the cicadas. The sounds reminded me of the hot summer days in my own backyard when I was a kid. It was easy to understand why this place felt safe to a couple of kids from Williamsburg, Brooklyn.

"I have already been cooperative," Anita said. "My husband is handling the rest of the matter, and, if you don't mind, we don't have a lot of time before it gets too hot out here."

That was the third time she told me her husband was taking care of everything. When someone keeps repeating things, it makes me wonder what they're avoiding.

"When was the last time Frankie and Milagros were here, Mrs. Roberts?"

She looked at me again and realized I wasn't going to go away as soon as she would have liked. "Gracie," she said, and leaned down to whisper something into her daughter's ear. The little girl twirled around a few times, showing off her dress, then ran toward the swing set in the backyard. Anita gave her attention back to me. "Christmas," she said. "We bring them up for a week during the vacation and again in the summer. So they were here last at Christmas. Frankie *and* Milagros."

"Mee lah grows." Gracie was pushing a swing back and forth, singing the name she'd just heard her mother speak. "Mee lah grows."

Anita and I shared a smile. "Can we talk in the shade?" I gestured to the patch of grass under the maple tree by the swing set.

"I don't know," she said. "It's getting close to Gracie's nap time and—"

I reached inside my jacket, pulled out the picture of her house, and handed it to her. "Frankie had this picture in his school notebook, Mrs. Roberts, and Milagros had a drawing of it on the refrigerator. Your house is very important to the both of them. I really just have a few quick questions, and I'll be on my way."

She looked at the picture and then up at the scaffolding. No work was being done at the moment, and that struck me as odd. It was just past noon on a Friday. Anita held the picture for a few more seconds and handed it back. "Five minutes," she said.

"Absolutely," I answered, following her under the tree. Anita Roberts picked up her daughter and placed her in the swing. Gracie held on to the chain and closed her eyes as her mother slowly pulled back and let go. The girl kept her eyes closed and squealed as the breeze played havoc with her hair.

"I really don't know what more I can tell you, Detective," Anita said. "I hadn't seen Francisco for months. He works—worked—for my husband."

"And you haven't seen the kids since Christmas?"

"I speak to Frankie every other week or so when I call to check on my aunt. I only speak to Milagros if she happens to be there."

"Mee lah grows," Gracie sang as the swing slowed down. "Mee lah grows."

"How often is your husband down in Brooklyn?"

"Every week," she said. "He—we—have an apartment down there."

"And you?"

"I haven't been down since Christmas."

"Ball!" Gracie yelled, leaning forward as the swing started to slow down. "Baaallllll."

"Okay, okay," her mother said, just barely getting her arm around the girl before she jumped off the swing. "*¡Cuidado!*"

Gracie jumped down, sprinted after the ball, and kicked it into the corner of the yard.

"She's got quite a lot of energy," I said.

"Yes," Anita said, placing her hand on her pregnant stomach.

"Is she growing up bilingual?"

"No," Anita said, realizing it had come out a bit harsh. She allowed herself a long breath. "It's getting very warm, and we only have a little more time to play outside. If that is all . . ."

"When are you due?" I asked, to keep her talking.

"Two months."

End of July, I thought, and again looked up at the workerless scaffolding. They were cutting it close with all the work that needed to be finished before the new baby.

"Gets hot up here over the summer," I said. "Can you run the air conditioner with all that open space on the top floor?"

"We'll go up north for a while," she answered. "John's parents own a house in Maine."

"Nice."

The soccer ball came rolling to a stop at my feet and Gracie came over. She eyed me cautiously and watched as I maneuvered my foot under the ball and lifted it over her head toward some bushes. She gave me a smile and ran after it.

"Yes," Anita said, watching her daughter pull the ball out of the bushes. "I don't remember you showing me any identification, Detective."

"Excuse me?"

"Your identification. A badge. Detectives do carry badges, don't they?"

"Of course," I said. "But I've taken up enough of—"

"MUN NEE!" Gracie yelled from the bushes. We both looked over as the little girl sang out again. "MUN NEE!"

She came running over to us, waving what looked like a dollar bill. She handed it to her mother, who looked at it and said, *"¡Ay dios mio!"*

"Problem?" I asked.

She held out the bill for me to see. It took me a few seconds to realize that it was not a dollar bill. It was a hundred. *Ay dios mio,* indeed.

I held out my hand and she gave me the bill. I then did what most people do when holding a bill of that denomination: I took it by the edges and pulled. It was real. I turned it over and saw that it had Anita's address written on the back. There were also some numbers: 710 and 410 and the letters "PA."

"This is Frankie's handwriting," I said to Anita.

"How can you be sure of that?" she asked.

"I recognize it from class," I said before realizing my mistake. "From some classwork of his I've seen."

Anita Roberts squinted at me, studying my face.

"Gracie," she said. "Come here."

Her daughter did as she was told, reacting more to the tone of her mother's voice than to the actual words. The two of them stood there as one, holding hands, looking at the stranger who had invaded their privacy.

"Who are you?" Anita asked.

"I told you," I said. "I'm looking for Frankie and Milagros."

"Who are you?" she repeated, taking a step back toward the door she had come running out of a short while ago.

"Frankie's teacher."

A few seconds went by as my words sunk in. Anita said, "You've got to be kidding."

"No, ma'am, I'm not."

"Why did you tell me that you were a detective?"

"I never told you that," I said. "You assumed, and I didn't correct you."

Anita looked at me and gave me something close to a smile. "You talk like a cop." The smile disappeared. "Why are you here?"

"Because I knew the cops wouldn't make the trip, and I wanted to speak to you and your husband about Frankie."

"To see if we knew more than we told the other—Detective Royce."

"Something like that." I held up the bill. "This proves they were here, Mrs. Roberts. This *is* Frankie's handwriting. Are you telling me that he came all the way up here and you didn't know about it?"

"That," she pointed to the bill, "proves nothing. And I'm not telling you anything. Please leave, mister . . ."

"Donne."

"Oh, so that much is true? Good-bye, *Mister* Donne."

She turned to take her daughter back into the house. When she got to the side door, I said, "Frankie and Milagros are still missing, Mrs. Roberts. That doesn't bother you?"

She looked over her shoulder and gave me a look that could have boiled water. She opened the side door. "Go inside, Gracie. Mommy will be right in."

"Mee lah grows?" the girl asked.

"Inside," her mother repeated and gave Gracie a light tap on her butt. Gracie gave me a little wave and went into the house. When the door shut, Anita turned back to me. "Do not dare take that tone of voice with me in front of my daughter, Mr. Donne. And do not dare presume to know what bothers me and what does not."

"There it is," I said.

"What?"

"The accent. I picked it up before when Gracie almost fell off the swing and now again when you slipped back into that tough *chica* from Clemente."

"You want me to sound like Clemente?" She looked at the door to make sure it was shut. "Get the fuck off my property or this tough *chica* is going to have you arrested for trespassing."

"Then you can explain to the police how this"—I raised the hundred-dollar bill again—"ended up on your property." She thought that over. "They were here, Anita. Why would they come all this way just to disappear again? Did something happen to them up here?"

"I DON'T KNOW!" she screamed. Again, she looked to the door her daughter had gone through. After a few seconds, she calmed down. "I don't know. Please"—her eyes were filling up with tears now—"show that to whoever you want, just leave us alone."

Anita Roberts ended our conversation by walking into her house and making sure the door did not slam behind her. I slipped the bill into my pocket and went back to the car with one thought: Frankie and Milagros got out of their father's apartment and made it all the way up here.

The tank was a little too close to *E*, so I pulled into a service station just past the entrance to the thruway. I filled up, ran a squeegee over the front and back windows, and went inside to pay and pick up another jolt of caffeine for the ride home. A Trailways bus rumbled by as I opened the door.

The ruddy-faced kid behind the register looked up from his wrestling magazine long enough to give me change. "How far into town is the bus station?" I asked.

He looked at me as if I'd asked him the average surface temperature of Jupiter. He rubbed his chin and said, "Never really thought about it before. Half mile or something?"

"Thanks."

I got back in the car and headed a half mile or something into town and pulled into the Trailways station. Outside on the wall, the schedule was posted, and I followed along with my finger and found the two buses that left from New York City: 7:10 A.M. and 4:10 P.M., from Port Authority. I took the hundred from my pocket and checked out what Frankie had written: 710 and 410 and "PA." He and Milagros got up here by bus. Then what? Walked the five miles to Anita's? I looked across the street and saw another service station: Downey's Taxi.

Inside the office, a very fat man sat in a recliner reading a newspaper. A floor fan was oscillating in the corner, moving the air-conditioned air around. He looked up and waited for me to speak.

"I was wondering if you could help me," I said.

"If ya need a ride or gas, I can," he said.

"Actually, I was hoping you could give me some information."

He pointed out the window. "Go back up another two blocks and make a left. College is three blocks in on your right. They got lots of information there and get paid to give it out. Me? I sell gas and drive people places. See the difference?"

Okay. I gave him my best Parent/Teacher Night smile and tried again.

"It's about some customers of yours," I said. "A couple of kids."

"Get lots of kids, mister. It's a college town."

"No, these two were—are—fourteen and eight. Boy and girl. They would have been going over to Highland. Bevier Court, within the past few days."

He looked at me and then down at his paper again. With a great deal of effort, he lifted himself out of his chair. He took five steps toward me and reached under the counter. He came up with a large binder notebook.

"Let's see what we got here," he said. "What day ya thinking of?"

"I'm not sure. Within the last couple, though."

"The last couple," he repeated, making sure I could hear how ridiculous my request was. "I don't know . . ."

I reached into my pocket, pulled out my last twenty, and placed it on the counter. "Could you just look, please? Twenty bucks for two minutes."

He tried to lean forward. "You a private eye or something?"

"Or something."

He scooped up the twenty like it was a doughnut and slipped it into his shirt pocket. He began flipping through the pages.

"Coupla runaways?" he asked. When I didn't respond, he said, "Oh, yeah. I bet you're not at liberty to discuss that." He gave me a wink and went back to the book. "Highland, Highland. Would help if I knew what time of day you were thinking of."

I thought back to the bus schedule and said, "About ten in the morning or seven at night. Just after the bus gets in from the city. My guess would be night."

"Let's try night then." He moved the big book to the side, reached under the counter again, and pulled out a single-subject notebook, the kind my kids used. "That'd be Jimmy's shift, and he likes to keep his own ledger," the big man explained. "College kid. Don't usually hire 'em 'cause they're quick to leave when they get another job or graduate. After all the training I give 'em." He opened up the notebook and found what he was looking for. "Monday . . . nope. Tuesday . . . nope. Wednesday . . . bingo! Two to Highland. Seven forty-five. Bev Court."

"That's it," I said. "Is it possible to talk to Jimmy?"

"You're asking a lot for twenty dollars, mister."

"It's all I have," I said. "Honest."

He looked me over to see if he believed me. I guess he did, because after a while, he picked up the phone and dialed. After another thirty seconds, he said, "Jimmy. Downey. No, no, we're fine. Got a question for ya, about a fare ya took over to Highland on Wednesday." He listened. "Seven forty-five? Two kids." Another pause. "Fifty? Shit. Got a guy here wants to talk to ya." He handed me the phone.

"Jimmy," I said. "My name's Raymond Donne."

"You a PI?" he asked. He sounded like his mouth was full of food.

"Those two kids you took over to Highland, how'd they look?"

I waited while he thought about that. Or maybe swallowed.

"Tired," he said. "Especially the girl. Boy seemed real nervous. Kept looking out the back window, telling the girl to keep it down. Like I cared what they were saying."

"What were they saying?"

"No idea. Had my mind on other things, and they mostly spoke in Spanish."

"You dropped them off on Bevier?"

"At the corner."

"Was there anyone there to meet them?"

"Said they'd walk the rest of the way. Kid seemed to know where he was going, so . . ."

These were two kids, I thought. Alone, in the early evening. Far from home. I wanted to reach through the phone and rip this guy a new one, but I needed a little more info.

"So you saw no one else?"

"Nope." He chewed a little more. "Kid asked for a card, though. Figured he wanted to have a number to call for a return ride."

"You figured that, huh?"

"Yeah. Hey, if you see them two?"

"Yeah?"

"Tell them I said thanks for the tip."

"Tip?"

"Gave me fifty. Kid said, 'Keep the change.' Like a real big shot."

It took all the control I could summon not to slam the phone into the counter.

"You didn't think," I asked, "to question that? Two kids giving you a fifty dollar bill?"

"Hey, man. I'm a grad student. Someone throws me a fifty, I ain't asking for ID. That's half a textbook." He took a sip of something. "Tell Downey I'll see him tomorrow at five."

After listening to the dial tone for a bit, I handed the phone back to Downey. "Thanks."

"No problem," Downey said. "Those kids gonna be okay?"

Good question. "I don't know."

The fat man studied me for a little while. "You ain't a private detective, are you, mister?"

"No," I said. "I'm just a schoolteacher."

He laughed. "Schoolteacher. Thought you were at least a cop. Here," he said, pulling out the twenty I had given him. "You need this more'n I do."

"Keep it," I said. "You earned it."

He pushed the bill at me. "Use it to pay for the gas home. Better yet, charge them kids for the trip. They seem to have some cash on hand."

"Yeah," I said, taking the money. "That they do. Thanks, Downey."

"You take care, mister."

I got back in the car and, five minutes later, I was on the thruway heading back to Brooklyn with some answers, but more questions than I had started with.

I pulled into the last service station on the thruway to stretch my legs and use the men's room. On my way out, I passed a bank of pay phones and had an idea. It took me three calls to reach Uncle Ray. His personal cell phone instructed me to leave a message. His wife, Reeny—"Why haven't we seen you for so long?"—gave me his work cell, which was answered by someone who introduced himself as Officer Jackson. Jackson told me my uncle was in Manhattan at the Chelsea Piers driving range hitting golf balls at New Jersey. When I told Jackson I would be there in an hour, he assured me that they would still be there.

When I was a kid, Uncle Ray would tell me, "You need directions, ask a map. You need help, ask a cop." I needed real help and I was going to ask the biggest cop I knew.

Chapter 11

I FOUND MY UNCLE ON THE GROUND level of the multitiered driving range. He'd never fool around with the upper levels; they didn't give an accurate account of how you were swinging. Uncle Ray was dressed in a short-sleeved golf shirt, blue uniform pants, and a baseball cap with the words "City Island Yacht Club" written in bright, yellow letters. The sweat marks on his shirt reached just above his belt. A young black uniformed cop was off to the side by a cooler. I watched as the automatic tee repeatedly disappeared below the artificial grass and resurfaced with a fresh golf ball. My uncle would then drive it into the early evening sky. He did this about a half dozen times before he acknowledged my presence.

"Officer Jackson," he said without looking back. "This is my nephew, Raymond Donne."

Jackson came over and offered me his hand. "Mr. Donne, sir. A pleasure."

"Ray," I said. "And the only 'sir' around here is my uncle."

He gave me a smile and a nod as my uncle said, "Have Jackson make you a drink, Nephew. He puts together a fine Diet Coke and Jack."

"No, thanks," I said. "I haven't had dinner yet."

"Jeez," Uncle Ray said, bending down and picking up a plastic cup. "This *is* my dinner." He drained the remainder of his drink in one long sip. "Another please, Jackson."

"Yes, sir."

Jackson went back to the cooler, the latest rookie to be "adopted" by my uncle straight from the academy. He'd serve for six months as personal secretary, chauffeur, caddy, and bartender. The hours were long, the days many, and just about everything about the position was against PBA rules. But no one complained about it because, if you lasted the half year, you were well on your way to a detective's shield. If you were one of "Donne's Boys," you were golden.

Jackson finished making the drink and brought it over to my uncle, who turned to face me for the first time. When I was a kid, Uncle Ray was the biggest man in my world. He had about six inches on my father, and my memory of him coming over to our house was him ducking as he came through the door. He removed his cap and ran his fingers over his sweaty gray hair. He took a long sip and said, "To what do I owe the pleasure, Raymond?"

"What?" I said. "I can't just drop by and visit my uncle?"

"Sure you can. You never do. Now, what is it that you want?"

I thought about it for a moment and decided the best approach would just be to dive right in. My uncle's tolerance for bullshit was lower than my own.

"I wanted to talk to you about a . . ." Jesus, Ray. Slow down. "One of my students is in trouble. Missing, actually. His sister, too. Their dad was killed over on the Southside last week."

"Rivas," he said.

"How did you know that?"

"Your name—shit, *my name*—shows up as a wit on a murder scene report, and you don't think it's gonna make its way to me? What the hell were you doing over there, Raymond?"

"Looking for my student."

"God," he said. "Is that what they got you doing now? Truancy shit?"

"I was there on my own, Uncle Ray. I swung by Clemente first to check with the grandmother. The kid hadn't been in for a—"

"It was a murder scene, Raymond."

"I didn't know that at the time."

"No," he said. "Just after you committed a little B and E."

"I didn't break in," I said. "The neighbor gave me a key."

"The detective didn't give you shit on that?"

"A little, but he didn't push it."

Uncle Ray grinned. "He didn't push it because your last name's Donne."

"He said he took a course with you at the academy. Detective Royce?"

He thought about the name for a bit. "Big black guy? Looks like he coulda played defensive end in college?"

"That's him."

"Yeah. He did pretty well, if I remember correctly."

"Said you were a hard-ass as an instructor."

"Don't know where he got that idea." Uncle Ray finished his drink and held the empty out for Officer Jackson. "So, what do you need me to do? Royce change his mind and decide to break your balls on illegal entry?"

"No," I said. "We're past that, I—"

"Past that? You know better than that, Raymond. You don't enter an apartment just because some neighbor gives you a key. You knock, you wait, but"—he tapped his golf club on the fake grass to accent the next four words: "You. Do. Not. Enter. You call it in."

"Call what in?" I asked. "You think the cops are going to rush over to the Southside because I can't find a fourteen-year-old?"

"What the hell was the goddamned rush?"

"There was a dead body in there."

"You didn't know that at the time."

"I felt something was wrong, Uncle Ray. And I was right."

"Ahhh." Uncle Ray leaned his golf club against the wall next to his pitching wedge. "Here we go."

"Here we go, what?"

"You're still getting those . . . *feelings.*" He wiggled his fingers in the air and added a spooky quality to his voice. "Something's rotten in the state of Denmark."

"I was taught to go with my instinct. By you. What? That's all bullshit now?"

"*Instinct,*" he repeated. "What you're describing is intuition. Cops have instinct. Psychics . . . women . . . have intuition." He picked up his pitching wedge. "If you honestly felt that something was wrong, you should've called it in. For Christ's sake, you coulda called me, and I coulda sent a car over there. Instead, you entered a private residence *illegally* and risked contaminating a crime scene. You know better than that. At least, you should."

I looked at my uncle's face—the wrinkles a little deeper and the circles a little darker than I remembered—and said, "I'm coming to you now."

Uncle Ray turned away, and with the business end of his pitching wedge, tipped the golf ball off the tee. He lined himself up and stroked the ball about thirty yards away, where it landed just short of a yellow flag. Out beyond where the ball fell, past the nets I doubt anyone could reach, a green and white Circle Line boat headed south on the Hudson, filled with curious folks who wanted to see what New York City looked like from the water.

"Coming to me for what?" Uncle Ray asked, lining up his next shot. "You said they're not pressing you on the entry. Something else they're squeezing your nuts over?"

I reached into my pocket and felt the hundred-dollar bill. "I found something."

"Good for you, Nephew."

"Regarding the case."

He drove the next ball.

"Excuse me?" he said, turning back to face me.

I had a sudden craving for a Diet Coke, so I went over to the cooler and grabbed a can from the ice. I took a sip and faced my uncle.

"I went by to see Royce yesterday," I said. "To see how the case was progressing."

Uncle Ray leaned forward. "You did what, now?"

"On my way home," I said. "I had this—"

"Urge to stick your nose into an active investigation?"

"I didn't stick my nose into anything. I thought I had something to offer him."

"What," my uncle said, not trying to hide his annoyance with me, "could you possibly have to offer the lead detective in a homicide case?"

I was about to say, "A clue," but I wasn't in the mood to hear another one of my uncle's Encyclopedia Brown jokes.

"I thought there was an avenue of investigation he may have overlooked."

He laughed. "Listen to my nephew, Jackson." Jackson took a tentative step toward us, uncomfortable with having been drawn into this conversation. "'Avenue of investigation.' Where'd you pick that up? A televised police drama?"

"I'm trying to help someone out, Uncle Ray. You don't need to talk to me like I'm a kid."

"Then don't act like one," he said. "Damn, Raymond." He shook his head and gave me the look. "You're still collecting strays."

I hated the grin he had on his face. It was the same one my dad used just before telling me where, and in how many ways, my thinking had been wrong.

"What does that mean?" I asked.

Uncle Ray turned to Jackson again. "I ever regale you with the story about my nephew and Lassie, Jackson?"

"No, sir," Jackson answered. "I don't believe you have."

"What was the name, Raymond," my uncle asked, "of that crazy guy used to live around your block? Security guard for Grumman."

Crazy guy around the— "Borrelli?" I said, the name coming from somewhere in the back of my head. What the hell did this have to do with . . . ? Oh.

"Borrelli, that was it. The wacky wop." Uncle Ray chipped the ball into the air. "I forget the name of his big old collie, but I just called him Lassie."

"Bandit," I said.

"Whatever. Old Man Borrelli used to treat that dog like a red-headed stepkid. Anyways, Jackson, one day Lassie—Bandit—shows up on Raymond's front lawn, lying there like it'd been hit by a truck. Raymond's dad is away on business, so Raymond takes the mutt in. Gets a bunch of old pillows and blankets and sets up his own veterinarian's office in the back shed."

"I was just trying to take care of him," I explained.

"Right," Uncle Ray said. "Too bad you never got your dad's okay, huh?"

Yeah. Too bad.

"Well, my brother finds out what's been going on in the backyard for the past few days, and he loses it. Takes the dog—which by now was looking a world better, but still can't walk too good—puts him in a wheelbarrow, and brings him back to his master. Borrelli goes nuts. Screams bloody murder, threatens to have the boy arrested for dognapping. Christ."

It was up there with the angriest I had ever seen my father. I wasn't sure what he was more furious about: that he didn't know about it, or that my mom kept it from him. Maybe if he'd been home more often.

"Two days later," my uncle continued, "the dog shows up again on the Donne Family's front lawn. Only this time, he's dead. Ray's mother, bless her Catholic heart, calls the animal control folks, and they take it away. I thought the old guy dumped it on the lawn like that, but Ray here explains to me that dogs know when they're going to die and find a safe place to spend their final moments."

I used to believe that. I remembered looking out the living room window at Bandit and wanting to go to him. But between my dad and Borrelli, I was too scared to do anything. It wasn't until my mom made the call that I knew for sure the dog was dead.

"You wanna tell the rest of the tale, Nephew?"

"What's left to tell, Uncle Ray? Bandit died. I cried for a couple of days and then got over it. That about covers it."

"Not quite. What about the part about Old Man Borrelli's house?"

"I never knew anything about that," I lied. "Even Dad said—"

"I know what your dad said. I was there."

"So," I said to Jackson, "end of story." To Uncle Ray, I said, "Thanks for the trip down Memory Lane."

"Not done until we get to the good part," he said as he chipped another ball off the green surface. "What happens next, Jackson, is that a few days after the dog's taken away, Old Man Borrelli comes a-knockin' at the Donne Family door—screaming bloody murder again—only this time, seems that sometime during the wee hours, when Borrelli was off guarding airplane parts or some such, somebody busted every window on the old fuck's house. Every. Single. Goddamned. Window." Uncle Ray used his club again to accent the last four words.

Officer Jackson looked at me and said, "You?"

I shook my head.

"Bullshit," my uncle said. "Borrelli starts screaming he's gonna have the boy arrested and sue my brother for everything he's got. Now, I'm over there having a cup of coffee on my way out to Montauk, and I'm watching and listening, and finally I ask my brother does he want me to badge the guy, threaten to kick his ass. And my brother gets this look in his eye I swear I never saw before. Tells me, no, he'll handle it, and walks across the front lawn toward Borrelli—I mean John Wayne walks—goes right up to the guy, grabs him by his shirt, and pulls him in real close. Then he whispers something into the guy's ear and pushes him away like he's nothing.

Borrelli's standing there, trying to come up with something, but he can't. After about a minute of this, he skulks away like the douche-bag dog beater he was. Remember that, Raymond?"

"Yeah," I said. Good times.

"What did he say to the guy?" Jackson asked.

I had no idea, so we both waited for Uncle Ray to finish.

"Told him that no one accuses a member of his family of wrongdoing unless he's got a shitload of evidence to back it up. And if he wanted to go ahead and press charges, my brother would file a countersuit, call the ASPCA, and get together with his lawyer buddies down at the county offices and see what else they could come up with."

"See," I said. "He knew I had nothing to do with the windows being busted."

"Wrong, kiddo. He knew that you did."

"If he thought I had anything to do with that, he'd have grounded me for life and made me spend the rest of my childhood paying off those windows."

"Unless," Uncle Ray said, "he thought you were right."

Whoa. "Excuse me?"

"Your old man figured Borrelli got what he had coming. Thought he deserved a little more, actually—but what you did?—your dad figured leave it go at that and let Borrelli make noise if he wanted to."

"So the point of this story is . . . ?"

"Understand what you're getting into when you mess with strays, Raymond."

I'd had enough of this. "Look, Uncle Ray. I need your help. Two kids need your help."

"Save the dramatics. Whatta ya want me to do? Call Detective Royce and let him know you've had another intuition, and would he please do what you say?"

I reached up and squeezed the area between my eyes, just above the nose. I'd been going since seven in the morning and had to remind myself that Uncle Ray deserved my respect. Especially if I was asking for his help. I pulled the bill out of my pocket and held it at my side.

"I drove up to Highland today," I said. "I wanted to talk to John Roberts. He is—was—Rivas's boss. The victim. Frankie had a picture of the house in his notebook, and I figured . . ."

"You might as well interfere with an active police investigation? You were out the day they covered obstruction of justice at the academy?"

"Are you going to let me finish?" I waited for a response, and when none came, I continued. "I spoke with Roberts's wife, Anita. She's Frankie's cousin, on his mother's side."

"The kids' mom?"

"Died a while ago. Anita says she has no idea where the kids are and hasn't seen them since Christmas."

"So?"

"So she asked me to leave . . ."

"Smart woman."

". . . after I found this on her property."

I held out the hundred, and Uncle Ray took it. He turned it over a few times. "This your boy's handwriting?"

"Yes." And before he could ask, I said, "I know Frankie's handwriting. I've had him for two years now."

Uncle Ray nodded. "This would be what we in the police academy call a 'clue.'"

"I know," I said. "I was there that day."

Uncle Ray handed the bill to Jackson, who slipped it into his front pocket without so much as looking at it.

"So your boy—Frankie?—was up at the Highland house?"

"Yes."

"And the cousin says she had no idea?"

"That's what she said."

"You believe her?"

"Yeah," I said. "She seemed genuinely surprised when I found that." I left out the part about the bill being found by a three-year-old girl and my dumb luck. "But that's when she decided she didn't want to answer any more of my questions."

"And now you'd like me to . . ."

"Show the bill to Royce. He needs to know that Frankie and Milagros were up at that house. If I bring it to him, we'll waste a lot of time discussing what I was doing up there."

Uncle Ray considered all that for a few seconds, then turned back to his golf. He leaned the wedge against the wall and picked up the driver.

He moved his hips, mumbled something about "tempo," and swung. I watched as the ball traveled in a beautiful arc and landed just shy of the *250* marker.

"If you're right, Raymond," he said, "they're running from something."

"Or some*one*."

"What's Royce think about your boy?"

"What do you mean?"

"Does he like him for knocking off his dad?"

"I don't think so. He's got it out there as a possibility, but I don't think he really believes Frankie killed his father."

Uncle Ray grinned. "You obviously don't."

"No," I said. "I don't. Not possible."

"Because you know him?"

"Because I know the kind of kid he is. Yes."

The grin mutated into a laugh. "And what kind of kid is that? The kind that wouldn't murder his father?"

"I know *this* kid, Uncle Ray." I wanted to get loud, but stopped myself. "You are not going to suck me into this conversation. Let me know what you decide to do with Royce and the hundred-dollar bill." I stepped over to Jackson and said, "Good luck to you. I'm sure you'll make a good detective."

"Thank you, sir," Jackson said.

"Good-bye, Uncle Ray."

"And just what conversation was I going to suck you into, Raymond?" he asked.

"The one," I said a bit too loudly, but, shit, I was tired, "where you remind me that the world is mostly black and white and I try too hard to see the gray."

"You do," he said. "Tell me, Ray. What kind of kid *would* kill his father? Ask any mother on the street, ask 'em if their kid would kill them. Or commit rape. Or steal. Whatever. You know what they say? 'Oh, never. Not my child.' Then who's committing all these rapes and murders and shit? Gotta be somebody's kid, right?" Uncle Ray took a deep breath and pointed his finger at me. "That's what you did on the job, kiddo. You thought too damn much."

"And that's a problem for a cop, right? Thinking?"

"Too much," he said, tapping his finger against his temple. "I said thinking *too much.*"

"Make sure you're getting all this down, Jackson." Jackson gave me a look that said he wanted no part of this. "I'm heading home, Uncle Ray. I'll talk to you when I talk to you."

I turned to go, but I stopped when my uncle said, "Ahh, don't be in such a rush to head out, Raymond." He came over and put his hand on my shoulder. "Give me a minute or two to lighten my load a bit, and we'll talk some more. In the meantime, chat with Officer Jackson here. Hell, talk about me behind my back. I don't mind."

When my uncle had been out of sight for fifteen seconds, Jackson said, "He'll do what you asked."

"You sure about that?"

"You presented him with a good case and a solid piece of evidence. He's got to give you shit about the way you obtained the evidence, but that doesn't mean he'll ignore it."

"You're learning a lot from him, huh?"

"You know that grin he gave you?" Jackson asked. "Right before the dog story?"

"Know it? It used to send chills down my spine as a kid."

"It took me a while to get it. I used to think it was condescending, but it's not. It's him saying, 'I'm right until you prove to me otherwise.' You did."

"I hope you're right about that."

"I am." Jackson grabbed my uncle's driver and set himself up in front of the tee. He moved his hips as my uncle had and hit the ball just shy of the *200* marker. "He talks about you a lot, you know. How good a cop you were and how sorry he was when you decided to leave."

"That decision was kind of made for me, Jackson. I got banged up pretty good."

"I know. He told me. He also told me that he could have arranged it so that you'da stayed on and still moved your way up."

"I didn't want it that way. I wanted it to be on my terms." I was suddenly very aware of my knees. "My body wouldn't let me be the kind of cop I wanted to be. I don't think my uncle understands that."

"He hears ya. He's not there all the way, and maybe never will be, but he does hear ya."

"How long have you been with him?" I asked.

"Three months."

"Halfway home."

"I guess."

"You don't sound too enthused."

Jackson reached into the cooler and pulled out a soda. He took a sip and pressed the can against his forehead.

"I'm learning a lot. Shit they'd never teach you at the academy. I want to learn it all."

"But . . ."

"I want that detective shield so bad I can taste it. But, like you said, I want it because I proved I'm a good cop, not because I know when he wants his drinks strong or what club he wants next."

"Hey," I said. "You make it through six months with my uncle, you deserve whatever they give you."

Jackson smiled. Damn, was this guy even twenty-five?

"Twice a week," he said.

"What?"

"You were looking at me wondering if I was old enough to shave, and I'm telling you. Twice a week."

I gave a slight nod and said, "You're going to be fine, Jackson."

"Chief Donne's talking about putting me in narcotics."

"That's a place to show what you know."

"I know it. I just don't think I want it that fast. Remember when you first started on the streets? The juice. The high?"

"Yeah."

"I don't," he said. "Never got the chance. Chief Donne snatched me right out of the academy. Made sure I was posted at One P.P. I never got the streets I wanted."

"Which streets were those?"

"Where I grew up. Bed-Stuy."

"Really," I said, not trying to hide my surprise.

"Yeah. I'm still young enough—your uncle'd say naïve—to think I can make a difference there. All the guys I ran with when I was younger?

The ones who got their college, they didn't stay around the neighborhood. That's what they got their college for, to get out. These kids growing up there now, what do they see? Same old dealers and knuckleheads ain't going anyplace. I want them to see me and then . . . I don't know. I just want them to see someone who made it out and came back."

"Then why get involved with my uncle? You had to know where this was going."

"And be known as the *black* cop who said no to Chief Donne?" He smiled. "You're a teacher, right?"

"Yeah."

"You wanna be a principal?"

"No. I like the kids too much and have all the paperwork I can handle now."

"Then you feel me. I'm not saying I don't want what your uncle's offering, just don't want it so quick, is all."

"See?" my uncle's voice boomed as he approached. "I knew you two'd find something to talk about."

"Comparing notes on you," I said.

"My favorite topic," he said. "I'll call Royce for you, Raymond. You came up with a valuable piece of info he's gonna want to know about, and you're right. It'll save a lot of time if it comes from me. But I will tell him how you got it."

"I can live with that."

"You'll have to."

"Thanks, Uncle Ray," I said and went over to shake his hand. He just looked at it and said, "Yeah, right," and pulled me into a hug. A sweaty one.

"I'll see you at the memorial service," he said. "You driving in with Rachel or staying at your mom's?"

"I'm not sure," I said, not willing to tell him I wasn't planning on attending.

"Well, either way, we'll see you there. And Reeny wants to have you both over for dinner. She'll cook up a special meal for the lot of us."

"That's supposed to entice me?" I asked.

"Hey." He gave me a playful slap on the shoulder. "She's been taking lessons. That's the great thing about second wives, Jackson. By definition, they know they can be replaced and are always looking for ways to improve."

"I'll keep that in mind, sir," Jackson said.

"See, Raymond? I teach more than good policing. I teach life."

My uncle's life lessons were often accompanied by the smell of Jack Daniels. "Whiskey and Wisdom" my mother called it.

"Thank you," I said.

"Be well, Nephew. Don't let those kids get the best of you."

"Good luck," I said to Jackson, shaking his hand again.

"Thanks."

"Okay," Uncle Ray said. "Enough talk. Time to get serious here."

"Yes, sir."

I left them there—teacher and pupil—and found myself wondering what Royce would do with the evidence my uncle was bringing him. And where were Frankie and Milagros?

A lot can happen in twelve hours, so as I was driving back to Brooklyn over the Williamsburg Bridge, I decided to swing by the Clemente Houses again. For all I knew, Frankie and Milagros were safe and sound, the police had their father's killer in custody, and my Uncle Ray would never have to give the hundred-dollar bill to Detective Royce. A lot can happen in twelve hours.

I circled the block a few times before finding a place to park. I got out of the car and walked toward Frankie's building. A small group of girls was hanging out on the concrete barrier that surrounded the small bushes. Another group—boys, about six of them—was taking turns playing daredevil, going down the steps that led to the sidewalk on their skateboards and bikes. In the waning light of the day, I could make out a figure walking in my direction. I remembered the outfit before I recognized the person wearing it.

"Mr. Donne," Elsa said. "Raymond."

"You working a late shift?" I asked, realizing too late the obvious answer.

"They just called," Elsa explained. "The hostess had to go home. An emergency with one of her kids, so . . ."

"Any word on Frankie and Milagros?"

"No. I was at Mrs. Santos's when I got the call. She has not heard anything new since you were here yesterday."

"And she never called the police about the break-in?"

"No," she said. "I'm sorry." Then she said, apologetically, "I have to go."

"Can I at least give you a ride?"

She looked at her watch. "Thank you, but it would be quicker to take the train . . . because of the traffic on the bridge."

"Right," I said. "Okay. I guess I'll see you around."

"That would be nice."

She gave me her hand. "What are you doing tomorrow?" I asked.

The question took us both by surprise. "I have finals next week," she said. "And a lot of studying and reading to get done this weekend."

"Finals?"

"I'm taking some psych courses at Baruch," she said.

"I have to work a cop party tomorrow anyway. At The LineUp?"

"Work?"

I explained the situation and how I had allowed myself to be coerced into helping out Mrs. McVernon. She smiled and let go of my hand.

"Good night, Raymond."

"Yeah."

She headed off in the direction of the subway, but before she got twenty feet away, she turned back. I was just about to unlock the driver's side door.

"I guess I have to eat sometime," she said.

I smiled. "You know The LineUp?" I asked.

"I know where it is, yes," she said.

"Meet me outside about six?"

"That would be nice."

"Good. I'll see you there."

"Good night."

"You, too," I said and watched her walk away.

Before heading to Queens, I drove over to the river and watched the sun set behind Manhattan. I sat there in the car, thinking about fathers, sons, and missing kids. I rolled down all the windows; a cool breeze was coming off the river. It almost felt like it was ready to rain.

Chapter 12

"THERE'S A LOT OF ROOM BACK here, Mrs. Mac."

We were standing in the rectangular area outside the back door of the bar. My best guess put it at about fifteen feet by forty, a bit smaller than my last apartment.

"We used to use it all the time," Mrs. McVernon said. "Years ago. We had four or five tables back here. Then we started getting complaints from the neighbors." She pointed up at the windows above us. "So, we started using it for storage. Yesterday, the Freddies cleared out everything. Threw it in the garbage or stored it downstairs. I don't know why I hold on to things. They cut back the bushes and weeds, too. It was a mess. Now . . ."

"It looks great," I said. "Billy's food come yet?"

"This morning. And he sent over those two grills."

I looked at the "grills"—two halves of an old oil drum that had been turned over, filled with coals, and propped up on metal braces. Billy. Real "down-home" cooking, Brooklyn–style.

Mrs. Mac put her hand on my head, pulled it down, and gave me a kiss on the temple. "This means a lot to me, Raymond. Thank you."

"Thank me when it's over," I said. "It's going to be a long day."

Half past noon, the first guests were arriving and gathering around the pool table. The Freddies had placed a huge piece of plywood over the table and covered it with a red, white, and blue cloth. This is where the plates, cups, and assorted munchies were laid out. The cooking would be done outside, the eating inside at the booths or the bar. Mikey and I were behind the bar, and Gloria started taking orders for drinks. Mikey would do anything that required mixing. I'd work the taps and bottles.

I was handing a tall, shaven-headed guy two Buds. "You don't remember me, do ya?" he asked. I studied his face for a few seconds and was about to apologize when he said, "I used to have hair." He ran his hand over his scalp, scratched the hair on his chin, and smiled.

"Neal O'Connor," I said. "What's with the lid?"

"I was losing it anyway, so I figured I'd give Mother Nature a hand. So this is what you're doing now, huh?"

"Part-time," I said. "I'm a schoolteacher now."

"The fuck you are. Really. Whatcha doing with yourself?"

"I'm really teaching now, Neal. Not too far from the precinct."

"Shit."

"You still working out of the old house?"

"No," he said. "Got transferred over to the other side of Brooklyn. Sheepshead Freakin' Bay. The 'burbs. Guess I spoke English too good to stay in the 'Burg, y'know?"

"Right," I said. "I heard they're making a lot of changes over there."

"For the worse, man. They want it, let 'em have it." He grabbed his two beers without having to explain who "they" were. "See ya next round, Ray."

"You bet."

A group of six—four men and two women—got my attention from the opposite side of the bar. The guys all wanted Buds; the women, vodka cranberries. Mikey was busy down at the other end wrestling with the blender, so I put the mixed drinks together. One of the guys tried to hand me some money. I waved him off.

"Billy says the first five hours are on him," I explained. "If you're still standing after that, I'll be glad to take your money."

"Thanks, man," the guy said and tossed a five on the bar.

"Thank you." I pocketed the bill. A few more guests like that, and I'd have dinner with Elsa paid for.

"Ramón!"

I turned and looked into the face of Victor Rodriguez. Victor had grown up on the streets of Williamsburg and started at the precinct a year before me. He showed me the ropes, taught me the difference between *mofongo* and *mondongo,* and clued me in to which bodegas had stashes of

Cuban cigars in the back. He leaned over the bar and pulled me into a head hug.

"*¿Como estás, Ramón?*"

"I'm good, Victor."

"*Bueno.*" He turned to the woman next to him. "This is my fiancée. Alice. Alice, this is Ray. From the house."

Alice was tanned, skinny, and in her mid-twenties. She was wearing cut-off denim jeans and a red shirt tied so that you could see her flat midsection. Alice looked like she'd just walked off a farm in Iowa.

"Nice to meet you, Alice," I said. "How'd you get stuck with this guy?"

"We met at Coney Island," she said, grabbing Victor by the elbow. As much as her appearance said Midwest, her voice said Brooklyn, born and bred. "He chased away some lowlifes who were bothering me."

"You should have seen what she was wearing, Ray," Victor said, shaking his hand as if he'd just touched a hot stove. "A priest would have bothered her."

"Be good," Alice said, giving Victor a playful slap to his upper arm. "Nice to meet you, Ray. What precinct are you at now?"

I told her I was a teacher now, and Victor added, "Ray got hurt on the job. He mistook a fire escape for a diving board and—"

"That's too bad."

"Life's like that sometimes," I said. And then to Victor, "You're not still at the house?"

"No, transferred to Coney Island. Made detective. Told you my last name would come in handy one day."

"You did." I considered telling him about my visit to Royce the other day, but decided against it. "What can I get you two?"

"Bud and a vodka cranberry."

After putting their drinks up, Victor handed me a ten. I explained the first-five-hours rule, and Victor put a couple of singles up on the bar. I slid them back.

"Not from you, Vic."

"All right, *maestro.* I'm going to walk my Alice around these *cabrones,* and then you and me are having a drink. And I won't take no for that."

"Wouldn't think of it. Have fun. Alice."

I spent the next fifteen minutes opening bottles and pouring pints.

When I finally had a chance to look up, the place was packed, and Edgar was sitting at the end of the bar under the TV set. He was wearing a dark blue T-shirt with a matching baseball cap and had the look of a kid on the first day of a carnival. I poured him a Bass and placed a can of tomato juice next to it.

"Your best behavior, Edgar."

He raised his right hand like a boy scout and said, "Promise." He reached into his pocket and pulled out an index card. "Hey, I gotta show you something."

"Later. I'm working here."

"This is important." He waved the card. "Yesterday—"

"Later," I repeated and walked down to the other end of the bar. Mrs. Mac was over at the food table straightening up. She glanced over at me, smiled, and gave me a thumbs-up. If I had any lingering doubts about helping her with the party, they were erased. Taking care of cops was what Mrs. Mac did best.

A roar and a round of applause turned all of our heads toward the front door where Billy Morris was making his entrance. The triumphant host—his loyal wife, Susie, by his side—raised his hands in victory as he was patted on the back and high-fived. He made a big deal out of checking his watch and yelled, "Y'all got four hours left before you're buying your own. So stop cheering and start drinking, 'cause at five o'clock, I stop buying, ya cheap coppers!"

Another cheer went up, and Billy accepted a bottle of Bud someone thrust into his hand. He took a big sip and looked over at the bar. When our eyes met, he pointed at me. I stepped out from behind the bar where Billy took me into a bear hug and then quickly backed off.

"I'm not hurtin' ya, am I, son?"

"I'm okay, Billy," I answered. "Just keep me off my knees."

"Your knees," he said, "are the last place I'd wanna see *you*." He held me out by the shoulders and grinned. "Boy, you don't look so bad. Could afford to drop a few, but . . . Where ya been hiding yourself?"

"I've been busy, Bill. School, rehab . . ."

"Bullshit," he said. "Rehab. Muscles said he ain't seen you since you were released from the hospital. You seeing another physical therapist?"

Billy Morris knows everything. "I've been busy," I repeated.

He had a look in his eyes that told me he was thinking about pushing the issue, but settled for "Whatever." He turned to his wife. "You remember Susie?"

"Absolutely." We kissed hello. "How are you, Susie?"

"Good," she said, although her tone said something else. "The work on the house is taking longer—and costing more—than we had hoped. But somebody"—she looked at her husband—"keeps making the job bigger."

"And *somebody* wanted a hot tub. I tell ya, son," Billy said, "I ever have six months to live, I wanna hear it from a contractor. Anyway, we are here now, and we are ready to party. How long you gonna be behind the stick?"

"A few more hours. It's still too busy to leave Mikey by himself."

"Let me make the rounds. Then we'll do some catching up." He looked at me again and shook his head. "Damn, it's been a long time." Billy Morris took Susie by the hand and walked to the back of the bar. He was right. It had been a long time. I was starting to feel better that Mrs. Mac coerced me into this. I missed these guys, the buzz I got just being around them. I'd almost forgotten about the buzz. I got behind the bar just in time to be greeted by a flustered Mikey.

"Damn, Ray," he said. "I gotta take a leak, man."

He didn't wait for a response, just headed off in the direction of the men's room. I served a few more rounds of drinks, collected a few more tips, and watched as Edgar made a production of fanning himself with the index card. I brought another pint over to him. "Okay," I said. "What's so important that it can't wait?"

He handed me the card. "I had a busy day yesterday. Very busy."

I looked at the card. It had a set of numbers and letters on it.

"What's this?" I asked. "Some kind of code you're working on?"

Edgar leaned forward and said, "I swung by the Clemente Houses and Rivas's block yesterday." He lowered his voice. "While I was working."

Great. "So?"

"So, that's a plate number belonging to a vehicle I observed outside the houses at . . ."—he pointed at some other numbers at the bottom of the card—". . . oh-seven-hundred, thirteen-thirty-hundred hours and down the block from Rivas's at twelve-hundred."

I looked at my watch. "Edgar, I'm going to kick your ass out of here at fourteen-hundred hours if you don't get to the point."

He smiled. "Why would this vehicle be parked outside the Houses and down the block from Rivas, Ray?"

"Because he lives or works in the neighborhood?"

"Maybe." He pointed at the plate number. "A white van. No markings on the outside."

"So it was a contractor working in the area. Someone making deliveries."

"Nope. There was always at least one guy sitting inside. Sometimes two. They were waiting for something. Or"—he paused for effect—"some*body*. And, come on, Ray. It was outside both places."

I looked at the card again. Edgar had penciled in the letters *"wv"* next to the plate number in question. I shook my head.

"Don't you have to account for your time while you're at work, Edgar?"

"Hey! I get more done before noon than most of those guys get done in the whole day. My supervisor knows that and leaves me alone." He tapped the card. "You should get one of your buddies to run that plate."

"Why would I want to embarrass myself like that?"

"You got two missing kids, a dead father, and a van doing surveillance outside the LKA of one of the kids. Why wouldn't you want to run the plate?"

LKA. Last Known Address. Edgar loved that cop talk. If this conversation kept going, I was sure he'd work in BOLOs and APBs. I slipped the index card into my back pocket and said, "Thanks, Edgar. I'll consider it."

"Consider it?" I wasn't taking him seriously enough. "Ray, if I were you, I'd—"

"Ask you to leave?" I warned. "I wouldn't think of it. You're on your best behavior, Edgar. Keep it up."

"But . . ."

"Keep it up."

The kid-at-the-carnival face disappeared and was replaced by the whatever-you-say-Dad look. I poured him a shot of Jack Daniel's to ease the pain.

The door to the bar opened again, and Jack Knight filled the doorway. Just like that, the room grew darker. Damn, twice in two days. He had a case of Heineken under his arm and swung it on top of the bar. When he saw me on the other side, he leaned in for a closer look. His breath smelled as if he'd already started his celebrating.

"Well," he said. "Found something you could do without hurting yourself?"

I ignored the shot and pushed the case of beer back at him. "You probably forgot bars have their own beer. That's how they make money."

"Didn't know if this hellhole carried my brand, Teach. Whyn't you just open me up one and put the rest on ice like a good boy?"

The people within earshot of our conversation stopped, listened, and waited for what I would say next. Neal O'Connor stepped out of nowhere and put his hand on Jack's shoulder.

"Glad you could make it, Jack," Neal said. "C'mon in the back and have a burger."

"Soon as the teacher here serves me my beer," Jack said, removing Neal's hand by the middle finger and locking his eyes on mine. "I'm waiting."

"I think Whack's had enough, Neal," I said. "Wouldn't want him to take a nap while driving home."

Jack leaned in again, quicker this time. "Nobody calls me that anymore, Raymond."

"Maybe not to your face, Jack. But trust me . . ." I looked around the bar and then stage-whispered, "They do."

"Still the wise-ass son of a bitch." Jack pushed Neal away and made his way to the service station at the end of the bar. That's where he bumped into Billy Morris.

"Problem, Jack?"

Jack looked at me and said, "Nothing I can't handle, Billy."

"Good, good. Glad to hear it. I can smell ya been drinking. Eaten yet?"

"No. Not yet."

"Well, I can fix that. Where are those car keys I've heard so much about?"

"What?"

"The car keys. How's about I trade ya a beer for them."

"I got my own beer," Jack said. "Just waiting on Raymond to give me one."

Billy looked over to where I was standing and winked. "And he will. Soon as you give me those car keys, we'll have ourselves a time."

Jack looked at me and then at the crowd around him. After a few seconds of silence, Billy leaned into him and whispered in his ear. Jack smiled, reached into his pocket, and dropped his keys into Billy Morris's outstretched hand. I popped open a Heineken and placed it on the bar, a few feet away from Jack.

"There ya go," Billy said, slapping Jack on the shoulder. "No blood, no foul."

Jack slithered over and grabbed his beer. He took a long sip and eyed me up and down. "We'll talk later, Teach. Count on it."

Billy spun Jack around and gave him a shove toward the back of the bar. He then came over to me. "Sorry about that, Ray."

"You think that was a good idea, Bill? Inviting Jack?"

"You don't exactly *invite* Jack to a party, Ray. He hears about it, and he comes. You wanna tell him he's not invited?"

I thought about that for a bit. "He starts in again, he's leaving."

"He'll be fine. I just gotta keep his keys away from him."

"What'd you whisper in his ear, anyway?"

Billy grinned. "You want the exact words or an approximation?"

"Paraphrase it for me."

"Told him not to waste his time with you. Now." He slapped the bar. "You and I are having a drink."

"I'm working."

"You can't pour and drink at the same time?"

I knew better than to argue with Billy. "Okay." I reached into the ice and pulled out a longneck. Billy and I clinked our bottles and drank. "Thanks."

"No prob. Hey, I heard about the two missing kids and their old man. The boy went to your school, didn't he?"

"How'd you know that?"

Billy Morris shrugged.

"He's one of mine," I said. "I called in the body."

"Crossed my mind that mighta been you in the papers. What's the latest?"

"How much time you got?"

"Talk, son," Billy said, pulling over an empty bar stool. "I am all ears."

I got behind the bar and told Billy about my visit to Detective Royce, my trip upstate, and the hundred-dollar bill with Frankie's handwriting on it I'd given to my uncle the day before.

"How's the chief doing these days?" Billy asked.

"Same as always. He said he'd bring the bill to Royce. Then he chewed my butt off for getting too involved."

"Sounds like Chief Donne. A steady diet of asses and other people's balls." Billy took another sip. "Tell him I said hey next time you see him."

"I'll do that."

"Anything else?"

"Not really." I remembered Edgar's index card with the license plates on it and took it out of my pocket. "Well, maybe . . ."

"What?"

"How much would I be pushing it if I asked you to run a plate for me?"

Now he looked surprised. "You? Wouldn't be a push at all. What's up?"

I handed him the card. "That top one with '*wv*' written next to it?" He nodded. "I'm kind of interested in who owns it."

"And why would that be?"

"How about," I said, "I tell you that I think it might have been involved in a ding-and-dent with one of the teachers I work with?"

Billy's grin got bigger. "And how's about I pretend to believe you but you tell me the real story later?"

"I can live with that."

"Gimme your number, and I'll call ya Monday."

I pulled my newly charged cell phone out of my front pocket along with the slip of paper that had my new number on it. I read it off to Billy, who wrote it on the index card.

"Your memory going in your old age, Ray?"

"I just renewed it this morning. Got a two-year plan and a new number."

"All right, then." Billy shook his head and put the card into his pocket. "Going to Clemente and the Southside? Up to Highland? And now asking me to run a plate for a 'friend.'" He rolled his shoulders and did a little juke with his hips. "You getting back in the game."

"I'm not getting back into anything," I said. "I'm just trying to help a kid."

"Right."

"You don't know everything, Billy."

"Well," he said, "if there's something I don't know, I don't know what it is."

"You know, for a Brooklyn boy, you sound a lot like a country song."

"Gimme a pickup truck and a banjo any day."

Mikey was giving me his unhappy look, so I figured it was time to get back to work. I finished up my beer and offered Billy my hand.

"Thanks again, man," I said. "I appreciate your help."

"Son, this don't come close to paying you back. I still owe you huge."

"Don't start. I appreciate your help. Leave it at that."

"Whatever you say. But I know what I know."

"I'll see you before I head out."

"What? You got a date or something?"

My turn to grin. "Something."

"Oooh wee! That's my boy. Back in the game."

Billy Morris knows everything.

"See ya, Billy," I said and headed down to the other end of the bar, where Edgar sat with an empty pint glass. When I filled it, I saw that his happy face had returned. "What?" I asked.

Edgar shrugged. "Nothing. I just saw you hand the license plate number to your good buddy, Billy Morris. Guess I wasn't as far off as you thought, huh?"

"All right, Edgar. Maybe it means something, maybe it doesn't. I'm betting it doesn't. But you do not do anything like that again. I keep telling you, this is not some TV show." I realized I was sounding like my uncle. "Got it?"

"I got it, Ray." His smile grew bigger. "Just happy to be of service."

"You are this close, Edgar." I showed him a quarter-inch of space between my thumb and forefinger. "This close."

"You know," Edgar said. "If things jumped off over there—with that Jack guy?—I want you to know, I had your back."

"That's what kept me going, Edgar."

"Just saying, is all."

"Right."

During the next two hours, I served a few hundred adult beverages and cleaned the same number of glasses. I met a few more guys I used to know, and Billy did a good job of keeping Jack away from the bar area. By the time I was able to take a breath, I looked up at the clock. Nearly four. I needed some real air and told Mikey I'd be stepping outside for a bit.

The Saturday traffic buzzed past the weekend construction work on the BQE above me. By the time they finished the present round of construction up there, it would be time to start the next one. Some guys probably put their entire thirty years in on one stretch of road. Working their whole lives rebuilding a ten-mile-long piece of highway, handing the job down to their kids, and starting the whole cycle over again.

I found a spot in the shade and used a bike rack next to a row of garbage cans to do some stretches. My knees were aching from the hours of standing and bending behind the bar. It felt good to let the blood flow. I was halfway through a thirty-second runner's stretch, when a voice behind me said, "Did you finish early?"

I turned and saw Elsa. She had on a white sundress. With the sun behind her and a slight breeze blowing through the dress, she was a mirage, and I was a man dying of thirst.

"No," I said, slowly lowering my leg to the ground. "I just needed some air."

She looked up at the hazy sky. "Out here?"

"Different air. I expected you at six."

"I finished my reading and thought it would be interesting to see how the police party. Research for my final paper."

"Paper?"

"For my Abnormal Psychology class."

I laughed. "That's good."

She looked at the front door of the bar. "Would you like to buy me a drink?"

"Absolutely."

The air inside The LineUp felt better than it had before. Maybe it was the heat outside. Maybe it was Elsa. I got back behind the bar. She was standing next to Edgar, who was trying not to breathe too hard.

"Edgar," I said. "This is Elsa."

Edgar offered his hand. "Edgar Martinez O'Brien."

"Elsa."

"Edgar was just about to offer you his seat."

Edgar practically jumped off of his stool and made a big gesture of wiping it off and displaying it for Elsa.

"Are you sure?" she asked.

"Absolutely," he said, eyes on me. "I insist."

Elsa slid into the seat as I asked, "What'll you have?"

"Cuervo Margarita," she said without pause. "Frozen. No salt."

I shook my head and grinned.

"What?" she asked.

"Nothing. That's the third time in five minutes that you've surprised me."

She put on a serious face. "Do I look like the Shirley Temple type?"

Not in that dress.

"No, it's not that, it's just . . . I don't . . . Let me get that margarita for you."

Along the way to the other end of the bar, I opened a few Buds and poured three pints. By the time I brought Elsa's drink to her, she was engaged in a deep conversation with Edgar. Edgar said something I couldn't hear, and Elsa threw her head back in laughter.

"What'd I miss?" I asked.

Elsa thanked me for the margarita and took a sip. "Edgar was just telling me a story about his work. A conversation he overheard."

"Overheard or eavesdropped on?"

Edgar got defensive. "I may have . . . accidentally . . . tapped into the wrong line. It's easy to make a mistake with all those wires."

"And so hard not to listen after you . . . accidentally tap into the wrong line." I thought about Edgar's trick earlier in the week with the cell phone. "Edgar," I said, "is a bit of a techie."

"Techie?"

"A high-end nosybody."

"And Raymond," Edgar said, catching the look on my face, "is one heck of a guy."

"Yes," Elsa agreed, her eyes resting just above the rim of her margarita glass as she took another sip. "He seems to be."

"Is this the 'something' you mentioned earlier?"

"Billy," I said, turning to the voice. "Didn't see you there."

"I've added stealth to my long list of admirable qualities." Billy raised Elsa's hand and brought it to his lips. "Billy Morris, ma'am."

"Elsa Ramos."

"Raymond hinted that he had someone coming by, but he neglected to elaborate."

Edgar stuck out his hand. "Billy. How are ya? Edgar Martinez O'Brien."

"Nice to meet ya, Edgar." Billy studied Edgar's eager face for a few beats and said, "We know each other?"

"No, no," Edgar said and cleared his throat. "I'm a friend of Raymond's."

"Then we know each other now." Billy looked from Edgar to me and asked, "You guys work together?"

"Not yet," Edgar said.

"No," I corrected. "Edgar is . . . just a friend."

"Just a . . . I gave Ray those—"

"Who was just thinking about leaving," I said.

Billy clapped Edgar on the neck. "Ahh. Too early for that. We're just getting started."

"Yeah, Ray," Edgar said. "We're just getting started."

"We," Elsa jumped in, "have dinner reservations for six o'clock."

"Yes," I said. I looked around the bar and over to the food table. "Things seem to be under control. Maybe we should think about heading out."

"You gonna leave my Q early? You know the rules, son."

I gestured with my eyes at Elsa. "Sometimes we gotta break the rules, Billy. Based on . . . exigent circumstances."

"I hear that," Billy said and took a deep breath. "Don't mean I gotta like it. Mrs. Mac needs, I can always jump behind the bar for a spell. But we are going to get together soon. You gotta come over and see the new digs." He placed his hand on Elsa's back. "Maybe you can bring a friend. Or something."

"That would be nice," I said.

"And I'll do my best about that other thing," he said. "The van plates."

"Thanks."

I grabbed my umbrella and explained to Mikey that I had to leave. Before he could argue, I walked out from behind the bar. I said a few quick good-byes and made it over to where Elsa, Billy, and Edgar were. Billy gave me another hug.

"Take care of yourself, son."

"You, too, Billy."

Elsa took my hand and said, "It was nice meeting you both."

"You, too."

"Same here, Elsa."

I told Edgar to make my apologies to Mrs. McVernon and escorted Elsa out of the bar into the hot Brooklyn air.

"Thanks," I said.

"For what?"

"For the six o'clock reservation idea. I haven't been around those guys for a long time. I forgot how exhausting they can be."

Elsa smiled. "I am . . . something, aren't I?"

"All right. That was just something I told Billy," I explained. She gave me a blank look. "He asked if I had a date, and I didn't know what to call it so . . ."

"I understand. Really."

"Good. The restaurant's only a few blocks away. I figured we could walk it, and then I can get you a car service back to your place."

"We'll see." She took me by the hand again. "We'll see."

I found myself liking the tone of her voice the more she spoke. Asking her to dinner had been a good idea.

"Hey, Teach!"

I tightened my grip on Elsa's hand and picked up the pace a little.

"You gone deaf?"

I stopped and turned. Jack Knight had a beer in one hand and a cigar in the other.

"Go back inside, Jack," I said.

He took a few steps closer and said, "You ain't gonna introduce me to your friend?" He squinted at Elsa. "You datin' civilians now, huh? That figures."

To Jack, any member of the nonwhite, noncop population was a "civilian." It was a much more acceptable word in public than "nigger" or "spic."

"Go back inside, Jack."

"Your boyfriend tell ya what a great and honorable policeman he was, Missy?"

"I was hoping to hear about it over dinner."

"Ouch," Jack said. "She speaka the English real smooth there. She do the horizontal mambo the same way?"

I let go of Elsa's hand and stepped in front of her. She held on to my elbow as I said, "Watch your mouth in front of the lady, Jack."

"It's nothing, Ray," Elsa said. "Let's go eat."

"Yeah, Ray," Jacked mimicked. He took a drag of the cigar and exhaled it slowly. "Go eat. Then go home and eat a little more." He winked. "Spicy. You gonna tell her about the time you chased the street monkey up the fire escape?"

"You're pushing it, Jack," I said.

He took another couple of steps. Ten feet separated us now. Elsa tried to turn me by the elbow, but I wouldn't let her. I moved my right foot slightly forward, shifted more weight onto the right leg, and held the umbrella at my side.

"Let's just go," Elsa said.

"I think Jack wanted to apologize first," I said.

"Looks like you'll be missing dinner then." Jack bent over and placed his beer and cigar on the sidewalk. " 'Cause I ain't apologizing for shit."

"Please, Ray." Elsa tried pulling me. "He's drunk. It is not worth it."

I shrugged Elsa's hand off my elbow and said to Jack, "You never did learn how to behave in front of real people, did you?" For effect, I added, "Whack."

"And you never learned when to shut the fuck up."

"Not when I'm right. No."

He shook his head and laughed.

"That's what it's all about, ain't it? You being right."

"Think what you want, Jack."

"Oh, I will," he said. "I will."

He looked down at the ground, pushed off on his back leg, and came at me. He was drunk and not all that graceful, so I was able to sidestep his charge. He spun away, and his momentum carried him into a pile of garbage bags and tied-up newspapers. Jack got up, rubbed his hand across his mouth, and smiled.

"I'd like another shot at that, Teacher."

I spread out my arms, telling him I wasn't going anywhere. As he gathered himself together, I took a quick look at Elsa, who was standing between two parked cars.

"Are you okay?" I asked.

"I want to go," she pleaded. "You don't need to—"

I held up my hand. "In a minute."

Jack approached me, slower this time, realizing speed was not on his side. I eased into the middle of the sidewalk and balanced my weight evenly. I was thinking maybe I had been lucky the first time. Jack had quite a few inches and pounds on me and seemed to learn from his mistake.

"Just say you're sorry, Jack, and you can go back to drinking yourself into a stupor."

Jack smirked as he crept closer, his breathing heavy but rhythmic. He was about three feet away when he threw his right hand at me. I leaned away from it, only to realize too late it was a feint, and he was able to smack me across the face with the back of his left. I stumbled back a few feet, where someone caught me.

"The fuck is this?" Billy Morris said, holding me up by my armpits. "Ain't no dancing allowed out here."

Jack took a few steps closer to us. Billy stopped him with a pointed finger.

"Enough!" Billy said. "You both seem to have gotten your shots in, so just cool the fuck out." He turned to Elsa and said, "You okay?"

She nodded.

"You," he said to Jack. "Get inside and drink."

Jack picked up his cigar and beer and tipped an imaginary hat at Elsa. "Ma'am." He strolled down the sidewalk and into The LineUp.

"And you," Billy said as he picked my umbrella off the ground. "I expect that shit from the Whack, but you? Damn, Ray. Go have dinner with your friend." He reached into his pocket and pulled out a tissue. "Wipe the blood off your face first."

Billy turned away and headed back inside. I touched the tissue to my nose and it came away red. Shit. Elsa took the tissue and wiped my face. When she was done, she walked over to an open garbage can and dropped the bloody tissue inside.

"I'm not hungry anymore," she said.

"Excuse me?"

Elsa shook her head. "That was just . . . stupid."

"I know. Jack gets out of control sometimes."

"I was talking about you."

"Me?" I asked. "I was defending myself."

"No. You thought you were defending me."

"Elsa . . ."

"Three times I asked you to stop. You didn't listen."

"He was verbally abusing you. I wasn't just going to let—"

"Do I look so helpless, I need my honor defended?" She took a step back and pointed at a red mark on her dress. "That is blood. Your blood." She paused. "I almost didn't come here because I was worried about the cops at the party. Too much . . . testosterone. I didn't think I had to worry about you."

"You didn't. You don't."

"You could have walked away from him. He was drunk. Instead you had to prove you could stand up for yourself. Stand up for me. I have had too much of that . . . that machismo shit." She waited for me to come back with an answer. When I didn't, she said, "What would you say to your students if they acted as you just did?"

"That's not fair," I said. "This was completely different."

"Because he started it?"

I tried to keep my tone calm. "Don't talk to me like I'm a child."

She shook her head. "You are not so different from that Jack as you would like to believe."

"What's that?" I asked, ignoring the little voice inside my head telling me to shut the fuck up. "Some of the psychology crap they teach you?"

She looked at me with what could only be called pity and shook her head. She looked up and down the avenue and crossed.

I followed her to the other side. "Where are you going?" I asked.

"Home." She pointed at a bus sign. "I can take this."

"Elsa. Can't we just have dinner?"

"Not tonight. I'm sorry." She looked over my shoulder. "The bus is coming."

I turned around and saw the blue and white city bus making the left under the BQE.

"Let me take you home," I tried.

"I can take myself home."

The bus pulled in front of us, opened its doors, and let off a handful of passengers. I thought about getting on the bus with her. Telling her about my trip to Highland, the clue I had found. She would see by my actions what kind of man I really was.

Maybe she already had.

Chapter 13

"HOW'S THAT FEEL?"

"Like someone's sticking a hot needle into the back of my legs."

"Excellent." Muscles Marinaccio looked down at me and grinned. "That means you're doing it correctly."

I did another one. The sharp pain began just below my knees and turned into a bright light as it moved its way north.

"I must be doing it very correctly," I said, exhaling and easing back into a squatting position. "Because it hurts like a bitch."

"That's the lactic acid rushing into the muscles," he continued. "If you'd been doing these consistently for the last four years, you'd know that. Also, it wouldn't be hurting so bad."

I was on a piece of gym equipment that required me to wrap my hands around two rubber grips, squat, and then stand up, raising the padded bar connected to the weights. Once my legs were straight, I was to count to three and then slowly—"Very slowly! There are two parts to this exercise!"—return to my original position. I've seen pictures in textbooks of similar devices that were used during the Spanish Inquisition to punish the unfaithful. This one was used to punish delinquent patients with torn ligaments behind their knees. As Muscles watched, I did five more, for a total of ten, and stopped.

"I said this to you four years ago, Raymond. You didn't just tear the meniscus." He touched below the back of my right knee and brought his finger up and around the kneecap. "You tore your ACL and pretty much fucked around with both patellas."

"Don't get so technical, Doc."

"How about this? Your knee bone ain't exactly connected to your leg bone the way God meant it to be. That dumbed down enough for you?"

"Sorry."

"You should be." Muscles reached into his shirt pocket and pulled out two white pills. "Take these," he said.

"Ibuprofen?"

"Wintergreen. Every time you exhale, I get hit with a faceful of vodka. Where the hell'd you go last night?"

I popped the mints into my mouth. "Every bar between The LineUp and my apartment. I had some thinking to do."

"You pissed off at your liver?"

"Just pissed," I said, and told him about last night's aborted date with Elsa and the fight with Jack Knight.

"No offense, Raymond," Muscles said, "but Jack could break you in two."

"He was drunk."

"That would just give him more reason to want to. That why you're back here today? After all these years of neglect? Tired of getting sand kicked in your face?"

"That's part of it."

"What's the other part?"

"This morning," I said, "when I was drinking my coffee with *The New York Times* spread out on the carpet?"

"Yeah?"

"It took me five minutes to get up off the floor."

Muscles shook his head and offered his hand to help me out of the contraption. As he did, his left bicep ballooned to the size of a cantaloupe. All he needed was a tattoo of an anchor and a can of spinach to complete the image. "The surgery was not the end of your problems," he said. "You should have been coming here every week for physical therapy."

Here was Muscles Marinaccio's gym-slash-rehabilitation center on the top floor of an East River–front factory building that housed mostly artist studios and a few illegal residences. If you wanted to work out in a no-frills, no aerobics, let's-not-do-some-carrot-juice-afterward environment, this was the place. Since Muscles was also a licensed physical therapist, you could use his facilities and expertise to recover from an injury. I had come to him after my accident, just like the doctor had ordered. Then I didn't feel like coming anymore. The pain became a part of me, something I deserved.

"Why would you put yourself through that?" Muscles asked, sliding the palm of his hand over his crew cut. "I'll never understand it. It's not like you're stupid."

He was looking at me like I was stupid.

"I don't know," I said. "I've been busy."

"Busy? Bullshit. Busy limping around Brooklyn making the damned thing worse, and feeling sorry for yourself. So last night and this morning got to you, huh?"

"Yeah."

Muscles looked at me for ten seconds and said, "What else, Raymond?"

I took a deep breath. "I guess I just got tired of the pain."

"About fucking time." He pointed over at the blue padded table by the window. "Go over and do some stretching. I'm going to search the archives and see if I can unearth your file."

As Muscles walked away, I went over to the table, placed my leg on top, and reached for my toes. I got about as far as the ankle when the burning started again. I settled for placing my hand on the knee and leaning forward. I felt pain in muscles I had forgotten were there.

There was only one other person in the place. A woman, about fifty or so, working up a sweat on the stair machine. We acknowledged each other with brief smiles and nods, and went back to our tasks. I looked out the window at the river in an attempt to keep my mind off the fire behind my knees. It was calm out there today. A light mix of smoke and clouds hung above the city, the sky once again not committing itself to either rain or sun.

"Should I bore you—again—with the details of the MRIs and X-rays?" Muscles's voice brought me back inside.

"No."

"Good. You wouldn't be able to follow most of it anyway." He pulled up a stool and sat next to me. "The bottom line is—if you're serious this time around—you need to be coming to see me three times a week. There was a lot of damage to both knees. It's still there. Like I said, the surgery took care of some of it, but . . ."

"I've got to do the rest," I finished for him.

He closed up the folder. "For someone as seemingly bright as yourself, you're taking a hell of a chance with your physical well-being. You looking forward to spending the last half of your life not moving around too much?"

"No."

"Then quit fucking around."

"I am," I said. "I will. That's why I'm here."

"All right then." He took out a piece of paper and handed me what appeared to be a spreadsheet. "That is your plan for the next six weeks."

I took some time to look over the paper. He had me scheduled for three days a week, including one on the weekend, Saturday or Sunday, my choice. Under each day was a series of empty boxes, and next to them, initials.

"Translate this into English for me?" I asked.

"That's more for me than you." He touched his index finger to the initials. "These are the exercises you'll be doing. In these boxes, we'll fill in your reps and weights. When the six weeks are up, we'll analyze your progress."

"And after that?"

"We schedule another six weeks." He saw the look on my face. "This isn't a sprint, Raymond. It's a marathon. A lifelong marathon."

I took another look at the sheet. "What's this about abs and quads? I thought I was working on getting my knees back."

Muscles leaned into me and grabbed my stomach. He pinched the two inches or so of flesh between his fingers. "Any other questions?"

"Jesus."

"The Lord's got nothing to do with this, Raymond. It's just you, me, and all this modern rehabilitation equipment."

I handed the paper back to him. "About the cost of all this . . ."

"You got insurance, don't you?" he said.

"Yeah, but I don't think they'll cover this. Working out?"

"It's called *rehabilitation therapy*," he said. "You got an orthopedist?"

"No."

"I do." He produced a business card between his fingers like a magician turning a trick. "He'll write you a scrip for six weeks of therapy, three days a week. I will bill your insurance. You won't have to fork over a dime."

"Copayment?"

"Please."

"I appreciate that. What if I can't make it three days a week?"

"I still bill the insurance. Three a week is standard. They have any qualms, they'll request copies of your X-rays and MRIs. Believe me, after they see the damage you did to your knees . . ."

"So you get paid whether I show up or not?"

"That's the way it works, yeah."

"That doesn't sound . . ."

"It's the way it is. But it doesn't really matter, does it?" He placed a hand just above my knee and squeezed. "Because you will show up. Right?"

"Absolutely," I answered.

"Good." He stood up. "Now give me ten minutes on the stationary bike. I'll hit you with the ice and electric stim on the knees, and you're done for the day."

"Electric stim?"

"Relax. It'll feel like pins and needles. Speeds up the recovery."

"The insurance covers that, too?"

"Hell, Raymond. I'm going to charge them for the ice and bill them just for this conversation. Sorry. 'Consultation.'"

I waited for him to smile or wink. When he didn't, I held out my hand. "Thanks."

"Welcome back, Raymond. Now hit the bike." He walked toward his office, turned back, and said, "And stop picking fights with drunk cops twice your size. I can only do so much."

Less than an hour later, I was showered and still in pain. "Good pain," Muscles had called it. "Replacing the bad." Either way, I was buzzing with endorphins—or whatever it is that gives you the high after working out—and felt myself deserving of a treat. I stepped out into the heat thinking of chicken with garlic sauce from the place by my apartment. Not watching where I was going, I just about knocked Detective Royce off the top step.

"Mr. Donne," he said.

"Detective," I said, not hiding my surprise. "You looking for me?"

He gave me a what-do-you-think? look. "I found you, didn't I?"

"How did you—?"

"Part of the job description, last I checked." He moved the gym bag he was carrying from his left hand to his right. "Speaking of which, I had a little talk with your uncle yesterday."

"I figured you might have," I said.

"Actually, he had a talk. I had a listen."

"Sorry about that. I just—"

"Sorry about what?" Detective Royce asked. "Messing with my case even after I told you not to? Or sorry about screwing up my weekend, which I just would have wasted on time with my family anyways?" He swung the bag over his shoulder. "Nothing I like more than coming into work on my day off. By the way, Mr. Donne," he took a step closer, "you look like shit."

I ran my fingers through my hair and said, "I just had a workout. And I'm getting over a little something."

"Smells like"—he leaned in—"you're getting over a little vodka."

"Did you have a question for me, Detective? If not, I'd really like to go home and eat."

"Matter of fact, I do have a couple of questions. Tell me why you went up to Highland."

"I wanted to talk to Frankie's cousin and her husband."

"Even after I told you to stay out of my way?"

"I had the funny feeling we wouldn't be running into each other up there."

Royce looked as if he wanted to take a bite out of my face. After a few seconds and a deep breath, he said, "And . . . ?"

"And what?"

"What kind of feel did you get off of them?"

I smiled. "I only spoke with her. The husband was down here."

"Yeah?"

"She told me he was planning on talking to you."

"News to me," he said.

"And . . . she didn't like the idea of the—of me—coming to her house. She kept telling me her husband was handling everything."

"Mr. Donne," Royce said, "you didn't tell her that you were police, did you?"

"I didn't tell her anything. Until she asked. When she found out I was Frankie's teacher, she lightened up a bit." I thought back to the spacious backyard and the light breeze moving through the maples. "Then I found the hundred and I was asked to leave."

"She didn't ask for the bill back?"

"She seemed to want me and it off her property as soon as physically possible."

Royce pondered that for a few seconds before saying, "And he was down here?"

"That's what she said. Why?"

"I called his place of business," Royce explained. "Around the Horn Travel. They said he hadn't been in for a few days."

"He owns some apartment buildings, right?"

"Yeah. I guess he coulda been busy with them, but they made it seem like they hadn't heard from him in a while."

"Covering for the boss?"

"Maybe."

I wiped some sweat from my forehead. "Anything else?"

"Yeah," he said, changing his tone to remind me who was the cop here. "Next time you take a field trip, you better have a bunch of kids with you. Because of you, I may have to take a two-hour ride up to the Hudson Valley tomorrow."

"Hour and a half if you go seventy," I joked. If Royce found me funny, he was hiding it well. "I brought you a clue, Detective."

"Fuck your clue. You stepped on my toes, Mr. Donne. Even though your uncle is not my direct superior, I don't like being made to look like I dropped the ball."

"Don't worry. My uncle read me the riot act on this one."

"Good."

I looked up and down the block. Before going down the steps I asked, "You wouldn't want to give me a ride home, would you?"

"Actually," Royce said, tapping the side of his bag, "I'm here to work out."

"So . . . you weren't looking for me?"

"I come here on the odd weekend when I'm called in . . . unexpectedly . . . and can't get home to my own gym. By my house."

"I hear you. And again, I'm sorry." I took the first few steps toward the sidewalk and then remembered something. "You get anything off that bill?"

He smirked. "Not gonna bother running it for prints if that's what you mean. I'll just get a mix of the kid's, the cousin's, yours, P.O. Jackson's, and Inspector Donne's. Called in the serial number to the feds. Waiting to see if it rings a bell with them, but I'm not waiting by the phone."

"Good luck to you, Detective."

"And to you, Mr. Donne. And, no offense, but the next time you get an idea about this case, give me a heads-up, okay?"

"No offense," I answered, "but I thought I did."

If he said something after I went down the steps, I didn't hear it.

As I waited for the light to turn, my biggest concern was whether I was feeling well enough to have a cold beer with lunch. That changed when I started to cross the street and almost walked head-on into a van that screeched to a stop in front of me. Asshole.

I took a few steps to walk around the front. Its windows were tinted, so I didn't have the pleasure of making eye contact with the driver. The van pulled up three feet, blocking my path. What the fuck? I counted to five and then tried again. Again I was blocked, and this time the side door slid open. I looked inside and saw the driver, his huge hands on the wheel and the eyes in his very large head looking forward. There was nobody in the passenger seat.

"You got a problem?" I asked the driver.

No reaction from him, but from behind me came a low voice. "Get in, Mr. Donne." Something sharp touched my lower back, telling me it would be a bad idea to get overexcited at that moment.

"Just get in," the voice repeated. "Before your detective friend comes back and your time at the gym becomes a complete waste."

There was nothing but metal floor in the back of the van, and the only light came from the small, rear-door window. A solid partition separated the back from the front, so I couldn't see the driver. The guy with the knife got in the back with me and held on to a leather strap connected to the side door. I couldn't tell where we were going, only that the driver was making a lot of lefts and rights, and making them harder than he needed to. I had to make my way to the rear of the van and grab the door handle to have something to hold on to, or I would have rolled all over the back. My knees were screaming. The guy with the knife watched me as I tried the door handle. Locked. He gave me a smile that sent a wave of fear down to my toes.

"You want to tell me what this is about?" I asked, trying to keep my voice steady.

He put his index finger to his lips. "Shhhh."

Another sharp turn, and my head hit the metal door. The guy kept on grinning, enjoying the ride. He closed up the knife and slipped it inside his jacket. Now that my eyes were adjusting to the lack of light, I could see he was wearing a dark blue business suit. I tried studying his face, looking for any distinguishing marks. Nothing.

"Watch your head, Mr. Donne."

Okay, I thought. He knew my name, so any discussion about his having mistaken me for someone else was worthless.

"The Clemente Houses," he said. "The old precinct. Highland. Field trips are very educational. I am sure you will find this one very much so."

I took a breath. I wanted to speak, but my pain and fear were making it hard to form the right words. I tried anyway. "Why don't you just—?"

Suit shook his head and again placed his index finger to his lips.

"No more talking," he said. "When we get to our destination, you will listen. If all goes well, you will have a nice walk home and enjoy the rest of your Sunday."

About a minute later—after a few more hard lefts—the van came to a stop. I heard the driver get out, and then he appeared as the side door slid open. Suit put on a pair of sunglasses and exited the van. He held out his hand for me to follow. I moved across the floor on my butt and, ignoring his hand, slid myself out.

Suit grabbed me by the elbow and squeezed. "If you draw any attention, you will go back inside the van and not get out again for days. Do you understand me?"

I tried to free my elbow, but couldn't. "Yeah," I said. "I understand."

"Good."

He released my arm and pushed me into the driver, who placed his hand on my shoulder. This guy was dressed in a sweatsuit the exact color as his partner's business suit. He was also about twice my size. His big head and long arms gave him an apelike appearance.

"You recognize this block?" Suit asked.

I looked around, and as my eyes readjusted to the bright sunlight, I felt my stomach clutch as I realized exactly where we were. Across the street from where the three of us were standing was the building where I had my accident and a kid had died. Except for a few overgrown weeds on the front steps and a faded, yellow NO TRESPASSING sign on the front door, it looked exactly as it had five years ago. Just like it looked in my nightmares. I thought the city would have knocked it down by now. Or at least sold it to some real estate developer. How the hell did these guys—?

"Of course you do, Mr. Donne. Good. Then we do not have to waste a lot of time discussing what we know about you and your history."

Anger was mixing with my fear. I got the nerve up to say, "What the fuck do you—?"

Ape squeezed my shoulder, almost bringing me to my knees.

"As you can see," Suit said, "not much has changed on this block. Even now, a beautiful Sunday afternoon, it is empty. Nobody on the front steps, no kids riding their bikes in the street. A shame. With the market the way it is, someone could do quite well here. But maybe some things are meant to stay unchanged. To remind us of our pasts, yes? As a teacher, you are familiar with what they say about those who refuse to learn from history?"

I thought it was a rhetorical question until Ape squeezed my shoulder again. I nodded and said, "Yeah."

Suit smiled. "So," he said. "The lesson here is we need to be very careful what doors we go through. We never quite know what will be on the other side. And we need to ask ourselves, 'Is it worth the risk? This search for knowledge?' " He turned to me and said, "Would you care to go inside, Mr. Donne? I understand that a part of the fire escape still clings from the back wall."

"No," I said. "You've made your point."

"I do not think we have," Suit said. "Yet."

"You want me to stay away from Frankie's," I said. "And the police."

Suit grinned and looked at his partner. Ape did not grin. Suit said, "That is a bit of a . . . cliché, isn't it? No, we are not here to tell you to stay away from anything. In fact, we wish for you to continue with what you are doing."

"Excuse me?"

"You are very good at this," he said. "And you can talk to certain people who would, for obvious reasons, not wish to talk to us."

"Like the police?"

"When you talk to these people, we want to know about it. Immediately."

"And why would I want to do that?" I asked, right before Ape tightened his grip. This time I did go down. Hard. My fear, nausea, and anger now had pain to keep them company.

"Because if you don't," Suit said, looking down at me, "that is when the harm will come to you." He leaned over. "Much more harm than this." He reached into his jacket pocket, and I was sure I was going to see his knife again. Instead, he pulled out an envelope and tossed it to the ground in front of me. "Now," he said, "excuse one cliché . . . we will be in touch."

Ape let go of me, and I had to hold out my hands to avoid hitting the ground with my face. I watched as the two of them got back into the van—a white van, it occurred to me—and drove off. No back license plate for me to commit to memory. Just like that, they were gone. I picked up the envelope and got to my feet. I looked around. Suit was right. The street was empty.

I opened the envelope. Another wave of fear and nausea coursed through my body as I realized what I was looking at. A photograph of my sister Rachel's front door.

Chapter 14

YOU DON'T JUST HAIL A CAB in the middle of Williamsburg, Brooklyn. That's a Manhattan thing. In Williamsburg, if you need a car quick, you call a service and hope for the best. I remembered there was one around the block and got there as fast as I could. I checked my pockets for cash and only had a twenty, so I hit the ATM a few doors down from the car service and got another hundred. I got lucky; a driver was just pulling in. I got in his backseat before he could get out of his car.

"I am off duty, sir," he said. "Perhaps if you went inside."

I showed him two twenties. "I need to get to Queens real quick. It'll take less than a half hour." As he pondered the bills in front of his face, I took out another. "Twenty more if I can use your cell phone." I had left mine home since I had only planned to go to the gym.

"Twenty dollars," he said, "just to make a phone call?"

"Sixty all together. The ride and the call."

He took the sixty bucks, put the car in gear, and handed me his phone. I dialed Rachel's number and got her voice mail.

"Rachel," I said, trying to mix a little calm in with the sense of urgency, "if you get this before I get to your place, go upstairs to the . . ." —what the hell was their—"the Burkes's. I know. Just do it. I'll explain when I get there." I couldn't think of anything else to say, so I closed up the phone and was about to give it back to the driver. Instead, I dialed nine-one-one and told the operator that I'd heard gunfire. I gave my sister's address and hung up before she could ask any questions.

"You said one call," the driver said.

"Just drive," I said, handing the phone over the seat.

We flew past what little traffic there was on the BQE and the Long Island Expressway. There was a bit of a snarl on Queens Boulevard, but the driver took the service road and cut down a few side streets, getting me in front of my sister's apartment building—right behind the patrol car responding to my anonymous nine-one-one call—in just over twenty minutes. The guy had earned his sixty bucks.

I looked around. No white van. I went straight to the front door as the police officer was radioing back to his command. They might be able to track the call to the driver, but I didn't really care. I buzzed Rachel, and she let me in.

"What the hell was that all about?" she asked as I entered her apartment. I smelled coffee brewing. Rachel looked me over and considered my appearance.

"Where were you?" I asked.

"Food shopping. I just got in. What the hell—?"

I reached out and hugged her. After a while, she said, "Ray? What is it? Is it Mom?"

"No," I said, letting her go and taking a step back. "No. Mom's fine. I guess."

"Then what is it?"

I looked at my little sister. If something ever happened to her . . . because of something I got involved in . . .

"Can I get a cup of coffee first?"

"Yeah. Sit down. Give me a minute."

When she went into the kitchen, I stepped over to her window that looked out onto the street. The patrol car had gone, and there was still no sign of the white van. Ape and Suit had wanted to scare me with that photo. They had succeeded. Would they show up? Or was that picture just to let me know that they knew about me? Like the trip to the scene of my accident. Who were those guys?

"Ray?"

I turned around to see my sister holding a mug of coffee in each hand. I went over to her and she handed me mine. "Now, talk," she said.

I took a sip and let it work on me. "Remember Frankie?"

"The missing kid?" she asked.

"Yeah."

"The one whose father you found murdered?"

"Yeah, that's the one."

"What's going on, Ray?"

I brought her up to date: Frankie's grandmother's apartment, the trip up to Highland, Uncle Ray, and the two guys who'd just taken me for a ride. When I was done, Rachel waited a full minute before talking.

"You borrowed my car so you could play private eye?" she asked.

"That's not what I did, Rachel."

"It's exactly what you did, Ray. I can't believe you." She walked over to the window. I was about to ask her not to do that, but she turned back. "No, that's not true. I do believe it. It's exactly the kind of thing I'd expect from Dad."

"What the hell does that mean?" I asked.

"Did you even think about the repercussions? How playing Sam Spade might come back and bite you in the ass? Or worse?"

"Rachel," I said, "if I had any idea that something like this could have happened, I'd never have gotten involved."

"That's just it, Ray. You didn't think past what you wanted to do. How getting your cop rocks off might affect others."

"Come on, Rache."

"No," she said. "This is the kinda shit Mom says Dad used to pull, only with him it was the long hours, the road trips, no sleep. Why do you think he had the heart attack?"

Shit. "This is nothing like Dad," I said. "I was trying to help a kid. You told me the other night how great it was I was reaching out to someone."

"Reaching out, yes. Not sticking your nose into official police business."

"Now *you* sound like Uncle Ray," I said.

"Better than sounding like Dad."

"I do not sound like Dad, Rachel."

"Yeah, well . . . here we are, Ray." Her eyes filled up. "Here we fucking are."

I took a step toward her. She held out her hand. "Don't."

"I need to make sure you're safe, Rachel."

"I'm a big girl, Ray. I can protect myself."

"Not from these guys," I said. "Trust me."

I could tell she wanted to argue the point, but the look on my face must have stopped her. In a low voice, she asked, "So what do you want me to do?"

"I want you to take that trip to L.A. your boss wanted you on."

"Just like that?"

"Call him," I said. "He'd be thrilled, right?"

"Probably," she said as she thought it over. I've never known Rachel to respond well to having decisions made for her, and she was not one to scare easily. I was prepared to give her as much time as she needed. Up to a point. "I'll make you a deal," she said.

"What kind of deal?"

"I'll call Les. Tell him I changed my mind about going. He's gonna give me shit about the ticket price, but too bad. I'll go to L.A. You call Uncle Ray."

"I don't think that's a good—"

"You said these guys scared you, Ray. I can see that. That's the only reason I'm willing to go on this trip. You have to protect yourself now, too." She walked across the room and came back with her phone. "Call Uncle Ray. Now. You can both take me to the airport."

I took the phone and said, "You're a lot tougher than you used to be."

"Which is why my boss wants me on this trip. I'll be packed in fifteen minutes."

Rachel left the room, and I called Uncle Ray's house. I got Reeny again, and she gave me my uncle's cell phone. He was between holes when he picked up.

"This better be good," he said.

"It's me."

"Nephew! Twice in one week. This must be my—"

"I'm in some trouble, Uncle Ray," I said, and then told him why.

"I'm on my way," he said. "Less than half an hour. Stay away from the windows, and don't answer the door. You see anything makes you think twice, call nine-one-one."

"Thanks, Uncle Ray."

"Thank me when I get there," he said, and hung up.

I went into the kitchen and helped myself to another cup of coffee. I looked out the window that faced the courtyard. The trees were all green now and stroller marks crisscrossed the grass. Each corner of the lawn had a picnic table with benches. Rachel and I would have dinner down there once in a while. Sandwiches and a beer from the gourmet deli up the block. The six-story buildings did a good job keeping the sounds of Kew Gardens from getting in. We always seemed to wind up on the grass, telling stories about growing up and how weird it was that we both ended up in the boroughs our parents couldn't wait to move out of. We had outgrown the tree-lined streets and manicured lawns of Long Island and wanted more. Things only the city could offer. To not be like our parents. To make different choices. Different mistakes.

"How'd your date go the other night?" Rachel yelled from her bedroom.

"Not so great," I yelled back. "Kinda got into a fight."

"With your date?"

"No," I said. "With a guy I used to—never mind. I screwed up is what happened."

"You call her and apologize?"

"Not yet."

"Do it, Ray," Rachel said. "Soon. Before you look like an asshole."

Might be too late for that. The cordless rang. I forgot it was still in my hand.

"Hello," I said.

"I'm five seconds from the front door." Uncle Ray. "Buzz me up."

One thing about my Uncle Ray: the man can fill a doorway.

"You and I," he said, tapping my chest twice with his huge index finger as he stepped into Rachel's apartment, "are going to have a long talk after your sister's on her way to La La Land." He then gestured over his shoulder. "You remember Jackson."

Officer Jackson walked in and removed his blue baseball cap. He was dressed like my uncle, in khaki pants and a yellow golf shirt. Like a couple of undercovers and their colors of the day. We shook hands.

"Thanks," I said.

"No problem."

"Raymond," my uncle said. "We will take your sister to the airport. Jackson will take up a position down the block in my car and keep an eye out for anything out of the ordinary."

"Like a black guy sitting in a parked car in Rego Park?" I turned to Jackson. "Sorry."

"No problem," he repeated, not concealing his amused grin.

Uncle Ray pondered that. "Right. Jackson, take a position up here by the window until we get back." He walked over and pulled up the shade but let the curtain fall into place over the window. "Anything you think I should know about, call me."

"Understood."

Rachel came into the living room holding a large suitcase. She put it down and gave our uncle a hug. When the embrace ended, she turned to Jackson and said, "Hey."

Jackson smiled. "Ma'am."

"Ray tell you the story, Uncle Ray?" Rachel asked.

"And he will again," my uncle replied. "After we get you in the air. Your car?"

"Around back."

"Give the keys to your brother. He's driving."

Rachel went into the kitchen and returned with her car keys. She flipped them to me.

"Bring it around front," Uncle Ray said. "Three minutes."

I did as instructed. Three minutes later, I pulled away from the curb on the way to LaGuardia with my sister and uncle in the backseat.

Uncle Ray badged our way into a parking spot in the red zone. We got Rachel ticketed, her bag checked, and we were able to wait with her by the Passenger's Only gate. Uncle Ray again flashed his shield so we could escort my embarrassed sister onto the plane. Her fellow passengers checked her out, as they probably would during the next five hours.

When we got back to the car, Uncle Ray took the keys. "I'll drive." I was about to object when he added, "Keeping my hands on the wheel will quiet the urge I have to smack you."

We drove back toward Rachel's in silence.

Chapter 15

"YOUR LITTLE GAMES HAVE GOTTEN you in over your head, Nephew."

We were sitting in a booth at the pizza place under the BQE, not far from my place. Uncle Ray was drinking an espresso. I had an iced tea. Jackson sat in the car, across the street, with a Diet Coke.

"I wasn't playing games, Uncle Ray."

"Yeah," he said. "You were. And you got caught not watching your back. It's over now. Your . . . involvement in all this. Let the real police do their job."

"The real police," I said, "were sitting on their asses while I took a ride upstate and found something pretty damned important."

About a year after my dad died, Uncle Ray caught me in the back shed smoking a cigarette. He smacked me so hard I felt it for days. He had the same look on his face now.

"Great," he said through his teeth. "I'm real proud of you." He pointed at me with his cigar. "Now look at the fucking results. Two of the people I love most in this world are in danger. How's that make you feel about finding a *clue*, Raymond? Was it worth it?"

"If it helps get Frankie home . . . yeah."

"Goddamn, boy. Is this kid so fucking special he's worth all of this?" He shook his head, and before I could answer he added, "I'm thinking of sticking *your* ass on a plane. Get you out of town until this kid's found." He paused to make sure I was listening. "One way or the other."

"He was alive a few days ago," I reminded him. "He's a smart kid. He got himself and his sister upstate. Maybe back."

"Well, if he's all that smart, Raymond, you need to consider the very real possibility he does not want to be found. By you or the police. Why would that be?"

"He's scared," I said. "He doesn't know who to trust. Something made him not tell his cousin he was up at her place. Maybe he saw something that spooked him. Or someone."

Uncle Ray shook his head. "You got a whole lotta answers, don't you?"

I got a whole lotta nothing, he meant. He was right.

"You wanna disappear for a while?" Uncle Ray asked.

I shook my head. "I got school. I can't just *disappear* for a while."

"School fall apart without you?"

"Yeah, Uncle Ray. That's what I meant."

"You'd be smart to lose the sarcasm, Raymond." There was that look again.

"I'm going to live my life," I said. "If these guys wanted to hurt me—I mean really hurt me—they had the chance. I'll just mind my business until this all gets settled."

"You'd better." He finished his espresso. "In the meantime, I'm gonna have some patrol cars pass by your apartment for the next few days. The school, too." Before I could object, he said, "Don't worry. They'll be discreet. We—I—am also gonna have another talk with Royce. I'll set that up for tomorrow. See if anything rings a bell with him regarding the two guys you ran into today."

"He's not going to be happy."

"That's not my problem, Raymond. In fact, he's probably already unhappy that I made an inquiry to the ME's office into the COD."

Cause of death. This got my attention. "What'd they say?"

"Blunt force trauma," he said. "No big surprise there. But they're not quite sure which blow did the deed. The heavy object or the shot to the nose. Doc I spoke to seems to be leaning toward a combination of the two."

"What's that mean?"

"Means that either injury by itself would—ordinarily—not've been enough to kill the guy. Put the two together, though, and you got yourself one unlucky son of a bitch."

Ordinarily. "So . . . what?" I asked. "Rivas got hit in the head by a . . . something heavy and then got punched in the nose?"

"Or vice versa, Raymond. Can't even be sure how much time passed between the injuries, or if they were inflicted by the same person."

"Great," I said.

"It is what it is, Nephew." He stood up. "Let's get you home." He handed me the keys to Rachel's car.

When we got outside, Uncle Ray explained the plan to Jackson. "Yes, sir."

"I'm going to hang back," Uncle Ray said. "Make some calls and get a ride back to the Island. Maybe get a slice or three. Jackson'll follow you home."

Again, Jackson said, "Yes, sir."

I thanked Jackson, and before I could cross the street to Rachel's car, my uncle took me by the elbow. "Be careful, Raymond."

"I will be," I said.

He pulled me into a hug, and then held me at arm's length. I'm not sure what he saw when he looked at me, but I saw my father's brother. The man who'd hurt you if he thought it would keep you from hurting yourself. The man I had wanted to be so many years ago.

It took three minutes to drive to my apartment and another fifteen to find a parking spot. It was two blocks away, and I'd have to get up early to move it, but this day was almost over. Jackson was parked across the street from my place and would be until he was relieved at ten. I was unlocking the second door to my apartment building, when it occurred to me that I hadn't heard the first click shut behind me. I turned and saw why.

A small girl—seven or eight years old—was standing there, holding the door open with her foot. A dark blue book bag hung from her shoulder.

"Are you Mr. Donne?" she asked, barely above a whisper.

"Yes," I said.

"I am Milagros," she said. "Frankie's sister?"

Shit.

Chapter 16

"AND SHE JUST SHOWED UP AT your place?"

"Yeah," I said.

"No sign of the boy?"

"No."

"She give you any idea where the boy—"

"His name's Frankie," I said.

"She give you any idea where Frankie was? Or is? Or might be?"

"No. She said Frankie told her not to tell anybody anything."

"Well, damn, Mr. Donne, then maybe you won't mind telling me why you got that shit-eating grin on your face."

"I guess I'm relieved Frankie's still okay, Detective. Relatively speaking."

"Relatively speaking." Detective Royce turned to Jackson and said, "You see anything, Patrolman?"

"Just the little girl, sir," Jackson said. "I was keeping my eyes out for the two suspects described by Mr. Donne earlier today to Chief Donne and myself. When Mr. Donne identified the young female as the missing girl, we came here immediately."

"Here" was the precinct's detective squad, quieter now than the last time I'd visited, but still busier than you'd think for an early Sunday evening. Two other detectives were working at the moment: one on the phone, the other filling out a report, clicking away on an outdated computer keyboard. Royce leaned back in his chair and stared at Jackson for a few more seconds, wanting to chew him out just a little, but knowing that Jackson had done everything by the book and was smart enough to drop my uncle's name into his verbal statement. Royce turned his tired eyes to me and took a deep breath. The three of us looked over at Milagros, who was sitting at a desk and talking with a female officer in between bites of Chinese food.

"God damn," Royce said and squeezed the bridge of his nose. He hadn't made it home today either. And I was to blame. "Girl's gonna have to get checked out over at the hospital. Make sure she gets a clean bill of health before . . ."

"Foster home?" I asked.

"Until we figure out something better."

"How about the grandmother's?"

"It's not my call. I'm still waiting for someone from Children's Services to get back to me. Tough to get a social worker this time on a Sunday."

I gave that some thought and figured the last thing we needed was some overworked, underpaid city employee who wouldn't be too happy to trek out to Williamsburg on a Sunday night. "You need a licensed social worker to sign off on that, right?" I asked Royce.

"That's why I called ACS, Mr. Donne."

"What if I can get someone here quicker?"

"Licensed?"

"Woman I work with at the school."

"You think she can pull off a temporary kinship foster with the grandmother?"

"That's what I'm thinking."

Royce thought about that for a while. "It's worth a shot."

"Can I borrow your phone?"

Royce handed it to me. "Dial nine first."

I got Elaine's home number from information. She said she'd be there in a half hour. I called information again and asked for Elsa's number. I got a recording telling me it was unlisted. Royce was able to get it by identifying himself and giving his badge number to a supervisor. I called Elsa and, after an awkward greeting, told her what was going on. She said they'd be at the precinct as soon as they could get a ride. I gave the phone back to Royce.

"Want me to arrange for you to get a ride home now, Mr. Donne?"

"Actually," I said, "if it's okay with you, I'd rather stay."

"Yeah," Royce said. "I had a feeling." He turned to Jackson and pointed to the big coffee machine across the room. "You know how to work one of those?"

Jackson stood. "I'll figure it out. Sir."

"There's a good rookie." Royce turned back to me. "Since you're gonna be here for a while longer, you wanna give it another go with the girl? Maybe she'll be more cooperative now that she's had something to eat. I'd try again myself, but I don't think she's warmed to me yet."

"Yeah," I said and walked over to the desk where Milagros was sitting. The female officer gave me a forced smile, and I gestured for her to leave Milagros and me alone. Milagros looked like she was feeling better now and began spinning the chair around, making humming noises. I put my hand on the back of the chair to bring it to a stop and crouched down to be at her eye level. "Hey," I said. "You like that food?"

"It was a little spicy," she said. "But it was good. Thank you."

"You feel like talking now?"

" 'Bout what?"

"About Frankie."

"He told me not to tell anybody anything," she said. "I promised."

"I know you did," I said. "But sometimes it's not really breaking a promise if you are trying to help somebody."

"Are you trying to help Frankie?"

"Yes. I am."

"Then he said you would understand."

"But that's just it, Milagros," I said. "I don't understand."

"Yeah," she said, nodding her head.

"Okay, let me try to help you understand. If you can tell me where you were before you got to my apartment, that would be a big help."

"I was with Frankie."

"I know that, Milagros, but *where* with Frankie?"

"He told me not to tell anybody anything." She sounded like a recording. "I promised."

"Okay," I said, barely hiding my growing frustration. "Just tell me *how* you got to my apartment. Did you take the subway? A taxi? What?"

"We took a taxi to Anita's house," she said with a smile. The smile went away and she added, "But we didn't go in and say hi."

"Yes," I said. "I know that. Why didn't you go in and say hi?"

"I don't know. We got to the front of Anita's house—by the bushes—and then Frankie said 'Let's play hide-and-seek,' so we went behind the bushes and stayed there for like a thousand minutes but nobody found us, so I guess we won."

I guess you did.

"And Frankie never told you who you were hiding from?"

"Nope. I thought it was from Anita and John and Gracie, but then we never saw them, and then they never got a chance to hide. And then we left."

"And how did you get to my apartment?" I asked quickly.

"We took a—" She stopped herself. "Frankie told me not to tell any—"

"I know!" I slapped the side of the desk before I could stop myself. "Don't tell anybody anything. You promised." I realized that everybody in the room was now looking at me. Milagros started to cry. "I'm sorry, honey," I said, remembering that she must have been more tired and frustrated than I was. "I just need to—"

The little girl's tears increased. I got up and grabbed a few tissues off the desk and handed them to her. She began to shake. When I crouched back down and put my hand on her shoulder, she shrugged it off. The female officer came up from behind me, put her hand on my shoulder, and said, "Mr. Donne."

I stood up. "Yeah," I said. "Thanks."

I walked back over to Detective Royce, who was pretending to go through some papers on his desk. Without looking up, he said, "That went well."

"Yeah," I said. "I'm thinking of working with children someday."

Elaine Stiles arrived wearing a Brooklyn College sweatshirt, blue jeans, and sneakers. I guessed we hadn't interrupted anything too important. I introduced her around. She looked over at Milagros, who had a can of Diet Pepsi tilted over her open mouth.

"You called the hospital?" Elaine asked.

Royce answered. "Yes."

"Good. If you'd let me on your computer, I can download the paperwork we'll need to allow her grandmother to take her home." Royce got up and motioned for Elaine to sit. She pressed a few keys, got online, and pressed a few more keys. "In absence of the legal guardian, the time and day, I don't think it'll come back to bite us. She tell you where Frankie was?"

"No," I answered. "He told her not to."

Elaine gave me a look, let out a sigh, and went back to pressing keys and moving the mouse around. "Where's your printer, Detective?"

Royce pointed across the room.

"Would you mind?" Elaine asked.

Jackson walked away, returned with the printouts, and handed them to Elaine.

"This'll take some time," she said, handing me the paperwork. "Let me talk to Milagros, explain to her what's going to happen. Tell me when you're done with page two."

I started in on the paperwork as Elaine crouched down and spoke to Milagros. The little girl seemed much calmer now. She listened with a serious look on her face and kept nodding her head. When Elaine was done, I could read Milagros's lips. "Okay."

I filled in all the information I could regarding Milagros and Frankie: addresses, schools, and names of family members. I had no phone numbers with me. When I got to page three, the rest had to be filled out by a licensed social worker. I held up the pages to signal I was done. Elaine excused herself from Milagros and came back over.

"That," she said, "is one well-adjusted, tough cookie."

"She tell you anything about Frankie?" I asked.

"About as much as she told all of you. It'll take some time before she trusts anyone besides her brother."

I wondered how much time we had.

"Can you finish that up on the way to the hospital?" Royce asked, pointing at the pages in Elaine's hand.

"Shouldn't we wait for the grandmother?"

"Might save some time if we got the girl over—"

Royce cut himself short as something over my shoulder caught his attention. I turned and saw Elsa holding the swinging gate open for Mrs. Santos, who eased through, her walker in front of her. Right behind them was the guy from the church I'd met the other day. Elijah Cruz.

"The grandmother," I said to Elaine and Royce.

We all watched her make her way over to Milagros and bend down to exchange hugs with the little girl. They both started crying. When the embrace ended, Mrs. Santos held Milagros by the shoulders and said, *"¿Dónde está Francisco, chica?"*

I couldn't hear the girl's response, but it was followed by more tears and a shake of the head. Mrs. Santos was not pleased and stood up slowly. *"Ay dios mio,"* she said and turned to Elsa and Cruz. Milagros said something to the three adults, and Elsa shot me a look. Yeah, I raised my voice to a little kid. I know. The four of them spoke for another half minute. When they were done, Cruz came over to us.

"Mr. Donne," he said, shaking my hand. "Again you have proven yourself to be a true friend to this family."

"Milagros showed up at my door, Mr. Cruz."

"Ah," he said. "Because Francisco trusted you with his little sister. Don't underestimate your contribution to the girl's safe return." Cruz turned to Detective Royce and said, "I am Elijah Cruz, Detective. I . . . represent the family. Can we take the girl to Mrs. Santos's home?"

"Not right away, Mr. Cruz," Royce explained. "Procedure is we have to get her checked out by a doctor first and then file some paperwork. But yeah, by the end of the evening . . . I don't see why not."

"Good," Cruz said. "Good." He turned to Jackson and offered his hand. "Elijah Cruz."

"Police Officer Jackson, sir." Jackson caught Cruz checking out the golf clothes he was wearing and added, "I was called to Mr. Donne's when the girl showed up. Sir."

Cruz smiled at the explanation and turned back to me. "Can we talk, Mr. Donne?"

"Sure," I said and waited.

Cruz said, "Privately." And then to Royce and Jackson, "No offense, gentlemen."

They both shrugged, and Cruz and I walked over to the swinging gate. I waited for him to say whatever it was that needed to be said in private.

"The girl," he began, "has said nothing about Francisco?"

"No."

"Mrs. Santos is rightfully upset about this, Mr. Donne."

"I know how she feels."

"Yes." He turned toward the window, away from where his face could be seen by Royce or Jackson. "Is there nothing she said to you about her brother?" he asked. "That you haven't shared with the police?"

"Why would I withhold information from the police, Mr. Cruz? I was the one who wanted them brought in the other day."

"And, I assume, the one responsible for the three patrol cars that showed up at Clemente shortly after you left?"

I ignored the question. "Milagros told me what she's told everyone tonight. Nothing." I gestured over to where Elaine was talking with Elsa and Mrs. Santos. "Ms. Stiles, the school counselor, feels that Milagros doesn't trust anyone but her brother. It'll be a while before she says anything."

Cruz nodded. "She has good reason to feel that way. She and her brother have been through much these past few days." He fingered the patch of hair under his lower lip as he looked over at Frankie's grandmother. "Is there any more that I can be doing?"

Now, you want my input?

"Yeah," I said. "Milagros has to get examined by a doctor before she can be placed. They"—I gestured toward Royce and Jackson—"called the hospital."

"Which?" When I told him, he shook his head. "No." He walked over to Royce and asked, "Ms. Stiles is a licensed social worker?"

"That's why she's here."

"The family may choose a doctor to examine the girl, correct?"

Elaine overheard that and came over. "Yes."

"Then we will go to the family's doctor."

Elaine looked at her watch. "He has office hours on Sunday evening?"

Cruz smiled. "He will be in his office." He took his cell phone off his belt and dialed a number. "You will accompany us, Ms. Stiles?"

Elaine looked at Royce and me. We shrugged.

"Yes," she answered. "I'll be right behind you."

"Good." Cruz walked away and spoke into his phone.

"He's from the grandmother's church," I explained to Elaine. "He works in the medical field. Sort of."

"Can he get a doctor at this hour?" Elaine asked.

"I guess we'll find out."

Cruz returned in less than a minute. "It is settled. Dr. Matos will expect us in twenty minutes. Is there anything else, Detective Royce?"

"We'll need to interview the girl tomorrow," he said. "Maybe she'll decide to answer some of our questions. The grandmother might be some help in that area."

"Yes," Cruz said and offered his hand to Royce, Jackson, and me. "Tomorrow then." He gave Royce a card. "Senora Santos has no phone at the moment, so this would be the best way to reach her."

The way this guy made building superintendents and doctors appear, I figured he could have done something about getting an old woman a phone.

"Good night, gentlemen. And Mr. Donne, again, our sincerest gratitude."

"Glad I could help," I said.

Cruz returned to Frankie's grandmother, Milagros, and Elsa. Elsa looked over and gave me something that was not quite a smile.

Elaine got my attention and said, "I'll see you tomorrow, Ray."

"Oh, yeah," I said and gave her a quick hug. "Thanks, Elaine. I owe you one."

"Let's just hope we get Frankie home now," she said.

"Yeah," I said. "Let's hope."

She went over to the other group and put her hand on Milagros's shoulder. Milagros smiled and looked back at me. She took a deep breath, ran over, and stopped in front of me. I crouched down again. My knees were buzzing.

"Milagros," I said. "I'm really sorry for raising my voice like that."

"It's okay, Mr. Donne," she said. "My daddy used to yell sometimes."

Great. Now I'm like her dad.

"No, Milagros. It's not okay. I shouldn't have done it. I'm sorry."

"Me, too. But Frankie said you would understand."

"I know he did, honey."

"He also said he's gonna call you."

I crept closer. "What did you say?"

Elijah Cruz came over before she could answer.

"Let us go, Milagros," he said, taking her by the hand. "We need to get you home."

"Good night, Mr. Donne," Milagros said.

"Can you give me one more minute, Mr. Cruz?"

"We do need to get her home, Mr. Donne. I'm sure you understand."

Why did everyone assume I'd fucking understand when I didn't understand a goddamned thing? I stood up, trying to hide my pain and frustration.

"What do you mean, he said he'd call me?"

She made as if she hadn't heard me. They all left the detective squad together, leaving Royce, Jackson, and me standing by Royce's desk. "You feel okay going home by yourself?" Royce asked.

"Yeah." I looked over at Jackson. "I think I'm covered."

Royce picked up his briefcase and jacket. "Then I guess we'll call it a day," he said. "One long fucking day."

He wasn't going to get an argument from me. One kid home safe, the other still out there. Milagros's words stuck in my head: Frankie said he'd call you. *When?* I thought. *From where?*

This was turning into a game I didn't know how to play.

Chapter 17

I MADE IT ALMOST TO THE TOP of the subway stairs before I had to stop. My fellow travelers brushed past me, annoyed, as they went on their way to their very important jobs, pissed off they had to navigate around the guy who was out of breath and practically doubled over his umbrella. Knees throbbing with pain, hungry from skipping breakfast, and working on less than two hours of sleep. What the hell was I doing going to work today? I closed my eyes, waited for the pain to subside, and tried to avoid the obvious answer.

Like it or not, it was Monday morning. And on Monday mornings, teachers go to school. I was a teacher.

Not a cop, as my Uncle Ray was quick to remind me. That's why he had one stationed outside my apartment when I left this morning. Jackson's replacement had offered me a ride, but I chose my regular routine and told him I'd see him later, outside the school. I should have taken him up on the offer, but I wanted to prove I could take care of myself. It was time to cut the shit, get back to my life. I had a pile of paperwork waiting for me on my desk that wasn't going to get done by anybody but me, and a group of eighth graders who were not going to get exposed to the poetry of Walt Whitman or the complexities of basic algebra by the Education Fairy.

A few students were hanging around the front of the school, too cool to be early, most of them waiting until just before the side doors closed; a couple were playing tag, slapping each other's book bags. A rather large guy was leaning up against the rusty metal fence. He was dressed in an army jacket and matching pants. He had one foot up against the fence and a cigarette burning in his left hand. Too old to be a student, too young to be a parent. Probably an older brother or cousin dropping someone off and grabbing a quick smoke before heading off to work. As I neared the opening, he straightened himself up and blocked my path. I stopped with about three feet between us.

He put the cigarette in his mouth and looked me over, starting with my shoes and slowly making his way to my face. A smirk crossed his lips. "You Mister Donne?"

I said, "Yes," and took the time to check out his face. He had to be at least twenty. A mess of brown whiskers I'm sure he'd call a mustache lay between his nose and upper lip. His eyes were bloodshot, and he had the kind of complexion my mother would have described as olive, with pimentos. I didn't know him. "May I help you?"

He took the cigarette out of his mouth and let out a lungful of smoke. "Yeah." Like something out of a bad western. "You can stop hasslin' my girlfriend."

"I teach *here*, man." I gestured with my head at the building. "Middle school. I don't know your girlfriend. Try the high school around the block."

I took a few steps to go around him. He matched those with his own. We were now too close for comfort. I could smell the smoke on his breath, the sweat coming off the rest of him.

He looked down at my umbrella. "She said you'd be the cripple."

I took a step back. "What's your name?" I asked.

He took a last drag of his cigarette and flicked it into the street. He rolled up his left sleeve, revealing the name "Zeke," which had been tattooed into the hairless part of his arm. It was homemade, probably made with the ink from a ballpoint pen. The kind of thing you might do when killing time in a juvenile detention center.

I nodded. "Like I said, Zeke. I don't know your girlfriend." I started to make my way around him again. "I really have to—"

He stepped in front of me and grabbed my arm.

"Lisa said you been hasslin' her. Gettin' her pops all upset and shit."

"Lisa?" I said. "Lisa King?"

"Yeah."

"She's your . . . girlfriend?"

"Uh-huh."

"Lisa's fourteen."

"So?"

"So you're, what? Twenty?"

"What can I say?" He grinned, spreading out his arms. "I like 'em young."

"Her dad know you like 'em young?"

"Ain't none of his business," Zeke said. He took his right index finger and poked me in the chest. "Yours neither."

Yeah, I thought, taking a calming breath and waiting for the small circle of pain to spread out and go away, today would've been a real good day to stay in bed. It was about thirty seconds before I thought of something to say.

"Tell ya what, Zeke. Why don't we go inside and talk about this?" I made a show of looking around at the kids and teachers heading into the building. "Too many people out here minding our business."

"Nah," he said. "I ain't going inside. You think I'm stupid or somethin'?" Before I could answer, he added, "'Sides, I got things to do and people to see."

Busy guy, Zeke. "Okay," I said. "You want me to mind my own business? You got it. I gotta get to work now."

I moved around him yet again, and again he grabbed me. This time, one of my fellow teachers noticed. Josephine from the second floor.

"Everything okay, Mr. Donne?" she asked.

"Yeah, Jo. Fine. Do me a favor, though, will ya? And ask School Safety Officer Jenkins to come outside? Tell her I need to touch base with her."

She hurried up the steps into the school.

To Zeke, I said, "You might want to leave now. Officer Jenkins has the power to arrest, and, what with you trespassing and all . . . You got people to see, don'tcha?"

"What the fuck, trespassing?" He took his hands off me and held them up in the air. "I'm just standing outside a public building. 'School Safety Officer Jenkins,'" he mimicked. "Fucking wannabe cop."

"Threatening a public schoolteacher. Guy like you"—I let him notice as I took a long look again at his tattoo—"on probation. Not going to look too good to your P.O."

"Fuck you know about my P.O.?" He grabbed my shirt again. I had my umbrella in one hand and my backpack weighing me down. This would have been a good time for one of my uncle's patrol cars to swing by.

"Z!" A voice came from behind us. "*Z!*"

We both turned to see Lisa King entering through the gate.

"Whatchoo think you're doing, Z?" She stopped a few feet away. "That's my *teacher!*"

"You said he was bothering you," he said through gritted teeth. "I'm taking care of it."

"You not taking care of nothing, Z. Get your hands off him."

His grip on my shirt tightened, and he gave it a twist. I looked over my shoulder at the street. Still no blue-and-white.

"Don't talk to me like that, Lee. I told you about talking to me like I'm slow."

"Then why you acting slow, Z?" As Lisa squinted at her boyfriend, he let go of my shirt. I took the opportunity to lean my umbrella against the wall, freeing up both hands. "What? You think I'm gonna be impressed? You coming down here, messing with my teacher?"

"Wasn't gonna beat him up," Zeke said. "Gonna scare—ask—him to leave you alone is all. You said he was—"

"I know what I said, and I'm handling it." She paused for a few seconds, and then added, "I'm not a little girl."

And at that moment, for the first time in the nearly two years I'd known her, Lisa King, all fourteen years of her, actually looked like a teen-aged girl.

"Everything okay out here, Mr. Donne?"

Officer Jenkins was making her way down the steps of the building with purpose.

"I think so, Jenkins." I turned back to Zeke. "Now that Zeke here has his hands off of me, I think I'll be fine."

As Zeke considered that, he looked at Lisa and then at Officer Jenkins, who was now within pouncing distance. His breathing grew deeper. The longer he contemplated the situation, the more I picked up the staleness of his breath. If I listened real closely, I could probably hear his mind working this over.

He had put himself in an unwinnable situation. Hit me, and his girlfriend was going to give him a world of shit. And he'd face an altercation with a school safety officer. A female school safety officer. Let it go, and he'd be backing down. In front of his girlfriend. I didn't believe old Zeke here had the brainpower to ease himself out of this one. I tried to help him out.

"Just let it go, Zeke. Officer Jenkins and I'll go inside, and you and Lisa can talk about this. You showed her you're looking out for her. Leave it there."

His eyes glazed over as he looked me in the eyes. I'm not sure he heard me.

WHOOP! WHOOP!

The four of us turned toward the street where a blue-and-white squad car was making a U-turn in front of the building.

Zeke grabbed my shirt again and twisted hard. "Fucking mother fucker!"

"I didn't call them, Zeke," I said. "I'm out here with you."

Over Zeke's shoulder, I saw two cops getting out of the car. They were about ten seconds away. Too far.

Zeke pulled me toward him. The pressure was too much for my already overworked knees, and I fell. It took all I could to not scream out loud. With his hand still grabbing my shirt, he looked down and grinned. I slipped my left arm through the book-bag strap so that it was hanging only on the right shoulder. Zeke cocked back his free arm and made a fist. He looked up to make sure he was being watched.

"Hold it!" one of the cops yelled.

"Z!" screamed Lisa. "Don't!"

Zeke wasn't listening. As he turned his eyes to me again, I let the book bag slip down, and with all the strength I could summon, swung it up as hard as I could. It hit him square on the left side of his head, spinning him around, and knocking him down to my level. The momentum threw me the rest of the way to the ground, where again I found myself looking up at Zeke. This time he was stunned, ignoring the blood oozing from his nose, and as he brought his arm back again, he was grabbed and wrestled to the ground by Officer Jenkins. One of the cops came up behind her and took over, while the other cop placed a knee on Zeke's back and reached behind his own back to get a pair of handcuffs.

"Holy fucking shit, Hector," the other cop said. *Holy fucking shit* was right. Jack Knight. "Did I tell ya it might be my old buddy, Ray, or what?"

"Yeah, Jack," Hector said, doing the work of getting Zeke to his feet. "You told me."

"Damn, Ray," Jack said. "Three times in one week. What're the odds of that?" He shook his head and smirked. "The call came in, said it was the school, I thought, 'Hot damn! Wouldn't it be great if it were Raymond?' And here we pull up just in time to see you cold cock that son of a bitch. Man!" He lowered his voice so only I could hear him. "Kinda like that cheap shot you gave me the other night, huh?"

"Not quite, Jack," I said.

Jenkins came over and offered me her hand.

"You okay, Mr. Donne?"

"Yeah," I lied, getting to my feet. "Nothing a new pair of knees won't fix."

"You fucking asshole!" Lisa screamed. She was in Zeke's face now, tears streaming down her cheeks, spit flying from her mouth. "You goddamn stupid fucking asshole!"

"Get her inside," I said to Jenkins. "Call her folks."

Jenkins went over to Lisa, and put her arm around the scared kid. After struggling a bit and letting out a few more screams, Lisa allowed Jenkins to lead her up the stairs and into the building. Right past my boss.

"Officers!" he yelled. "Ron Thomas. Principal." He stopped a few feet in front of Jack and his partner. Thomas looked at me like I was becoming an inconvenience. "Officers, I'm sure your report will clearly mention that this incident occurred outside the school building and was therefore not school-related."

As Officer Hector took Zeke over to the squad car, Jack took his notebook out of his back pocket and flipped it open. He rested the tip of his pen on the blank sheet of paper, looked at my boss, and said, "And you are?"

"Ron Thomas," Ron Thomas said. "Principal."

"You called in the complaint?"

"Yes. I was hoping to avoid it happening on school grounds." He took a loud, deep sigh. "Looks like we were just in time."

"Yes," Jack said. "*We* were." Jack bent over and picked up my umbrella. I reached for it, and he pulled me closer. "Feels good to hit one of the street monkeys, don't it, Ray?"

I ignored the question and turned away from Jack. My boss saw the way I was moving and asked, "Do you need medical attention, Mr. Donne?"

"I don't think so." My knees disagreed, but I blocked out their screaming by gripping the handle of my umbrella as tightly as I could. "Thanks."

"That was quite a shot you gave old Zeke there, Teach," Jack said. "Working out some anger issues, are we?" When I didn't answer, he went on. "Just out of curiosity, what you got in the bag?" He reached into the bag and pulled out the Whitman book, all four hundred pages of him. Jack grinned. "Yeah. Pussy shit used to kick my ass, too."

"So," Ron Thomas said, clearly not comfortable in Jack's presence, "we are done here?"

Jack Knight made a smooth gesture out of flipping his notebook closed. "Yes, sir." All professional now. "You'll get a copy of our report. Make sure you fill out one of your own. You can fax a copy to the precinct."

"But—"

"It's a school-related incident, sir. This here is school property and"—he gave me a dismissive, fuck-you look—"school personnel were involved. Have a good one. Sirs." Jack crossed the street and joined his partner in the squad car. My boss and I watched as they did another U-turn and headed off.

"Jesus, Ray. I don't need another incident report heading off to the D.O. And what the hell was that? You know that guy?"

"We used to work together," I said. "A long time ago."

I looked at my watch and started hobbling toward the steps.

"Where do you think you're going?" he asked.

"I work here," I answered. "I'm going to my classroom."

"No, no. You're taking the day off. You're hurt."

"I'm fine, Ron."

"I'm not asking, Mr. Donne. I'm telling you. Go home. I'll cover you for the day." I was about to argue when he raised his hand. "The last thing I need is you getting injured *inside* school. Besides . . . you look like shit."

"Can I at least sit for a while?"

"*Outside* the building. On the steps." And with that, Ron Thomas, Principal, entered the building he was in charge of.

I took a seat on the bottom step and closed my eyes. Inside, the first bell of the day rang, signaling to all it was eight twenty, and homeroom had officially started. A minute later, a blue, battered pickup truck pulled to the curb. Lisa's father came out and ran right at me.

"Where's Lisa?" he said.

"Inside," I said. "With school safety."

He took the steps two at a time and vanished through the front door. With the side doors now closed, a few late students made their way past me up the steps, some in more of a hurry than others. A delivery truck pulled up, and a guy in a brown shirt and matching shorts filled a hand truck with boxes of copy paper and eased them up the steps, one loud crash at a time. Fifteen minutes went by before Mr. King exited the building, his arm around Lisa.

"Go on," he said. "Wait for me in the truck."

Lisa walked down the steps and headed toward her dad's truck. She got to the gate and turned. "You okay, Mr. Donne?"

"Yeah, Lise," I said. "I'm fine."

Even from twenty feet away, I could see the tears in her eyes as she said, "Sorry."

"Not your fault, kiddo. I'll see ya tomorrow."

She turned away, went over to the truck, and slipped into the passenger seat. Mr. King stood above me. "You really okay?"

"Yeah." I got to my feet to prove it to him. And myself. "Fine."

"That . . . boy they were talking about. Zeke?"

"Cops took him to the precinct. I got a feeling he won't be around Lisa anymore." Or anybody else for the next three to five years, I hoped.

"He really her boyfriend?"

"I think you need to talk to Lisa about that."

"He . . ." The father's eyes teared up. "He responsible for those bruises on my girl?"

"I don't know, Mr. King. Take your daughter home. You and your wife talk to her. I'll ask Ms. Stiles to give you guys a call later."

"You think he . . ."

I watched his mouth twitch as those words came out. He was squeezing his keys so hard, I wouldn't have been surprised to see them melt.

"Take Lisa home, Mr. King." He turned his head in the direction of the precinct, five blocks away. "And stay away from Zeke. The cops'll handle it. That's their job. Yours is to take care of your own."

"If he hurt Lisa . . ."

"Let her make out a complaint. Along with mine, it'll help put him away for a while. Lisa could be in college before he gets out."

That brought a small smile to his face that disappeared as quickly as it had showed up. He reached down and grabbed my hand.

"Thank you, Mr. Donne," he said. "For keeping an eye out for Lisa."

"You're welcome," I said. "And I'm sorry."

"For what?"

"For thinking that . . . Lisa's bruise . . ."

"Thank you." With nothing left to say, he let go of my hand, got into his truck, and headed home. It was about time I did the same thing.

Chapter 18

I GOT AS FAR AS THE BODEGA by the subway and decided I wanted a cup of coffee. I filled the cup halfway and dumped in a lot of sugar. I had the guy fill the rest with ice, and I took the cup outside. Shaking it all together, I leaned against the entrance to the subway and watched as all the busy people hurried past me, up and down the subway stairs, across the avenue, and around the crowded intersection. I was the only one not in motion, and I felt a small sense of peace. I'd been moving a lot the past couple of days. Maybe Ron had been right to send me home.

I took a long sip of my coffee and thought about what I'd do with my unexpected day off when a car horn sounded, and a dark blue sedan pulled over to the curb in front of where I was standing. The car had a logo on its passenger side door that took me a few seconds to place. A snake wrapped around a cross. The passenger window rolled down.

"Mr. Donne," Elijah Cruz said, leaning across the seat. "I believe you are late for school."

"I got sent home," I said. "Sick."

"You do not look sick to me."

"That's what I thought until my boss told me I was wrong. How did everything go with Milagros last night?"

"The doctor said she was fine. No injuries or bruises. She was obviously disturbed by the events of the past week, but he cleared her to be released to her grandmother."

"Good news," I said.

"Can I give you a ride? You are going home, I presume."

I stepped over and placed my hand on the roof. The cool air coming out of the car tempted me. "That's what I was debating. Seems a shame to waste a day like this."

"You enjoy the heat?"

"To a point," I said. "It just doesn't seem like an indoor day."

The passenger door lock popped up.

"Exactly as I was thinking," Elijah Cruz said. "Come. I want to show you something that I believe will be of interest to you." And, as if sensing my hesitation, he added, "One hour of your time, Mr. Donne. Then I will take you home or wherever it is you wish to go next."

"Wherever?" I asked.

Elijah Cruz smiled. "Within reason."

He didn't take me far. We were about halfway to my apartment when he pulled over and parked illegally in front of McCarren Pool. "Excuse me." He reached into his glove compartment and removed a blue card with an official-looking seal on it. "Come." He placed the card on the dashboard.

"You have some business at the pool, Mr. Cruz?"

"Come."

We exited the car, and I followed him over to the pool's main gates, which have been chained shut for over twenty years. Not today. He swung open one of the gates and held it for me as if welcoming me to a backyard barbecue.

"It is okay, Mr. Donne," he said. "I have the city's permission."

"I haven't been inside here for years," I said, stepping past Cruz.

"You used to come here to swim?" he asked, surprised.

"When I was a cop," I explained, "we used to get called out here every week." I looked around at the knee-high weeds, old tires, pieces of lumber, garbage bags filled with God-knew-what, and the neglected, dying trees. "Kids partying in the pool, climbing the towers. I had to put out fires every once in a while."

"Yes," Cruz agreed. "My point to the city exactly. When you let a glorious place like this . . . fall into decay, you are asking for problems. It is only by building something positive that you make a change for the better."

If he were waiting for an "Amen" from me, he'd have to keep waiting. We took the stairs up to the arch, the once-grand pool entrance that welcomed thousands of people off the steamy streets of Brooklyn. Now nothing more than an easel for any knucklehead with a can of spray paint who wasn't afraid to crawl under, slip through, or climb over a barb-wired fence. We passed the admission booth and the bathhouses, and walked into the main pool area. You could fit a football field in here. In the middle of the pool, a few feet away from one of the many "islands" that rose from the floor, a man was looking through one of those scopes surveyors use. I spotted his partner about fifty yards away.

"Your business?" I asked Cruz.

Cruz stood beside me. "The city has graciously allowed me the day to survey the pool." He didn't hide his sarcasm. "I have two weeks to present my plan to the zoning board."

"Plan?"

"Look around you, Mr. Donne," he said, making a sweeping gesture with his hand. I looked around. "Now close your eyes." I kept my eyes open. Cruz had his shut as he went on, his arm held out in front of him, the palm facing the pool. "I envision a church, a temple for the people to worship in. I see"—he moved his palm over a bit—"a school the parishioners would be proud to send their children to. A recreation center"—again his hand moved slightly—"to exercise not only the body, but the soul, as well."

He stood like that for a few more seconds—silent, his hand out in front of him—before asking, "Can you see that, Mr. Donne?"

"I see an abandoned pool," I said, "hopelessly and unfortunately stuck between a public school and a public park, Mr. Cruz. Not to mention an old factory across the street that is probably going to be broken up into million-dollar condos in a year or two. Do you really think the city will let you put a church here?"

"Yes!" He bought his two hands together, making a loud enough noise that the surveyor closest to us looked over. "That," Cruz said, his hands still together, eyes still closed as if in prayer, "is my vision. The vision I share with you today."

I couldn't think of anything to say, so I kept quiet, waiting for Cruz to reopen his eyes. When he did, he turned to me and touched my elbow.

"Perhaps if my last name were Trump," he said. "You—they—would take me more seriously, yes?"

"Perhaps."

"Let them have the waterfront," he said. "Let them build their million-dollar condominiums with views of Manhattan. Fill them with those who work across the river and would not dream of sending their children to public schools." He fixed his eyes on mine. "I know the struggle that comes with no place to worship. My own childhood church was destroyed by fire when I was just a teenager. My dream is to rebuild the spirit of that church. Here, on this spot. This is what I ask for."

I held his stare for a few seconds and then said, "Sold."

Cruz laughed. "If only the city were as easily convinced."

"Maybe you should bring the mayor out here and have him shut his eyes."

"The mayor has little interest in abandoned pools. Or abandoned people."

"You're preaching to the choir," I said.

"Do you know, when they decided to shut this pool down, when they decided they could spare no more resources for the maintenance and security? That same year the millionaires running this country announced massive tax cuts. The federal government paid billions of dollars to the arms builders to produce weapons they told us they hoped to never use. They even found enough money to help other countries buy weapons and train soldiers and contribute to the culture of death."

Cruz bent over and picked up a piece of the pool bottom, its blue paint faded but still visible after all these years. He held it in his closed hand and crushed it, allowing the pieces to fall to the ground.

"Do you know where the children of Williamsburg go swimming now? The lucky ones take the hour ride by subway to Coney Island. The less fortunate and more daring take their chances by jumping into the East River off the decaying piers. Politicians prefer their pools like their schools: private."

I looked over at what used to be the children's pool. The tall, brown grass covering the swimming area swayed gently in the slight breeze, a miniaturized prairie.

"Yo!" We both looked over at the surveyor, who was waving his clipboard.

"Excuse me for a moment, Mr. Donne."

As Cruz went over to discuss business, I tried to imagine what this pool once was and what it had meant to this community. Standing here in the great, empty space, I could understand a little better what some of the old-timers had meant when they told me about McCarren. *"Our homes may not have been much, sonny boy, but we were close to the pool."* An oasis.

I walked over to where Cruz was finishing up his conversation with the surveyor. They were looking at the clipboard. Cruz pointed at something and the surveyor nodded. Cruz smiled. They shook hands, and the surveyor went over to his coworker.

"Good news?" I asked.

"The work I would like to have done can be done."

"Congratulations."

"One obstacle out of many," he said. "But it is enough to get me to the next one. Have you had breakfast yet, Mr. Donne?"

"Just coffee," I said.

"Would you join me then?"

"I'm not hungry yet, thanks. But I will take that ride now. Home."

"As you wish."

We were approaching the archway when Cruz stopped. He reached over and began gently fingering the leaves on a six-inch plant that was growing out of the floor of the pool.

"What would you call this, Mr. Donne?"

I stepped closer to get a better look. "A weed?"

Cruz nodded. "Most people would," he said. "But in reality, it is the same tree that grows just outside this fence." He pointed to a tall tree to the right of the pool's entrance. "That tree will grow to thirty or forty feet and was planted well before the city shut the pool. This one," he touched the leaves of the one at his feet again, "comes from the one outside. The product of a stray seed blown over by a storm. It may grow another foot or so and still be seen as a weed, but it is truly a small miracle. To be able to survive at all, to burst through the concrete and reach for the sun. Remarkable. And yet, for all its perseverance, it will always be considered a weed until it grows too big and demands more than the soil can provide."

"That's too bad," I said, as much to Cruz as to the weed.

"It will die here unless it is taken and placed where there is more water, more sunlight. If that happens, it will grow as mighty as any of its brothers and shed its status of 'weed' and be called a tree." He gave the leaves one more stroke. "What do you think, Mr. Donne?"

"You should take the pulpit every once in a while at that church of yours, Mr. Cruz."

He smiled. "I leave that for the real preachers. I am just a businessman. Which I must now get back to," he said. "Let me take you home."

By the time Cruz dropped me off, it was after ten. I picked up an egg sandwich, another coffee, and a newspaper at the deli. It was almost noon when I finished all of them. The message light on my phone was blinking. It was Billy.

"No go on those plates, Ray," he explained. "Used to be registered upstate, but that car was dumped and they ain't in the system anymore. Maybe your friend read it wrong. Sorry."

I hated dead ends. I took a second shower, then wasted half an hour channel-surfing, and another thirty minutes trying to doze off. Too many thoughts of Frankie made me feel helpless; too much caffeine had me wired. Looked like I was going to see Muscles after all.

Chapter 19

"I GUESS I DIDN'T MAKE MYSELF clear last time we spoke."

Muscles was spreading a jellylike substance on my knees as I was trying to get into a comfortable position on the training table.

"When I said it was about time you decided to get your knees back in shape, you thought I meant what, now?"

It's pretty easy to be sarcastic when you're the one holding pads with wires connected to a generator that looks big enough start a truck engine.

"Explain this part to me again," I said as he attached four pads to the sides of my knees.

"Transcutaneous Electronic Nerve Stimulation." Like he had invented the thing. "TENS. Once I turn on the generator"—he gave a sweeping hand motion—"you're gonna feel something along the lines of pins and needles. I'll increase the voltage until you tell me to stop."

After a few seconds, I said, "Okay." It took me a while to get used to it, but when I did, it felt . . . therapeutic. "This new tech stuff is great."

"Not so new, Raymond." Muscles stood. "High frequency electronic stim has been known to disrupt the pain signals in targeted parts of the body for years."

"I'm not buying one of these machines, Muscles."

"You could, though. This one here'll run you about eight hundred."

"And my insurance?"

"Covered," he said. "I may have to call it something besides TENS, but they'll cover it."

"Why's that?"

"Raymond. Do you really need a lecture on how our medical system—and the politicians they pay good money for—would rather spend billions of dollars on drug therapy instead of something like this that really helps? This device, you buy and pay for once. Where's the perpetual profit in that? Drugs? Now, there's the gift that keeps on giving." He reached into the cooler, pulled out two ice packs, and placed one on top of each knee. "Don't worry. There's no danger of leaking"—he wiggled his fingers—"and gzzzzzzz!"

"I trust you."

"When I submit your forms, I'll have to write 'Pain Management' instead of 'TENS.' Some insurance companies still consider this an 'elective procedure.' From the Latin for 'We don't wanna pay for it.' They reject, I appeal. Sometimes I win."

The pins-and-needles were doing their job, creating a pleasant sensation that started at my knees and rippled up the legs and down to the feet. I was tempted to ask Muscles to up the voltage, but it was my first time.

"How long do I lie here?" I asked, leaning back and shutting my eyes.

"Give it ten. You know, I really could hook you up with the home version."

"I'll be fine."

"Minimal cost," he continued. "To you, I mean. A little creative writing on the referral, get your ortho to spice up his scrip a little . . ."

"I'll be fine," I repeated. "Thanks."

The ten minutes went by too fast. I thought about taking a shower, but decided to just get dressed and take one at home. I was lacing up my sneakers when I realized I hadn't spoken to Elaine Stiles about Lisa.

This time, I remembered my cell and used it to call the school. Someone in the main office picked up.

"This is Raymond Donne," I said. No response. "Mr. Donne."

"Oh, hey, Mr. Donne." A kid's voice. "This is Juanita. I'm interning with the after-school program. How may I direct your call?"

"Is Elaine Stiles there?" I asked.

"I'll try that extension."

A short while later, Juanita was back. "No, Mr. Donne. I'm sorry. She must have left for the day. Can I take a message?"

"No, thanks." I was about to hang up when another thought hit me.

"Juanita. Would you mind going to my mailbox and seeing if she left me a message?"

"Your mailbox? Oh, you work here. Sure, Mr. Donne. Gimme a sec."

A sec later, she was back. "Yes, Mr. Donne. You have two messages in your box."

I waited a bit, but it was apparent I was going to have to ask.

"What are they, Juanita?"

"Oh. One's on white loose-leaf, and it's signed, 'Elaine.' I guess that's Ms. Stiles." Silence. "I'll read it to you. 'Tried you at home. NA.' That means 'No Answer.'" More silence. "'Doctor says Lisa's fine. I'll swing by the Kings on my way home.' That's it for that one."

"Good. Thanks, Juanita."

"You want me to read the other one?"

I wanted to say it could wait, but it came out, "Go ahead."

"This one's on a pink 'While You Were Out' slip. It's got today's date on it and it's from . . . Willy B. Says 'Four o'clock. Halfway point.'"

"And?"

"And . . . that's it."

Willy B.? "Who took that message, Juanita? Does it say?"

"Nope. Sorry. I came on at three fifteen, and the office was empty."

"Okay, thanks."

"Thanks for calling," Juanita sang. "Have a good day!"

Elaine was in contact with Lisa's family. Good. But who the hell was Willy B.? None of my students was William or Bill or Will. A parent? Four o'clock. Today? Tomorrow? I know Mary didn't take that message. Probably Edna. Halfway point.

Something about that name—Willy B.—rang familiar. Some kid's tag I've seen scrawled in black marker on the bathroom wall?

I said good-bye to Muscles, assured him I'd be back in two days, and walked out to the elevator. Willy B.? The elevator doors opened. Whoa! The Willy B. That's what the hipster locals and kids called the Williamsburg Bridge. That's why it sounded . . . but that didn't make sense. Juanita said the message was from—

Jesus. The halfway point. I must have told my students dozens of times that one of my favorite places in the city is the middle of the Williamsburg Bridge walkway. The constant hum of the traffic underneath generated white noise, giving the illusion of silence, providing one of the most unlikely places I've found in the city where I could actually think. But what—

Holy shit.

Frankie. He called.

I looked at my watch. I had less than fifteen minutes.

Chapter 20

MUSCLES PULLED HIS BMW UNDER the overpass and parked in front of the entrance to the pedestrian/bike pathway of the bridge. I picked up my water bottle and umbrella from the floor, mumbled thanks, and was about to open the passenger door when he grabbed my forearm.

"You gonna stick with that bullshit story," he said, punctuating it with a squeeze, "or do I go with you and find out what you're really doing here?"

I looked at his hand and realized there was no way of shaking it loose. I grimaced and said, "How about you let me stick with my bullshit story, and I'll call you later and let you know how it all turned out?"

"How about you just tell me the truth?"

I glanced over at the digital clock on the dashboard. I had less than five minutes.

"What gets me out of the car quicker?" I asked. "The truth or another lie?"

"Try the truth."

Muscles released my arm, and two minutes later, he was filled in on the details of Frankie's disappearance. I stopped when I got to today's phone call. "It may be something or maybe not. Either way I have to go by myself. I'll be okay."

Muscles stared at me for about ten seconds before he shook his head and smiled.

"What?" I asked.

"Nice to see you coming back, Raymond."

"What the hell does that mean?" I asked, remembering Billy's comment the other day.

"It's like the rehab," he said. "A little bit at a time."

"Whatever you say, Muscles." I slid the rest of the way out of the car and shut the door. "Thanks for the ride."

"How long you gonna be?"

"I have no idea."

"Call me, and I'll pick you up. No problem."

"What's your number?"

He took my phone and pressed a bunch of buttons. "That's my office," he said. "I'm not going home for a while. So give me a call, and I'll come get ya."

"Thanks," I said for the third time.

"You know what you're doing, Raymond?"

"No more or less than usual," I said.

Muscles gave me a shake of the head and then made an illegal, screeching U-turn up the wrong way of a one-way street. I took a long sip from my water bottle before turning around and walking up to the halfway point of the Williamsburg Bridge.

I got about a hundred feet before I had to stop. I did a couple of quick stretches, gulped down some more water, and tried to get my breathing and heart rate somewhere close to normal.

Frankie may not have been the best student in my class but he was always a good listener, and I guess he was paying attention when I told the kids about the bridge. It made sense for him to leave that cryptic message at the school. Especially with all that had been going on lately. He didn't trust most people on a good day, and I don't know when he'd last had one of those.

I was still a couple of minutes away from the middle of the bridge, so I took a little more water and started moving. Three Hassidic men were walking toward me, briefcases in hand, coming back home to Williamsburg after a day in the city. Behind them, I saw a couple of black kids on a bike. The one doing the pumping was doing it hard, using the downward momentum to build up to a real cruising speed. His buddy had his hands on the leader's shoulders and screamed with laughter as they frightened the three men, who split up to avoid getting run over. Another fun thing to do on the Willy B.

A minute later, I was standing at the midway point. I did a three-sixty. No sign of Frankie. I didn't even know which side he'd be coming from.

This was the spot I'd told my students about. A hundred feet above the East River, just as close to Brooklyn as to Manhattan. Watching from on high as the tugs, tourists, and other boats made their way up and down the East River. The slightly less-than-cool breeze coming off the water, the vibration of the bridge as the subway rumbled by. The collective hum of the tires on the asphalt just below me, creating a white noise, blocking out all the other sounds of the city. This was the place to come—in the middle of everything—to get away from everything else.

I grabbed the railing with both hands, took a deep breath, and did a slow bend. I held it for five seconds and came up slowly, releasing the air from my lungs as Muscles had instructed. The process took about twenty seconds. As I rose out of the last one, a voice came from behind me.

"Hey."

I turned and looked at Frankie. "Hey," I said back.

Resisting the urge to throw my arms around him, I watched as Frankie removed his Yankees cap and ran his fingers through his brown hair. It was longer than I'd remembered, but clean. There were dark rings under his eyes, and his face looked as if he'd lost some weight. He was wearing a long-sleeved baseball shirt with the sleeves rolled up and a pair of khaki shorts that looked as if they'd been recently cleaned and pressed.

"Where have you been, Frankie?"

"Thanks for coming, Mr. D." He looked up and down the bridge. I did the same. "I wasn't sure you got my message. Hadda say it twice for that lady at school."

"Took me a bit to figure it out, but I got it. Let's go home. I want to get you to the—"

"That's not why I called you, Mr. D. I didn't say nothing about going home."

"You didn't say *anything*. Where'd you call from, anyway?"

He lifted his shirt and showed me a cell phone clipped to his shorts. "A friend's," he explained. "I called you from where I been staying. How's Milagros?"

"She's good. Children's Services is letting her stay with your grandmother for now. They're both worried about you. What friends?"

Frankie just smiled. "Good," he said. "Tell 'em I'll be home soon and I'm sorry about being away so long."

"You're coming with me and telling them yourself."

He shook his head. "Can't do that. I got some shit I gotta figure out first."

"Can't do that? Frankie, your dad's been murdered, and the cops are looking for you. You don't have to figure out anything. You're fourteen years old."

He looked down at his feet. "I got Milagros and me all the way up to Anita's."

I nodded.

"And I got Milagros to you safe."

"That was a big risk, Frankie."

"I was watching from the corner when you got dropped off, Mr. D. I knew she'd be okay. I just need a few more days."

"Jesus, Frankie. You go all the way up to Highland and don't contact your cousin?"

"I thought we could stay up there for a few days, but then I seen that guy."

"What guy?"

"The big one I seen coming outta my dad's . . . the day . . . you know?"

"No, Frankie," I said. "I don't know. That's why you have to go back with me now so you can explain all this to the cops." I got a look telling me this kid was five seconds away from pulling another Houdini. "Okay," I said. "Start from the beginning."

He looked around again. When he was sure we weren't being stalked, he looked at my water bottle. "Can I get some of that?"

I handed it to him. "Finish it."

He did. In one gulp. He let it do its job and then said, "We were staying at my dad's. Milagros and me. He was real nervous the last few days. Not jumpy nervous like when he drank too much or scored something, but *real* nervous. Like he was expecting some shit to come down. He's not usually like that. That day he was gonna take us into the city, maybe the zoo. Showed me a buncha hundreds, like he was trying to impress me."

"He say where he got the money from?" I asked.

"Said he had a good week selling stuff. Did that a lot. Anyways, we're all getting ready to go, and he looks out the window, and something got him real jumpy, y'know? He starts to put all this shit into a case, gives it to me, and tells me to take Milagros up to the roof. Says he'll call up to us when it's okay to come down."

"So you went up to the roof . . . ?"

"Yeah. We get up there, and we're waiting for about a half hour and then he yells up that it's okay to come on down."

"Did he say who he was talking to?"

"Nah." Frankie scratched his head. "Probably one of his friends he hangs with when me and Milagros ain't around."

"What makes you think that?" I asked.

It looked like this question embarrassed Frankie a little by the way he shifted his feet and looked over my shoulder when he answered. "He was kinda slurring his words, y'know. Wasn't doing that before. He seemed a bit . . . sleepy. I seen him like that after he'd been smoking. Didn't smell no smoke, so maybe they opened a window in the front room. He don't usually—"

"Then what happened?"

"We start getting ready to go, and someone started knocking on the door. I mean banging. Dad tells us to get back on the roof again, and he'd let us know when it was chill to come down."

He was having trouble breathing. I put my hand on his shoulder.

"Take it easy," I said. I counted to twenty before asking, "How long were you up there?"

Frankie took a deep breath and swallowed hard. He closed his eyes and shook his head. "I don't know. Another half hour, maybe? I heard this door shut outside, and I go over to the side and see this big guy get in the driver's side of a van, and then the van pulled away."

"A white van?" I asked.

"How'd you know that?"

Had to be Ape, I thought. "The big guy, you saw him up at Anita's?"

"Yeah." He rubbed the back of his neck. "I keep waiting for Dad to call us down, but he don't. So after a while, we go down and he's . . . he's on the bed, and he's not moving, and there's all this blood on his face and the floor, and he's holding on to Milagros's book bag, and . . ."

"I know," I said. "I was the one who found him."

"I don't get it, Mr. D. I was just talking to him like this and then he's . . ."

Now the tears came, and he didn't try to stop them. I put my hand on his shoulder and kept my mouth shut. We stood like that for a few minutes as Frankie let the last week pour out through his eyes. A young couple walked by and gave us a look. The two kids on the bike sped past, the one on the back screaming, "Faggots!" Frankie was oblivious to the whole scene. It was just the two of us and some bad memories.

When he was done, he wiped both cheeks. "You saw him?"

"Yeah," I said. "I was looking for you. You promised you'd be in school every day for the rest of the year, remember?"

He managed a small grin. "Sorry about that, Mr. D."

"Don't worry. We'll take care of it when I get you home. This has gone on long enough."

"I don't know what to do now, Mr. D. That's why I called you."

"And I'm saying we have to go to the police."

He shook his head. "Nah, man. Not the cops."

"You can't just keep running, Frankie. It's just a matter of time before they find you. The cops or the guy in the white van. Shit, they found me."

"Who did?"

"The guy in the van," I said. "And he's got a partner." I told him the story about getting nabbed by Ape and Suit outside Muscles's the day before. I left out the part about my sister. "Did you see anyone in the passenger side?"

"Nah, had tinted windows. But damn," he said. "You okay?"

"I'm here," I said, trying to sound nonchalant. "Let me bring you to Detective Royce. He's the—"

"But I didn't do nothing!" he yelled. Then in a lower voice, he added, "Mostly."

"What do you mean *mostly*?"

He put his cap back on and adjusted the brim. "My dad's suitcase," he said.

"Yeah?"

"Had money in it, Mr. D. Stupid money."

"How much stupid money, Frankie?"

"About ten gees, more or less."

I leaned into him. "Ten thousand dollars?"

"In hundreds. Some fifties." He reached into his pocket and showed me a little green.

"Not a good idea walking around with that kind of cash, Frankie. Your dad tell you where he got that kind of money?"

He pushed the bills back into his pocket and said, "Like I said. Selling shit. But he was lying. He ain't never sold that much stuff in his life. Probably stole it."

It struck me how casual he was being about his substance-abusing father who stole shit for a living. Frankie stepped over to the railing and shut his eyes. After a few seconds he said, "You're right, Mr. D. Does kinda sound like a waterfall up here. Never noticed that before."

"Yeah, sometimes you just got to stop and smell the exhaust fumes." After a half minute of listening to the traffic hum by below us, I said, "So why'd you call me if you're not ready to go home?"

Frankie shoved his hands in his pocket and gave me a meek grin. "You know how in class you're always telling E to catch a clue?"

"Yeah?"

He pulled a pink piece of paper out of his pocket and handed it to me. "I think I caught one. About my dad."

I kept my eyes on Frankie as I unfolded the paper.

"It's a truck rental receipt," Frankie said. "It was in the suitcase. My dad rented a truck a few days before he . . . y'know."

"So?"

"Look at it. It's a one-way. To Florida."

He was right. His dad had rented a truck and was going to drop it off in Florida. "Did he tell you about this?" I asked.

"Just that he was gonna take me and Milagros away from . . . here . . . and we was gonna start a new life somewhere like a real family. Somewhere where Milagros could ride her bike every day, and I could play ball in the winter." He slapped the paper. "He was serious this time. My dad was looking out for us, Mr. D. He was gonna try Florida. My dad was getting us away from all this shit. He was putting stuff together to start a new life."

And look where it got him.

"That's great, Frankie," I said. "Where's the rest of the stuff from the suitcase?"

"It's with some people I hang with," he explained. "Gonna go pick it up after I leave here. I'm staying somewhere else tonight. At a friend's who's got a computer."

I folded up the truck receipt, slipped it into my front pocket, and said, "Let me tell you how I see things, Frankie. First—"

"No offense, Mr. D. But I don't got time for one of your lectures. I gotta—"

I surprised him—and myself—by grabbing his wrist. "What you gotta do is listen to me, Frankie." He tried to pull away, but I tightened my grip. "You're the kid here. I'm the adult, so just shut up and listen."

He looked at me with fear, a new round of tears in his eyes. "You're hurting me."

"Too bad," I said and immediately felt like shit. I loosened my grip. "You got the police thinking you're involved in your dad's death." He was about to interrupt, but I cut him off. "They figured you were probably dead, but once Milagros came back, they got to thinking maybe you have more to do with this situation than just bad luck."

"I didn't kill my dad, Mr. D."

"I know that. But you know how the cops look at things. And think about it," I said, slipping my hand off his wrist and into his hand, like a handshake. I lowered my voice. "Those guys your dad was so scared of, the ones who messed with me, they're looking for you, too. The best move— the *only* move—right now is for me to take you to the detective in charge of your dad's case. Royce. He's not a bad guy. Tell him your story."

He considered that for about ten seconds, and then said, "I can't do that, Mr. D."

I felt my grip tightening again. "*You can't do that?* Let me tell you something. You don't have a choice. I've spent the last week looking for you, and I've been pushed around a little too much for my liking. By the same people who are looking for you, because that shit your dad shoved into his suitcase? It belongs to them. I finally find you, and you tell me you—"

"I called you," he said.

"What did you say?"

"You didn't find me, Mr. D. I called you."

I took his hand and pushed him away from me. "You listen to me. This isn't just about you and your father anymore. They broke into your grandmother's apartment looking for what he took. You think they won't come back and try again? With your sister there?" I paused to catch my breath. Tears were coming down Frankie's face again. Too fucking bad.

"Twice I thought I was done with this shit. First with Milagros at my apartment, and now meeting you here. You can't have it both ways, kiddo. I'm in. You're coming with me if I have to throw you over my shoulder and carry you into the precinct myself."

Frankie glared back at me with angry, wet eyes. He pointed his finger at me, struggling for the right words. "Fuck you." He found them. "I came to you for help. I thought you, out of all people would understand—I found my father dead."

We stood, glaring at each other, waiting for the other to speak. I realized I had just told Frankie I was the adult. I took a deep breath. "I'm sorry about everything that's happened, Frankie. I am. But if you don't think I'll drag you in, you're mistaken. I've come too far to let you just—"

"*You* come too far?" he said. "And you think *I'm* being selfish? Listen to you. Just because you got me into that holy-rolling white-boy school don't mean you're in charge of me. You're not my father."

"You're right," I said. "I'm not your father. I don't do drugs and put my family at risk by stealing money from dangerous people who end up—"

Without a word, he charged at me. I slammed so hard into the railing that a shockwave of pain spread throughout my midsection, doubling me over. A low rumble of nausea started in my gut. I put my hand over my mouth and bit down on the fleshy area between my thumb and forefinger. I'm not sure how long it took before I was sure I wasn't going to vomit. It was the sound of Frankie sobbing that made me look up.

"I'm sorry, Mr. D," he mumbled. "I didn't mean to . . ."

Fuck this. I'd been getting knocked around too much lately. And now by the kid I was sticking my neck out for?

"Okay, Frankie," I said, straightening myself up. My knees were yelling at me to get back down, but I ignored them. "Do what you want. I'm out of it."

"I don't want you out of it."

"Then I'll ask one more time. Come with me."

"I can't do that right now."

"Then go." I motioned with my head toward the Manhattan side of the bridge. "Just get the hell out of here."

"You're not going to help me?"

"Jesus, Frankie. That's what I'm trying to do here. But I'm not going to help you get yourself killed. You're doing a pretty good job of that by yourself. I just don't know why you'd drag your sister and grandmother into it."

"That's not my fault. I didn't do that."

"Well, that's what happened, Frankie. They're in it, and the longer you keep running, the longer this plays out into something bad." I thought about Rachel. "Not just for you."

Frankie gave that some thought and took a step forward to let a Hispanic woman pushing a stroller and dragging another kid pass. He was next to me and leaned up against the railing. I felt behind my knees. I was hurting and glad the trip back to Brooklyn was downhill. The only question was whether or not I was going it alone. He either comes with me, or I'm out of it. Royce and my uncle were right: I wasn't a cop anymore and was probably doing more harm than good. Let the cops take it from here. It's what they do, and they're good at it.

"Okay," Frankie said. "I'll go with you."

I looked up. "Say that again?"

He took his hat off again and wiped his forehead with the back of his hand. "I don't want any shit to happen to my grandmother or Milagros. I'll go with you, but I gotta get that suitcase."

I straightened up, wincing as the back of my legs caught fire. A low moan came from deep inside me. It took all I had not to double over again. Frankie reached out and held my arm.

"Sorry about that, Mr. D."

"Me, too, Frankie. Why don't we wait on the suitcase?" I said, not wanting anything to get in the way of getting this kid home. "It's safe, right?"

"Yeah."

"Then we'll have the cops pick it up."

"Nuh-uh, Mr. D. I don't want my friends in no trouble with the cops."

Good point. "How about I send a friend of mine?" I was thinking about Officer Jackson. "He's a cop, but he'll be cool."

"You trust him?"

"Yeah."

"Okay, then. I guess."

"Good." I pointed to the cell phone clipped to his shorts. "Why don't you call your grandmother. Tell her to meet us at the precinct."

"Yeah, right," he said with a smile. "Be nice to see her again. She not gonna be too happy to go to the precinct, though. Grams don't like cops all that much."

"Tell her to bring Elsa with her."

"Yeah, that'd be good. Gotta call Elsa anyways, come to think of it. Grams's phone is probably still outta order."

He unfolded the phone and started dialing. I took out mine and speed-dialed Muscles's office to have him pick us up on the other side. As I listened to the ringing, I saw a cop on a bike coming our way. Frankie saw him, too. The nervous look came back.

"I don't know," I said. "He's probably just—"

"Hey!" The cop yelled, pointing with his walkie-talkie. "You two! Hold it!"

Frankie closed up his phone. "Shit, Mr. D. You called the five-oh?"

"No, Frankie. I swear. I have no idea . . ."

The cop started pedaling faster. "I said hold it!"

Frankie clipped the phone to his shorts again. "I trusted you, Mr. D."

"Frankie," I said, "I told you I—"

"Damn!" he screamed. He turned the other way and was just about run over by the two kids on the bike. They skidded out, and the bike flipped over, sending the two riders barreling into Frankie and me. Mostly me.

"I told you to goddamn stop!" The cop was about twenty yards away.

Frankie picked himself up, grabbed the bike off the ground, got on, and took off.

"Frankie!" I yelled, pushing one of the kids off my chest. "He's not here for you. I didn't call them!" He kept pumping. "Frankie!"

He didn't look back. He just rode toward Manhattan as fast as he could, weaving in and out of the pedestrian traffic.

"Damn it!" I screamed, rolling myself over and pulling myself up with the help of the railing. Someone touched my back, and I twisted around. "Get your fucking hands off me," I yelled into the face of the cop. "Damn it. I'm sorry, I just . . ."

"Sir," he said, pointing at me. "Calm. Down. Are you okay?"

"No," I said. "I'm not okay." I looked over at the two kids brushing themselves off and checking their arms and legs for injuries. "These two . . . kids almost killed me."

"That guy stole our bike, mister," one of the kids said as they both turned in the direction Frankie rode off. "He was with this guy. They was talking. We want our bike back." He turned his angry face to me and said, "Sue your white ass."

I took a step toward the kid, and the cop put his hand on my chest.

"Do you know the young man who took the bike, sir?"

"What?" I said, staring at the two assholes who just blew my chance of getting Frankie home. "Yeah, I know him. He's one of my kids. One of my students."

"You're a teacher, then."

"Yes." My breathing was getting steadier. "I'm a teacher."

"And you two," the cop said to the kids. He raised his radio. "I got two calls about you. What the hell do you think you were doing riding around like that?"

"Just havin' some fun, mister. Whatchoo gonna do about our bike?"

The cop took off his hat and used it to fan himself. "Why don't you come back to the precinct with me, and we'll fill out a stolen property report?" He paused to give a cop grin. "Get your parents to come pick you up."

The boys looked at each other for two seconds, and the verbal one said, "Nah. Bike was bootleg anyways. We'll just walk on home if that's okay with you."

"Why don't you do that? And don't get into any more trouble on your way."

The police officer stepped aside as the two did a junior pimp walk past us, their punk-ass grins in full mode, just begging to be slapped upside the head. They were about fifty feet away when the cop said, "Bootleg. Means it didn't belong to them."

"Thanks for the translation."

"I take it you're going to be okay, sir? What with the sarcasm and all?"

"I'll be fine," I said.

"And the young man you were with. Your student?"

I opened up the phone and called Muscles. "I don't know," I said to the cop.

"Okay, then," he said. "Try to have a good evening."

"Yeah," I said as he biked away. "I'll do my best."

When Muscles picked me up, I told him what had happened on the bridge. He was not happy with me. But it was the truth, and that's what I had promised in exchange for his driving services. He was less happy when I told him I had no intention of notifying the police.

"What am I going to tell him?" I pictured Detective Royce's face. "We had a meeting, I didn't bother to call the cops, and then let the kid slip through my fingers?"

Muscles started the car. "So the kid's talking to his dad one minute, and thirty minutes later the guy's dead, and all it looks like he's got is a bloody nose?"

"That's how I'm hearing it."

"Interesting."

He took me back to the office where he insisted I soak in the hot tub, undergo a not-so-deep-tissue massage—which hurt like hell just the same— and an icing down of the knees with another round of electric stimulation. When it was over, it still felt like a truck had run over me, only a slightly smaller truck. Muscles offered to drive me home, but I was starving and in no mood to fend for myself, so I asked to be dropped off at The LineUp.

Chapter 21

MIKEY GREETED ME WITH THE wave of a towel. "There he is!"

"Cheeseburger," I said. "Fries and a pilsner. And Tabasco." Muscles had told me about the capsaicin in the hot sauce easing the pain. I pointed to the empty pint glass next to the can of tomato juice. "Set me up next to Edgar, and get him another round on me, Mikey."

"If you say so."

I headed off in the direction of the men's room and ran into Edgar as he was coming out.

"You okay, Ray? You're walking a little funny."

"Too much horseback riding," I said. "I'll be right back. I gotta hit the head."

"Hey," he said, "you hear about—"

"I'll be right back, Edgar," I repeated. He got the message and went over to his stool as I entered the men's room.

As I was washing my hands, I took a long look in the mirror. I didn't completely fuck up on the bridge. I had Frankie coming home until that cop and those kids got in the way. I couldn't control everything, couldn't foresee every possible way a situation like that could go south. I did a decent job, got some new bruises for my troubles, and now it was time for some food and a few beers. Just like old times. Almost.

When I got back to the bar, Mikey had the Yankee game on. As I slid onto the stool, Edgar picked up right where he'd left off.

"You hear that the kid's—Frankie's—sister came back?" he asked.

I took a long sip from my pint glass and said, "You think I live in a vacuum?"

"Nah. It's just you're at work all day and then . . . well, whatever else you do when you're not at work. I thought maybe you missed the news."

"No, Edgar. I didn't miss the news. In fact . . ." I went on to tell him everything about Milagros's return up to the point of my leaving the precinct last night.

"Holy shit, Raymond," he said. "That makes you like some kinda hero, don't it?"

"No, Edgar. It makes me some kinda delivery boy."

"So what'd she say about Frankie? Where is he?"

"She didn't say. Just that he's fine."

"Well, why didn't he come in with her? Didn't the cops ask her that?"

"Yes, they asked her. She didn't say."

He poured a little tomato juice into his Bass and watched it make its way down the inside of the glass. After it had settled, he took a sip. "Did she say who killed her old man?"

"She doesn't know, Edgar." Mikey came over and put my burgers and fries in front of me. "Thanks," I said, and then to Edgar, "Let me eat a bit, huh? It's been a long day. If you're good, I'll tell you another story when I'm done."

"Don't talk to me like I'm a kid," he said. "I get enough of that from the other guys."

I poured some ketchup onto my plate and some hot sauce on top of that. "You're right, Edgar. I'm sorry." I pointed to the TV. "Watch the game. Then we'll talk."

He did, and I was able to make it through my dinner and start a second beer in peace. I convinced myself the combination of red meat, carbs, beer, and Tabasco aided in my recovery efforts. I relaxed and let my attention drift up to the TV, and when the Yanks ended the second inning with a bases-loaded pop-up, Edgar cleared his throat. I went right to the highlight.

"I saw Frankie today," I said, and for the next two minutes, Edgar *was* a kid. His mouth practically hung open, his eyes the size of shot glasses. It was the longest I could remember him keeping silent. When I was done, it took him a full minute to speak.

"Cheese and crackers," he said. "You had him."

"I know."

"Damn kids and that cop. What the hell was he thinking?"

"It wasn't his fault. He had no idea about Frankie and me."

"Yeah," he said. "I guess, but still . . . Whatta you gonna do now?"

"Not much I can do," I said. "At least I know he's okay. For now."

Edgar nodded and closed his eyes. He did that when he thought about something deeply. Usually it was figuring out someone's batting average or who had the majors' lowest ERA in 1957. I took the opportunity to sip some more beer.

"You said he gave you a truck rental receipt," he said, his eyes now open. "Still got it?"

I pulled the receipt out of my pocket. "Yeah."

He took it and studied it for a bit. "I know these guys. They're good. We rent from them at work when we're short on fleet."

"Okay."

"They use a GPS to track their vehicles. Global Positioning System."

"I know what GPS means, Edgar. I'm just wondering why you're telling me this stuff."

"The company can keep track of their vehicles. They say it's in case they get stolen or something, but it's more Big Brother than that."

"What do you mean?"

"They use the GPS to see if you've gone out of state without telling them or if you violated any speed limits. I've heard some places use that info to pad their bills."

"That sounds illegal."

"The Supreme Court said so."

"This is all very interesting, Edgar, but . . ."

"But how does it help you?"

"That's what I was thinking."

"Well," he said, taking a sip from his beer and teasing me with the pause, "we could probably locate this truck. If you were interested, that is."

"Let's say I was," I said. "I don't have access to their GPS system, and I sure as hell can't just walk into their offices and say, 'Hey, can you find this truck for me?'"

Edgar leaned into me and whispered, "Tell me you're interested."

"What?"

"Tell me," he whispered again, "that you're interested."

I probably should have sat at the other end of the bar. "Okay," I whispered back. "I'm interested. Now what?"

Edgar straightened up. "I've got this friend," he said. "And my friend's got this computer, and this really cool software."

"Your friend got a name?"

"Deadbolt."

"Deadbolt," I repeated. "Is that his first or last name, Edgar?"

"Just Deadbolt," he said.

"And he can tell us where this truck is?"

"If he can't, I don't know who can."

I didn't ask about the legality of all this, because I already knew the answer. It would be nice to have something to take to Royce, though. Maybe Frankie really did catch a clue.

"Okay, Edgar," I said. "When can we meet with Deadbolt?"

"What's today?" Edgar asked.

"Monday."

He looked at his watch and said, "How's fifteen minutes sound?"

Twenty minutes later, we were sitting in Edgar's car at the East River. The pier we were parked in front of was fenced off. The city had finally had enough of large chunks of aging concrete crashing into the water while Grampa was trying to teach Junior how to fish and cut bait. Deadbolt was sitting in the backseat with a silver laptop on his knees. He reached into the front pocket of his overalls and pulled out a device about the size of a stick of gum. He inserted it into the side of his computer, pressed a few buttons and said, "This'll take a few."

He leaned forward and stuck his head between the headrests. It was the first good look I got of him. Even in the early evening light, I could tell this man did not get enough sun. His skin was two shades too pale, and he had bags under his eyes big enough to pack a lunch in. His breath smelled like fresh bread.

"I remember you now," he said to me. "Emo said you used to be a cop. You were the one took that plunge about four or five years ago. Didn't a kid get killed?"

"And you were the one," I said, "who was suspected in about a half dozen break-ins over at the industrial park."

"Suspected," he repeated. "Never charged."

"Nothing was ever taken in those break-ins. Detectives had a hard time figuring that out."

"Maybe someone was trying to teach the businesses the importance of high-tech security systems."

"And you're in what legitimate business now?" I asked.

"I design and install high-tech security systems." His computer started beeping. He put it back on his lap and punched the keys for a few seconds. "Read me the redge, Emo."

Edgar looked at the rental slip and read off the numbers. Deadbolt keyed them into the computer and after five seconds said, "Voy lah." He turned the screen around so Edgar and I could see it. Deadbolt pointed at the red circle on the screen. "That's right in the neighborhood."

After I got my bearings on the grid map, I could see that the truck was five blocks from where we were sitting. Not far from where Frankie's father used to live.

"I know that corner," Edgar said. "It's an old gas station. Owner let the thing run down, and now he makes his nut by letting people park there."

"Which means it's locked," I added.

Deadbolt leaned forward again and let out a deep breath. If my eyes were closed I would have sworn I had walked into a bakery.

"You're not a cop no more, right?" he said.

"Right."

"And you don't go telling on people to the cops, right?"

"Not if they don't tell on me," I answered.

Deadbolt reached into his computer briefcase and pulled out a small tool. "You know what this is, right?"

I took it. "Sure. It's a low-tech security device." I turned the lock pick over in my hand. "Took a lot of these off a lot of people back in the day."

"I use it in my work sometimes. Consider it a gift." He leaned back and turned off his computer. "Use it in good health. It's a good one. Made in China."

"Says here," I said, looking at the side of the lock pick, "it's from Japan."

"What's the diff?" Deadbolt had his computer all packed up and he was ready to go. "Always a pleasure, Edgar." They shook hands, and then he offered his to me. "Officer."

"Whatever."

"Thanks, DB," Edgar said. "I owe ya one."

"Please. This is one of the ones I owed you."

I slipped the lock pick into my front pocket and said, "Good night, Deadbolt."

"Gentlemen."

After Deadbolt was gone, Edgar turned the key and started the car. "Where to now, Ray? Back to The LineUp? Home?"

Both of those were excellent ideas, I thought. Beer, baseball, and bed. Tomorrow after work I could head over to the precinct and tell Royce that not only had his murder victim rented a truck before he died, but that I knew where it was parked.

Then I heard myself tell Edgar, "Let's go check out that truck."

We were parked about a hundred feet off the intersection. One corner housed the parking lot, the other three consisted of an old automotive repair shop that had been out of business for about ten years, a defunct bar with a nautically themed exterior, and a five-story apartment building that had seen its best days about forty years ago when this part of Williamsburg was known more for meatpacking than for being the next area ripe for picking by real estate developers. With a little imagination, I could picture a pair of ten-story condos rising into the Brooklyn night with an upscale coffeehouse across the way. In two years, this corner will look as unfamiliar to me as some town in Iowa.

After waiting for about three minutes, seeing no pedestrians and only a handful of cars and trucks go by, I turned to Edgar. "You ready?"

"Oh, yeah," he said, a little too eager. "I'm ready."

"Remember, Edgar," I said. "You are a lookout. Any sign of trouble—cops, whatever—give me one long honk of the horn, and you get out of here. No use both of us getting screwed."

"I got it, Ray. You notice the lot's full?"

Three medium-sized trucks and five cars. Probably netted the landlord over three thousand dollars a month, maintenance-free. A full lot meant I wouldn't be bothered by someone coming in to park. I looked at my watch. Just after nine. I doubted anyone would be picking up a vehicle at this hour.

"Okay," I said. "I don't expect to be in there that long. Ten minutes, tops."

"How about I give the horn a couple of toots when ten minutes have gone by?" Edgar asked. "In case you lose track of the time."

I gave that some thought. "Yeah. Good idea."

Edgar opened his glove compartment and pulled out something that looked like a cigar holder. He twisted the end, and the front seat of his car filled with light. He handed it to me. "This'll help, huh?"

"Yeah," I said, taking the flashlight and twisting it into the off position. "It'll help." I opened the car door and said, "I'll be right back."

"Ten minutes."

"Ten minutes."

I got out of the car, walked to the corner, and waited. There was nobody coming from any direction, so I crossed over to the parking lot. I glanced up at the apartment building. All the windows that faced the lot were covered with curtains. I took the lock pick out of my pocket and rolled it between my thumb and forefinger. The padlock on the gate was a good one, but it was designed more to keep away the casual troublemaker looking for kicks. Not someone determined to get in. Someone with a lock pick.

I inserted the pick into the lock and let it catch. When it wouldn't move anymore, I gave it a turn and the lock opened. That was easy. Almost easy enough to make me forget that what I was prepared to do was called breaking and entering. I thought again about just going into Royce's office the next day with what I knew, but what I knew wasn't enough.

I thought of Frankie's grandmother and sister. Frankie finding his father the way he had. Royce ready to put this one on the bottom of the pile. How far was I willing to go to get this kid home? The answer came when I took the lock off the gate and slipped through to the other side of the fence.

I relocked the gate on the off chance some bored cop or security guard might come by and check things out. I pocketed the lock pick and took out Edgar's flashlight. It was no problem finding the truck Frankie's dad had rented. I had committed the plate number to memory. It was about the size of a mail truck, and the rear was facing away from the street. Nice bit of luck there.

There was enough light coming off the streetlights for me to check out the back door of the truck. It had one of those security hooks that looks like a pick ax inserted into a U-ring. I focused my attention on the actual lock. It was of decent quality and would keep out most people. I stuck the pick in and waited for the catch. This time it took a bit more maneuvering, but I got it, turned it, and lifted the hook out of the way.

The door rolled up without a sound—I hadn't considered an alarm until then—and the smell of hot air laced with artificial pine wafted out. I turned on the flashlight and looked inside. There were a dozen or so boxes along the right side, neatly stacked. On the left were a rolled-out sleeping bag and a suitcase. I used the bumper to help me get up onto the floor of the truck, and I swung my legs over so I was completely inside. When I figured out the headroom situation, I stood up slowly and then lowered the door.

I went over to the boxes. They all appeared to be factory-sealed and contained brand-name electronics: a large-screen TV, DVD/VCR combination, two identical videogame systems, some stereo equipment, a convection oven, phone and answering machine, computer, printer, a minifridge, and two air conditioners. All the right stuff for someone who was planning to start a new life in Florida.

The suitcase was an older model, the kind my mother still used, with the hard shell. I bent over and opened it. Inside were a pair of blue jeans, a hooded sweatshirt, some boxer shorts, and two pairs of socks. All clean. The sleeping bag looked well worn but in decent shape.

I went up to the front and tried the glove compartment, where I found the truck's registration and insurance info. Nothing under the passenger-side seat, and the door's storage pocket contained only a map of Florida. I slid over and sat behind the wheel. There was nothing in the door and nothing in either of the sun flaps. I reached under the seat and pulled out a manila envelope. I opened it. A bunch of receipts and some credit cards wrapped in a rubber band. I took the envelope, got up, and made my way to the back of the van. One more sweep with the flashlight. I'd seen all there was to see and decided not to push my luck any further.

I exited the truck and the lot as easily as I had entered, and when I opened the side door of Edgar's car, he pressed a button on his watch and said, "Eight minutes, thirty-seven seconds. That was quick and easy."

He couldn't feel my heart beating. "Let's go."

"Anything good in there?" he asked, looking at the envelope.

"I'll let you know when I check it out, Edgar. Right now, just go."

•   •   •

Edgar and I were too juiced to call it a night, so after he parked his car outside my apartment, we ducked into the McDonald's on the corner. We grabbed a couple of large decafs and sat at one of the tables in the back, away from the windows. An employee came by with a mop and explained in a mix of Spanish and English that the area where we were sitting was ready to be closed for the night. I told him we'd only be about ten minutes, and put a five-dollar bill on the table. He smiled and headed to the front. I opened three packs of sugar and dumped them into my cup. Then I told Edgar about what I had seen in the van.

"You gonna open that?" Edgar asked, staring at the envelope on my lap.

"Relax," I said. "Enjoy your coffee."

As he took a sip, I put my hand under the table and opened the envelope. I pulled out the receipts and credit cards, placed them on my lap and glanced down at them.

"What?" Edgar asked.

"Some credit cards and receipts," I said.

I removed the rubber band and checked out the cards. There were five of them, all from different companies, and all had the same name on them: Felix Villejo. I could tell they had all been issued recently. They had that new shine on them that only lasts for a few weeks. I put the rubber band around them again and dropped them back into the envelope. Then I took out the receipts. They were from four different stores. The electronic equipment I'd seen in the truck. All had the same date on them, a few days before Frankie's dad was killed.

"You're killing me here, Raymond. Whatcha got?"

I put the receipts back, folded the envelope in half, and stuck it under my left leg. After taking a sip from my cup, I said, "Credit cards, all issued to a Felix Villejo. The guy used them at four different stores. Why not just use them all in the same place?"

Edgar put on his serious face—complete with squinty eyes and furrowed brow—as he contemplated the question. He was loving this and was going to make it last as long as he could. I was about to repeat the question when he said, "And what's all that stuff doing in a van rented by a dead guy?"

"There is that," I agreed. "Rivas holding for Villejo? No, Rivas was getting ready to move himself and his kids down to Florida."

"So . . . let's say Villejo buys the stuff and sells it to Rivas."

"Maybe," I said, "but why go to four different places and pay with four different cards? And if Frankie's dad was walking around with the kind of cash Frankie said, why'd he need someone else's credit cards to help him out?"

Edgar bit his lower lip while he made little circles with his stirrer for ten seconds. "They weren't his cards, and either Villejo or Rivas was afraid of maxing them out. It's a bit less obvious to spread the purchases out over a few stores and not run up too much on any one card."

"Edgar," I said, "your next four beers are on me. That's pretty good."

After a little beaming, he added, "That still leaves the question as to why Rivas has—had—the stuff with him."

"It's possible," I said, "that Rivas bought the stuff off Villejo because Villejo needed the cash. If he were afraid of maxing out the cards, it'd make sense he was low on money."

"I guess," Edgar said, sounding a bit disappointed.

"What's the matter?" I asked.

"Ahh. Just hoping for a more exciting alternative, I guess."

I took a final sip of coffee. "Edgar," I said, "I just committed a felony. That's excitement enough for me." I walked over to the trash can and deposited my cup. "I'm going home."

"You going to work tomorrow?"

"I'll see how I feel in the morning." I was reluctant to admit how jazzed up the events of the evening had left me. I doubted I'd be going to work tomorrow.

"See ya at The LineUp then?"

"You bet," I said, giving him a slap on the back. "I owe you four beers."

Chapter 22

AN ANGRY GARBAGE TRUCK HAD interrupted a dream where I was locked in a dark room, my sister and Frankie screaming and banging on the other side of the door. According to the church clock, it was five minutes after six, and now I was drinking coffee and watching the sun rise over Brooklyn. Maybe it was the way the hazy, orange sky was slowly changing to yellow that made me think of the first—and only—time my dad took me fishing.

I was seven years old, thrilled to be riding in the backseat of my Uncle Ray's convertible Caddy with the top down, driving toward Robert Moses State Park while it was still dark. My dad and my uncle were in the front seats drinking coffee out of extra-large to-go cups, while I drank orange juice from a pint container. We got to my uncle's boat just as the sun was coming up. Within minutes I was decked out in a bright red life preserver, and we were pulling away from the dock. Just the guys. After a breakfast of hard-boiled eggs and doughnuts, it was time, Uncle Ray said, "to get our dicks wet." I loved it when he spoke that way in front of me, but I was careful not to let my dad see how much.

We baited the hooks and got our lines in the water. My dad and uncle sat back in the comfortable chairs while I sat on the side, checking for any bites. After about a half hour of nothing, I started to get bored. I said something to my dad and uncle, who proceeded to lecture me on the virtues of patience as they sipped from their whiskey-laced coffees.

"Look over the side," Uncle Ray said. "See what's going on down there."

I finished my doughnut, brushed the powder off my life jacket, and leaned over the side of the boat. "I can't see anything," I said.

"Keep looking," my uncle said. "Patience."

I did as I was told, leaning a bit more over the side when I felt a hand on my back. The next thing I knew I was in the water looking up at the two men I admired most: my uncle laughing his ass off, and my dad, also laughing, but not quite as hard as his brother.

"Lesson to be learned, Nephew," Uncle Ray said as my father helped me up the ladder. "Patience is a beautiful thing. But always watch your back."

I thought back to last night and considered myself lucky. Breaking into the van was a stupid chance to take, but I did learn Frankie's dad really had been planning on moving to Florida, and he'd been using someone else's credit cards to help him get there. Another question answered, another question posed.

Sometimes, Uncle Ray taught me later in life, you don't know enough to know what questions to ask. I wanted to know more.

After calling school and informing them I was still too shaken up to work, I showered and put on my suit. A call to Information told me Around the Horn Travel was located a block from the Williamsburg Bridge and would be open for business at nine. I had another cup of coffee and a bagel while wasting another hour flipping through the channels. Time to go.

I popped a piece of gum in my mouth outside the office. I had decided not to call ahead, so John Roberts wouldn't be expecting me, and I didn't need bad breath adding to the list of my offenses. The hazy sky and humid breeze coming off the river got me thinking maybe today would be the day it finally rained. I was glad I'd thought to bring my umbrella. As I chewed away the coffee taste, I watched the traffic come off the Willy B and negotiate its way around the construction that was still in progress on this side of the bridge.

I straightened my tie and entered the travel agency. It was about twenty degrees cooler inside, and there was a slight flowery fragrance. The smell of someplace one might wish to go to on vacation. The agency was one long room with four desks, two on each side, and lots of posters of places far away from Williamsburg, Brooklyn. Only two of the desks were occupied, both by women: one middle-aged, white, and talking on a head-set phone; the other one young, black, and seemingly free at the moment. She took off her headset, stepped out from behind her desk, and walked toward me, her white skirt floating around her.

"Now, you," she said, with a smile and a hint of the Caribbean in her voice, "look like a gentleman in need of a vacation."

"You read minds," I said, taking her well-manicured hand.

"And faces," she said. "Come, sit and tell Caroline all about it."

"Actually, Caroline," I said, very aware of her smooth, dark fingers and orange nails, "I'm here on a different kind of business. I was hoping to speak with your boss."

"John," she said, taking her time slipping her hand out of mine. "Mr. Roberts will not be in until later this morning. Was he expecting you?"

"Only if he shares your gift of mind reading. I'm here about his nephew . . . his wife's cousin. Frankie."

"Oh. Have you found him?"

"No," I said. "No, we ha—he's still missing. I wanted to talk to Mr. Roberts about Frankie's father, Francisco, Senior."

"He's dead," Caroline blurted out. "But I guess you know that."

"Of course."

"I read in the paper they got his sister back."

"Yes, she's staying with her grandmother for the time being."

"Thank Jesus for small blessings," she said. "I'm sorry, I didn't get your name."

"Raymond."

"Well, Detective Raymond, I can tell you a thing or two about Francisco." Just as she finished the offer, I heard the door open behind me, and Caroline's eyebrows shot up. "Oh," she said, her hands smoothing out her skirt, "you're in luck. Mr. Roberts is early."

I turned to see a man who already seemed to be in the middle of a very bad day. John Roberts's hair was slicked back by sweat, the same sweat that was soaking the upper part of his light gray dress shirt. He had given up on the tie and jacket, and held them in the same hand that carried his briefcase. He was shorter and heavier than I had expected and about ten years older than his wife. To his credit, when he noticed me talking with Caroline, he put on his game face, grinned, and said, "Next time I'm gonna skip the bridge all together and jet-ski on over. I'd get here earlier and drier." He put down his briefcase. "Morning, girls."

"Good morning, Mr. Roberts," the two women said.

He stepped toward me and stuck out his hand. "John Roberts."

"This is Detective Raymond," Caroline said, speaking for me while handing her boss a couple of tissues. Then in a whisper, "He's here about Francisco."

"Really?" Roberts said, unable to hide his surprise. He rubbed his eyes. "I thought I'd covered . . . all that with the other detective. Royce, was it?"

"Yes." I released his hand. I should have corrected him about being a detective, but I decided to wait. "I have a few questions and hope you can spare me a moment."

"Shoulda called me on my cell. I had a lot of spare moments over the East River." He picked up his case. "Come on into my office, Detective. I think I can give you a few."

"Thanks." I gave Caroline a smile as I followed Roberts. We passed the white woman, who was talking on her headset. She gave me a brief smile as Roberts opened his office door.

"Come on in," he said. "Excuse the mess. We're in the process of giving me more space back here." I stepped inside. The mess he was talking about was some wallboard, boxes filled with stuff that I guessed used to be on the walls, and a few gallons of paint. The room had no windows, only an air conditioner built into the back wall, which Roberts switched on. To the right of that was another dress shirt hanging in a dry-cleaning bag. The man was prepared. "Gonna knock the walls down and take over some of the main area there."

"Why not expand out?" I said, pointing to the back door.

"It's an alley. Not part of my lease."

I nodded. "How long had Mr. Rivas worked for you?"

Roberts put his briefcase on his desk. "On and off, five years. He wasn't a regular employee." He took the clean shirt off its hook and tore open the plastic bag. "I used him for odd jobs, some maintenance, some travel I didn't want to do."

"Where'd this travel take him?"

"Caribbean mostly, sometimes Florida."

"He ever mention anything about *moving* down to Florida?"

"Not to me." Surprised. "Why?"

"How about a Felix Villejo?" I tried. "Does that name mean anything to you?"

"No," Roberts said. "Should it?"

I shook my head. I could tell by the look on his face, he had no idea what I was talking about. "Something someone said," I explained. "Nothing important."

"No offense, Detective, but if it's not important . . ."

"You know, Mr. Roberts," I said. "I never actually said I was a detective."

Roberts draped the shirt over his chair. "Excuse me? You told Caroline—"

"I told her I had some questions about Rivas. She assumed the rest."

"And you didn't correct—" A small smirk crossed his face. "You pulled this same shitty routine with my wife." He snapped his fingers. "Raymond. Donne. You're the schoolteacher." I stayed quiet long enough for him to add, "What the hell is wrong with you?"

I paused. "I'm trying to find Frankie, Mr. Roberts."

"Oh, please. That's the same line of crap you fed my wife. Impersonating a police officer is what you're doing. Trespassing, too." He reached into his desk, pulled out a business card, and picked up his phone. "Why don't I call Detective Royce and see what he has to say."

"I'd rather you didn't."

He laughed. "Damn right, you'd rather I didn't. How dare you harass my family like this and treat us as . . . Jesus . . . treat us like suspects." He slammed the phone down. "You're not even a goddamned cop, and you're treating us like we're hiding something. Coming to my home, into my business." He pointed his finger at me. "Something's wrong with you."

"I'm trying to find Frankie," I repeated. "I thought if I learned a bit about his father, it might help me figure out where he went."

"His father," Roberts said, "was a sinking ship. The only reason I gave him work was because no one else would, and he was . . . family. My wife felt sorry for his kids, so I threw him some work now and then and held my breath he didn't screw it up. And look what happened."

"Are you saying his death *was* related to the work you gave him?"

"See?" he said, sticking his finger in my face now. "You're— Get the fuck out of my . . . business, or I swear to God I'll call Royce and have you locked up."

"Thanks for your time, Mr. Roberts," I said.

"Go back to your real job, Mr. Donne."

I left his office and headed right out the front door to the street. The temperature seemed to have gone up ten degrees. I took off my jacket and thought about all the shit I had waiting for me back at school. Maybe I could swing by, say I felt better, get a half day in. Damn it. More time wasted.

"Now you really look like you need a vacation."

I spun around as Caroline took one last drag from a cigarette, dropped it to the sidewalk, and stepped on it with an expensive-looking shoe.

"Was John able to answer your questions, Detective Raymond?"

"I'm not a detective, Caroline. I'm a schoolteacher."

"Ahh," she said. "I knew you were too cute to be a police officer. But, excuse me for asking, what are you doing here asking questions about Francisco?"

"I'm Frankie's teacher." As if that explained everything. "I don't know, to be honest. I'm just trying to . . ."

"You're just trying to help," she finished for me. "That is good of you."

"Yeah, but I think I just ran out of helpful ideas."

Caroline walked over to me and took my hand. "Perhaps," she said, "I can give you some ideas, Mr. Raymond."

"Donne," I said. "Raymond Donne."

She rubbed her orange-tipped thumb over mine. "Are you getting any good ideas?"

"One or two."

"Good. I work late tonight, but tomorrow would be a very good time for you to ask me to dinner, so I accept."

"What time should I ask you for?"

"Seven would be nice," she said. "Meet me at Shorty's." She took her hand back and pointed down Broadway. "It's under the tracks. I'm sure you'll find it."

"I know it."

"Good. I have to get back to work now, Raymond."

"I'll see you tomorrow," I said.

"Yes. You will." She turned back to the travel agency. As she opened the door, she glanced over her shoulder to make sure I was still watching. She smiled and waved good-bye with a wiggle from those wonderful fingers.

Chapter 23

THE COMBINATION OF AIR-CONDITIONING, unlimited iced cof-
fee, and a page of box scores kept me in the diner longer than I had wanted.
The thought of having free time when I really wanted to be out doing
something for Frankie would have driven me crazy if not for this game I
play when reading the box scores: I try to find which pitcher had the best
game the previous night based on innings pitched, base runners allowed,
and earned runs. I do the same with hitters by checking the in-game
batting average, on-base percentage, and runs batted in. Unfortunately, both
showed up on the team that played the Yankees last night, blowing them
out by six runs. By the time the waitress dropped the check in front of me,
it was early afternoon.

With baseball heavily on my mind, I remembered what day it was and
that Frankie had told me this was a practice day for his traveling team over
at McCarren Park. The practices ran from three thirty until six. Maybe the
coach could spare me a few minutes. He knew Frankie as well as anyone.
It was worth a shot, even if it was a long one.

I got to McCarren Park a little before three thirty. Students from
Automotive High School were crossing Bedford Avenue to the park side,
paying little mind to the buses or cars that shared the road. Some of the
kids cut through the park. Others went left or right, depending on which
subway they were taking home.

I walked over to the ball field as a stocky Hispanic man dressed in
shorts and a sweatshirt dumped the equipment bag he was carrying at home
plate. I heard the disappointing sound of aluminum hitting aluminum.

Metal and baseball don't mix. The man pulled out a bat and a few balls. A boy about Frankie's age dragged a red cooler over to the fence, then ran out to the shortstop position. He did some deep knee bends and a few stretches. After a minute or so, the man standing at home plate yelled, "You ready?"

"Yeah," the shortstop said, raising his glove above his head and then touching it flat to the ground. "Go."

The coach's name was Herrera, and the boy was his son, Rafael. Frankie had told me he didn't like the kid much because of the conceited way he carried himself. It seemed like every coach wanted his son at shortstop, and every coach's kid thought he belonged there.

Herrera tossed a ball into the air and proceeded to smack hard grounders at his kid at the rate of about one every fifteen seconds. Rafael would scoop each one up just as smooth as someone serving ice cream and then toss the ball toward the backstop. One of the grounders hit a rock or something on its way to the kid and he picked it off his hip and waved his glove in the air. Maybe he did belong there.

"I don't need no show," the man yelled. "Jus' get the ball back in, Rafi."

"Having a little fun, Dad," the shortstop said. "Coach."

"Save the fun for some other time. This is baseball. Move in another five feet."

Rafael did as he was told, and his dad smashed a one-hopper that the kid took off the shoulder. He grimaced, but made no sound that I could hear.

"That's what happens when you show off," Herrera said. "Here's another."

Just as promised, the ball took a bounce about two feet in front of Rafael, and the kid practically hit the ground getting out of the way. He looked at his father, who just picked up another ball and tossed it up in the air, this time catching it.

"Why you move, Big Man? Afraid you take one in that pretty face?"

I could hear Rafael's voice crack as he said, "Okay, Coach. I get it. No more. Please."

Herrera looked at his son with disgust and waved him back to the shortstop position. "You think about that next time you put on a show."

"Yes, Coach," Rafael said, looking down and testing the dirt with his toe.

I bought a bottle of water from the vendor behind the backstop and took a seat in the bottom row of the third-base-side bleachers. The coach gave me a five-second appraisal through the fence and went back to hitting balls at his son. The wind picked up a bit, and a small, brown tornado formed behind second base. The kid glanced over at it, and a sharp grounder skipped on past him into centerfield.

"You got one minute to get that ball and the other two you missed back to the plate. And pay attention. You wanna watch dust fly, you can do it from the bench."

As Rafael sprinted after the errant balls, his dad went over to the cooler. He walked with a slight limp. He squatted down like the catcher I figured he used to be and pulled out a can of something. I walked over to him.

He acknowledged me as he rose with an almost inaudible grunt, popped the pull-tab on his soda, and said, "Don't tell me. You're a major league scout slumming it."

"No." I laughed. "But if I were, I'd be pretty impressed with that boy of yours."

"He's gettin' there. Gotta learn to keep his eye on the ball, though."

"People tell me the same thing," I said, looking for a smile. It didn't come, so I stuck out my hand. "Raymond Donne."

He shook it and said, "And . . . ?"

"I'm Frankie Rivas's teacher."

"Oh, yeah. You the guy got him into Our Lady."

"Frankie got himself into Our Lady. I just made sure the right guy saw him."

"Keenan," he said, as if recalling an old wound.

I nodded. "Eddie's been a friend for a few years. Does a good job with that team."

"I'd do a nice job, too, I had that church money backing me up."

"I don't think Our Lady spends a lot of money—"

"They hand out some juicy scholarships, though, huh?" he said, taking a long sip from his drink. We both watched as his son raced toward home plate with the errant balls. "Give 'em out like winning lottery tickets to those white boys in Queens."

"Have you ever played against Our Lady, Mr. Herrera?"

"In tournaments, yeah. Why?"

"Then you know that they're a pretty mixed team."

"Mostly white, though."

I reminded myself I had not come here to get into an argument. Rafael came over and handed the balls to his dad. He was breathing heavily but smiling as he looked at me.

"This is Mr. Donne, Rafi."

"Frankie's teacher?" the boy asked.

"Yeah," I said, pleased that Frankie had mentioned me to the team.

"They find him yet? The cops?"

"No," I said. "Not yet. That's sort of why I'm here."

Herrera gave me a look. "I don't get that."

"Did the police talk to you, Mr. Herrera?"

"Over the phone, yeah. Called me at work. Asked if I'd heard from Frankie, when's the last time I seen him. Stuff like that."

"What kind of work do you do?"

"Mechanic." He gestured across the street with his thumb. "Went to Automotive twenty years ago. Played ball for them. Almost won the city one year."

I nodded like I was impressed. "Were you able to tell the police anything helpful?"

He thought about that for a few seconds. "Helpful? Like what? I found an address on a piece of paper? Frankie once told me if he's ever missing, call this secret number? Who the fu— Why are you asking me all these questions? You're a teacher."

"I'm trying to find something the cops may've overlooked. If I can bring them something they missed, it might jump-start them a bit."

He shook his head.

"Go run a few laps, Rafi. Before the others get here."

Rafael was about to object, but the look on his dad's face told him he'd better not.

"Yes, Coach," he said and ran off.

"You," Herrera said after his son was out of earshot, "are one nosy son of a bitch."

"I'm just trying—"

"To stick your nose all into Frankie's life."

"To help find him."

"Ahh, I see. You a teacher during the day . . ."—he wiggled his fingers—"and a superhero at night."

This guy was making it real easy not to like him. The kind of guy who got into arguments for sport. Watching the way he related to his son, I could tell he spent his days and nights not getting along with people.

I tried again. "Coach . . ."

"You can call me *Mister* Herrera," he said. "Only my players call me Coach."

"Mr. Herrera," I said, "if there's anything you might have thought of since you spoke to the police, the detective on the case needs to hear it."

Herrera grinned and pointed his finger at me. "I got you figured now," he said. "You're the guy makes himself feel good by doing things for other people. That's why you got Frankie into Our Lady. Helping the less fortunate and going home to Long Island or Jersey and telling yourself you did good."

"I wish I had the time," I said, "to tell you how wrong you are about so much of the crap that just came out of your mouth. You don't want to help me—help Frankie—that's your choice. Just understand what you're doing."

"I understand that because of you, I'm losing the best pitcher I got—ever—from my team 'cause he's going to that Catholic school."

"That Catholic school," I said, "is the best chance Frankie's got to get a good education. It's probably his ticket to college."

"Fuck college," Herrera said. "And fuck you."

"Nice. You teaching your kid to talk like that?"

He raised his finger again. "Keep Rafael out of it, Mr. Donne."

"Absolutely. The world needs another angry kid from Brooklyn. Good work."

He took a step toward me and said, "Get the hell out of here."

When he was close enough, I reached over the fence and grabbed him by his sweatshirt. "You think you got me figured out?" I said. "Let me give *you* a try. Your knee? You blew it out playing ball. I'm guessing some rich, white kid from a Catholic school crashed into you at home plate. And when the knee went, so did your chances of making it to the next level. Now you find yourself fixing other people's cars and coaching a team of other people's sons so that maybe, one day, you find an arm like Frankie's and you can relive those glory days of when you had the world by the balls." I leaned into his face. "In the meantime, don't kid yourself. You're nothing but a bitter, selfish loser who treats his son like shit."

Herrera's eyes welled up with anger. I looked over to home plate, where Rafael was taking a break from his laps. I let Herrera go.

"You're lucky," he said, brushing off the front of his shirt and checking to see if his son had caught what just happened. He hadn't. "That this fence is here."

"This fence has nothing to do with it," I said. "Your son is the only reason I'm not kicking your sorry ass around the bases."

I turned away and picked up my umbrella. I had gone a few labored steps when I heard him laugh behind me.

"You don't walk so good either, teacher."

"No," I said. "But at least I'm not angry at the whole world because of it."

I kept on walking, my heart beating too fast and my knees throbbing. Yeah. I *was* angry. Angry at my body for constantly reminding me of my limitations. Angry at the feeling of taking two steps back for every two forward. And angry for letting this asshole get to me. With nowhere else to go and not feeling like sitting at home alone, again, I headed off in the other direction.

Chapter 24

"SO WHY DIDN'T YOU HIT HIM?"

"Because his kid was there," I said. "Because he was trying to get me mad and he succeeded, and I don't like being played like that."

Edgar and I were eating dinner at The LineUp. I needed some comfort food and drink. Where else was I supposed to go? The cheeseburger and fries were exactly what I wanted at the moment, but the beer wasn't going down too good.

"I'da slugged him," Edgar said.

"Yeah, well, it would've made me feel better for about five seconds, then I'm left with a bruised hand and the knowledge that I let some knucklehead push my buttons."

"You're probably right," he said. "You gonna hang around and watch the game?"

I tried another sip of beer. It still wasn't working. The mood I was in, if I was going to drink it was going to be for real, and I didn't want to go there. "No," I said, taking a twenty out of my pocket. "I think I may just cut my losses and call it a night."

"Me, too. Besides, I gotta go by and hit the ATM at my bank. I'll swing you home after."

"Yeah, why not."

"Let me go take a quick leak," he said, "and I'll meet you outside."

"You got it," I said.

Mikey came over and began to clear our places. "You and Edgar got a date tonight? Dinner and a romantic drive?"

I put my hand to my ear like I didn't hear him. "What's that? You say you don't want the tip I was going to leave you?"

"Nothing," Mikey said. "You two have a good time."

.

Edgar took a bunch of side streets, and in about five minutes we were parked outside his bank by the Williamsburg Bridge. I looked at my watch: almost eight o'clock. Edgar jumped out of the car and was back in two minutes. "Ready?" he asked.

"Yeah," I said. "I'm starting to drift off here."

"Let's roll."

Edgar took a different way home, and before I knew it we were in front of Roberts's travel agency. The neon sign had been shut off for the night. A white van was parked in front. There must be thousands of white vans in Brooklyn, but this one was parked in front of a place that was connected to Rivas. Curiosity got the best of me, and I asked Edgar to pull over in front of a pile of stacked construction cones less than a block away from Roberts's.

"Why?" he asked. "What's up?"

"Nothing. I thought I saw someone I know." I undid my seat belt and turned around to get a better look at the travel agency. "Give it a minute, okay?"

"Take your time, partner. I got all night."

Partner. Right. "I don't think it'll come to that."

And as if on cue, the front door opened and out walked two men: one short, the other large. Holy shit. Ape and Suit. Suit was holding a briefcase and wearing a light gray jacket with matching pants. Ape had on a sweat-suit the same color. I watched as Ape got into the driver's side of the van and Suit opened the back door. The back license plate was missing.

"Turn the car around, Edgar," I said.

"What? You see your friends?"

"Something like that."

Edgar did a U-turn, pulled over along the chain-link fence that was supposed to keep intruders out of the construction area, and asked, "What now?"

"Switch seats with me," I said. "I'm going to drive for a while."

"You know how?"

"Yeah, I know how. Come on. Move."

Edgar got out and walked around the car while I slid over to the driver's seat. Down the block, Suit was closing the back door and heading to the passenger side. Edgar was about to say something as he sat down, but I put my hand on his arm. "Don't get too excited here, but see that van parked in front of the travel agency?"

"Yeah."

"As soon as it pulls away, we're going to follow it."

Edgar got a look on his face like someone had just told him Christmas was coming twice this year. "You're not fucking with me, are you, Ray?"

I pointed out the front window. "They're moving, Edgar," I said. "Buckle up."

"What's going on here, Raymond?" he asked as he put on his seat belt.

"I'll tell you on the way. Right now, I just need you to be quiet. Please."

"Okay, okay," he said, trying to sound serious, but not able to get the twelve-year-old kid out of his voice. "This is so cool."

"We'll see how cool it is later."

I pulled away from the fence and followed the van as it made a left turn onto Union Avenue and then stopped at the red light. I made sure to stop a car-length behind and to the right, just in case Ape decided to look in his rearview mirror. Then again, it might give Suit a better view of me if he decided to look behind him. It was dark out, but with the streetlights on . . .

"You got a hat I could borrow, Edgar?"

He opened up his glove compartment and pulled out a faded Mets cap. "You mind wearing this?" he asked.

I pulled it down low on my head and checked myself out in the rear-view mirror. In this light, I didn't think they'd be able to see my face.

The light turned green, and the van drove on for two blocks and then made a right. After three more blocks, it made another right, and then another, and pulled into a spot just before the next corner. I drove by and found an empty spot just past the intersection. I adjusted my side view and watched as Ape and Suit, the briefcase in his hand, got out of the van and headed across the street to one of the newer apartment buildings on the block. If I remembered correctly, it was one of those senior citizen residences the city had built a few years back after condemning and knocking down a bunch of abandoned buildings.

"Edgar," I said, "do me a favor and get me the address of that building."

"You got it." He again reached into his glove compartment and this time came out with a notepad and pencil. "Anything else?" he asked. "You want me to copy the names and apartment numbers off the buzzers?"

"Just the number of the building. See if you can make out the front license plate on the van, too. And stay on this side of the street, understand?"

"Yeah, I understand," he said. "Hey, Billy ever get back to you on that plate?"

"It was a no go," I said. "If you see those two guys come out, just keep walking and go around the block. I'll meet you at the corner. You got that?"

"Got it." He got out of the car and stuck his head back in through the window. "I tell you how cool this is?"

"Go, before I change my mind."

He did. I watched in the rearview mirror as he made his way down the block in that kind of forced casual walk you do when trying too hard not to be noticed. He was probably whistling nonchalantly. I checked out the front of the building. Nobody was coming or going at the moment, so Edgar should be back in less than a minute if he didn't stop to tie his shoe. I started counting, and before I reached forty, he had returned.

"I got it," he said, showing me the number on his notepad. "No front plate, though. What are we going to do next?"

"We are going to wait," I said, as I ripped out the page from his pad and slipped it into my pants pocket, "and see what they do next."

"So we have some time for you to tell me who those guys are, right?"

"Yeah, but first, let me move this thing." I started the car up again and shifted it into reverse. A spot was open on the near side of the cross street, and I wanted to be in position to follow the van in case it made the right turn instead of going straight. I backed out slowly and did a reverse U-turn into the spot I wanted. I couldn't see the van anymore, but since they were parked on a one-way street, they had only one way to go: past me.

"You did that rather nicely, Ray."

"I did go through the academy, Edgar. Driving's part of the training."

"Sorry," he said. "So those guys . . ."

"Those guys," I began, "kidnapped me the other day."

"No shit? Kidnapped! For real?"

"They forced me into the van and took me for a ride. By definition, that's kidnapping. They threatened me—threatened my sister—if I didn't give them any new information about Frankie from the cops, or that I find out on my own by the next time they catch up with me. Not that the cops are telling me anything. I told my Uncle Ray, and he told the lead investigator on Frankie's case."

Edgar looked at me silently and when he realized I was done, he said, "Holy shit. Shouldn't we call the cops?" Again, he reached into his glove compartment. This time he came out with a phone. "I mean, let's get those guys. You want me to dial nine-one-one?"

"And tell them what, exactly?"

"That we spotted the van that— Hey, that's not the same white van I saw last week is it?"

"I think so, yeah."

"Hey!" Edgar said, pointing out the window. "There they go."

I shifted the car into drive and followed as the van took a right at the corner. Less than two minutes later, two more rights and a left, they pulled over again. Instead of passing them, I stopped the car a half block behind, double-parked, and shut off the headlights. Ape and Suit got out and crossed the street. Suit had the briefcase again. They entered another apartment building, this one taller and older than the last. They didn't have to buzz to get into either building. They had keys. I remembered that Roberts owned some apartment buildings in Brooklyn. This was getting interesting.

"You want me to get the number of that building, too?" Edgar asked, clutching his notepad and reaching for the door handle.

"We'll get it when we pass it," I said. "Relax."

"Okay, okay," he said. "It's just that this is—"

"I know. It's so cool." I took a deep breath and added, "The hardest part of doing a stakeout is waiting, Edgar. If you really want to get good at this"—and I knew he wanted exactly that—"you have to learn patience. You do not *make* things happen, you react when they do."

He wrote that down. "If you've planned it right and you've got people to relieve you, you take some water, a couple of apples, and maybe some mixed nuts. If you're by yourself or don't know when your backup's coming, you want an empty bottle in the backseat. Just in case."

"Got it."

"Good," I said. "Now, get ready, 'cause we're moving again. Get that building number."

Ape and Suit were getting into their van. We followed them as they took a straight shot almost back to Union Avenue. We drove by as they pulled over. I stopped at the next corner and watched as Suit got out with his case and crossed the street. Ape remained in the van.

"They changed their pattern, Ray."

"I see that, Edgar. I'm going to circle back. I want the address of that building."

"Why'd they change up like that?"

"Playing it safe, probably. Making sure nobody's doing what we're doing."

I drove around the block, and as we passed the apartment building, I read the number off to Edgar. "Now what?" he asked.

"Now," I said, driving past the van, "we go back to the travel agency and wait."

"You think they're going back there?"

"That's what I want to find out. They're collecting something. If they do go back to Roberts's, then we can assume whatever they're picking up belongs to him."

That, I thought to myself, would tie Ape and Suit even more directly to Roberts and give me enough strong information to bring to Detective Royce, even if I had to explain how I came across the connection. I'm sure he'd be real pleased when I told him that story. It's not like I had intended to tail these guys. I was on my way home, saw the van pulling away from Roberts's, and what was I supposed to do? I'll just tell him the truth and let him handle it.

I pulled over alongside the construction fence and looked at the travel agency.

Edgar asked, "How long do we wait?"

"As long as it takes," I said. "You got plans?"

"No, no. I'm good."

"Hungry, thirsty, gotta pee?"

"Nope."

"Excellent."

"What exactly are we going to do if they do come back here?" he asked.

"I'll call Royce first thing in the morning and hope he gets suffi-
ciently motivated to drop by and rattle Roberts's cage. I would have loved
to have pushed him more this morning, but we both knew he was well
within his rights to bring charges against me."

"How come he didn't, do you think?"

"I thought he didn't want the extra hassle. Now I'm thinking he's
happy keeping the cops out of his life as much as he can. I'd like to start
making his life a little more uncomfortable."

"You've done a lot already, Ray."

"Not enough, Edgar. It's not going to be enough until Frankie gets
home."

"Hey," Edgar said, motioning with his head out the windshield,
"speaking of coming home . . ."

The van was pulling up in front of Roberts's. Suit and Ape got out,
and Ape went to the security gate, bent over, and unlocked it. As he lifted
the gate up, Suit came around with the briefcase and punched some numbers into the alarm pad located to the right of the front door. When he
was done, Ape unlocked that, and the two men stepped inside the travel
agency.

"There we have it," said Edgar. "You think that's enough for the detective?"

"Should be," I said. "Let's give it a little more time though, okay?"

"I was hoping you'd say that."

Edgar unbuckled his seat belt and opened his door.

"Where are you going?" I asked.

"Got something in the back that might come in handy. Okay if I get
it?"

I thought about it and said, "Yeah, fine. Just be quick about it."

Less than a minute later, he returned holding a small black case. He
placed it on his lap, opened it, and pulled out a pair of binoculars that
looked like they'd just come out of the factory.

"Got these last week," he explained. He put the binoculars up to his
eyes and adjusted the lenses. "Freaking beautiful," he said. "You really do
get what you pay for in surveillance equipment, Ray. These are special
night-vision glasses, and they rock. Here, take a look."

I took the binoculars and peered through them. They gave the evening a light green tint and were as good as Edgar had said. So good, even

from this distance and in this low light, I could make out the numbers on the alarm pad. Which gave me an idea.

"Edgar," I said, "if this place has a back entrance, what are the chances it would have the same alarm code as the front?"

"Better than excellent. Who wants to bother with two codes? Especially if you don't use the back door all that much. Why?"

"Just thinking out loud."

Before Edgar could respond, the front door reopened and out stepped Ape and Suit. Suit no longer had the black bag with him. He turned to reset the alarm, and I focused the binoculars on the pad. "Write this down, Edgar." I watched Suit's hand. "Five, six, four . . ." Ape stepped in front of Suit as he finished pressing the buttons. "Shit," I said. "Five, six, four, what? Dammit."

Suit went over to the van as Ape pulled down the security gate and relocked it. They hadn't been in there for more than two minutes, which meant they had probably just dropped off the bag. Ape got in the van, and they pulled away.

"We gonna follow them, Ray?"

"No," I said.

"Why not?"

"Because I want to know what's in that briefcase."

"Won't the cops do that?"

"That case'll be gone as soon as Roberts knows Royce is coming over. That is, *if* Royce comes over. Even if it were still there, Royce would need a warrant to take a look at it, and he's not going to get one because he only has my word to go on, and that's thin to begin with."

"So how are you . . . ?" It came to him before he could finish his question, and he gave me that big smile he's got. "You're thinking about going in there and getting the case, aren't you?"

"Shut up a second, Edgar. I'm thinking about it." I paused for a few seconds and then said, "Can't do anything unless we know the last number of that code."

"Gotta be something zero through nine," Edgar said, thinking out loud.

"Thanks. What happens if you press the wrong number?"

"Most systems give you a second chance. Like your ATM card. They're programmed to allow one mistake. They figure anyone can touch the wrong button. You make a second one—and *ding ding*—the alarm's activated."

"So a one-out-of-five chance of getting it right."

"And four-out-of-five of not."

"Fuck," I said.

I took the time to run the first three numbers through my head. Five, six, four. Too few numbers to spot a pattern. Maybe it was an important date, but that wasn't going to help. I knew next to nothing about Roberts and his family. I looked over at Roberts's place again. AROUND THE HORN TRAVEL AGENCY. I had seen no posters inside the other day that would make me think they booked trips like that. And in this location, it didn't add up. So why name your place after a destination most of your clients couldn't find on a map?

"Edgar," I said to hear my thoughts out loud. "What do you think of when you think of that name? If you just saw the words, without knowing it was a travel agency?"

He made a face as if someone had just suggested sucking on a lemon. "I don't know, Ray. I guess I'd . . . maybe . . ."

"Baseball," I said. " 'Around the horn.' Third, second, first."

Edgar—whom I'd seen fill out hundreds of scorecards while watching baseball on TV at the bar—smiled. "A five-four-three double play. Throw in the shortstop and . . ."

"Five, six, four, *three*."

"Pretty clever."

"If we're right."

"Well," he said quietly, "there's only one way to find out."

"I know." I thought about the two places I'd already entered illegally this week. "Fuck it," I said. "Let's find out."

"I was hoping you'd say that," Edgar said and, once again, slipped out the side door.

Chapter 25

THE UPPER HALF OF EDGAR'S BODY disappeared inside the trunk of his car. When he reemerged, he was holding a beaten-up brown leather case. "Let's see what we have in here," he said, closing the trunk and putting the case on top.

I had moved the car a few more blocks away from the travel agency, into an area with a little less light and traffic. After the decision to break in, I realized we needed more privacy to work out the details, possibly even reconsider the whole thing. The first thing Edgar pulled out of his case was about the size and shape of a deck of cards. "Clip this onto your belt."

I fingered the box, found the clip, and did as he said. "What's this do?" I asked.

Ignoring me, he began unrolling a black cord, which was wrapped around a headset. He handed me the jack and, with about three feet of cord between us, said, "Plug that into your end." When I did, he stepped over and slipped the headset over my ears.

"Dammit, Edgar. That's digging into my scalp."

He gave me a look like that was my fault, removed the headset, and readjusted it. "Here," he said, "*you* put it on."

I did, carefully this time, and it felt better. "That's good."

"Now lower the mike." He waited while I did that. "How's that feel?"

"Like I'm working the drive-through window at Burger King."

Edgar has little sense of humor when it comes to his techie stuff. He reached under his shirt and removed the cell phone from his waist. He punched in some numbers. Five seconds later there was a ringing in my ears.

"Push the button on the side of the receiver." When he realized I had no idea what he meant, he said, "The receiver. On your belt. There's a button on the side."

I reached down, found the button, and pressed. The ringing stopped. "Okay."

"Come here, Watson," Edgar said. "I need you."

"Neat," I said.

"Two thousand dollars' worth of technology, and all you can say is 'neat'?"

This from a guy who thinks breaking and entering is "cool."

"You're right, Edgar. This is pretty impressive stuff."

"Thank you," he said, giving me a slight bow. "You can get cheaper shit these days, but most of that's line-of-sight crap or stuff for parents who don't wanna lose sight of their rugrats. This"—he tapped the box on my belt—"goes through all sorts of building materials, and it'll give you a range of two miles most of the time and won't drop out like a cell phone."

I removed the headset. "Just as long as it goes—what?—a quarter mile?"

"Not a problem." He reached into his bag of tricks and came out with the flashlight I had used last night in Rivas's rented truck. "I put new batteries in," he said. "It's good to go. You remember how to work it?"

"It's a flashlight." I took it from him and put it in the front pocket of my pants.

"How you planning on getting that back door opened?" Edgar asked.

I smiled, reached into my other front pocket, and pulled out the lock pick that Deadbolt had given me. "You got any WD-40 or something to make this work a bit easier?"

"I think I can oblige you there." He went back to his trunk, practically skipping. Here I was, about to commit my second felony break-in in two nights, and Edgar was acting like he'd just won the science fair. When he returned, he was holding a small can with a three-inch tube coming out of the top. "Stick this end into the lock, or just spray it on the pick, and it'll slide in and out quicker than a twelfth grader's dick on prom night."

We spent the next ten minutes going over what was starting to sound like a plan. It had one central theme: the simpler, the quicker, the better. I would head over to the alley behind Roberts's. Edgar would pull up to the alley and drive past slowly, making sure I got inside.

"If we're wrong about that code," I said, "I wanna get out as quickly as we can."

"Agreed. You think those two are gonna come back?"

"I doubt it," I said. "They pulled the security gate down." I thought for a bit and added, "I want you to keep the car moving once I'm in. Keep an eye out for the van. Any vehicle or foot traffic, you let me know."

"Agreed."

"That includes the cops."

"Obviously."

"Also," I added, "I'm going to need you to keep track of the time for me. I wanna be in and out of there in five minutes. If Roberts has some sort of secondary alarm system, I don't wanna find out the hard way."

"Gotcha," Edgar said. "You wanna synchronize watches?"

"Just let me know when two minutes have gone by. Then we'll go minute by minute." I tapped the box attached to my belt. "This thing is charged up?"

"Fully."

"Good," I said. "Dial me up."

He did, I pressed the button, and Edgar said, "You ready?"

"Yeah." The situation played around inside my head for a few seconds, and I was flooded with the events of the past week. Frankie was still missing, even though I'd just seen him and lost him on the bridge. The cops were nowhere finding whoever killed his father, and I'd been stalked, threatened, and tossed around. I'd had to get my sister out of town, and I was frustrated, exhausted, and more than a little pissed off. Was I ready to break into somebody's business in order to . . . what? Prove I could still play with the big boys? Save Frankie?

"Yeah," I said again. "I'm ready."

"Then let's do it," Edgar said, slapping me on the back. "Let me know when you're in position at the back door. I'll be circling around if you need me."

"Thanks. Why don't you go around first? Make sure things look okay."

"You got it. See ya on the other side."

Right.

A minute later, I was in the small alley behind the agency. No cars had passed, and there was nobody walking around. The smell of urine and garbage greeted me as I made my way to the back exit. I took the lock pick and spray out of my pocket. Sweat was starting to run down my back. I took a deep breath and realized how hard my heart was beating. I leaned against the wall and closed my eyes. Shit, I could almost hear it, ready to come out of my chest. Still time, I thought. I could call this whole thing off, face the scornful disappointment of Edgar, but be back home within fifteen minutes. The alley filled with light from a passing car, and I flattened myself against the wall. Just my luck. Getting caught behind a place of business with a flashlight, a can of WD-40, and a lock pick. When the alley went dark again, I let out the breath I was holding and whispered, "Was that you, Edgar?"

"Was what me?"

"Never mind."

I closed my eyes and pictured how I wanted this to happen. Spray the pick, slip it into the lock, turn, and open the door. Step inside, punch in the four numbers on the keypad, and shut the door when the alarm was deactivated. Use my mini-flashlight to find what Ape and Suit had dropped off, reset the alarm, and slip back outside and into Edgar's car. Sounded good to me. It'd be all over so quick. Like I didn't do a thing.

I held the lock pick about two feet away from my face and sprayed it. I returned the lubricant to my pants pocket, turned on the flashlight, placed it in my mouth, and aimed it at the lock. Then I slipped the pick into the lock and turned both the pick and the door's latch at the same time.

Technically, that was the "breaking" part. Now all I had to do was push open the door and go inside to complete the "entering." I wondered whether anyone in the history of criminal justice had ever gotten popped just breaking and whether or not it mattered. I forced the thought out of my head, took one more deep breath, and pushed open the door.

I heard a beeping, went over to the keypad, and pressed five, six, four, three. The beeping stopped, and I allowed myself to breathe again. I shut the door, and I was in.

On the other side.

"I'm in," I mumbled.

"Starting the clock," Edgar replied.

I took the flashlight out of my mouth and went over to Roberts's desk. I rolled the chair back and sat down, as much to get my breathing under control as to get at the drawers. All of which were locked. The thought of going at them with the pick crossed my mind, but I wanted to cause as little damage as possible and decided to save that for later, if I had the time. The top of the desk was about as minimalist as could be. A phone, a legal pad attached to a clipboard, and a pencil holder containing one sharpened pencil and three pens.

There was a safe to my right, next to three moving boxes stacked on top of one another and marked "Office." If Ape and Suit had put their night's work in the safe, that was the end of that. Breaking and entering, anyone could do. Safecracking was for the pros. I swept the walls with my light. Nothing much beyond travel posters and an empty bulletin board. I stood and walked over to the file cabinet. It was small, about chest-high, with four drawers that opened easily but held nothing more than empty hanging folders and a huge plastic jar of beer pretzels.

"Two minutes, Ray."

Shit. It felt like thirty seconds. "Thanks, Edgar. I think I'm almost done."

"You find anything?"

"Not yet. Let me know when I hit the four-minute mark."

"Copy that."

I leaned against the file cabinet and placed my arm on top. My heart and breathing rates were still faster than normal, but I was getting over the initial anxiety of my crime. I thought about making a run through the front area. Another clue would be nice. Make this B and E worth the time and effort. Maybe I should just take the pretzels and go. As I removed my arm from the top of the file cabinet, my hand brushed across the top, which felt uneven. I shone the flashlight on it and, sure enough, the top of the cabinet was dented in. I redirected the light to the ceiling and saw old fireproof tiles, two-by-twos, probably made of asbestos. The one directly above the file cabinet looked slightly out of place.

I rolled the desk chair over and carefully got myself into a sitting position on top of the cabinet. It wasn't easy or painless, but I was able to get myself onto my knees and stretch up enough to touch the tile. I pushed up gently, raised the tile, and was able to turn it enough so it could be removed. I was high enough to stick my arm in where the tile had been and reach around. After a few seconds, I hit something solid. I spun it around until I found a handle and removed a briefcase. I lowered myself into a less painful sitting position, my legs dangling over the side, with the case resting on my lap.

"That's four minutes, Ray."

"Copy," I said.

I placed my thumbs on the left and right latches of the briefcase and pushed. The case snapped open. Of course it did. It's not like Ape and Suit were expecting anyone to open it before Roberts in the morning. I popped the lid and found some cash, a few envelopes, and a small spiral notebook. I flipped open the notebook and leafed through a few pages. I recognized a few of the addresses Ape and Suit had visited earlier, and other numbers I'd try to figure out later.

"Ray?"

"Coming, Edgar." I closed the case and replaced the tile. I slid off the file cabinet and pushed the chair back to the desk.

"Patrol car just swung by."

Shit. Maybe Roberts did have a secondary alarm. "They make you?"

"I don't think so."

"Good. Just count to twenty and come a—"

"Shit. They pulled a huey. Coming back."

Damn it. "Just relax, Edgar." I went over and reset the alarm.

"Nothing, officer." Edgar talking to the cops. "Engine seized up on me coming off the bridge. Wanted to let it rest before getting back on the BQE."

I went out the back door into the alley, shutting the door to Roberts's behind me. Not knowing which side of the building Edgar and the cops were on, I crouched down against the wall, making myself as invisible as possible.

"Thanks for checking," Edgar said. "It'll be fine." Pause. "You, too."

I waited about thirty seconds. "Edgar?"

"They're gone, Ray. What's your twenty?"

"Meet me on the corner across from where we parked. Drive around the block once, though, okay?"

"That's a copy."

Two minutes later I got in Edgar's car, and he pulled away slowly.

"That was exciting," he said.

"Nice job, Edgar."

He looked at the case on my lap and said, "What's that?"

"Something that's going to piss off a few people when they find out it's not there in the morning, I hope." I placed my hands on top of the case and said, "Let's go home."

"Copy that," my partner said.

Chapter 26

"YO, MR D! WE HEARD YOU WAS DEAD."

I waited until he walked past me and into the classroom before I answered.

"Greatly exaggerated rumors, Eric."

"The lunch ladies said you were in the hospital," Annie said, genuine concern on her face. "Said you got stabbed."

"Nah," Eric said. "They said you got mugged."

I spread my arms out and did a three-sixty.

"Do I look like I got stabbed? Or mugged?"

The two kids took their time assessing me. Angel, Julio, and Dougie strolled in, looking like they weren't quite sure they'd ever see me again either. After a while, Annie said, "No."

"But you don't look too good, though," added Eric. "Maybe you should go back home for another week or something."

"I'm going to look even worse," I said as I stepped over to my desk and opened my attendance book, "if you have to see me during summer school."

"Ooooh," the others chimed in, daring Eric to risk a comeback.

Eric gave that some thought, managed a big grin. "That's a good one, Mr. D." After a pause, he added, "You kidding, right?"

"Of course. You know I don't teach summer school, E."

"Ahhhh."

"Okay, guys and girls! Let's get going. It's been . . . a few days." It seemed more like a few weeks. I came in early to get myself up to speed, and I had to open all the windows because the room smelled . . . I don't know . . . closed off. Stale and unused. The teachers who had covered my classes had taken my kids elsewhere. "We have a lot of catching up to do." I waited until the moans and mumbling wore down and added, "I am fine, and yes, I missed you all, too. Math books. Page two-forty-five."

I walked around the room for the next thirty minutes, checking the work. Half of them were getting it—the usual ones—and the other half weren't. If we didn't review this stuff over and over, work it, and practice it again and again, it didn't stick all that long. Like rehabbing your knees. I looked at my watch. We'd have to come back to this later. I hated doing math with them twice in the same day, but I didn't see another option.

"Okay," I said. "You've got gym next, then library. Anybody gives Ms. Walsh a hard time, I'll hear about it." I looked at Angel, and he knew why. "After lunch, we'll get back on that ferry with Mr. Whitman." The bell rang. I pointed to the door. "You may go!" And they did.

"Just tell me what you're looking at."

"That's why I'm calling you," I said, flipping through the pages. "I don't know."

I was on the phone in the copy room with Rich, the one ex-boyfriend of Rachel's I could actually stand. Rich was an investigator for the district attorney's office in Manhattan and the first person I thought to call after going over the papers I had taken from the travel agency. "Well," Rich said, "where'd you get them?"

"I can't tell you that."

"Or who you got them from, I guess."

"No."

"Glad you called, Ray."

"Can I fax them to you?"

"You got a fax?"

"My boss does."

"Yeah." He gave me his fax number. "And this is school-related?"

"A class project."

"Can I point out what a pain in the ass this is turning into?"

"Absolutely. While you're drinking all the beers I am going to buy you if you make any kind of sense out of this stuff."

"That, my friend, is a deal. Maybe you can invite Rachel. What time is your day over?"

"Three o'clock."

"Nice schedule, Ray. No wonder you guys need the whole summer off." He paused for a few seconds. "Call me at three thirty and I'll tell ya what I can tell ya."

"Thanks, Rich."

"Thank me later, Ray."

"See?" I asked. "Whitman's asking how much time has passed—'how long is the distance'—between when he's writing these words and you're reading them."

"Not long enough," Eric mumbled.

I ignored him.

"What's he talking about?" Angel wanted to know. " 'Brooklyn of ample hills'? Ain't no ample hills around here. This guy smoking something when he wrote this?"

After the laughter died down, I spoke. "Back in the day," I said, "you could look south or southwest from the ferry as you were crossing the East River to Manhattan and see the hills of Brooklyn clearly. Before all the buildings went up and the highways and bridges were built, you had a clear view of Brooklyn Heights."

"That's why they called 'em 'Heights,' genius," Eric said.

"Yeah," Angel said. "Like you knew that before Mr. D said something."

"What about the next part?" I asked before they could go on.

"He talking about taking a bath in the river?"

"Swimming. You could do that back then. Before all the factories and ships and polluters came along, people swam in the East River. And the Hudson."

"Damn," Dougie said. "I've seen some kids jump off the old piers by the bridge and come up gagging."

"And those white boys with their wave runners? They run you over and not look back."

"Yeah," I said. "I wouldn't recommend doing that these days, but back then, they didn't have public pools—or wave runners—they had the river."

"My uncle eats the fish he catches outta there," Angel said.

"Your uncle's a Porta Rican," Eric said. "He'd eat anything that's free."

Angel let that sit for a bit and said, "Tell your moms not to give it away no more then."

"All right!" I yelled. "I don't think Walt would appreciate this kind of discussion. I know your mothers wouldn't, so quit it."

The room grew silent and stayed that way until Annie raised her hand.

"Yes, Annie," I said. "Please."

"That part right before that," she said. "Where he says, 'others who look back on me because I look'd forward to them'?"

"Yes?"

"First time I read that, I thought that he was talking about the people on the boat with him, but . . . he's talking about us, ain't he?" She had the whole class's attention now and seemed a bit embarrassed. "Like he's writing to us and . . . we're reading him, so in a way, we're looking back at him. Right?"

"You," I said, "just made my day, Annie." I turned to Angel and Eric. "When you stop messing around and pay attention, you can pick up on stuff like that. Mr. Whitman hoped that, one day, people would be reading his words. He was sending them a message: I looked at the same sun reflecting off the same water as you and had the same worries, the same thoughts."

"So that ferry he was on," Dougie said, sitting up straighter now, "they been running for all these years?"

"No. In fact, the bridges—the Brooklyn and the Williamsburg—put the ferries out of business for a while. People could walk to Manhattan, take the train or a horse and carriage."

"My grandfather . . ." Angel said and then looked at Eric, waiting for a smart comment. When none came, he went on. "He said his dad and them used to call the Willy B 'The Jew Bridge' back in the day."

"Yeah," I said. "Not so politically correct, but the Williamsburg Bridge was the biggest reason the Jews from the Lower East Side crossed the river to live in Brooklyn. They could live here and work in Manhattan."

"You mean, without the bridge we wouldn't have all these Hasseedics around?"

"Taking up all our housing?" Angel added, trying to sound political.

"Remember, before the Jews it was the Germans, and the Irish, and the Italians. Most of your folks"—I looked out at the eight nonwhite faces looking back at me—"came after they did. Every immigrant group has its stories to tell. Some of them are happy, some unhappy. Life's like that." The bell rang, ending that thought and reminding me how quickly a period can go by.

"All right. Tonight, finish reading the poem and jot down at least five words from it you don't know. You know what the math work is. Both should take a total of less than an hour, so no excuses. Get your stuff together and . . ."—they waited for it—"you may go."

"So what are they?"

"Plain old Social Security numbers, my friend." Rich had been at his desk when I got him on the phone just after three thirty. "You got some DOBs, and they match with the SSNs, and this ain't no class project, Ray. What is this?"

I hate lying to friends, but Rich worked for the DA, and I didn't want him involved in anything that might cause him grief at work.

"One of my kids," I began my lie, "said he found the papers on his way to school. He thought it looked like it might be something, and he knows I used to be a cop, so he gave it to me. I thought I'd have a little fun and play detective for him. But . . ."

"Yeah," Rich said. "A big but. Either your kid is lying to you or you're lying to me, and I don't wanna know which. I have access to this kind of info, and I doubt a junior high kid could pull it off, but it's not a great leap to having someone's Social and their DOB, getting their name and residence, and causing some trouble."

"What kind of trouble?"

"Hypothetically?"

"Absolutely."

"I guess you could mess with their benefits. Find out when their checks come in. I mean, according to the DOBs, these are seniors we're talking about. The SSNs are also their Medicare numbers. Instead of using the three-two-four combo, they use a five-four setup. Bottom line, it's information you don't want other people having, you know what I mean?"

"You're right," I said. "I'll tell the kid to forget it. That I lost the papers."

"That's a good idea, Ray. In fact, it's such a good idea, I wish you'd have come up with it before you faxed this shit to me. Now, what about those beers?"

"I'll call you."

"I'll try to find something to keep myself busy until you do. You talk to Rache yet?"

I got back to my apartment just after four and had enough time before my date with Caroline to take a shower, turn up the AC, and try to doze off in front of the repeat of last night's Yankee game. They still lost, and I was still awake. I checked my answering machine. Two messages. Rachel had called from L.A. and said the trip wasn't as bad as she thought it would be, but she'd still prefer to be back home. Of course, I could make it up to her if I just cut out my immature bullshit and show up at our dad's memorial service next week.

"We'll have dinner when I'm allowed to come home," she said, "and we'll talk more about it then."

The second call was from my mother, who had also heard from my sister, and how was Rachel ever going to find a man when she spent all this time gallivanting—my mother actually used the word—around the country?

"Anyway," my mom concluded, "call me when you get the chance. I'm thinking of heading down to Florida after your father's service and could use some help with the train arrangements." My mother hated flying about as much as she hated my sister being single, and don't get her started on grandkids. "Nice to hear you had a visit with Uncle Ray. Call me."

I erased both messages and thought about changing the outgoing message to one that invited only those who did not want to talk about my father's goddamned memorial service to leave a message.

The notebook I had taken from Roberts's last night sat on my coffee table. I leafed through the pages. Initials and numbers. I wanted to see if I could connect the names with the buildings Ape and Suit visited last night, but I didn't have much time before my date. I found Edgar's phone number and got his voice mail. I read off the addresses of the buildings and asked him if he could find out who owned them or managed them or both.

I added that if he couldn't do it, I didn't know who could. After hanging up, I took the notebook and put it inside my school bag.

I checked my closet for something appropriate to wear for a first date. All my clothes—of which I did not have a lot—seemed suddenly very boring. I opted for my only clean pair of jeans and a red, long-sleeved shirt, untucked, sleeves rolled up.

Styling, Mr. D.

Chapter 27

SHORTY'S BAR AND GRILL WAS located on a corner not far from Roberts's travel agency. The wave of urban renewal that had swept through this section of Williamsburg had stopped a few blocks shy of this place. Small businesses stood vacant, and some of the buildings had plywood where the windows should have been. Men in suits and women in dresses walked by quickly on their way to the subway and on to homes in other, better parts of the city. A few were probably on their way to the Long Island Rail Road and back into suburbia.

On the front door of Shorty's was a sign advertising LIVE JAZZ on Friday and Saturday. A gust of cool air greeted me as I entered and made my way to the bar. It was dark inside; the kind of lighting that took a minute for the eyes to adjust to and didn't exactly invite newcomers. The aroma of hamburgers cooking hung in the air. I remembered skipping lunch that afternoon, grabbed the stool nearest the door, and hoped Caroline would show up soon.

A trio of black men was seated at the other end of the bar under a TV set. They all glanced my way, considered me for a few seconds, and then went back to their conversation. I pulled a twenty out of my pocket, placed it in front of me, and cleared my throat. Again, the group looked at me. One of them rose and took his time walking around the bar and then down to my end. He was about my age, thirty pounds too heavy, with a short Afro and a goatee that was mostly gray. He picked up a rag and wiped down the area in front of me.

"Can I do for ya?" he asked without really meaning it.

"What do you have on tap?"

He turned to his friends, smiled, and made a big show of looking all around and even under the bar. "Don't seem to have a tap, sir."

"Well, then," I said with a smile of my own, "what do you have in a bottle?"

"Don't have no tap," he said again, "guess everything we got's in a bottle."

That brought a round of laughter from his buddies. I chuckled along with them and looked at the selection behind the bar. A hand-written sign by the clock said all domestic beers were three dollars from four to seven. I had two minutes left. "I'll just take a Bud Light."

He nodded and said, "Bud Light. For the Man."

He spun around, headed back to his pals, and resumed his conversation. I guessed "the Man" was just going to have to wait for his beer. I busied myself by perusing the selection of top-shelf liquor, recalling the ones I'd had the pleasure of tasting and ranking them in order. After about five minutes, the bartender remembered my beer and brought it over to me.

"That'll be four dollars."

I looked up at the sign. "Don't I have a few more minutes of happy hour left?"

He looked at the clock, took my money, and shook his head. "Happy hour's over." He went over to the cash register, broke the twenty, and returned with my change. "Enjoy."

I raised my bottle. "Thanks."

After a few minutes, the door behind me opened. The men at the other end looked up and waved. The bartender walked over with a lot more energy than when I arrived. "Caroline!"

Caroline slipped into the seat next to me as the bartender placed a napkin in front of her and leaned over for a kiss.

"Willy," she said, placing her hand on my arm. She was wearing a tight-fitting flowered shirt that showed off her well-tended midriff and a pair of equally tight white pants. The come-away-with-me look that I was sure only a handful of travel agents could pull off. "I hope you've made my friend Raymond feel at home."

"Whyn't you tell me you was a friend of Caroline's?" He offered his hand.

"I didn't want any special treatment," I said. "You know, being 'the Man' and all."

He smiled at that. "Caroline?"

"The usual, Willy." He went to get her drink. Caroline asked, "What was that about?"

"Just getting to know the regulars. I guess you come here often, huh?"

"Willy's my cousin. Shorty was my uncle. Hope you didn't feel uncomfortable waiting."

"Not the first time I've been the minority." I adjusted myself in the stool to better face her and get the full effect. "Excuse me for saying so, but you smell wonderful."

She gave me a practiced giggle. "I prepped before locking up the shop. Not every day a girl gets to have dinner and drinks with a respectable schoolteacher. You are respectable?"

Before I could answer, Willy returned with Caroline's drink. "Whiskey sour for the lady." He put a dollar bill in front of me. "Forgot that last drink was on happy hour."

"No harm," I said. "Put Caroline's on mine, would you?"

"Caroline don't pay for drinks here." He leaned in close. "Sorry about that before. Thought you mighta been a cop."

"What makes you think I'm not?"

He straightened up. Then, seeing the look on my face, he broke into a huge grin and tapped the bar with his finger, and then pointed it at me. "That's a good one. Got yourself a funny friend here, Caroline." Willy shook his head. "'What makes you think I'm not?' That's good. Anything else I can get you two, you let me know."

"Those burgers smell good," I said.

Caroline nodded. "Willy may not be the best—or friendliest—bartender in the city, but he does make a good cheeseburger."

Willy slapped the bar. "You two grab a table, and I'll bring a couple of platters out."

Caroline led me to a booth along the wall. There were two framed pictures hanging on the paneling, both of black men playing the trumpet. Caroline tapped the one closest to me.

"He played here," she said. "In the early sixties. Said my uncle made the best ribs he'd ever had." She saw the look on my face. "You have no idea who that is, do you?"

I shook my head. "Not unless he played for the Yankees."

"Sonny Rollins?"

"If you say so. I never quite got into jazz to be honest."

"Jazz is not something you 'get into,' Mr. Donne." She ran a red fingernail along the frame. "Jazz is something that gets into you. Into your essence. Slowly . . . and over a long, long time."

A warm sensation hit the center of my chest. "You make it sound . . . very Zen-like."

"Damn. I was trying to make it sound like sex."

I took a long sip of my Bud. "That, too."

She laughed, and after a while Cousin Willy came over with two plates filled with sweet potato fries, pickles, and the biggest cheeseburgers I'd ever seen.

"You two can get started on these," he said. "I'll be over in a bit with a coupla more drinks for ya." Before he left, he gave me a wink and a big slap on the shoulder. Buddies.

Between bites, she spoke more about jazz, and I filled her in on some of the finer points of baseball. After half an hour, I'd finished my second beer and barely half of the burger. I pushed my plate away and leaned back.

"Don't worry," Caroline said. "Willy'd be disappointed if you actually finished the whole thing."

"He may have spoiled breakfast for me tomorrow."

"He'll be happy to hear that." She reached into her bag and took out a pack of cigarettes. She slid one out and passed it under her nose. "So that poor boy is still missing?"

"Going on two weeks now." I got Willy's attention behind the bar and stuck two fingers in the air. "How well did you know the father? Francisco Senior."

"Too well." She took a final sip of her sour and whirled the ice cubes around. "Man didn't walk so much as he slithered, know what I mean?" She gave me a fake shudder. "Man made my skin crawl every time he came into the office."

"Which was how often?"

"Too often. Except near the end . . . near the time he was killed."

Willy came by with our drinks. As he was clearing the table, he asked, "Anything else?"

"Just two more of these in a bit," Caroline said. Then to me, "That okay with you?"

I nodded, detecting the beginning effects of alcohol on her. "Absolutely. Thanks, Willy."

After he left, Caroline said, "I've been wanting to ask you something. How come—you being a schoolteacher and all—you're so interested in Mr. Francisco Rivas?"

"I'm more interested in getting Frankie home," I said. "Knowing more about the father might help me do that."

"Shouldn't the cops be doing that?"

"Cops got a lot on their plate. Besides, how high on their list of priorities do you think a dead sleazeball and his missing son rate?"

She smiled. "You gotta point there."

"And you were so eager to talk to me about him because . . . ?"

"Like you said, I figured somebody's gotta be lookin' out for that kid. I'm impressed that you're taking the time to do that." She picked the cherry out of her whiskey sour and placed it up to her lips. "Anything else you care to impress me with?"

"Maybe later," I said, as the cherry disappeared into her mouth. "What exactly did Rivas do for Roberts?"

"Mostly just building maintenance. Upkeep. Even did that sleazy."

"How do you mean?"

"One time," she said, "the boiler at one of Mr. Roberts's apartment buildings goes out. He sends Rivas over to see what he can do to fix it. Rivas comes back saying it's more than he can handle. Mr. Roberts gives him a few hundred dollars to give to the regular repairman. Next day, Rivas says it's done. That's it."

"That wasn't it?"

"A week later, the thing blows again. Did a lot of smoke damage to the lower units. Mr. Roberts called up the repairman to chew him out. Turns out the guy was never called to the job. Mr. Roberts finds out that Rivas had his own guy, some loser friend, come in and patch up the old one while Rivas pockets the money. That's what I mean by sleazy. If there was a dollar in a bucket of cow shit, you'd find Rivas's hand in it." She put her fingers over her mouth in an exaggerated motion. "Excuse my language."

"Don't let it happen again."

She touched my hand. "You'll have to excuse me. I need to powder my nose."

She slid out of the booth and made her way to the back, past the small stage. She looked back to make sure I was watching. Just like the first time we'd met. The bar was now filled, and most of the patrons were watching the Mets game. They were up by two in the sixth. Caroline returned, nose freshly powdered.

"Did I tell you that the office was broken into last night?"

I gave her a shocked look. "No. What happened?"

"Came in through the back door. Picked the lock."

"They get anything of value?"

She smirked. "Like what? Blank tickets? Any cash comes through that place is out before five. Everything else is done over the phone. Credit cards."

"Why would anyone bother to break in then?"

"Probably just some kids screwin' around." She took a sip from her drink. "To see John—Mr. Roberts—though, you'd think it was the end of the world."

I nodded. "That's understandable. His place of business was violated. People react strongly in that kind of situation. What did the cops say?"

"He didn't call them." She leaned into me, still smelling like a vacation. "I can see why Willy thought you were a cop. You talk like one."

Our faces were inches apart. "Teachers, cops. I guess we all kind of sound the same."

"I guess so," she said. "Feel like movin' on?"

I looked at my watch. "It is getting late."

She took my wrist in her long fingers. "I didn't say the evening was over."

"No," I said. "No, you didn't. Let me take care of the bill."

"Just leave some money on the table." She stood up and smoothed her hands over her pants. "Willy'll figure it out."

I did a quick calculation in my head, took a last sip of beer, and left two twenties under the empty bottle. Caroline grabbed my hand and led me to the door. She waved over to the bar. Willy waved back. "See ya," he shouted to us as we exited.

Outside, the air was sticky and warm. After sitting for so long, my knees took a while to warm up. I don't think Caroline noticed. There was little traffic on the street as she took both my hands in hers and asked, "Now what, Mr. Donne?"

"Are you going to call me Mr. Donne all night?"

She pulled me close and whispered in my ear. "I just might. And how long do you think all night might be?"

"I don't know," I said. "It is a school night."

She released my left hand and readjusted her bag over her shoulder. "Wanna see if we can find us some music around here?"

"That sounds good."

"Good? Boy, you don't know the half of it." She reached into her bag and pulled out her lighter. She rummaged through it for a few more seconds, and instead of pulling out her pack of cigarettes, she said, "Shit."

"What?"

"I left my wallet at the office." She closed her eyes. "Middle drawer." She squeezed my hand. "I'm sorry. We have to swing by the agency."

I held out my arm. "Let's go."

It took less than five minutes to stroll to the office, and arm-in-arm with a sweet-smelling, beautiful woman was the way to do it. Caroline got out her keys, and the two of us lifted the gate. Once inside, she punched in the alarm code and locked the door. She didn't bother turning any lights on as she carefully made her way over to her desk. After opening the middle drawer, she spun around to face me, waving her wallet.

"Ready when you are," I said.

"You know, Mr. Donne. We do have this whole place to ourselves."

I looked around. "And a very romantic place it is at that."

"Oh, come on." She took a few steps toward me. "We could have just as much fun here as we could listening to music." When she reached me, she put her arms around my waist and pulled me into her. "You ever do it on an office desk before?"

"No."

"This could really be your night, then." She leaned forward and kissed me. I could taste the burger, whiskey sour, and cigarettes as she slid her tongue into my mouth. She ran her fingers up and down my back before she pulled away. "You kiss pretty good for a white guy."

"I'd like to think I kiss pretty good for any color."

She laughed and kissed me again, this time taking her hands around to my front and looping her thumbs on my belt. "Pick a desk," she whispered.

"Excuse me?"

"Any desk." She pushed me back. "How about Marsha's?"

"You don't think she'd mind?" I asked, my butt resting up against what I assumed to be Marsha's desk.

Caroline smiled as she slowly unbuckled my belt. "She would totally come undone." I could feel my belt slipping through the loops of my pants. I took Caroline's face in my hands and kissed her again. She dropped my belt and I moaned as her fingers worked to get the top button of my pants undone. When she'd succeeded, she slowly pulled down the zipper.

"Shit," she said.

"What? Is it stuck?"

"Not that." She pulled the zipper up quickly and stepped back. "That." She pointed toward Roberts's office.

I looked over and saw what she meant. There was a light coming from under the door. We were not alone.

Caroline put her finger to her lips. "Shhh." She took a step toward the office and turned to me. "I was the last one out of here tonight. He must have come back."

I gestured at the front door. "Let's go."

She took another step. "I don't hear anything. What's he doing in there so late?"

I shrugged. "Let's just get out of here, okay?" I had the feeling if Roberts saw me one more time, he might just call Detective Royce, and I did not need that kind of trouble.

Caroline waved her hand at me, went over to the office door, and placed her ear against it. After a few seconds, she put her hand on the doorknob and turned it. She was halfway through the door when she screamed.

I ran over to her as she stumbled back out of the office. She grabbed me hard and started to breathe heavy through tears. I took her by the shoulders and said, "What?"

She motioned with her head to the office. "Oh, my god."

I loosened my grip on her and opened the door the rest of the way with my foot. There was Roberts. Slumped over his computer, looking like he'd fallen asleep while working late.

Except for all the blood.

Chapter 28

"JUST THAT ONE TIME," I SAID for the third time in the past half hour. "Yesterday. Here at his office."

Roberts had been taken away by an ambulance almost an hour before. He was still alive, but from what I overheard from the EMS crew, he'd be lucky to make it to the hospital. I was being interviewed by a detective, Lund or Lind, I didn't quite get his name, as he seemed rather annoyed at working at this late hour and had a bad habit of slurring his words. He had his jacket hanging over the driver's side door as we stood outside Roberts's in the late-night humidity. The sweat stains under his arms were threatening to reach his belt. He was a tall man. Tall and fat. The kind of fat you get from sitting on your ass eight hours a day for ten or more years. The kind that makes it difficult to see your shoes.

"And you were here, why?" he mumbled.

"Then?" I asked. "Or tonight?"

He looked down at his notebook. "Tell me both. Again."

I reminded myself to keep my tone respectful. "I was here the other day to ask about his nephew. A student of mine. Tonight, because Ms. Pierre left her wallet behind."

Still looking at his notebook, flipping through the pages, he said, "You're a teacher, is that right?"

"Yes. Can I see Ms. Pierre now?" It was pushing ten, and I hadn't seen Caroline for almost thirty minutes. She was inside being interviewed by this guy's partner.

"Soon as Detective Vincent's done with her." He gave me a look, more guy-to-guy than professional. "You planning on taking her home tonight?"

"Just as soon as the other detective's through. She's had a rough night."

"Right." He flipped to a new page. "How long you known Miss Pierre?"

"Less than a week," I said, because it sounded better than "two days."

"Whaddaya think?"

"I don't understand your question."

"You think she coulda taken a swing at her boss's head?" He locked his eyes on me in an attempt to come across astute.

"No," I said. "She was with me all night. I told you that."

"She was here until seven. Coulda done the deed, locked up, had dinner and drinks with you, and brought you back so you could both discover the body." He made that quotation mark gesture with his fingers to highlight the word "discover."

"Not possible. She was perfectly calm when I saw her."

He smiled. "C'mon, Mr. Donne. Looker like that? Ice water in their veins. And the black ones?" He got close enough to my face where I could smell the coffee on his breath. "How'd you think she got the keys to this place? You ask me, Mr. Roberts is the victim of Jungle Fever."

"You're an asshole." Maybe I was too tired, too frustrated, or just too pissed off, but the words came right out, and I didn't care. I waited a few seconds for his reaction.

He leaned away from me. Instead of shock or anger, he gave me a grin that bordered on delight. "Maybe so," he said, pointing his pencil at me. "But I think I'm right." He flipped his notebook shut and turned to go back inside the travel agency. "Stay here. Please."

After a few minutes, I placed my hands on top of his car and started to stretch. I was beginning to feel the effects of the evening from my neck down to my hip. I was about to reach for my toes when I heard a voice behind me.

"Sorry about the wait, Mr. Donne." I looked up to see the other detective exiting the building. This one looked as if he spent much of his free time in the gym. He offered his hand. His grip was impressive without being intimidating. "Detective Vincent," he said.

"Your partner's an asshole," I returned.

"And a racist. He's also grossly overweight, smokes way too much, and has breath that'd make a camel cry. He'll probably be dead in less than two years, and he's not my partner. Still, I'd appreciate it if you didn't talk about him like that."

I put my hands up. "Sorry. It's been a long night."

"For all of us." He took a look at his notes. "Raymond Donne. Is that right?" I nodded. "I had an instructor at the academy with that exact name."

"I have an uncle who sometimes instructs at the academy with that exact name."

Detective Vincent smiled. If he was surprised or impressed, he didn't let it show. "Sorry if Lynn gave you a hard time. He doesn't know any better."

"How'd you get stuck with him?"

"I'm the guy with the shiniest new shield, so I get the honor of riding with the big man. Paying my dues. I know it's a pain in the ass, but would you mind going over what you already told Detective Lynn? I'd like to hear it from you."

It took less than three minutes to once again recap the night's activities. Vincent listened carefully, didn't interrupt once, and never wrote one word down in his notebook. When I was finished, he repeated the key details for me to verify. "So neither you nor Ms. Pierre saw Mr. Roberts this evening, is that right?"

"Yes. Caroline—Ms. Pierre—said she closed up the agency just around seven and came right to the restaurant."

"Shorty's? Willy bust your chops?"

I smiled. "Tried to."

"Best burgers this part of Brooklyn. You understand I'll have to check on your story?"

"Sure. Can I take Ms. Pierre home now?"

"Just let me make sure Detective Lynn is through questioning her."

Must be tough for this guy, working with someone you know is an idiot and yet having to go through the motions of respect. I admired the ease with which he did it. A minute later, Caroline came out of the agency, followed closely by the two detectives.

"We've called the wife," Vincent told me. "Gonna take her a while to get someone to watch her kid and get down here. Lives upstate, you know."

"What's the word on Roberts?"

"Made it to the OR. See what happens after that."

Detective Lynn stepped forward. "Thanks for all your help, Mr. Donne." All respectful now. I guessed he'd had a brief chat with his partner regarding my uncle. "Hope we didn't cause you too much inconvenience."

I shook my head and took Caroline by the hand. "Not at all. We can leave now?"

"Yes." Vincent stepped forward and gave me his card. "If you think of anything . . ."

"Absolutely," I said. "You going to tell us not to leave town?"

He laughed. So did Lynn, after a second or two. "Wouldn't think of it. Thanks again."

The two of them went back inside and a couple of uniforms stayed in front of the building. Caroline took my hand and led me up the street. When we were a block away, she turned and wrapped her arms around me. She began to shake and cry and held on to me for a minute. When she was done, she stepped away.

"I'm sorry," she whispered. "I was holding that in and didn't want to do it in front of those detectives."

"I understand," I said, and she gave me a look that told me I really didn't. "You want me to take you home?"

She shook her head. "Just walk me to the car service."

"Sure."

As we continued up the street, she told me that the detectives had taken Roberts's keys and would lock up. When Roberts's wife showed up at the hospital, she'd get them back.

"What did you tell them back there?" I asked.

"Not much I could tell them. That one guy—the fat one—kept pushing it. Like I knew something I wasn't saying."

"Did you tell them about Rivas?"

"Yes, I did. You don't think—"

"They will check it out," I said. "Did you mention last night's break-in?"

"I wasn't sure if John—" She stopped. "What the hell is going on?"

"I don't know. Let's hope the cops figure it out before someone else gets hurt."

She shivered at that thought, and I put my arm around her. When we made it to the corner, I put Caroline in a car and gave the driver a twenty. I leaned in through the window and kissed her on the cheek.

"Get some sleep," I said. "I'll check on you tomorrow, okay?"

She nodded. "Thanks."

I went back inside the car service. As I waited for the next available driver, it occurred to me that being associated with Roberts's travel agency was not good for one's health.

Chapter 29

A HALF HOUR AFTER SCHOOL LET out the next day, I was heading down the front stairs of the school when I noticed Detective Royce leaning up against his car, smoking a cigarette. His jacket was off, sleeves rolled up, and his tie loosened an inch or two.

"Detective," I said.

He pointed at me and smirked. "Teacher," he said, and flicked his cigarette into the gutter. "I'm glad we got that straight."

"Excuse me?"

"Don't push it, Mr. Donne." His smirk was gone. "I got a call from the two detectives you spoke to last night."

"Oh."

"You've been at more crime scenes these past ten days than most cops I know."

"Hey, I had no idea that—"

"You just happened to be at Roberts's late at night with one of his employees?"

"That was a date," I said.

We looked at each other for a few awkward seconds before I broke the silence. "I'm getting a beer, Detective. You're welcome to join me."

Royce grabbed me by the elbow. "You're coming close, Donne."

"To what, Detective? Figuring something out before you?"

He threw my elbow back at me. "Fuck you."

"Always good to have an adult conversation after a day with the kids," I said. "Is that it?"

He stared at me and then reached up and squeezed the bridge of his nose. With his hand in front of his face, he said, "Get in the car."

I snorted. "You taking me in?"

"I think I need a beer," he said. "How about you?"

I smiled. "You know how to get to Teddy's?"

"I'm a detective. I'll find it."

Royce finished almost a third of his pint in one gulp. When he opened his eyes he said, "This is brewed in Brooklyn?"

I pointed out the window. "Used to be, you could go outside, walk three blocks north and one block west. Brewed upstate now, I think."

"Brooklyn Pilsner."

"Think globally," I said. "Drink locally."

And we did. In silence, while we both finished our pints and then ordered two more.

"You didn't follow my advice, Mr. Donne."

"I didn't know I had to, Detective Royce."

"I'm just about at my desired level of bullshit for the day," Royce said. "I phrased it as advice out of respect for your uncle. Now I'm going to be a bit more direct. Stay out of the Rivas case and away from anyone who has anything to do with the Rivas case. Is that clear enough?"

"With all due respect, Detective, you can't tell me who I can talk to and where I can go."

"I can when it— Jesus Christ, Donne." He took out a cigarette and placed it between his lips without lighting it. "You're getting in way over your head here. That guy you described to me, the one who took you for a ride the other day? The short one in the suit?"

"Yeah?"

"I ran his description past some guys at the house, and it sounds to them like it may be Jerry Vega. Small-time trying to become big-time."

"Connected to Rivas and Roberts?"

"Don't know. Thing is, Vega's been off the radar for a while now. At one time, he was connected all over. Name came up with some PRs, some Dominicans, even some Nigerians. Just about anyone having anything to do with stolen IDs and bootleg credit cards, shit like that. Nothing big on its own, but for a little man he had his fingers in a lot of pies for a while."

"And now?"

Royce took another long sip. "Been quiet for something like two years. Guys at the Nine-Oh thought maybe he took his show on the road. Florida. Maybe West Coast."

"I wonder how he fits in with Roberts then. Or Frankie's father."

"That's the question I was—" He stopped himself. "That's the problem with good beer. It makes me chatty. We can't be having this conversation, Donne."

"Come on," I said. "Two guys shooting the shit about work over a few pints."

"Yeah, but only one of us is a cop."

"Make you'd feel better if I talked a little algebra? Maybe Walt Whitman?"

Royce didn't smile. He just took the unlit cigarette out of his mouth and rolled it around in his fingers. He leaned back on his stool and took in the atmosphere.

"See those two guys over there drinking longneck Buds?"

Royce nodded.

"Guy on the left writes for *Sesame Street*. The other one's a pastry chef."

"Definitely not a cop bar."

"Well . . ." I spun around and faced the back of the bar, where the bathrooms were. "See the tall, white-haired guy at the juke box?"

"Yeah."

"He's an investigator for the city health department."

"Not a real cop," Royce said.

"We make do with what we got." I took another sip and raised two fingers in the direction of the bartender. "So," I said, "Rivas and Roberts and Vega?"

Royce ignored that and took his time finishing his beer. He glanced up at the stained-glass window and said, "Who the hell was Peter Doelger?" He slid the empty pint glass to the side and brought the new one in. "This is it for me," he said. "I still gotta drive home." Then he looked me square in the eyes. "You miss it bad, don't you?"

I placed a hand on the cold pint in front of me and said, "Miss what?"

"The job," he said. "Police work."

I took a sip and shrugged. "I don't think about it all that much."

"Bullshit." He took his unlit cigarette out of his mouth and placed it on the bar. "I mighta bought that a week and a half ago. Just some dumb-ass schoolteacher who got unlucky enough to stumble across a DB. But now? You're the guy who steps in a pile of shit and just keeps on walking."

I spun my glass around a few times. "I'm just trying to get Frankie home."

"If that's all you wanted, you'd leave it to the cops."

"Who are doing such a damn fine job of it, right?"

"Fuck you, Donne. You think you could—"

"Do better? Yeah, I do. In fact—" The beer was making me run my mouth, too. "Look, I know you've got your hands full, and Rivas is not exactly at the top of your to-do list. I get that. But Frankie should be. He is to me. Frankie needs to be found."

"And you can't leave that to the cops?"

"I want Frankie home, Detective. Where he belongs."

Royce put both hands on his glass. "I know what you're trying to do, Mr. Donne."

"I'm not keeping it a secret."

"That's not what I mean."

"Then, please, tell me what I'm trying to do. Please."

"I know about your accident." He took another sip. "The kid. Raheem Ellis."

"Detective," I said, leaning back and placing both hands on the edge of the bar. "With all due . . . whatever, you don't know shit. And I think our little talk is over." I pushed my stool back to get up, and Royce grabbed my wrist.

"That's why you left," he said. "Not because you couldn't see yourself behind a desk. Because you couldn't see yourself as a cop anymore. Not after what you thought you'd done."

"What I *thought* I'd done?" I got to my feet and leaned into the detective's face. He tightened the grip on my wrist. "I got a kid killed, Royce. Raheem Ellis is dead because of me."

Royce held my stare, but leaned back an inch or two. "You followed a juvenile into an abandoned building. You had no way of knowing about the structural faults, the condition of the fire escape. You were doing your job, Donne. You were being a cop."

"'Structural faults,'" I repeated. I closed my eyes. Royce let go of my wrist and I sat back down. "All that kid—Raheem Ellis—did was call me a pig," I said. "It was the end of a long, hot day. I was going back to the house to change out of my uniform and get really drunk on the way home. And this motherfucker—this *boy*—called me a pig. I kept going and he did it again. 'Yo, pig. Why don't you go back to Long Island and watch your own kind.'" I took a sip of pilsner. "A few hours earlier, I'd removed a four-month-old from a bathtub. Barely five pounds. Took her out of the tub after a neighbor finally called when she *stopped* hearing the baby screaming. I spent the morning canvassing the neighbors, all of whom *knew* something bad was gonna happen one day. Just didn't know which day it was gonna be. And this thirteen-year-old boy called me a pig and told me to go back and police my own kind?"

The look Royce gave me made me feel like a rookie. Again. "You're not the first cop to lose perspective, Donne. The kid got to you. Doesn't make it your fault."

"It was my responsibility," I said. "If I don't chase him, life goes on as usual."

"And if he didn't mouth off—"

"He was a kid!" I shouted. The bartender and a few of the customers looked over. I raised my hand and lowered my voice. "He was a kid. Repeating some shit he'd heard over and over in the projects. He didn't know better. I did. Or should have."

"And now you're trying to balance things out."

"I'm just trying to get Frankie home."

"And if playing cops-and-robbers is part of the game, all the better for you."

We both took sips and pretended to be interested in the other drinkers. After a minute, Royce shook his head and looked at his watch. "So what'd you learn from your date last night?"

"Caroline," I said, hiding a small grin. "Rivas Senior gave her the willies. And Roberts wasn't around all that much."

"Nothing wrong with that. Guy's doing well. Expanding."

"I guess. She didn't seem all that shocked that Rivas got what he got, though. And"—I was being careful now—"did you know Roberts's place was broken into the other night?"

"No."

"Yeah, Caroline said he was obviously all upset, but he never reported it to the cops."

"Curious. You got that from one dinner, huh?"

"I'm a good listener."

"Maybe it would be worth my while to have a face-to-face with Roberts."

"That may have to wait a few days, Detective," I said, trying not to sound too smug.

"Fuck."

"I'm sure Caroline would be happy to talk to you, though. I could put in a good word."

"Thanks," Royce said. "And fuck you. But I'm not going to be able to get a warrant if all she knows is what she told you."

I was glad to hear him talk about warrants. "What if," I said, "some more information happened to find its way to your desk?"

"How would that happen?"

"I'm speaking hypothetically."

"Oh, good. I just love hypothetical shit." He looked at his watch again. "I suppose, if an interested third party—who was not encumbered by the same Constitutional restrictions as I am—were to come across information pertinent to an ongoing investigation, and that information happened to show up on my desk in an unmarked envelope, I'd be obligated to look at it."

I smiled. "You speak hypothetical real good."

"Took it at the academy. Anyways"—he took a sip from his beer and stood up—"I have to head home, play Daddy for a few hours." He raised his glass to mine and said, "Here's to the anonymous tipsters in the world."

"Here's to 'em," I said, clinking his glass with mine.

"Don't be out too late, Mr. Donne. It is a school night."

"Drive carefully, Detective Royce."

"I always do," he said. "Don't wanna get pulled over by them Long Island cops."

As I watched him leave, the bartender came over and said, "You okay?"

"I don't know about that," I said. "But I'm not done drinking yet." I finished what was left in my pint glass and slid it toward him. As I waited for my next one, I thought about Elsa, and Rachel's advice to give her a call. I pulled out my cell phone, looked at it, and remembered I didn't have her number. Just as well. I still hadn't figured out what to say to her, and three beers weren't going to help.

The bartender put my fourth beer in front of me and told me it was on the house. I thanked him and went back to thinking about kids. Missing ones, dead ones, and the ones I'd have to teach in the morning.

Chapter 30

FRIDAY AFTERNOON, THREE THIRTY. The school week was over. The halls were quiet, the kids and most of the teachers gone until Monday. Normally, I'd be out of here myself, on my way over to the Northside, ready to sit down at Teddy's or the Ale House, maybe Mugs if I felt like something from Belgium. Knocking back a few happy-hour pints and making sketchy plans for my well-deserved weekend. That was another time, though. A time before Frankie went missing.

I locked the door to my room and spread out the papers I'd stolen from Roberts the other night. They still didn't make any sense: the same bunch of numbers and letters I assumed to be initials. I opened the notebook and tried to make a connection between the information in there and the information on the papers. I recognized the symbols, but they meant practically nothing.

I heard a knock on my door and looked up to see Elaine Stiles on the other side of the small glass window. I let her in.

"Working late, Raymond? On a Friday?"

"Catching up on some paperwork." It's not a lie if it's true.

"Well, don't stay too late. You look like you need some rest."

"Thanks," I said. "I guess I do."

"Oh," she said. "Mary upstairs gave me these. They were faxed over an hour ago." She handed me a few sheets of paper. "You know someone named Emo?"

I looked at the papers. The cover page read, "ATTENTION RAY-

MOND DONNE!! IMPORTANT!! EMO." Edgar can be described with many adjectives, but subtle is not one of them.

"Yeah. Thanks."

"Does that have anything to do with Frankie?"

"No," I said. "Something personal."

She gave me a look that made it clear she didn't quite believe me, but she didn't push it. "Okay, then. Get some rest, Ray. Really."

"I will, Elaine. Really."

After she had gone, I went back to the table with Edgar's fax. One more piece of the puzzle. Edgar had confirmed not only who resided in the buildings Ape and Suit had visited the other night, but also who owned them. Some company called ATH Holdings, and immediately I thought of Around the Horn—ATH. Roberts owned the buildings. Ape and Suit made pickups from the buildings. Somewhere in front of me was the answer—or answers—I was looking for, and pretty soon those answers would show up on Royce's desk in an unmarked envelope.

Edgar had sent me a separate sheet for each building: addresses and a list of the individual units, broken down by floors. There were either one or two names next to each unit identifying the residents by last name and first initial. It was just a matter of time and patience to match the residents with the initials on the papers from Roberts. I did that successfully for about twenty minutes and realized I wasn't learning anything much beyond who lived in what apartment and most of the residents had Hispanic last names. According to the dates of birth, most of the residents were senior citizens.

I walked around the room a bit, pushing in a few chairs, straightening some desks. I picked up the sheets of names and went back to pacing. I read them in the order Edgar had sent them and then backward. I mentally tried to put them in alphabetical order, which proved to be difficult, as there were over seventy-five names. I even read them out loud by first initial and last name, and that's when my mind clicked.

"M and F Villejo," I said to myself a few times. "Villejo." The name on the credit cards I had found in the truck rented by Rivas. "First name was . . . Felix." F Villejo had to be Felix Villejo, and I had his address right in front of me. Now what? I could give that info to Royce, but then I'd have to explain how I found out about the credit cards and addresses. I didn't want to do that. And it wasn't enough. There was only one viable option I could come up with.

I went to my closet and put on the jacket and tie I kept back there for parent/teacher conferences. I also took off my sneakers and slipped on the black shoes I wore for the same occasions. I found my unused Department of Education ID badge, attached to its chain, and put it around my neck. I grabbed a fresh legal pad, some blank DOE forms, and the papers from the travel agency and clipped them to my clipboard. I took the ones Edgar had faxed over and locked them in the bottom drawer of my file cabinet under empty folders.

I went back to the closet, took a look at myself in the mirror, and straightened my tie. There. I looked like a decently dressed employee of the City of New York, and I was going to make a house call to one Felix Villejo.

The building I was standing in front of had been an empty lot five years ago. Before that, it was a bodega, a cleaners, and a video store that sat below three floors of apartments. The businesses had all failed, and when the apartments fell vacant, the squatters moved in. About four years ago, the city took ownership, "relocated" the squatters, and decided to sell off the land. That's when the fan got dirty and smelly.

One paper had played it up as "New vs. Jew" and others as "Latino Against Black." Everybody felt they had a bigger stake in the community than the next group, and everybody had a sign and a chant to prove their point. The Hassidim were being pushed out, the Latinos kept out, and the Blacks left out. The yuppies? Well, they were already taking over the Northside, so why didn't they just leave the Southside alone? In the end, the city chose to sell the land to a developer for low-income housing. For all. Which really meant for the Latinos and the Blacks, because the Hassidim got another deal on the other side of the bridge and the yuppies don't do low-income housing. Somewhere along the line, this building became senior housing.

The developers had done a nice job. Six stories of light orange brick-face with double-sided windows and white trim. A pair of potted trees by the entrance announced the residents of this building lived with dignity. The buzzer marked "F Villejo" was one of thirty in a patchwork. Five apartments per floor. It took three attempts at the buzzer before a female voice responded.

"Yes?"

"Mrs. Villejo?" I said. "Raymond Donne."

"Yes?" came the response.

"From the City, ma'am."

A five-second pause, then, "—ep over."

"Excuse me?"

"Step over," slower this time, as if she were talking to a kid.

I leaned away from the buzzers and looked at the door. I hadn't noticed it at first, but there was a small video camera about two feet above the entrance behind the heavy-duty glass. I put on my best I-work-for-the-City smile and lifted my ID, careful to keep my fingers over everything except my picture. It was ten seconds before the front door buzzed. I entered the building and walked directly to the elevators on a freshly vacuumed carpet. On the elevator door, there was a sign in English and Spanish reminding the residents of Saturday morning's bus trip to the Fulton Mall. A short time later I was outside the Villejo apartment, being appraised by an elderly female.

"Everything is okay," she said.

Unsure if that were a statement or a question, I said, "That is the reason for my visit, Mrs. Villejo."

She considered me for a while longer, her eyes barely above the chain that connected the door to the wall. I gave the impression I had nothing better to do than wait outside her apartment all afternoon. She eventually let out a deep sigh, the door closed, then reopened. Mrs. Villejo stepped aside, allowing me—the City of New York—into her home.

What a week I've had, I thought. Withholding evidence from the police, impersonating a cop, breaking and entering, stealing. Now I was lying to a little old lady, because I wanted to talk to her husband about his relationship with a dead guy.

The room was sparsely furnished with a recliner, sofa, coffee table, and a small entertainment center in the corner. There were two lamps in the room, but both were off at the moment, as a good amount of sunlight came through a double window. There was one painting on the wall: a landscape of the sun setting over a tropical forest.

"I call and I call," Mrs. Villejo said, her faint accent becoming a little more pronounced. "*Pero*, I get no answer. Just recordings, and then I am asked to press many buttons. After a while, I stop calling."

"I hope I can answer your questions, ma'am." I tucked my ID badge inside my shirt, in case she thought of getting a closer look. "And I have a few for you and your husband, as well."

"Felix?"

I smiled and pretended to look for something on the clipboard by flipping through the papers. "Yes," I said. "Felix."

"*Pero* . . . " she began. ". . . but he is dead." She took a breath. "Two years now. But the checks . . ." She stopped herself, making me think she had said more than she had wanted.

"I'm very sorry." I wrote Felix Villejo's name on the top sheet. "I'll check our records, Mrs. Villejo." I faked a cough. "Can I bother you for a glass of water?"

"*Si,*" she said. "Is no bother."

She went into the kitchen, and I took the opportunity to open what I guessed was the bedroom door and peek inside. There were two beds: a regular one and the kind you'd see in a hospital room. There was also an oxygen tank and motorized wheel chair, with Elijah Cruz's decal on it, tucked away in the corner. The way that Mrs. Villejo had just moved to get my drink, I doubted the chair was for her. I closed the door and stepped back into the living room before she returned with two waters.

"Thank you," I said, as she handed me one. "Your medical equipment. Is everything in proper operational form?"

She took some time decoding my bureaucratic speech. "Yes. Is all working. All proper."

I wrote "Proper" on a piece of paper in the area reserved for Student's Name and said, "The oxygen tank. The wheelchair? The bed?"

"That is why I call," she said. "The bed was for my husband. Two years now, and I no need the bed. Two years. You can take it away?"

I smiled. "I'll make a note of it." And I did.

"Yes. I tell Mr. Jerry, but he say there is nothing he can do."

"Mr. Jerry?" Jerry Vega, the name Royce had mentioned. Suit.

"The man from the building. The landlord's . . . ?"

"Representative," I finished for her. "Of course. Did you contact Medicare directly?"

"*¡Ay Dios!* Those are the ones with the pressing buttons and not calling me back. Mr. Jerry said he take care of. I give him all the mail, and he say he take care of it. Not for me to worry. Every month, the same thing."

"And Mr. Jerry takes care of it?"

"That is what he says, but still the bed . . . is bad luck."

"How often do you see Mr. Jerry?"

"The end of the months. I give him the mail, and sign for him the checks."

"The checks?"

"*Si.* Still with the name of my husband. Two years now. I sign for him and he makes for me the bank deposits."

I nodded and wrote this information down.

"You will speak with Mrs. Brown, too?"

"Mrs. Brown?"

"*Si.* Upstairs. Angela. Five A. She has same things, same problems. And Mrs. Cuevas. Imelda. On the first floor. But her husband . . ."—she rolled her eyes—"*that* one is still alive. We all go on the bus trip together. Every Saturday."

I smiled and wrote those names down and put a question mark next to each.

"I will speak to them," I said.

"Good. Thank you."

I finished off my water and placed it on the coffee table.

"Thank you for your time, Mrs. Villejo. And the water. Will you be taking advantage of the bus trip this Saturday?"

"Ah, *si.* Yes. We shop, we eat, we laugh. Very nice."

"Yes. It sounds like it would be."

"That is the church."

"Excuse me?"

"The bus trips. Shopping, into the city. They take us every week to the doctors. Next week, *Las Mujeres,* we are to go upstate." She breathed in deeply. "For the fresh air."

Las Mujeres? That is Frankie's grandmother's group. From Cruz's church.

"How many of you go on these trips?" I asked, trying to sound casual.

"We all go. We are all of the church. The bus, it even picks us up for

Sunday. Is very nice." She paused for a few seconds and added, "Why does the City not do such things for us?"

"Budget cuts," I said. "Hard to do more with less."

"Ahh." She waved that away. "You seem like a nice man, but the City, they no care like the church."

"No," I agreed, at least sneaking in one truth before ending my visit with Mrs. Villejo. "I guess we don't."

Chapter 31

ANY GUILT OVER MY ACTIONS of the past week and a half—including lying to Senora Villejo—was overshadowed by the feeling that I was finally putting this all together. Rivas, Roberts, and now Cruz—the church. They were all connected. I wasn't all the way there yet, but I figured a lot of the missing pieces were somewhere in all that paper I had locked up back at work. I wasn't sure how much closer I was to getting Frankie home, but I had a hell of an idea what I'd be sending Detective Royce's way real soon.

I stifled the urge to whistle as I unlocked the door to my apartment building and went over to check my mailbox. Empty. As I put the key into the lock of the second door, I realized something. For the second time that week, the front door failed to click shut behind me.

I awoke to the sound of organ music and the smell of incense. *Heaven?* It felt as if I were squeezed into a box. My back and my head—which was pounding at the moment—were pressed up against a hard surface. I opened my eyes and gave them thirty seconds to adjust to the lack of light. When they had, I slowly pulled my throbbing knees toward my chest. The hard surface was a door to the very small room I was in. A few feet above my head was a tiny window with a metal screen in front of it.

The music stopped, but the incense continued to hang in the air. I took a deep breath and slowly got to my feet. The only light came from above, a low-wattage bulb behind some smoky glass. I went over to the door and tried the knob. Locked. I tried looking through the window, but the curtain on the other side prevented me from seeing anything. Directly below the window was a small bench covered with a dark carpet.

Christ. I hadn't been in one for so long that it took me a while to realize I was inside a confessional. Someone's idea of a joke?

My head throbbed on, and I had a brief recollection of getting hit real hard and then going black. I'd never made it through the second door of my apartment building.

The organ started in again, and a small bit of light appeared at the window as someone drew the curtain aside. I didn't have to wait long.

"Mr. Donne," a voice said—male—just above a whisper.

I stepped to the window. The shape of a head appeared on the other side, but the metal screen and lack of light made it impossible to make out the face. That's what confessionals were designed for. Anonymity.

"Yeah," I answered, like there was gravel in my throat. I grabbed the back of my neck where the pain was coming from and squeezed as hard as I could.

"Good. You are awake. I was afraid you were badly hurt."

Depends on your point of view. "What do you want?" I asked.

A short laugh came from the other side. "That is good," the voice said. "Not 'Where am I?' or 'Who are you?' but 'What do you want?' Direct and to the point, as if you know more than you do. You do not disappoint me."

I knew the voice. It was just a matter of time before I realized whom it belonged to.

"I want," the voice said, "what belongs to me."

I took a step closer. "And you think I can help you how?"

"I understand you are in possession of what was taken from me."

"And if I told you I have no idea what you're talking about?"

"I would not believe you."

"Then I'm not sure what we have to talk about."

The light on the other side of the window gradually grew brighter, as if someone had turned up a dimmer. I could now make out the face behind the voice. Elijah Cruz.

"Oh," he said. "I believe that we have much to talk about."

He disappeared for a few seconds and then returned with his hand on the back of Frankie Rivas's neck. I leaned in, the tip of my nose touching the screen.

"Frankie," I said. "Are you okay?"

Frankie didn't respond. The look on his face told me that Cruz's grip was growing tighter. I was about to turn and try the door again, when someone grabbed my neck and pushed the side of my face up against the window screen.

"Son of a bitch!" I said, my teeth scraping the inside of my mouth.

"The boy is fine," Cruz said. "That is, however, a fluid situation." He must have squeezed harder because Frankie groaned. "Give me what I want, and we can end this quickly."

"Tell me what you think I have," I said. "And I'll do my best to— Ahh! Fuck!" My face was pushed harder into the screen.

"This conversation will end unpleasantly if you continue to lie to me, Mr. Donne. The boy has told me that he has passed my property on to you. You will not 'do your best.' You will simply return my property."

"I don't have— Goddamn it!" Something small and hard was jammed into my lower back, and my knees slammed into the wall. "All right," I said and tried to turn around. "I can't get it right now. I need some time."

"Where is it?"

"My uncle's office," I said, impressed with the quickness of my lie.

"Your uncle's office," Cruz repeated, weighing the credibility of my words.

I braced myself for another burst of pain. None came. Cruz waited for a moment and then gestured with his head toward the door. I was pulled out of the confessional and into the main part of the church. Cruz stepped out and handed Frankie over to Suit. The hand on my neck belonged to Ape.

"Mr. Donne," Frankie said. "I'm sorry. They grabbed me—when I tried to go home—my dad's. They made me . . . tell them that . . . I delivered it to you."

"It's okay, Frankie," I said as Suit dragged Frankie away. "It's okay." I tried to take a step toward him, but Ape grabbed me by my belt and pulled.

Frankie and Suit exited through a side door. As Cruz made his way toward the altar, Ape pushed me in that direction. I don't remember ever wanting to hurt somebody as badly as I did then. Ape read my face and showed me the palms of his hands as he held them out about waist-high. He grinned, daring me. There was so much anger and fear coursing through my body, I could barely stay on my feet, let alone make any kind of run at this sadistic giant. We locked eyes for a few more seconds. This was not the time to push my luck. I took a deep breath, turned back around, and followed Cruz. He stopped at the front row, genuflected, and slipped into the pew.

"Where are you taking Frankie?" I asked.

"Please," he said, caressing the polished wood. "Sit."

I looked up at the altar, flanked by candles flickering through their red glass holders. The main part of the altar was shrouded in darkness, except for a miniature spotlight that illuminated Christ on the cross. I sat down and heard a wooden pew creak, as Ape settled his huge frame a few rows behind us.

Again, the music stopped. I looked around and saw no organ. Recorded church music.

"The boy is safe for now," Cruz said. "He thought he would be safe at his father's . . ." He rested his arms on the back of the pew. With his eyes up on the altar, he said, "Are you a religious man, Mr. Donne?"

"Not for a long time," I replied.

Cruz smiled. "There is still some faith left in you, though. I can feel it."

"Is that why you brought me here? To discuss my personal theology?"

"There is still in you that little Catholic boy, filled with guilt and fear, who wants to please others by doing good. That is why you became a policeman and, when that came to an end, a teacher. That is why you have invested so much of yourself in the well-being of Francisco. You two are very much alike."

"How are we going to do this, Cruz?"

"It must have been very difficult for you after your father's death," he said, turning to check my reaction. I gave him none. "To lose your father at such a young age is unimaginable."

"If your point is you know a lot more about me than I know about you," I said, "or that you are in charge here, consider it taken. Tell me how we are going to do this, Cruz."

"I told you of the fire that destroyed my childhood church. It also led to the tragic death of our family priest," Cruz said. "That crucifix"—he pointed up at the altar—"is the only thing left from Father Rodrigo's church. It became the foundation of mine." He blessed himself. "After the fire," Cruz continued, "I made a decision. Someday I would build another church. In His name. Bigger and more worthy of Him. That day is upon us."

Our conversation in McCarren Pool. How Cruz had spoken about his "vision."

"The medical supply business must be very good," I said.

"Do not play ignorant, Mr. Donne. You have just returned from a visit with Senora Villejo. The video cameras provide more than security for my people. Surely, you must have wondered how she can afford such a . . . comfortable lifestyle."

"I'm getting the idea it has something to do with your business and your church."

"Please. The government and the politicians are more than willing to dole out money and tax breaks to the pharmaceutical and insurance industries. They are much more reticent to do so for those who are truly vulnerable. The citizens who have the audacity to be both poor and sick. I help make up the difference. The politicians do not want to do what's right, so I play their game against them. I can show you dozens like Senora Villejo, who, without me, would be living day to day, not sure where their next meal is coming from or whether this is the time their husband or child will not get well."

I thought back to Frankie's grandmother. How she had called Cruz instead of the police after her place was broken into.

"You seem to be doing quite nicely for yourself," I said.

"God has been very good to me, yes."

God. The government. What's the difference?

"You will go to your uncle's office, Mr. Donne, and retrieve what is mine. When that is done, I will consider this matter to be concluded."

"Just like that?" I asked.

"You do not trust me."

"Probably about as much as you trust me."

He laughed. "If I wished you harm, it would already have befallen you. I only wish to have my property returned."

"And I want the boy home safely and his family left alone."

"We are in agreement then. No harm will come to the boy or his family."

"Like his father?"

Cruz shook his head. "That was not done on my word. Yes, the father stole from me, but his death did not solve anything. We are here now, are we not?"

He had a point.

"I need some time to get into my uncle's office."

"You will do it tonight. My men will take you there."

I took a shot and added to my lie. "I can't just walk into my uncle's office. He's a deputy inspector. I can't get into the building without him being there."

Cruz considered that. "I will give you until Sunday morning. Before first light."

"Excuse me?"

"Sunday morning at four thirty. You will have my property by then."

Four thirty? "Or . . ."

"You may use your imagination," he said.

"And what happens when this deal is completed?"

"This is not a *deal*, Mr. Donne. A deal is made when one party has as much to gain or to lose as the other. You have much more at stake here than I. It would be in your best interest to keep that in mind."

Cruz could teach a thing or two to the politicians he so greatly despised about not answering questions.

"There is a small park along the river," Cruz continued. "A block north of the oil tanks and across from the old mustard factory."

"I know it."

"There is a phone booth. At four thirty, you will answer it and be given instructions."

"Why don't you just give me the instructions now?"

Cruz smiled. "You have chosen your friends—and family—wisely, Mr. Donne. An admirable quality. I failed to recognize that when we first met. The expeditious way in which you removed your sister was impressive."

"I'm like that when my family's been threatened."

"Another thing you have in common with the boy." He paused for a bit. "You will pick up the phone at four thirty. You will listen and act accordingly."

"You still haven't told me what happens to me when you get your property back. And how do you know I won't just turn it over to my uncle and let the power of the New York Police Department come down upon you and your church?"

Cruz listened, and when I was done, nodded. Like he'd had his answer all ready.

"Unlike you, Mr. Donne, I am open about my faith. And I believe you when you say you only wish the boy home and well." He leaned forward, close enough for me to feel the heat of his breath. "That will not happen if you vary in any way from the arrangements I have made." After a moment, his face turned away from me, and his eyes returned to the altar. To the crucifix. The foundation of his church.

"As for what happens to you . . . we all make sacrifices." He closed his eyes and without opening them again, said, "You may leave now."

With those words, Ape pulled me out of the pew and thrust me a few feet toward the church's exit. I turned back, hoping to get a little more information from Cruz, to keep the conversation going, but Ape's body blocked my view. I craned my neck to see past him. Just before Ape gave me one last shove through the massive church door, Elijah Cruz stepped up onto the altar and kissed Christ's feet.

I stood outside on the steps of the church and watched the low clouds as they raced against the darkening sky for what seemed like an hour but was probably no more than five minutes. The last of the sun's light was barely visible, and it was time to go home. Again. I was scared, angry, tired, and in pain.

What the hell was I going to do now?

I needed help. Who could I go to, looking and feeling like shit at seven thirty on a Friday night who wouldn't ask any questions? I took out my cell phone and dialed Edgar's number. His recorded message told me he wasn't home, but my call was important to him and I should leave a brief message. As I was doing so, he picked up and explained he was screening.

"You never know," he said, then told me he'd pick me up in ten minutes.

It's good to have friends.

Twenty minutes later, I was sitting on Edgar's couch with my eyes closed, an icepack on my head, and a cold Diet Pepsi in my hand.

"Pizza'll be here in ten minutes," Edgar said. "I asked them to rush it."

"You got any ibuprofen?" I asked.

"I'll do you better than that." Edgar vanished into another part of his basement apartment and returned a half-minute later with a small bottle.

He rattled it like a salesman. "Friend of mine got these in South Africa. Can't get them here. Three of these'll put you right out."

"I can't afford to be put out, Edgar. Just give me two, okay?"

He shook a couple of small blue pills out and handed them to me.

"Two'll do you fine. This friend? Former Special Ops. Swears by this stuff."

"Terrific." I chased the pills with a sip of soda. "Thanks, Edgar. I really appreciate this."

"Please."

Even with my eyes closed, I could feel Edgar staring at me. Dying to know the latest developments. I could hear his breathing and imagined him about to fall over with curiosity. When I got to the part where I called him from the pay phone, the pizza showed up.

Edgar opened the box. "So go to your uncle. Tell him everything. He'll help get—"

"Frankie killed," I said. "I'm back to square one here, Edgar. Cruz has Frankie, but I'm not sure where. I have shaky proof—at best—of any wrongdoing on his part and, oh yeah, the guy's a fucking freak. Frankie wouldn't stand a chance, and I wouldn't put it past Cruz to do as much damage to my life as he could."

We ate a couple of slices in silence before Edgar had an idea.

"You gotta call your buddy," he said. "Billy."

"You haven't been listening, Edgar. Cruz said no variations. That means no cops."

"He's your friend. I got the feeling at the Q he'd do anything for you. Was I wrong?"

You don't know how right you are, I thought. But was I willing to do that? Put a friend's career—or more—on the line? This was my fight. I picked it. Now I had to pussy out and rope in a buddy to bail me out?

"You'd do it for him," Edgar said.

I leaned back, thought about it for a few seconds, and said, "Give me the phone."

He already had it in his hands.

"Can't do much about it tonight, partner." Billy told me he was sitting out on his almost-finished back deck. The girls were down for the night. His wife was out with the ladies, and he was smoking a cigar and drinking a cold beer. I had forgotten about his daughters and was about to tell him to drop the whole thing when he said, "La Casa Diner. Tomorrow at eight."

"You sure?" I asked.

"I'm gonna pretend you didn't ask that, Raymond."

When I hung up, Edgar came into the living room carrying something that looked like a parachute. He unrolled the most comfortable sleeping bag I'd ever seen and laid it out on the carpet. He'd probably gotten it from his friend in Special Ops.

"I'll sleep out here," he said. "You take the bed."

"I'm not taking your bed, Edgar."

"I insist."

"Just get me a towel and a toothbrush. I'll be fine." He was about to insist again when I put my hand on his shoulder and squeezed. "Thanks, Edgar. You came through big-time. You're a good friend."

He put his arm around me and gave me a half hug. "So are you," he said. I could swear there was a tear in his eye as he turned away. "Towel and toothbrush are in the bathroom." His back was to me as he spoke. "Take your time. Good night, Ray."

"Good night."

Chapter 32

BILLY MORRIS WAS SEATED AT ONE of the back booths at La Casa Diner with enough scrambled eggs, sausage, bacon, and bagels on the table to feed a family of five. He poured himself a cup of coffee while eyeing Edgar as the two of us slid into the booth.

"Thought this was gonna be just me and you, partner," Billy said, picking up a plastic bear full of honey and squeezing some into his coffee.

If Edgar's feelings were hurt by Billy's greeting, he hid it well. He fixed himself a big plate from the family-style portions on the table as I poured myself a cup of coffee. First things first.

"You look better than I thought you would," Billy said.

"Edgar took good care of me. Slept like a baby."

"Good to know." That got a smile from Edgar. "Now, I know you gave me the *Reader's Digest* version last night, but I wanna hear it all again. Slowly, and don't worry about boring me with the smallest of details. Go."

I did, and when I finished, Billy nodded.

"Ya had no clue this Cruz guy was involved before last night?"

"No."

"Or that those two bad guys worked for him?"

"Never saw them together. No."

"Jesus." He drank a little coffee.

Edgar took the opportunity to pick up the honey bear and pour a little into his own coffee. He took a sip and didn't do a very good job hiding his disgust.

Billy smirked. "Least I could do is call up the old house, see if they know anything about this guy . . . Vega?"

"He said no cops."

"Hey," Billy said, spreading out his hands, his sign for me to take it easy. "Just a friendly chat between old friends is all."

"I mean it, Billy. Anything goes wrong, Frankie's in a shitload of trouble. Me, too."

Billy shook his head. "I don't get it, Ray. I mean, why for fuck's sake did you get involved in this to begin with?"

"He's one of mine, Billy. If I had known it was going to develop into this, I would've called my uncle and stepped back. But I didn't. Shit got real deep, real fast. I had to find out what was going on."

"Not like you to get caught leaning, partner."

"I know."

"You think maybe you shoulda seen this coming?"

"I fucked up, okay!" I said, loud enough to make the waitress step back as she brought us another pot of coffee. She took away the old one and placed our bill under the sugar dispenser. I gave her an apologetic smile and lowered my voice. "Now I need to fix it. You think it's easy coming here, asking for help? I'm putting you in a bad position, Billy. I know that. I wouldn't be asking if it weren't important."

Edgar shifted uncomfortably. He picked up his coffee cup, remembered the taste it had left the last time, and chose a glass of water instead. We were all silent for about a minute.

"Okay," Billy said. "You got absolutely no idea what Cruz thinks you have?"

"No."

"And the reason he thinks you have it . . ."

". . . is because Frankie told him I did."

"How long has he had the kid?"

"Good question," I said. "Long enough to know Frankie's not in possession of what he told Cruz I have."

"I see why you like this kid so much. Forget I said that." As he thought, I grabbed half a bagel and spread some butter on it. "Can what he's looking for be at your school?"

"Possible," I said. "But I doubt it. I checked my box yesterday."

"Home?"

"I never got a chance to find out."

"We need to do that." He turned to Edgar. "You can swing Ray by his place, right?"

Edgar sat up straighter. "Yes, sir. I . . . Billy. Yeah. Absolutely."

Billy grinned and said, "Good. I'm gonna drive by the park and check it out. See if I can figure out why Cruz wants the meet there."

"How about we all do that?" I said. "Cruz told me to wait at the pay phone."

"Yeah?"

"Edgar," I said, "tell Billy about that trick you did with the phone at The LineUp."

"It's not a trick, Ray. It's a—"

"Just tell him."

He did, and when he was finished, Billy nodded.

"And you could do that right now?"

"I don't see why not. I got the equipment in my car."

Billy stood. "Let's go to the park first, boys." He took a final sip of coffee and slid the bill toward me. "Don't forget to leave a good tip, Ray. Ya scared the shit out of Carmen."

Chapter 33

I CAN'T SWEAR TO IT, BUT I'D bet good money that River Street Park is the smallest park in the city system. It looks like someone noticed there was about sixty feet of unused riverfront space between the old sugar factory and an oil storage facility and decided to put in a few picnic tables, post a green sign with a Parks Department maple leaf on it, and call it a park. According to the historical plaque on the restored smokestack, ferries used to leave from this spot every five minutes before the Williamsburg Bridge was built in 1903.

Edgar parked right behind Billy's Jeep. Before I could get out of the car, he was over at the pay phone, checking it out.

Billy gave me a grin. "That guy's something else."

"If he says he can do it," I said, "he'll do it."

Edgar came back to his car, popped the trunk, and took out a toolbox.

"You guys got my back while I work my magic?" he asked.

"Anyone asks you what you're doing," Billy said, "tell 'em to call a fucking cop."

Billy and I walked over to the water as Edgar made his way back to the phone. Billy put his foot on a rock and looked across the river toward Manhattan. Two men in baseball caps fished, and an older man made his way around the rocks picking up empty cans and putting them into a garbage bag. A good breeze was coming off the water. With the dark clouds sailing eastward over the city skyline, I was almost convinced it might rain.

"I don't like the location, Ray," he said. "A meet like this has a higher likelihood of going bad when there's more than one viable exit or entrance."

"You think a boat could get in here?" I asked, watching as the waves crashed against the rocks and the foam retreated into the river.

"Mine could. Be a bit rough, but it's doable. Enough to let someone off."

"Or on."

"That, too." He shook his head. "Don't like it. Means we need a man on the water." He stepped back and did a three-sixty, taking in the small park. He pointed up at the three-story, gun-metal gray tower adjacent to the oil tanks. "Could just situate my heavily armed self up there and wait for them to show up."

"I won't even justify that with a response," I said. "What about Edgar?"

"For the meet? He may be good at the techie shit, but no way I'm trusting a wannabe with this kind of job. I'd like to find someone who can handle a boat. Preferably their own."

"What about yours?"

"If it wasn't up on blocks in my backyard. Suffered some structural damage last week, courtesy of my asshole brother-in-law, who can't read a fucking depth chart. Was gonna fix it this weekend, but I don't have the necessary materials, and even then it's a six-hour job at least, and we don't got that kind of time."

"Can you borrow one?"

"It ain't a lawn mower, Ray. I can't just call somebody and ask if I can borrow his boat for an early-morning errand. Not without dealing with a whole lot of questions you don't want answered."

My inner light bulb went off. "What if I knew someone who could fix yours?"

"This time of year? Anybody any good'll be booked for a few weeks at least."

"But if I did know someone?"

"Do you?"

"I might," I said, taking out my cell phone.

It took a little while for me to remember the name of the company Lisa's father worked for. When it came to me, I called information and had the phone company connect me. I wasn't sure if Mr. King worked on Saturdays, but after three rings he picked up. After exchanging hellos and how-you-doings, and his telling me how grateful he was for my helping

Lisa—who would definitely be back in school come Monday—I told him what I needed.

"I can free myself up in an hour," he told me. "What kinda job are we talking about?"

I handed the phone back to Billy to let him work out the details. I joined Edgar over at the pay phone. He was holding the hand piece and using a small screwdriver to implant something.

"One of the newer ones," he informed me, with more than a touch of sarcasm. "Designed to prevent just this kind of interference. I tell you, Raymond, when I retire, these guys are gonna pay me big bucks to show them how to do this right."

"You almost done?"

"Couple more turns of the screw," he said. "And there we have it." He put the mouthpiece back where it belonged. "As good as when the company first installed it."

A minute later, Billy came over. "You save this guy King's life or something?"

"I was there when his daughter made an important life decision," I said.

"Sounded like he'd take a bullet for you. Anyways, he'll be at my house in less than two hours. I called the wife and told her to expect him." Billy looked at the phone and then at Edgar. "You done already?"

"Call the number," Edgar said and unclipped his cell phone from his belt. Billy looked at the pay phone's number on the small, white part above the keyboard, and when he was finished dialing, the phone rang. Edgar told me to pick it up. I did, and Edgar said, "Say hi."

"Hello."

Edgar handed his cell phone to Billy. "Keep talking, Ray."

"Check. One, two, three."

With Edgar's cell phone up against his ear, Billy smiled and slapped Edgar on the shoulder. "All righty, then. We're in business. What kinda range we got?"

"Not even a consideration," Edgar said. "For all intents and purposes, they're the same unit. I just can't use mine at the same time as when we want to hear the talk on the pay phone."

"Excellent." Billy looked at his watch. "I gotta make some calls. See about getting a little help for tonight . . . tomorrow. Cutting it kind of close, though."

"I know," I said. "Edgar, can you take me home now? I've been wearing the same clothes since yesterday."

"You sure it's safe?" Edgar asked.

"Cruz has no reason to mess with me until tomorrow morning. He's got every reason not to. I wouldn't put it past him to have my place scoped out, but I don't think he'll bother me."

Billy reached into his pocket, pulled out one of his business cards, and handed it to Edgar. "Call me in an hour, and we'll see where we're at."

Edgar and I shook hands with Billy, who gave us a grin, got in his SUV, and pulled away.

"Home?" Edgar asked.

"Yeah," I said. "Please."

"You're not gonna find a place to park around here," I told Edgar as he pulled in front of my building. "Just circle the block a couple of times. I want to get a change of clothes and maybe check my messages. I can shower at your place, right?"

"No problem," he said.

I got out of the car, gave Edgar a wave, and unlocked the first door. I watched and listened as it clicked shut. I emptied my mailbox—nothing but junk mail—opened the second door, and headed up to my apartment. An oversized envelope was leaning against my door, addressed to me in Frankie's handwriting. I ripped it open and found a piece of paper, another envelope, and two computer discs. I unfolded the paper and again recognized Frankie's handwriting.

> *Mr. D,*
>
> *This was in my dads stuff that he gave me the day he got killed. I was gonna give it to you on the bridge but those guys on the bike came and then the cop and well you know. Its got something to do with why they did that to him. Right? I didnt have a computer where I was and thought maybe you could do better then me anyway. Thanks again for taken care of Milagros. I hope I didnt cause you to much trouble.*
>
> *Frankie*

I ripped open the smaller envelope; a whole lot of fifties and hundreds held together by a rubber band. I'd count it later. Right now, I couldn't wait to pack my stuff, get over to Edgar's, and see what was on the discs.

I don't have a lot of things in my apartment, but most of what I do own had been thrown around the place. Clothes, books, and papers were all over the living room and bedroom floors. The closet had been ransacked. Every cabinet and drawer in the kitchen had been emptied, the contents tossed. In the bathroom, the medicine cabinet was open, and the back of the toilet had been removed. It seemed as if Ape and Suit had left no stone unturned in their search for what they thought I had.

I looked around the apartment again. *My home.* The place where I convinced myself I was safe from the outside world. The one place I felt was mine and mine alone. Few people had come here, and they came only when I invited them. That's the way I liked it, the way I *needed* it. Now, my home had been violated. I wanted so much to pick up some clothes and throw them against the wall, kick some books, maybe break a few dishes. I wanted to throw a fucking temper tantrum, like a kid who'd had enough of being picked on.

Instead, I found my overnight bag in the closet and packed it with enough to get me through the weekend. I left my apartment—careful to lock up behind me—and went downstairs to find Edgar. I needed his computer.

Chapter 34

EDGAR, OF COURSE, HAD A RIDICULOUS computer system and accessories that probably cost more than a midsized car.

"I already got my eye on the Twenty-two Hundred that comes out in the fall," Edgar said, as he slipped Frankie's disc into the Twenty-one Hundred's drive. "A friend overseas says he might be able to get his hands on one by mid–August."

He punched a series of buttons, and within seconds a selection of files appeared on the screen. I had no idea what was in any of them, so we clicked on the first one, and a spreadsheet came up. There were those Social Security numbers again, followed by dates, dollar amounts, and then two more multidigit numbers that meant nothing to me. We scrolled down until we ran out of numbers. Socials, dates, dollar amounts, and two other numbers.

"Any ideas?" Edgar asked.

I told him what I knew, or thought I knew, and confessed my ignorance regarding the fourth and fifth columns of numbers.

"Social Security numbers are Medicare numbers, right?" Edgar asked.

"Yeah. And . . . ?"

Silence from Edgar. I went back to the top and then scrolled down slower this time, hoping something might click. Nothing. So I did it all again, and it started to make a little sense.

"Okay," I said, using Edgar as a sounding board. "Patients are IDed by their Socials. Let's go ahead and say these," I ran my finger down the column of six-digit numbers that seemed to follow a pattern, many starting with a zero, "are dates of service. And then we have . . . what? Payments? To whom?"

"The providers," Edgar said.

"That's got to be one of the other numbers," I said. "Get your phone, will ya?"

I dialed information and got the number for Muscles's. The man himself picked up.

"Raymond," he said after I identified myself. "I hope you're calling to reschedule those appointments you missed."

"Not exactly," I said. "But I will. I got some questions for you."

"When?"

"Right now," I said.

"No. When are you coming in again?"

"Monday," I said. "After school."

"I'm writing it down," Muscle said. "Monday, four P.M. What are your questions?"

"When you send the bill to my insurance, what info do you have to give?"

"Name, member number—in your case, your SSN—the dates of service, what service or services you received, and my name and provider number."

"You describe the service?"

"I just give them the codes. It's all numbers, Ray."

"Same with the provider?"

"I *am* the provider. If you're asking do they give a shit about my name, nope. As long as my number's valid, that's all they care about."

"If I gave you some numbers, could you tell me who the providers are?"

"That depends," he said. "Give me a second." I was expecting him to ask why I would want this information, and I was prepared to lie. He didn't want to know why, I guess, but when it came to my missing an appointment . . . "Whatta ya got?"

I read off the first number. I listened as he worked a keyboard on his end.

"That's a service code," Muscles said. "Not a provider. Respiration therapy."

I wrote that down and read off the number next to that one.

"That's a Medicare provider," Muscles said and gave me the name and address of the doctor. It was not far from Roberts's travel agency. Under the same Medicare number, I noticed all the provider numbers were the same. I read off the matching service codes, and Muscles was able to find the corresponding medical procedure. There were eight of them. I told Muscles they all had the same date, and he told me to check again.

"I did," I said. "Twice. All eight services on the fifteenth of March."

"That's not kosher, Raymond. Too many services for one visit."

I scrolled down again and saw the pattern. Same patient, same provider, at least five services rendered on the same date. Quick math had each provider billing over a thousand dollars per patient, per visit. Many of the same patients were seen on the same day as each other. Mrs. Villejo told me the church sometimes took a whole group to the doctor's.

Muscles gave me the names and addresses for all the providers listed on the first file. The other files could wait. For now.

"Thanks, Muscles," I said. "I owe you."

"Pay me back by getting your ass—and your knees—in here on Monday. I *penned* you in for four o'clock."

"I'll be there."

"Hey," Muscles said, "one more thing."

"Yeah?"

"I've been thinking about what the kid told you. How his dad died."

"Go on," I said.

"You said the kid went up to the roof for a half hour, came down, and thought his dad had been smoking some shit, right?"

"Yeah."

"Then he goes back up to the roof for another thirty minutes, and when he comes back down the dad's got a bloody nose and he's dead."

"That's what he said."

"Right. So the injury above the ear was the first blow and not enough to kill the guy, but maybe it was enough to give him a subdural hematoma."

I put those two words together. "Bleeding in the head?"

"Around the brain. Worse than a regular concussion, not enough to kill a guy. Usually."

"Usually?"

"The ER docs call it 'Talk and Die.' You get a blow to the head—like your guy did—you shake it off and think you're gonna be okay. After a while, you start to slur your words, your vision gets blurry. You think it's gonna pass. What you don't realize is you're bleeding inside the head. If you don't seek some professional help soon, it ain't gonna stop on its own."

"And a punch in the nose . . ."

"Pretty much seals the deal."

"So," I thought out loud, "the first time Frankie and his sister go up to the roof, someone clocks the dad in the head and leaves."

"Right, with no idea what they started."

"And the second guy comes along, gives him a punch . . ."

"And within minutes, your guy's dead."

"Jesus," I said. "Guy couldn't catch a break."

"Not sure if he deserved one, Raymond. I'll see ya Monday."

"Absolutely." I hoped.

After I hung up, Edgar pointed at the computer screen and said, "I put in the other disc."

"Edgar, we don't have the—"

"Seems like a lot of money was going from EC Medical to Around the Horn Travel."

I slid over and took a look at where he was pointing. He was right. Again.

"I need copies of this."

"I'll burn it onto a CD," he said. "How many?"

I thought about that. One for me, definitely. I figured I'd hand over the original and a copy to Cruz in the morning. And a few extra for friends and family.

"Hold on," I said. "We got two different things going on here. One's fraud, the other's money laundering, right?"

"That's what it looks like. And whatever scam Rivas was pulling with the credit cards."

I thought about what information I'd want to get to Royce, if necessary. "Let's keep the discs separate."

"Why?"

"Separate crimes, separate discs. Can you do five copies each? Please."

"It'll take a while," Edgar said. "But yeah, no prob."

"Great." I called Billy while I waited.

• • •

"This guy, King," Billy said, "is a freaking miracle worker. He's been here about an hour, and he's almost done. Found something with my motor, too, and he's gonna give that another look-see. I think I'm in love."

"I'm very happy for the both of you," I said. "Any luck getting some back-up for tomorrow morning?"

"Bad luck, yeah. Everybody I trust is on duty tonight or gone for the weekend. I got a couple more calls to make, but I'm not too optimistic." He paused for a few seconds. "I may have to consider your geek buddy."

I looked over at Edgar, busy copying the discs for me. Doing what he did best. What he lived for. Impressing others with his technological prowess.

"I don't know about that, Billy."

"Just keeping the option open, partner." When I didn't answer, Billy said, "We'll talk again, Raymond. One hour. I gotta get back to my new best friend."

"See ya."

I hung up, and Edgar handed me a Diet Pepsi.

"That last part was about me, wasn't it?" he asked. "About helping out with the meeting tomorrow morning?"

"Yeah, but I don't know, Edgar. I feel weird enough putting Billy in that situation, and he's a cop. You're a—"

"Nerd? Computer geek?"

"I was going to say civilian. You want me to be honest? All you know about this stuff is what you see on TV or overhear at The LineUp. Shit. I'm scared to death, and I used to do this for a living." A long time ago. "No offense. What you've done for me? I owe you big. But I'm not putting you in the line of fire just so I don't hurt your feelings."

"What if I signed a waiver or something? You know, legally absolving you from any responsibility if I get hurt?"

"Or killed. It's not a field trip, Edgar. Please. I don't want to waste time on this. I've got to stay focused."

His computer system made a noise, and Edgar said, "Your discs are done, Ray. I printed out the hard copies you asked for." He handed me the pages. "Thanks for letting me help."

He left me alone in the living room while he went into the kitchen and started moving stuff around, slamming cabinets shut, making enough noise to let me know how he felt. Better that than having to live with getting a friend into a situation I knew was more than he could handle.

I sat at Edgar's desk, looking through the pages he'd just given me. How many years did it take Cruz to set all this up? How much money was involved? Doctors, suppliers, providers, patients. How much did Cruz get? For his church? For himself?

If this situation got to the point where I—or others—had to report this to the authorities, how many people's lives would be screwed with? How many other people like Mrs. Villejo were out there depending on Cruz for their standard of living? On these sheets alone, I counted at least fifty patient numbers.

Was having this information enough to keep Frankie and me alive past sunrise tomorrow? I could think this out and make brilliant plans until five A.M. and still not be sure I was holding more cards than Cruz.

And he had Frankie. That much was clear to me. I needed more. I called Edgar back.

He walked in with his arms folded across his chest and said, "What?"

"Lose the attitude," I said. "I need your help."

"You mean you need *more* of my help?"

"Yes." I put on my teacher voice, the one I use to soothe a sulking kid. "Look, Edgar, you're the only one I know who could help me right now, okay? Shit, you're the best at this kind of stuff." He unfolded his arms. "You can do more from this desk to help me right now than any cop Billy can scrape up. Will you do it?"

He pretended to think about it and then pulled the other chair next to mine.

"Whatta ya need?"

"First," I said, "an address. In Puerto Rico."

He punched in some information, and a directory Web site came up.

"First and last name?"

"Right there's where I'm going to need your help."

Three hours later my eyes were hurting, my vision blurry, but I now believed I knew more about Cruz than he knew about me. Watching Edgar work his magic on the keyboard—and acquire access to a few sites he shouldn't have—was impressive, and I told him so. He just wiggled his fingers and smiled.

"Dinner?" he asked.

"I'm not hungry."

He looked at his watch. "Ten hours to go. How do you feel?"

"Like I need to do more to get ready."

"You got all this info, Ray. What more do you want?"

"I don't know," I said. "More."

Edgar gave that some thought. "I had a Little League coach once who used to—"

"You played Little League?"

"For a couple of years, yeah. Then I gave it up."

"What happened?"

"Video games happened. Anyway, this coach I had, Mr. Kammerer, used to tell us at the start of each season, 'Talent doesn't guarantee success. Preparation guarantees success.'"

"What's your point, Edgar?"

"You say you want more. So what's missing? What's left you haven't thought of?"

When did Edgar get so damned insightful? I was beating myself up because I'd overlooked something. All the times during the past two weeks I thought I was through with this mess, and here I was, a few hours away from making a trade for Frankie. What was it Royce had said about the search for redemption? It could kill you.

After all these years of hiding them from those closest to me, I'd let Cruz see my weak spots. First my sister, then Frankie. That's how Cruz got me back in the game and kept me in. That's how he was so sure he was going to win.

I needed to find his weak spot.

I shut my eyes and went over the details of the past twenty-four hours, and I kept coming back to the conversation in the church last night with Cruz. All the talk about faith and family and God. And Cruz's eyes drifting up to the altar. The crucifix.

"Edgar," I said. "Get your car keys."

He stood up. "Why?"

"We're going to church."

• • •

Edgar did his best to walk nonchalantly down the block to Cruz's church. He stopped once as he checked the time and then continued on to the front door. I was watching from the driver's seat of his car as he climbed the steps and pressed the church's buzzer. Edgar's cell phone was up against my ear. No one was picking up inside the church. Edgar rang twice more and then knocked a few times. Getting no answer, he stepped down and made his way to the alleyway that separated the church from the apartment building next door. He bent down to tie his sneakers. When he got up, he disappeared into the alley. My breathing stopped. This was not what we'd planned. He was to make sure no one was at the church. That was all.

The street seemed unusually empty for a Friday night, most of the locals safe inside their apartments. I hoped we had no window gawkers up there tonight. Edgar came back out of the alley a minute later, crossed the street, and walked up the block to where we had parked. He opened the back passenger door of his car, slid in and said, "No one home."

"What were you doing in the alley, Edgar?"

"Making sure there was no one inside," he said. "You wanted me to be sure, right?"

"And what if there had been, and you'd gotten caught?"

"I'd act drunk and speak a little Spanish," he smirked. "Fit right into—"

"I don't want you taking chances like that, Edgar. You hear me?"

"Yeah. Okay." He paused and then added, "There's a window off the alley. I think you can get in that way."

I pushed the redial button for the church again and listened to the ringing.

"I didn't see an alarm system," he said. "Pretty sure of himself, this guy."

"He's a pillar of his community. Who'd want to break into his church?"

"Besides you?" Edgar leaned forward and rested his head on the back of his hands between the two headrests. "So, what do we do now?"

"We wait." I closed the phone and put it on the passenger seat. "I want to make sure no one's coming back."

"You wanna tell me what we're doing here?"

"The less you know about this, the better."

"Okay, then," he said. "What's the story with you and Billy?"

"We partnered for a time before I left the force."

"The guy comes riding in on his white horse when you call, and you guys haven't seen each other for years? You don't hang out?"

"No," I said. "We don't."

"Why not?"

I let out a deep breath. "We live in different worlds, Edgar. Cops and schoolteachers don't usually make for good running buddies."

Edgar considered that for a while and then said, "Bull."

"Excuse me?"

"Bull. You don't wanna tell me, Ray, say so. Don't lie to me."

"I don't wanna tell you."

"Come on, Ray. What did he mean when he said he owed you? Please." He sounded like he'd go on until he got what he wanted. I decided to give it to him. Shit, he'd earned it.

"About a year before I left the job . . ."

Edgar leaned over more. "Yeah?" He might as well have been sitting up front with me.

"I testified on Billy's behalf in a departmental hearing."

"What happened?"

"Some local scumbag. Corner boy. Said Billy roughed him up, planted evidence on him. Got the ear of some assistant DA hoping to make a name for himself by busting a cop. If the hearing didn't go in Billy's favor, he was looking at dismissal and criminal charges."

"So . . . you testified . . ."

"I testified that Billy hit the guy only after the guy hit Billy. Twice. And the only reason he was making these bullshit charges was that he was carrying enough weight to put him away for the better part of ten years." I took a breath. "The brass looked at my record—shit, they all knew my uncle—and dropped the charges."

"Billy was lucky you had his back, huh?"

Edgar loved this stuff. Stories from the streets. Brothers in blue and all that shit.

"Yeah," I said. "Real lucky."

"I can see why he owes you, but why the rift? Why don't you guys—"

"I lied," I said.

It took a little while to sink in, and when it did, Edgar said, "What?"

"I perjured myself," I said, using the more accurate verb. "The guy never touched Billy. He was just a loudmouth piece of shit who picked the wrong cop to give lip to."

"Yeah," Edgar said, "but—"

"But nothing, Edgar. I lied under oath in an official departmental hearing." I wasn't sure I'd ever said that out loud before. "I put my job on the line to protect Billy's ass. Mine, too. I was there when Billy roughed the guy up and did nothing to stop it."

"Did Billy plant the evidence on him?"

"If he did, he's a goddamned magician, because I didn't see him do it. The perp owned up to carrying some coke for his own use. Said the extra stuff wasn't his, that Billy put it in his sock after he'd knocked his ass to the ground. Actually thought it would help his case to point out that he kept *his* coke in a plastic bag and the coke he said was not his was in vials. Upped the stakes from possession to possession with intent, turning a two-year bit into ten. Enough to make a scumbag corner boy lie about his own mother."

"Scumbag corner boy," Edgar repeated with a smile. "Hey, the way I see it, he got what was coming to him. Sooner or later, he was going away."

"That's not the way it's supposed to work. I didn't become a cop to jam people up."

"C'mon, Ray. You did what you thought was right. You—"

"No," I said. "You see? That's just it. I knew it was wrong and did it anyway. I looked at my choices and made the one that was best for me. Just like that." I looked back at the front door of the church. "I was becoming the kind of cop I told myself I'd never be."

"And then you got hurt?"

"About ten months later, yeah." I looked at my watch. "Okay, storytime is over. You want to hook me up?"

"Absolutely." He opened his case, which contained the equipment we'd used to break into Roberts's travel agency. The stuff was coming in handy, and Edgar could not have been happier.

"Okay," I said as I slipped the headset on. "You know the game plan."

"Anybody or anything looks like trouble, I give you a holler. Your knees okay?"

I ignored that. "I want to be in and out in five minutes. Keep an eye on the clock."

"How about I give you a countdown? You know, 'You now have four minutes.'"

"Fine," I said. "Give me a sound check."

He did. Everything worked fine. "You got your cell?"

"Check."

"And the camera?"

"Got it. See you in five minutes," I said, slinging my book bag over my shoulder.

Five minutes later, I got in the back of Edgar's car and said, "Let's go."

"That was quick."

"Drive."

Chapter 35

WHEN WE GOT BACK TO EDGAR'S, Billy was already waiting for us. We went inside.

"Your man King's a miracle worker," Billy said. "Had the job done in no time."

Edgar came into the living room with three cans of Diet Pepsi and a bowl of pretzels. After handing out the drinks, he placed the pretzels on the coffee table and sat in the recliner.

"What?" Billy said. "No dip?" Edgar was about to jump out of the chair when Billy raised his hand. "Just shittin' ya, Emo. Chill."

Edgar leaned back and smiled at Billy's use of his nickname. "I knew that."

"My boat's a go," Billy said. "Still waiting on some feelers I put out there, but I ain't getting any bites. Maybe if you were still on the job . . ." He let that idea float for a bit. "I hate to do this to you, but I think we're gonna need your boy here."

"Absolutely not," I said, standing up. "I'm not going to put—"

"Whoa, whoa, whoa," Billy said. "Why'd you call me in on this, partner?"

"What kind of question is that?" I asked. "I need your help, and you're one of the few people I could trust with this. Why else—"

"Then do what I say. If I say we need Emo, we need Emo. This ain't a two-man job. Not when one of the men is gonna be in the presence of un-friendlies." He looked at Edgar, who was now getting so excited he was practically falling off the recliner. "Take it easy, boy. I just need you behind the wheel of a car. Case I gotta be picked up from the river." To me he said, "Just wheels, Ray. He picks me up, I drop him off. No line-of-fire shit. I promise."

I looked at Edgar, sitting on the edge of the recliner, sipping from his can of soda and doing his best to stay under control.

"I don't like it, Billy."

"Hey," he said, "there's a whole lot I don't like about this, but you have to let me do what I do, and you don't gotta like it."

I walked over and glanced out the window that looked up to the driveway separating Edgar's house from his neighbor's. I'd go nuts living in a basement.

"Okay," I said. "He drives. That's all."

"And maybe not even that," Billy said. "We'll play it as it lays."

"Right."

Billy stood and drained the rest of his soda.

"What're your plans for the rest of the evening?"

"I don't have any," I said. "Except waiting."

"You might wanna think about catching a few hours' sleep. You look like shit."

"Thanks. I'll consider it."

The next morning, we met Billy not far from the bridge, in the construction area across from Roberts's travel agency. We got there just after three thirty. Edgar pulled up alongside Billy's Jeep so the vehicles were facing opposite directions, the drivers' sides almost touching.

"You good to go?" Billy asked.

I leaned across Edgar and said, "I think so. You?"

"As much as I can be, considering it looks like it *is* gonna be just the three of us."

"Looks like?" I asked.

"Got one more possible out there, but it doesn't look too good." He looked over at the exit ramp off the bridge. "Last time I was sitting under this bridge at three thirty in the A.M., I was backing up a buy-and-bust. I got the same feeling in my gut now. Not good."

"I hear you, Billy. But . . . what are you going to do?"

Billy reached into his backseat and pulled out a bag. He took out three red baseball caps and handed two of them to Edgar.

"Put those on," Billy said.

Edgar handed one to me. "St. Louis Cardinals?" he asked.

"Color of the day," I said.

"Gotta be able to make out the players from a distance," Billy said. "That Yankee cap of yours ain't gonna do the trick."

"Why does Edgar need one if he's just going to drive?"

"Just covering all the angles," Billy said. "Besides, he's part of the team, right?"

Edgar took off his hat and put on the Cardinal's cap. He checked himself out in the rearview mirror and smiled. "Color of the day," he said.

"When you are with Cruz," Billy said to me, "you feel you need immediate assistance, take off the hat. If I gotcha in my sights, I'll be coming."

"What kind of immediate assistance?" I asked.

"Depends on the situation."

"I don't want any shooting, Billy. Especially if Frankie's there."

"I hear you," he said. "You walking from here?"

"Yeah." I put my new cap on. "Not a good idea to be seen getting dropped off. Edgar'll park a few blocks over. He's got his cell on, and he gave me this—" I lifted my shirt to show Billy Edgar's phone. "GPS," I said. "You guys should be in constant contact. I can't be seen talking on a phone unless it's with Cruz."

"Good point."

"Actually," Edgar said, "I got some walkie-talkies." He reached over into the glove compartment and pulled out a pair, handing one to Billy. "I got it set for channel three. It's a four-mile range, so don't go too far."

Billy looked at the walkie-talkie in his hand. "Right." He gave me a thumbs-up. "Good luck, partner."

"I'll see you in an hour," I said.

"Let's do that." Billy shifted his Jeep into drive and eased out of the lot.

"All right, Edgar." I picked up my bag and opened the side door. "Thanks for the lift."

"I'll only be a few blocks away. Anything you need, I am there in a blink."

"That's good to know." I got out, slid my arms through the straps of the bag, and shut the door. "Thank you."

"Hey," Edgar said. "Thank me later."

"You got it," I said and started walking toward the park.

Except for a few trucks, a slow-moving station wagon, and a pair of dogs that strayed on the other side of the street, I was the only one out at this hour. Most of the bars were over by the L train and not too many people lived on this block, so I didn't expect a lot of company. Across the river, the skyline was asleep. The buildings turned their show lights off around midnight. I could make out their silhouettes in the darkness of the early-morning sky. Another breeze was coming off the river, reminding me that the weather folks had predicted some early rain for today.

I got to the park fifteen minutes ahead of schedule and walked over to the rocks. The waves seemed higher and louder than they had the previous day. I guessed the tide was coming in. I looked out under the Williamsburg Bridge and saw a boat—one bright light on deck—hanging out closer to the Manhattan side. Billy? Cruz?

I went to the pay phone and did some stretches as I waited for it to ring. It wasn't long.

"You're early," the voice on the other end said.

"Yeah."

"You were told not to deviate from your instructions."

"Who is this?" I asked. "Vega?" No answer. "I know what I was told. The point is I'm here, and I'm ready to do business." I waited a few seconds. "Are you?"

More silence. After a while the voice said, "Take down this number."

"I don't have anything to write with."

"You have a cell phone. Punch the number in."

I unclipped the phone. "Go ahead."

He read it off, and I entered the numbers.

"Now," the voice said, "hang up the phone and call that number."

"That wasn't what we decided on." Edgar was listening in on the conversation. I needed to stay on this line. "Cruz told me—"

"You . . . decided on nothing. And now you are being told something else." The line went dead, and I looked at the useless receiver in my hand.

"I'm switching to the cell," I said to Edgar. I dialed the number I had punched in, and the other end rang once.

"Now walk to the river. You may stop when you get to the rocks."

"Thanks," I said, and did as I was told. When I made it to the rocks, I said, "Now what?"

"Do you see the boat under the bridge?"

"Yeah."

"Wave good-bye to your friend, throw the phone into the water, and then turn around and start walking east."

"Excuse me?"

"I'm not going to repeat myself, Teacher." He hung up.

I looked behind me. He was around somewhere, but where? I didn't see any parked cars—I looked up—or movement on the rooftops above me. I turned back to the water, and the only boat out there was still idling under the bridge. Without waving good-bye, I tossed Edgar's cell phone into the East River. One more look around, and then I headed east, away from the river.

The streets were still empty, but the closer I got to the residential area, the more parked cars I passed. After about two minutes, I spotted the white van on my side of the street. I slowed down as I passed it. The driver's window was down, and behind the wheel was Suit. Vega.

The sliding door opened, and he said, "Get in."

After looking around, I got in. As the door closed, Vega stepped on the gas, sending me skidding into the back, just like the first time I was in this van. If not for my book bag, I would have hit the back door hard. We drove for about ten minutes before he pulled over. He got out, opened the side door, and told me to step outside. I looked around and had no idea where we were. He ran his hands over my body, checked my bag, and, when satisfied I was unarmed and had no more cell phones, said, "Get back in."

"Where's your partner?" I asked.

"Shut up and move."

We drove for another ten minutes and then stopped. Vega got out and opened the back door. I knew where we were now: McCarren Pool. Blocks away from where we had started.

He grabbed my arm and escorted me to the front gate, unchained and opened it. We stepped through the high weeds and grass and entered the pool area. With the small amount of light coming off the street, I could make out three shapes in the middle of the pool. Vega pushed me down the steps and into the pool toward the group.

"Mr. Donne," Elijah Cruz said, standing next to Ape, who had one hand on Frankie's shoulder and a laptop computer in the other. Frankie looked like he hadn't slept since I last saw him. "You have what belongs to me?"

"Like we agreed," I said.

"Good. Then this should not take much time."

He stuck out his hand. I reached into the book bag, removed the discs, and offered them to Cruz. Vega came over and took them. He stepped over to Ape. Vega opened the laptop and slid the first disc in. The screen lit up, illuminating Vega's face. He pressed some keys and nodded. He took the second disc and repeated the process.

"These are the discs," he said.

"Good," Cruz answered. "And the money?"

I took the bundle out of the bag and tossed it to him.

"That's what's left of it," I said.

"Of course," Elijah said, taking the cash and handing it to Vega. "I understand the boy had certain expenses the last few weeks." Cruz stared at me. "That is a new hat for you."

"I have a lot of baseball hats."

He stepped over to me and took it off. "The Cardinals?" he said. "No. A true fan does not show allegiance to another team."

"It's a different league."

"I don't like it," he said. He took the cap and threw it into the darkness.

We stood in silence for another minute, waiting for Cruz—his back still to the four of us—to speak. When that didn't happen, I said, "So, I can take Frankie home now?"

Cruz turned and eyeballed me. Then he laughed, as did Vega. Ape just smiled. Frankie tried to take a step toward me, but Ape pulled him back.

"I don't think that would be a smart business decision, Mr. Donne," Cruz said.

"Yeah," I said. "You're probably right." I reached back into the book bag and pulled out the two discs I had Edgar make for me. "You might want to take a look at these, Elijah."

"And why would I want to do that?"

"It might be a smart business decision."

Vega looked at Cruz, who was trying to make up his mind as to whether or not to humor me. After a while, he nodded. Vega took the first disc and repeated the steps he'd just gone through. "It's a copy, Elijah."

"Why," Elijah Cruz said, "would you go to the trouble of making a copy of the disc, Mr. Donne?"

"Another *four* copies," I said. "Of both discs. The first one has to do with EC Medical and Medicare. The other has quite a lot of info regarding your relationship with John Roberts." I pointed at the discs. "I labeled them."

Elijah Cruz digested this new information. "You have been busy since we last met."

I smiled. "Idle hands . . ."

"No matter," Cruz said. "They prove nothing. The information can all be explained away. Changed if necessary. They are of little significance."

"Not to my people," I said. "The same folks who'll be getting copies of those discs. And definitely not to the doctors, and service providers, and patients listed there. A lot of people's lives are involved here, Elijah. You said so yourself the other night."

Elijah Cruz said nothing. He was exuding complete control as he tried to figure out if I was bluffing; if I knew as much as I was letting on.

"Now," I continued, "are you willing to take a chance with all those people's lives? Your people? After all you've done so far?"

"What guarantee do I have," Cruz asked, "that this . . . information will not be delivered to your people if I choose to let you and the boy go?"

"All I want," I said in as clear and steady a tone as I could manage, "is for Frankie to go back home." I looked at Frankie, Ape's hand still holding him in place. As Frankie struggled, his eyes filled with anger and fear. "That's all I've wanted from the beginning. You let us walk out of here, I'm not going to give a second thought to your business dealings. You want to beat the government at their own game, fine. I honestly don't give a shit."

Cruz stared at me for a while, then turned and walked away. Ape, Vega, Frankie, and I watched as he made a slow circle, contemplating the situation before him. Ape and Vega exchanged almost imperceptible glances, and I could tell they had never before seen their boss caught by surprise. They looked at me like they wanted to do some real damage.

Just wait. It's about to get better.

Out of the corner of my eye, I caught some movement on one of the small towers at the other side of the pool. I couldn't look very long for fear of being noticed, but I thought I saw a flash of red disappear behind the concrete. Billy?

"You!" Cruz walked back to me. "Are not the one making decisions here. You . . ." His finger was about a foot from my face. "I am in charge here. I will tell what happens next."

"Now," I said, "you sound like Father Rodrigo."

That stopped him. Vega took two steps closer to us. Frankie moaned, and I guessed that Ape had increased the pressure on his neck.

"You," he said, quieter this time, "have no idea what you're talking about."

"It's amazing what information you can find online these days. Like the fire that destroyed the church." Cruz said nothing, so I continued. "The papers called it suspicious. The police suspected arson."

"There was nothing to prove. It was an accident."

"And all the allegations that came out," I said. "Years later, the rumors about Father Rodrigo and his boys. Horrible stuff."

"Again," Cruz said, "nothing. A bunch of unhappy young men, looking for someone to blame their weaknesses on."

"How long did it take, Elijah, before you'd had enough? Before you asked yourself what kind of god would allow that to happen?"

"You . . . you question my faith? You are a little man in the scheme of things, Mr. Donne. How long do you think it will take before you are forgotten by all except your family?" He allowed himself a small grin. "Your sister, Rachel. Your mother, Anna. She has a nice home, by the way. Close to the park."

"As nice as your mother's?"

Cruz flinched at the mention of his mother. I hoped that was a flash of red in the tower and not just my imagination.

"She's still down in Puerto Rico? Luquillo Beach?"

That stopped him again, and before he could think of something to say I went on.

"But her last name isn't Cruz. She still goes by Morales. You changed your name."

Cruz put his hands together and then brought them up to his mouth. He kept them there while he thought. "You are a smart man. Resourceful."

"You don't know the half of it." I looked over at Frankie. "We'll be going home soon."

"Good," Frankie said, struggling to get the one word out.

"Just like that?" Cruz said. "You come here with some computer discs and some information you found on the computer, and you think it is enough to intimidate me into letting *you* dictate the outcome of this morning? You are greatly overestimating the value of what you have."

"How about this?" I asked, reaching into my shirt pocket and pulling out my trump card: the picture of the crucifix I had taken a few hours earlier. I handed it to Cruz. "How much is that worth to you?"

Cruz just stared at the picture. His breathing became labored, and his confident stance wavered slightly, as if a cold hand were touching his back.

"You broke into my church?"

"Someone left a window open. You should be more careful in a neighborhood like that. It *is* still Brooklyn."

"You violated my church?"

"Yeah," I said. "But like I told you the other night, I've lost my faith. It's no more to me than, say, breaking into a travel agency." I took a step closer. "You took that crucifix from the church," I said. "But not *after* the fire. By then the cross would have burned up with the rest of the church. The news reports said everything in that church was destroyed." I pointed to the burn marks on Jesus' feet. "You took it during the fire, and the only way you could have done that is if you were there when the fire started."

Cruz reached out and grabbed me by my shirt.

"You have no idea what you're talking about!" he yelled.

I waited a bit. "Yes, I do." Looking over Cruz's shoulder, I definitely saw the flash of red again, moving left to right. My hat was off, and I hoped Billy wouldn't do anything reckless. "You set the fire, and now you use that cross as a symbol of your own power."

Cruz released my shirt and punched me in the stomach.

I straightened up and caught my breath. "How will your people feel," I whispered, "when they find out the foundation of your church is proof that you killed Father Rodrigo?"

"*No!*" Cruz shoved me to the ground. I stayed there, looking up at him. Vega went over to his boss, but Cruz held up a hand to stop him. He pointed his finger at me. "When I am through with you, you will see your father in Hell."

"If that happens," I said, getting to my feet, "I'd have to agree you were right after all. But when you don't believe in Heaven, Hell doesn't scare you all that much."

He turned away from me. I now noticed the gun Vega was holding. He looked like nothing would give him more joy than using it on me.

Elijah Cruz was not used to being spoken to like that. This was a man who lived his life in complete control. Smarter than the government bureaucracy he was so willing to steal from, and on the side of God. Who was I when it came down to it? A non-believing nobody.

A schoolteacher.

"It's like you told me the other night," I said. "A man has to believe in something." I took a step toward him. "What is it you believe in, Mr. Cruz?"

Elijah Cruz stared into my eyes for a half minute, took a step back, and motioned for Vega to join him. As the two of them spoke, I gave Frankie my best reassuring smile. Ape caught the smile and tightened his grip on Frankie's shoulder.

Cruz and Vega separated, and Cruz walked over to me.

"I have decided," he began, a touch of defeat in his voice, "to let you go." Cruz looked at Ape and nodded. Ape gave one more squeeze to Frankie's shoulder and pushed him toward me. I put my arm around Frankie and turned toward the exit. I wanted to get out as quickly as possible.

We had taken only a few steps when Cruz said, "Stop!"

I turned around to see Vega stepping toward Frankie and me with his gun raised.

"I cannot let you leave, Mr. Donne," Cruz said.

"You're willing to lose everything you've worked for?" I tried.

He shook his head. "You've left me with no choice." He sounded almost as if I had beaten him, yet I was the one with the gun pointed at me.

Vega came closer and aimed at my chest. The smile he gave me was one of long-overdue pleasure. It disappeared as a shot rang out, spinning him around, causing the gun to fall to the floor of the pool. Ape lumbered over to his wounded partner, held him upright, and looked around to see where the shot had come from. I took Frankie by the back and pushed him toward the exit. "Go!"

"But what about—?"

"Just get out of here!" I turned back as Cruz scrambled for Vega's dropped pistol.

"Don't do it!" A voice from the dark.

Cruz picked up the gun anyway and, before he could raise it, a second shot fired. Cruz fell to the ground. He looked at the gun in his hand, but seemed unable to raise his arm. "Alex," Cruz whispered. Ape just stood there, holding Vega, still looking around for the shooter.

I stepped over and removed the gun from Cruz's hand. I pointed it at Ape and thought about all the explaining this scene would take, and how much shit Billy and I were in for. I didn't know how badly Cruz and Vega were injured, and I was not going to wait around to find out. With the gun pointed at the three of them, I ran backward out of the pool as fast as my feet would take me.

I spotted Frankie by the corner and ran over to him. He looked like he was about to fall, so I put my arm around him. To our right, coming through the darkened playground, we saw a lone figure, head down, walking toward us. He was wearing a red cap and holding a black case, the kind pool players carried.

"Billy," I said. "You made it."

He looked up. It was Jack. Jack Knight. And he had a grin on his face you couldn't knock off with a shovel.

"Hey, Teach," he said. "Everything work out okay?" We looked at each other for a few seconds. "Oh. I guess Billy didn't tell you I was one of the ones he reached out to. He musta been scraping the bottom of the barrel when he got to me." He looked at Frankie. "Hey, kid. Sorry about having to take that guy out when he was so close to you and all, but, if I hadn't . . . we wouldn't be here talking now, would we? Of course, if I missed by a bit, probably would've hit your teacher here." He turned to me. "The old pussy got your tongue? Or you just searching for the right words of gratitude?"

"I don't know what to say, Jack," I said.

"That's a first. 'Thanks' might work for some people, but coming from you? I don't think so. I'm here for Billy."

"Yeah . . . well . . ."

"Thanks, mister," Frankie said.

"No problem, kid." Jack took a step closer, took off his red baseball cap, and placed it on Frankie's head. "I'm sure Mr. Donne here has taught you all that important stuff, huh? Like, just 'cause you think what you're doing is right, don't always make it so. That how it goes, Ray? Did I get that one?"

Before I could even think of a response, Billy pulled up in his Jeep. Edgar was right behind him. They both screeched to simultaneous halts and jumped out of their vehicles.

"Christ!" Billy said, rushing over to us. "I thought we'd lost you."

"You did," Jack pointed out.

Billy slapped Jack on the back. "Thanks for getting back to me in a timely fashion." He looked at the case Jack was holding. "I see you got my message and came prepared."

"It's the boy scout in me," Jack said.

"How did you . . . ?" I began and then stopped. I wasn't sure what question to ask.

"I was making a pass by the river when I spotted Ray here getting into the van," Jack explained to Billy. "Tailed them around for a bit, and then we ended up back here. Positioned myself above the action and waited to see how the shit was gonna come down."

"Outstanding," Billy said. "What's with the bad guys?"

"Three in the pool," I said. "Two injured." I nodded toward Jack.

"Okay," Billy said. "Let's get the hell out of here. We'll talk more tomorrow about this. I wanna hear all the details."

"Over beer?" Jack asked.

"Lots of them."

Jack Knight turned and walked away. I took a step after him, wanting to say something. Billy stopped me. "Let him go, partner. He's not going to hear you." Then he called Edgar over. "Can you take these two home?"

"You got it," Edgar said.

"Good work tonight."

"I didn't do anything. I just . . ."

" 'Just' nothing. You were there, man. Sometimes that's all you need to be." Billy turned to face Frankie and offered his hand. Frankie stepped forward and took it. "You must be one helluva kid, Francisco. My man Ray took quite a chance on you."

Frankie held Billy's hand and looked to me. "I know."

"I hope you don't disappoint."

"I won't, sir."

"Good." Then to me he added, "You're gonna have a shitload of explaining to do."

"I'll think of something." I stuck out my hand, and Billy pulled me into a hug.

"Keep it simple," he said. "Let's not make it too long before we get together, partner. I'm available for nonemergencies, too."

"Thanks." I searched for something more to say, but nothing came.

"I think it's time to go home," Billy said.

"Absolutely," I said.

On the way, Frankie and I went over his very simple story.

Chapter 36

DETECTIVE ROYCE LOOKED AT me and said, "So the grandmother called *you,* huh?"

"Right after she called you guys, I guess." We were standing on the balcony outside of Mrs. Santos's apartment. It was a few minutes after nine, Sunday morning, and the sun had just disappeared behind thickening clouds. A breeze was picking up, and I could make out the smell of the ocean. Weather coming this way.

"Gee," Royce said, jotting that down in his notebook. "Missing grandson returns early Sunday morning, and the second person she thinks to call is the kid's teacher, who rolls out of bed and gets here just before the police. That's pretty . . . impressive. Whose phone you think she used, Mr. Donne? Hers is out of service."

"She's pretty close with her downstairs neighbor," I said. "The one she's having coffee with in the kitchen."

"Right." He wrote something else down. "She's got a good-looking daughter, that one."

"Elsa."

"Elsa. Sure. She can make coffee for me anytime." He took a sip from the cup that had been getting cold on the outside table.

"What about you?" I asked. "You made it all the way in from Long Island on a Sunday just for this?"

"No, not just for this," he said. "I was spending some late-night quality time at the shop with my good buddy Oscar Thomas." I smiled at his use of cop slang for overtime. "Got a call about a gunshot victim at a local church early this morning."

"A church?"

"The one the grandmother goes to." He looked back inside and lowered his voice. "And when the responding officers arrived on scene, they found that guy we met the other day at the station. Elijah Cruz? That's why they called me."

"Elijah Cruz?" It looked like I had more explaining to do. "I'm not sure what Frankie—"

Royce held up his hand. "How about I tell you what I know, and then if you think you have anything of value to add, I'll let you do that."

"Okay," I said.

Royce took out his notebook. "Priest called it in. Father . . ."—he squinted at his writing—". . . something or other. Opened up this morning and found Cruz on the altar."

He went back to the church? "What did Cruz say?"

"Not much," Royce said. "He's dead."

"What happened?"

"Well," Royce said. "Here's the damnedest thing. Did you know that churches have security cameras?"

I thought about my late-night visit to the church. "No," I said, doing my best to keep my tone even. "I didn't."

"Yeah. 'Trust in the Lord, but everyone else—smile for the camera.'" Royce grinned. "Anyway, they got one camera, inside, focused on the entrance. Priest said they'd been broken into a few times the past two years, so—get this—Cruz springs for a little video surveillance."

"And?" I asked, thankful the church only had the one camera.

"And . . . we got Cruz coming into the church very early this morning. He's clearly alive, but he's practically being carried in. By two guys. One huge, the other not so much. And the smaller of the two . . ."

I waited a few seconds before saying, "Yeah?"

"Damned if he doesn't match the description of the guy you said was hassling you last week. Jerry Vega."

"Really," I said, trying for surprised.

"I shit you not," Detective Royce said. "We got some bloody prints the Crime Scene guys'll run. Today being Sunday we'll probably have to wait 'til tomorrow for the results, but it looks like him. You said he was with a big guy, right?"

"Yeah," I said. "If it's even him."

"Right. *If.* " Royce paused as he looked at his notebook again. "Oh, yeah," he said, almost as an afterthought. He reached into his pocket and pulled out a computer disc. "We found this on Cruz's person." He turned it around to show it to me. It read "Disc II" in my handwriting. I had just given that to Cruz a few hours ago.

"Is that important?" I asked.

"I'll find out when I get it back to the precinct," he said. "Makes you wonder though."

"What's that?"

"If there's a Disc One, where is it?"

As I pretended to think about that, it occurred to me that Vega had taken Disc One to protect himself. Maybe he knew he was also protecting those folks Cruz was helping. As far as Disc Two and John Roberts? Fuck him.

"I don't know, Detective," I said. "It's a mystery."

"That it is, Mr. Donne." He gave a solemn nod, glanced at his notebook again, and closed it. "Shame about Cruz, though. If he'd gotten to a hospital, he might still be alive. Vega's looking at depraved indifference, at least."

"Have you told Mrs. Santos yet?" I asked.

"Nah. Didn't want to ruin the joyous homecoming. She'll find out soon enough." He slipped his notebook into his back pocket. "So there I am trying to put that shit at the church together, and I get another call informing me that our prodigal son here has returned. I release the body to the ME and head over to listen to Junior's story about being dropped off by a van over by the river. Says after he got him and his sister upstate and then dropped the sister off with you, he got abducted. Not sure where he was the last week. Must be the trauma."

"Yeah. Frankie told me. That's some scary shit."

"Almost unbelievable." Royce gave me a long look. "Considering what coulda happened though? The kid was damned lucky." He walked over, opened the sliding door, and turned back to me. "I'm sure he appreciates all you did for him. Sometimes they don't come right out and say it, kids being kids and all."

"Thanks, Detective. But I really didn't—"

"So I guess you don't have anything else to add after all," Royce said. "Do you?"

"I guess I don't."

"Good," he said. "I don't need any more complications. How's it feel, Mr. Donne?"

"How's what feel?"

"Redemption."

"If I had to guess?" I asked. "I'd say not half bad. But, I'm just guessing."

He stuck out his hand, and I took it. "You keep sticking to that story, Donne. And let's hope the kid sticks to his." He held on to my hand a bit longer. "I bet you were one helluva cop back in the day. You give any thought to coming back?"

I smiled. He knew. "I did there for a while, but . . ."

"The knees?"

"That's what I told myself at first. But it was an easy out." I scratched my head. "I just got too damn tired of too many days that didn't end like this one. Kids like Frankie?" I motioned with my head into the apartment. "I'm better off seeing them inside my classroom. Out on the street, that's a game I don't want to play anymore. *Officer* Donne's retired. I'm gonna stick with being Mr. D. Shit, I'll be making your job easier."

"Wouldn't that be a pleasant change," Detective Royce said. "Good-bye, *Mister* Donne."

"Good-bye, Detective."

He went inside, and I turned around to watch the East River. The sky was getting darker now, and for the first time in what seemed like weeks there was a slight chill in the air. My cell phone rang. I had forgotten that Edgar gave it back to me. I slipped it out of my pocket. "Hello?"

"Raymond," my sister's voice said. "Your phone does work."

"Hey, Rache. Kinda early for you, isn't it? How's L.A.?"

"It *was* fine," she said. "But I took the red-eye back last night. Dad's memorial's today. Or did you let it slip your mind?"

Shit. "It's been crazy here, Rachel. I'll fill you in when I see you."

"Later today?"

"I don't know," I said. "I'll call you."

I considered going back inside, saying my good-byes, and heading home. The door to the deck slid open again, and Cousin Anita walked out, her pregnant belly leading the way.

"Mr. Donne," she said.

"Mrs. Roberts. How's your husband?"

"He is still in the coma, but the doctors are optimistic," she said.

"Good."

"I was on my way to the hospital when I got the call about Frankie. I came right over."

"That was good of you."

"We are family. That's what we do."

"Right."

"I spoke to Francisco," she said. "He told me . . ."—she looked over her shoulder—"everything. This family owes you a lot, Mr. Donne."

"Detective Royce has a disc," I said, not in the mood to hear who owed me what. "In a few hours, he's going to know about your husband's business arrangement with Elijah Cruz. Your husband kept very precise records."

Her look turned from grateful to concerned. "What does that mean?" she asked.

"It means your life is going to be changing drastically. Soon." I took a step toward her. "When your husband comes out of his coma, he's going to have a lot of questions to answer. You need to be prepared for that, Mrs. Roberts."

When she didn't reply, I made a move toward the door, but she stepped in front of me. "You don't like me very much, do you?"

"That's an odd question," I said, taking a step back. "We've met once. What difference does it make how I feel about you?"

"It might make a difference," she said, "if you knew—*thought* you knew— something about me."

I was beyond fried and not up to playing word games with this woman, but something came to me. I waited to make sure it wasn't the fatigue or hunger playing games with my head.

"When I showed up at your house," I began, "and told you I was looking into Frankie's disappearance, you thought I was a cop, and you got this look on your face. I couldn't figure it out at the time, but I just saw it again as you came out here to talk to me. It was fear. Not 'What can I do to help my cousin?' Fear. And then when you realized who I was, you couldn't wait to get rid of me."

"That is not true."

"Yeah, it is. And your husband acted the same way when I went to see him."

"I am not responsible for my husband's actions."

"He wasn't protecting himself," I said. "He was protecting you."

"So?"

"You didn't come here to see Frankie. You came here to see me."

"Why," she said, doing her best to not look away, "would I do that?"

She moved to the balcony and placed her hands on the railing. She was taking deep breaths, as if she was bothered by the humidity in the air. I walked over and stood to her left.

"Did you know Francisco had two head wounds when the cops found him?"

"I did not know," she said. "And I don't wish to hear about it now."

"Yeah," I continued. "One was a bloody nose. Most likely from a punch, the cops think. Broke the nose. Not enough kill him, just bleed a lot."

Anita put her hand on her stomach and closed her eyes. "Please," she said. "You are making me sick."

"The other one," I went on, too tired to care, "was a wound to the head just above the left ear. Made by an unidentified blunt instrument."

"Please," Anita said. "Stop."

"My guess is, someone got real pissed off at Rivas, picked up something like a baseball bat, and clocked him in the head. Not enough to kill him, but enough to cause some internal bleeding." This was all making sense to me now. Frankie told me that when he was on the roof he had seen the van pull away. But that was a half hour after his dad sent him up there. What if Anita had showed up before Ape and Vega? "Follow that up with a punch to the nose," I said, "and, well . . . we all know how that turned out."

Anita locked her eyes on me, and I watched as they filled with tears. She had a decision to make: deny everything or come clean. She wiped a tear away before saying, "I just wanted to talk to Francisco. To tell him—to explain to him—what he was doing to my husband. To our family."

"That was a pretty big risk."

"He stole from John. From Elijah Cruz. Elijah was holding John responsible." She paused to take a breath. "I just wanted Francisco to return what he had taken."

"And?"

"And he laughed at me. He said that no woman was going to tell him what to do. He denied stealing. He said I could look around if I wanted to. But that it would do no good. And anyway, if he did steal, it was *business*, and what did I know about that?"

"Your husband knew it was Rivas?"

"Yes, but he couldn't prove anything. Even if he could, what could he do? Go to the police? There was no way out."

"That's exactly the thought he should have had before getting involved with Cruz."

"You don't know," she said. "How could you know? The pressure my husband was under. Trying to do what was best for his family. That's why he did what he did. Why I did what I . . . It just got out of our control."

"That would be a hell of a lot more convincing if you weren't living in a house worth half a million dollars, Mrs. Roberts. It's not like your husband was stealing to put food on the table."

She took a step toward me. "How dare you! Do you have the slightest idea what a man like my husband would do for his family?"

"And look how well things turned out."

"Those people in there," she pointed at the glass door, "they think you are quite the hero. You got Frankie home. You . . ." She gave me a look of disgust. "You are not the man they think you are, Mr. Donne."

"Mrs. Roberts," I said. "I only know if your husband had done the right thing, Frankie and Milagros might not be grieving the loss of their father."

She tried to think of something else mean to say to me, but came up empty.

"But don't worry," I said. "Your secret is safe with me."

"You're not . . . you won't say anything?"

"To whom? The cops or your family? Who are you more afraid of?"

She took a moment before answering. "What is it you want from me, Mr. Donne?"

"Excuse me?"

"How much is your silence going to cost?"

I couldn't believe this woman. "You think I want money?" I almost laughed. "You've been living away from Brooklyn too long."

"Why else would you keep quiet?"

"Frankie knows who's responsible for killing his father," I said. "He's got someone to hate for the rest of his life. He doesn't need you in that group. You're family."

I turned to go inside. My hand was on the door when I heard Anita crying behind me.

"What am I supposed to do now?" she said.

"Your husband's facing some serious charges. I'm sure he has a lawyer?" She nodded. "Contact him tomorrow. Tell him everything you know about John and Cruz, and what's on that disc Royce has. With Cruz dead and your husband's cooperation, it'll probably go smoother."

A bad thought crossed her face. "Will John go to jail?"

"That's where they put criminals, Anita."

She winced and put her hand on her pregnant stomach. "We'll have to sell the house," she said. "Where will we go?"

"I don't know," I said, moving to the door. "You may have to come back home."

I went inside without either one of us saying another word. Mrs. Santos and Elsa's mother were at the kitchen table sipping from their cups. Elsa was leaning against the sink.

"I'm going to go home now," I said to the three women.

Mrs. Santos eased out of her chair and walked over to me. She took my hands in hers and gave them a weak squeeze.

"Gracias," she said. "Thank you."

I squeezed back. "You're welcome." We stood there for a few seconds, her eyes filling with tears. Before mine did the same, I said, "I'll see you at graduation, Senora."

"Si, maestro. Soon."

"Good." I let her hands go.

"I'll walk you out," Elsa said, getting a look from the two older women. "I have to get ready for work anyway."

I said good-bye again and let Elsa lead me by the elbow toward the front door. We stopped when we heard the bathroom door open.

"Mr. D!" Frankie said. He had a towel around his waist, and his wet hair was slicked back. "You going?"

"I gotta get some sleep, Frankie. I could probably use a shower, too."

"Gimme a minute, and I'll walk ya down," he said, and disappeared into his bedroom.

·

"Frankie's going to walk me down," I said to Elsa. "You're welcome to join us."

"No," she said. "I think he wants to talk to you alone." She opened the door and turned back to me. "What were you and Anita talking about?"

"Her role in Frankie's and Milagros's future," I said. "I think she's going to be more involved from now on."

"I thought I heard her raise her voice."

I didn't respond.

"You look different."

"I look tired."

"No, that's not it," she said. "I don't know what it is, but it will come to me."

"Let me know when it does."

"Maybe I'll do that." She stepped into the hallway.

"That'd be nice," I said as the door closed.

"You talkin' to yourself, Mr. D?"

"Yeah, Frankie. Don't sneak up on people like that. You'll give me a heart attack."

"Ahh," he said, pulling the door open for me. "You ain't that old."

We got to the elevator, and Frankie pressed the down button. He looked as tired as I felt. He'd lost a few pounds, and a few stray hairs were growing on his chin. When did that happen?

"How are you doing?" I asked.

"I don't know," he said. "Kinda all messed up inside, you know? I'm tired as shit, but I'm glad like anything to be home. *Home*, home. With my grandma."

"You didn't like hanging at your dad's?"

"For a weekend, yeah. Maybe a week over the summer, but . . ." He stopped for a bit, losing his thought. "Your dad still alive, Mr. D.?"

"No," I said. "He died when I was about your age. Heart attack."

"You cry a lot . . . after?"

"Yeah," I lied. "I guess."

"I been crying like a girl. Not in front of Milagros, though. After I got her to you. And not around my grandma, either. But . . ."

"It hurts," I said for him. "It hurts a lot, Frankie."

"Yeah."

"It's okay to let people know that," I said, wishing someone had told me that. Maybe they had. We stepped inside the elevator.

"You know what hurts the most?" he said. "That my dad's not gonna be around to see me get older, you know? Become a real baseball player. A man." He touched the button for the lobby and, without turning around, said, "Is it okay to be angry at somebody who's dead?"

You're asking the expert on that subject.

"I mean, my dad's dead, and I'm sad and all, but I'm angry, too, 'cause I think he . . . he didn't have to do them things that he did that . . ." Frankie started crying.

I put my hand on his shoulder. "Yeah, it's okay to be angry."

"This was gonna be it," Frankie said through the tears. "He promised this was gonna be the last time. He was gonna have enough money to take me and Milagros to Florida, he said. We was gonna move there soon as he got all his stuff together. It was gonna be the last time and then . . ." The elevator slowed to a stop, and the doors opened onto the lobby. Frankie ran his hands over his eyes, wiping away the tears but not the evidence that they had been there. "How you getting home?"

"My friend—Edgar—he said I could have his car for a while."

"Good." We stepped out of the building and into the empty common area, where I'd almost been run over by the kid on the bike twelve days ago. "I ain't gonna be in school tomorrow."

I thought about pushing it, but took a long look at Frankie and decided against it. "Okay," I said. "Tuesday then."

"My dad's church," Frankie continued, "they're doing a service for him in the morning, and then we're going to the cemetery after that." We took a left out of the courtyard to where I had parked Edgar's car.

"Something bothering you, Frankie?"

He looked at the ground and said, "You cry at your dad's funeral, Mr. D?"

"I guess."

"You guess?"

"I didn't . . ." I started and tried again. "I stayed outside on the steps of the church. I was too angry to go inside. I didn't want to hear . . . I don't know. I didn't want to hear the bullshit."

"All that god stuff? People saying good things about your dad?"

When did this kid get so insightful?

"Yeah."

"But didn't you have something to say?" Frankie asked.

"To whom?" I asked.

"Didn't you have something to say to your dad?"

We got to Edgar's car, and I pulled the keys out of my pocket.

"Like what?" I asked the fourteen-year-old kid in front of me.

"I don't know." He shrugged. "I guess that's why I'm askin' you. You been there and done that, I thought."

"You thought wrong," I said. My tone made Frankie take a step back. My hand closed tightly around the car keys. "I felt pretty much the way you do now, Frankie. My father's death was . . ." I found myself searching for the right word. ". . . avoidable. I've had a lot of problems dealing with that."

"How did you? Deal with it?"

"I became everything he wasn't," I said.

"Like a cop?"

"Especially like a cop."

"That help?"

"Not as much as I thought it would. Not at all, to tell the truth."

Frankie looked at me for a few seconds, digesting the spontaneous philosophy lesson. He stuck out his fist, and I met it with my own.

"See ya Tuesday, Mr. D," he said.

"You better," I answered. "I don't want to have to come looking for you again."

He smiled and turned away. I got in behind the wheel and started the car. Instead of shifting into Drive, I rolled down the driver's window and shut my eyes for a while. It would take me no time at all to get to my place. As much as I wanted that ten minutes ago . . . I thought about what Frankie had said, and what I had said, and suddenly I didn't feel like going home, dealing with the mess left by Vega and Ape. I called Edgar. He picked up after one ring.

"Yeah?" he said.

"When do you need the car back?" I asked.

"Not until tomorrow if you really need it. Got plans?"

"Yeah, I do," I said, looking in the rearview mirror at Frankie walking away. "I've got one more thing to do. Someone I need to say good-bye to. You mind?"

"No, Ray, not at all."

I thanked Edgar, closed up the phone, and pulled away from the curb. About a minute later, I had to roll up my window and turn on the wipers.

It had finally started to rain.